The Storks of La Caridad

Florence Byham Weinberg

Twilight Times Books
Kingsport Tennessee

The Storks of La Caridad

This is a work of fiction. All concepts, characters and events portrayed in this book are used fictitiously and any resemblance to real people or events is purely coincidental.

Paladin Timeless Books, an imprint of
Twilight Times Books
P O Box 3340
Kingsport, TN 37664
www.twilighttimesbooks.com/

First paperback printing, June 2005

Library of Congress Cataloging-in-Publication Data

Weinberg, Florence Byham.
  The storks of La Caridad / Florence Byham Weinberg.
      p. cm.
  ISBN 1-933353-21-X (pbk. : alk. paper)
  1. Pfefferkorn, Ignaz, b. 1725--Fiction. 2. Mexico--History--Spanish
colony, 1540-1810--Fiction. 3. Spain--History--Charles III,
1759-1788--Fiction. 4. Sonora (Mexico : State)--Fiction. 5. Political
prisoners--Fiction. 6. Missionaries--Fiction. 7. Jesuits--Fiction. I.
Title.
  PS3623.E4324S76 2004
  813'.6--dc22
                    2005006922

Cover art by Ardy M. Scott
Photo credit Dr. Florence Byham Weinberg

Printed in the United States of America

Acknowledgments

Here is my chance to salute those people, places and organizations that were indispensable in the creation of this book. To begin with, Dora Elizondo Guerra, Archivist of the Old Spanish Mission Historical Research Collection in the Library of Our Lady of The Lake University in San Antonio. It was she who advised me to consult a work by a certain Ignaz Pfefferkorn, S.J., *Sonora: a Description of the Province*, as a guide to plants of the Southwest. Professor Ralph Freedman of Princeton and later of Emory University patiently listened to every word of the novel in its earliest form and just as patiently gave me advice.

My friend, Father James L. Lambert, S. J., guided me in dogmatic and other ecclesiastical matters and was surprised (like everyone else) to discover who was the murderer in the end. A residency at the Hambidge Center for Creative Arts and Sciences provided the space, the silence and the stimulus to finish the first draft. The Daedalus Critique Group of San Antonio read chapters of the book in later incarnations and—what else—critiqued them, giving me valuable hints and information, and, finally, Gerald W. Mills, my editor, took the book in hand and honed off its rough edges, molding it into its present form. To all of them I am deeply grateful.

Florence B. Weinberg

Chapter I

Limbo

I am a priest. I am a Jesuit.

These words help me remember; help me believe. I've repeated them throughout my eight years of prison and pain, more so these past four sweltering days in this dusty coach. My wrists aren't infected yet, but surely my ankles are. With each jolt of these iron-shod wheels on the rough road, the manacles and leg irons cut deeper into my flesh, tormenting me.

We're four days north of Cádiz and its prison at the Port of Santa María. My next prison, the monastery of Nuestra Señora de la Caridad, Our Lady of Charity, is not far away.

I am a priest. I am a Jesuit.

୫ଓଷ

A storm was almost upon us. In the gathering gloom, I stared out the dirty coach window and watched black clouds ink out the sunset, trying to forget my pain. Flashes of sheet lightning lit the countryside every so often, reflecting on the man opposite me, riding backwards—my jailer. My plight was not his concern. He'd given me a little water and some dry bread, and allowed me to relieve myself on this journey, but I was baggage to him, nothing more. The horses were better treated.

In the space of a few heartbeats, gloom became darkness. A sudden, blinding flash and ear-splitting thunderclap lifted me from my seat. The horses bolted, tipping the coach almost on its side, and I slammed against the coach door. There was no way to lessen the impact, such was my surprise, and an involuntary cry escaped me as new pain mixed with old. Until that moment, I'd managed to endure my plight in silence.

I heard the coachman's angry shouts and the crack of his whip. He regained control, the coach righted itself with a jarring *thump* and I struggled back into my seat. The throbbing of my wrists and ankles now provided a dull background of pain to sharp new stabs from my shoulder, but I was still alive. I offered up a silent prayer, thanking God we were still upright, and reflected on my helplessness, mine and my brother Jesuits.'

We'd been helpless from the moment we were expelled from Spain and its colonies, and from all of Western Europe as well. Recently I'd heard our Society was suppressed completely by order of the Pope. Our Holy Mother Church had reduced us to nothing.

My own ordeal was now beginning its ninth year. I was arrested in 1767, near my mission in the Sonora Desert. I survived the death march across Mexico and that suffocating voyage in coffin-size cells on the prison ship bound for Cádiz. Twenty-six Sonora missionaries survived along with me, but twenty-four did not. Perhaps those martyred dead on the road to Vera Cruz were luckier than I.

Eight years of beatings and interrogations followed.

The excuse for keeping us was that we knew too much about classified Spanish installations in the Sonora Desert. But, in reality, the beatings and interrogations were about the gold. Always, the gold. No one, not even King Carlos III, believed we didn't know where it was hidden. There were gold and silver mines in Sonora, and we missionaries must each have had our secret hoards. After all, we were—once were—Jesuits! I shook my head with a bitter smile.

Another flash of lightning, almost as close. I caught sight of my reflection in the window glass, and a face still recognizably north European stared back at me. Yes, the eyes were still familiar, intense blue with pure whites. My hair was still blond, but now mixed with gray, cut short and combed straight back from my high forehead as always, plastered in place now by dust and grease. Otherwise, I hardly knew myself.

Repeated bouts of malaria had emaciated my frame. My left cheek was disfigured by a whip scar; a split right eyebrow testified to another whiplash, and a ruptured vein under the left eye to someone's fist. By some miracle, my hawk nose was still intact, as were my teeth. I'd been beaten, yes, but not yet broken. Not as long as I could remember who and what I was.

I am a priest. I am a Jesuit.

The lightning this time played back and forth across the sky, bringing with it a brief squall of rattling hailstones. Bracing myself against any further jolts, I pressed my face to the window. The stark white light revealed a walled complex of buildings ahead, atop a low rise. It had to be the monastery at last.

La Caridad! There lay my dark future, and an involuntary shiver shook me. That brief glimpse showed me a huge church dominated by a round tower over the transept, a separate bell tower rearing itself above the façade, several buildings and perhaps some ruins as well.

As I risked more pain to rub my shoulder again, my hands brushed against the edges of a letter, sealed with wax and tucked into the inner breast pocket of my robe. It was a message from Abbot Dom Gerónimo, Royal Inspector of Prisons from a Norbertine monastery in Madrid, to his peer in La Caridad, to be presented sealed and unread upon my arrival. He'd been abbot there once, and described the place to me. If his letter denounced my so-called crime committed at Santa María, my imprisonment at La Caridad would be real martyrdom. Yet, his friendship had saved me worse persecution up to now. Could it be my load of chains was simply official reaction to my 'misdeed?

The brief hail turned into pounding rain. The coachman cursed loudly and lashed the horses into a trot, only to slow them to a walk once they topped the rise. We turned right and halted before a massive gate in the monastery wall, surmounted by a fan-shaped iron grille under an ornate stone arch. The coachman jumped down and ran to the entrance, where he rang a bell and pressed close against the heavy double doors to shelter from the steady rain.

We waited for what seemed like many minutes. At last the bolt rattled and the doors creaked open. A hooded monk motioned him inside. The coachman took the nearest horse by the bit and led the whole equipage into a courtyard the size of a parade ground, past stone posts with heavy, ornate chains suspended between them, up to an open doorway. I could see light streaming out, glimmering on the streaks of falling rain, but no movement inside, just a stone wall with an arch and darkness beyond.

The church was straight ahead. A pair of wide stone steps led to heavy doors twice a man's height, hand-carved in square panels. Above them, barely visible in the darkness and the rain, loomed the bell tower. I squinted and made out the silhouettes of three bulky storks' nests, clinging to the side ledges and top of the tower.

My jailer stepped out first, then opened the door on my side and offered his hands to help me down. It was his first courtesy, a gesture I supposed was meant for show. My stiff legs threatened to buckle when I stood, and the pain in my wrists and ankles forced me to draw a sharp breath. I stared down. The coach's steps were twenty inches apart, but the chain between my leg irons only a foot long. Each time I'd left the coach during the journey, I'd hopped down, but this time I could not. Both his hands were extended, meaning I'd have to let go of the doorframe.

I managed the first step, but on attempting the second, the chain caught and I fell, helpless, my knees grazing the muddy cobblestones before the bailiff caught me, thank God! My knees were saved, but my ankles were cut still deeper, bleeding into my shoes as I shambled along.

I followed him through the pelting rain until we were inside the antechamber, where light from oil lamps flooded us with a warm, yellow glow. There, a stoop-shouldered monk met us, hands thrust together into the black sleeves of his robe. His face and even his tonsured head had high color compared to my own. The reflection I'd seen in the coach window during that lightning flash showed me as pasty white.

He'd seen my fall, I judged from the sympathetic twist of his mouth. After a moment's hesitation he extended a hand. "Welcome to La Caridad. I'm Brother Eugenio, the scribe here. You must surely be…?"

I squared my shoulders and took a deep breath, gritting my teeth once more against the waves of pain. My voice came out hoarse; my words were halting. I could not control my own hand's trembling as I met his.

"I am…Ygnacio Pfefferkorn, Society…of Jesus."

Chapter II

Holy Unrest

The monk seemed surprised. He shook his head and the crease between his gray eyebrows deepened. "The letter from Royal Council in Madrid gives your name as P...Pf...Pferkon.

He took my hand in his and my trembling stopped. It was the first such warmth I'd experienced in recent memory. I placed my left hand over his, wincing when my manacles clanked together, but nevertheless grateful for his simple act of kindness.

"That's close enough in Spanish, Brother Eugenio. It's good to be here. At least, all that traveling is over."

He tilted his head a bit sideways, eyes narrowing, then turned his attention to the bailiff, whom he thanked for good service. The short speech seemed recited, universal, something used for a messenger of any type. Finally he returned to me.

"Our abbot, Dom Gregorio Cañada y Lobato, is waiting. Come with me." He spun about before I could speak of my raw ankles, and moved away. The bailiff's hand was suddenly against my back, pushing me forward. I broke into a painfully fast shuffle, trying to catch up, but Eugenio paused just once before we reached a carved door, standing open. He waved me through ahead of him and followed on my heels, the bailiff trailing behind.

There, sitting behind a dark oaken table, its legs braced with wrought iron curlicues, a man wearing a simple black habit bowed over a document, not looking up. His tonsured head, fringed in gray, remained motionless above rigid shoulders as he drove a quill pen across the paper with angry, scratching sounds. Surely he knew we were there, just inside the door.

Brother Eugenio shifted his feet uneasily and warned me with a flash of his eyes to make no sound.

The abbot's breathing was harsh, as if he had been doing heavy exercise, and his voice rumbled with an occasional mutter or exclamation when he underscored a word with a slash of the quill. He dipped it once more in the inkwell to finish the paragraph, threw it down with a grumpy snap of his wrist, then stood and glared at us with face flushed, eyebrows knit into a single heavy line.

"The bishop's minion just brought His Grace's latest message," he growled through clenched teeth, emphasizing the honorific with heavy sarcasm. "Damned bastard's trying to destroy us, Eugenio. Worse than that Devil-sent earthquake not so long—"

Scowling, he stopped in mid-sentence, leaning first to one side, then the other as he examined me. His angry, brown-eyed stare was wilting, but I stood as erect as I could. Finally he threw his head back, slicing the air with his hands cupped into claws, fingers spread and arms gesturing as if to punctuate his words.

"What in hell have you drug in here on a night like this?"

I attempted a slight smile through my four-day beard, even though my heart was racing at the way his fingers curled. Hands like those could belong to a musician—or a satanic demon. His fingers were long and graceful, but that meant nothing. The hand that stroked a kitten could also hold a whip, and I feared more suffering at those hands.

Apparently in his fifties, a bit shorter than I, he was neither fat nor lean, but solid. His eyebrows had not yet gone gray, and his jaw was prominent, strong below an unremarkable nose. On the other hand, his full lips were nothing but a grim line as he inspected me from head to toe.

I was acutely conscious of my threadbare robe, patched and frayed around the collar and cuffs, dusty from the trip and splashed with mud in my fall from the carriage.

Eugenio, at last summoning courage, cleared his throat. "Domine, this is the ex-Jesuit, don Ygnacio Pfe…uh, Ferkon." He turned to me. "Dom Gregorio is our abbot—"

"Yes, yes, yes, yes…the ex-Jesuit Ygnacio, of course. The Council in Madrid informs me that he is to be our 'guest' for a time. Royal orders: that all German ex-Jesuits detained at Santa María be sent inland to one monastery or another, including this one. Devil take it! Another mouth to feed when we're going through hell, down from sixty-five to twenty-four monks and two postulants, and damned few donations coming in to support someone who can't pull his own weight." He turned his hostile glare upon the bailiff. "I assume you have keys to those shackles?"

The bailiff gulped, stepping forward as he groped in the pouch at his waist. "I do, yes, Dom Gregorio. They're right here." He held up an immense ring laden with various items, including keys.

"Why show them to *me*? Unchain the man. You brought him here trussed up like a wild beast. What folly made you think him a desperate criminal?"

"Forgive me, Domine," the bailiff stammered, "but those were His Majesty's orders."

To guard a criminal, I thought, *even though not desperate in the usual sense.*

"Yes, yes, yes, the King's orders…" The abbot moved away from the desk and moved closer, peering at my scars with lower lip extended. My chin came up as I withstood his scrutiny, and I began to understand how a slave feels as he stands on the auction block.

While the bailiff fumbled for the right keys, I drew in my breath. The letter! I might present it now; perhaps it would ease the tension. I held my arms to one side so the bailiff could work.

"Dom Gregorio, I bring you greetings from Dom Gerónimo Gómez Flores, Royal Inspector and Abbot of the Monasterio de San Norberto in Madrid. You know him well, of course, as your predecessor here. Over the past six yearly inspections, he and I had moments when we could talk. Thanks be to God, he seems to have taken an interest in me, and recommended that I be sent here. He wanted me to come to a place he knew… a healthy place… where he had friends. He wrote this—"

At that moment my hands were finally free for the first time since leaving the prison near Cádiz. They felt strangely light and expressive, now that the weight was gone. Quickly, I groped for the inner pocket of my robe and brought out the folded letter. I held it out to the abbot as the bailiff knelt to unchain my legs. Would the letter denounce me? Reveal my offense?

Apprehensive, I rubbed my raw wrists while my body involuntarily tensed in anxiety. This time I could not bring myself to smile.

Dom Gregorio broke the seal and began reading, but slowly. Gradually his features softened as a gentle smile replaced anger. My own tension began easing as well. Surely, my fears had been misplaced. Dom Gerónimo's words must have conveyed blessings, rather than an added burden. My emotional relief was punctuated by the sound of ankle chains joining the manacles in the bailiff's grasp. The pain was somehow different—an intense ache, but no longer sharp.

The abbot's smile remained as he folded the letter. "I have all too few instructions from the Council on how to treat you." He examined me again with a thoughtful expression, and turned to Brother Eugenio. "Take don Ygnacio and any personal belongings he might have to the cell I set aside for him, and if he wants to wash up, show him where the water tank is."

Then he turned to me. "We'll be singing Vespers, and after that we eat—probably around nine. Brother Eugenio will fetch you in time and escort you to the refectory. You'll eat with us. We'll talk later."

The monk who'd opened the gate poked his head through the open door, his robe dripping and muddy and clinging to the contours of his body. I guessed he'd guided the driver and horses across a muddy stable yard in the downpour. He was tall but delicate, thin, with a narrow nose and crooked teeth. The look he gave me was intense and sober, almost suspicious.

"Brother Tomás is our porter," the abbot explained, beckoning him in. "Tomás, this is don Ygnacio Pferkon. He'll be staying with us."

The expressionless monk nodded, handing me my battered cloth satchel. In it were my Bible, breviary, crucifix, rosary, a spare robe and underdrawers, my shaving equipment, and—precious to me—the folder with the remnants of notes I'd taken in the Sonora Desert. Tribes, fauna, flora, the properties of soil and rock formations—all there in preparation for my writing of a book some day, if ever I were given the chance.

I thanked him and he nodded once more, glanced at the abbot for permission to leave, and backed out, closing the door behind him. The trail of muddy water he'd painted on the stone floor made me wonder how my satchel remained all but dry.

Brother Eugenio laid a hand on my sleeve, nodding toward the door, and we took our leave. My first steps without fetters felt like a rebirth, but my ankles were afire. Eugenio seemed surprised when I begged him to wait while I inspected my injuries. He watched, but with detachment. Both ankles were black with bruises, chafed, and in places deeply cut from the iron bands. Dried and fresh blood made it hard to see the actual damage. I glanced up at him.

"I was afraid they might already be infected. Thank God, it doesn't seem so. I can heal all right if I get enough food—"

His elderly stoop straightened and his tone became defensive. "We eat well here, don Ygnacio. Were you told otherwise?"

"No, no. I was merely expressing hope. The secular authorities who saw fit to bind me hand and foot gave little thought to nourishment. I've been fed only enough to keep me alive."

That seemed to mollify him. We set out on a circuit around the cloister, he acting as guide. I surveyed the surroundings that would serve as my prison for an indefinite period. A beautiful prison. We paced along a majestic arched walkway floored with large, rectangular stones laid diagonally in a staggered pattern. For once, my mind was not focused on pain.

Eugenio's voice rang with pride of accomplishment. "Not long ago, we finished reconstructing the cloister and church—earthquake damage, you know. I wanted at least to show the cloister to you." Clearly, he enjoyed my wonder and appreciative nods. The colonnade ran around all four sides of a well-kept garden. In the flickering light cast by lamps hung along the walls at intervals, I could just make out several trees beginning to fruit. I saw peach and apple, perhaps pear as well.

We took a short detour while he showed me the water tank.

My cell was to be upstairs, where Brother Eugenio and the rest of the monks slept. We climbed a massive stone staircase to the second story, where the cloister looked out upon the garden below through regularly spaced, rectangular openings. Eugenio led me to the cell assigned me, tucked back into a corner abutting the transept of the church. It contained a narrow cot with a straw mattress and one blanket, a straight chair and table, a wax candle in a holder, a piece of flint but no steel, and two hooks in the stone wall for hanging clothes. That was all. The door could be closed, but not locked. Eugenio set my satchel on the bed and turned to leave.

It had taken me this long to understand I was not to be locked away like a wild beast, beaten, or starved. I had a clean and airy cell of my own; I was free to wash, even invited to eat with the brothers after Vespers. My energy level rose along with my curiosity. "Before you go, Brother Eugenio, I wonder if you can...or will...tell me why your abbot was so furious. What was it all about, this comment that you're going through hard times?"

Eugenio pondered my question for a moment. "It's a combination of things, don Ygnacio. Those French ideas coming in from the north...they've upset the Portuguese court and taken hold in Madrid. You should know all about that, don Ygnacio. They're one reason for your society's expulsion from Portugal, and probably from Spain as well." "You mean Voltaire? Or Diderot? Do the Encyclopedists have that much influence out here?"

"We're not as provincial as all that. Dom Gregorio has read Voltaire, and thinks the man's appeal to reason, especially his deism—his theory of a watch-maker God who sets the cosmic machine running and then abandons it—is extremely dangerous. Some of our most influential citizens have read Voltaire, too, and are convinced he's right. They are no longer sending their sons to us."

"Yes, yes, I see. But you said a combination of things. What else?"

Eugenio paused, his forehead furrowed. "I don't know if I should discuss these matters with you. They've caused division among our own ranks, and they're far from settled. Please don't think I expect you to take sides in this affair. But...the bishop of Ciudad Rodrigo...that's don Cayetano Antonio Cuadrillero y Mota...is trying to absorb the village of Robledillo de Gata into his diocese. Robledillo is one of the chief parishes that have sustained us...and we it...for many centuries. Since 1165, I think. We're interdependent, you see."

"And how do the villagers react to the bishop's interference in their traditional way of life?"

"It varies, don Ygnacio, it varies. On the one hand, we all know each other personally. The people travel all the way here for Mass on special occasions, as well as for other sacraments. That's about eight leagues, twenty-five miles. Several were at this morning's service. Perhaps you'll see one or two tomorrow, if you're up in time. They trust us, love us. They love our beautiful church and their own traditions bound up with ours, and they don't want to switch and pledge loyalty to Ciudad Rodrigo...at least not the majority. On the other hand, uncertainty about the outcome of the power struggle with the bishop has caused contributions to fall off, and young men are going to Salamanca for training to become diocesan priests; they're not choosing the religious life we lead here. I think they see that the power is going to the bishops these days, and flowing away from the abbots."

"You are saying that if Robledillo is taken away, the monastery will have fewer communities to tithe it, to contribute produce and manpower and all that."

"Exactly. The motherhouse will slowly starve." Eugenio's distress turned even the gloomy cell darker.

I was intrigued, however, hoping to learn more. "But where's the authority to annex Robledillo to Ciudad Rodrigo coming from?"

"Certainly from the archbishop; he's in on this. Maybe from higher up. I don't know."

"You said this is causing division among you? I'd have thought it would unify you."

"Many are taking the threat to the monastery personally. Then there are those who believe that obedience to the bishop is of supreme importance, even if it means our destruction. We're at each other's throats. But then there's the charter...."

He broke off his words with a suddenness that surprised me, leaving the taste of bitterness in the air. His lined face took on a new look, one of personal burden.

"Charter? What charter?"

"It's a complex matter. I've told you quite enough for you to understand our situation."

"But—"

An abrupt shaking of his head signaled the end of our exchange. For some reason, his reference to a charter seemed pivotal, but whose charter? Where was it? Who owned it?

But then there's the charter....

The words were spoken as if this charter could solve things, yet it was something he would not or could not discuss.

I analyzed their situation as I fished in my satchel for my shaving equipment. For Jesuits, the vow of obedience would have taken precedence over any sort of self-interest. I wondered whether the bishop's attempt to annex their parish had come as a direct order, or if it were a matter to be decided jointly, with political pressure from the episcopate and from still higher up. If the latter, the 'joint decision' would be weighted on the side of Ciudad Rodrigo. Whichever was the case, the monastery was resisting, perhaps with 'the charter.' That's how it sounded.

At any rate, Brother Eugenio's assignment had been completed. I turned to him. "With your permission, Brother Eugenio, I'd like to wash up, please."

He closed his eyes and bowed slightly, leaving me alone for the first time in many days.

My black wool robe reeked of four days' sweat from sitting chained in that sweltering coach, and a heavy layer of dust clung to it as well as to my face, hair and beard. I laid out my spare robe. It was slightly less threadbare, though patched and terribly wrinkled. At least it was clean.

I carried it and my shaving equipment as I made my way back downstairs and around the corner to the water tank. The monastery's water supply came from several small springs bubbling up into a foot-deep stone basin the size of a small room. Enough water was allowed to run off to insure that the basin always contained pure water. For me, it was a godsend. I drank my fill, then waded in and soaked my cut and aching ankles with great relief.

Later that evening I appeared in the refectory, clean-shaven and fairly presentable, though hungry and weak to the point of trembling. My designated seat, in full view of the abbot, priests and senior brothers, was slightly to one side of the 'bottom' of the circular arrangement of tables and benches, not quite opposite the lectern. There, a monk would deliver scriptural readings while the meal proceeded in silence. I sat as the youngest monks and postulants took their places near me on both sides. I, as prisoner, was counted as 'the least of these,' but I was grateful to be allowed to eat with the brotherhood, regardless of the rank I'd been assigned.

After the blessing and the opening prayers, which I repeated with them, the reading began along with the food service. Baskets of freshly baked, fragrant loaves were placed on the table. I barely resisted snatching one and devouring it on the spot, but I watched the others, waiting. As each man received a bowl of soup, he took one of the small loaves, tore bits from it and floated them on the soup. The serving went according to seniority or rank, my soup delivered last. A logical procedure, I thought, but a torment, since the enticing aroma from the nearby soup bowls made me feel faint.

As the reading continued, a competing passage of scripture from St. Paul invaded my mind, drowning out the reader. "We are fools on Christ's account, but you are wise in Christ; we are weak, but you are strong; you are held in honor, but we in disrepute. To this very hour we go hungry and thirsty, we are poorly clad and roughly treated...."

How long, oh Lord? I asked myself. *When do we eat?*

My stomach growled a loud protest in sympathy with my thoughts. I suspected the bailiff and coachman had been well fed in the kitchen, and were already sleeping off their abundant meal.

At last, a steaming bowl was placed before me. My hands shook so I could barely get spoon to mouth without spilling the liquid. Oh, if only I were allowed to pick up the bowl with both hands and gulp the contents down! I pictured myself scalding my mouth and spilling soup down the front of my robe.

At that moment, the scripture being read was particularly appropriate. Jesus was preaching to the multitude on the mount. *Therefore I tell you, do not worry about your life, what you will eat or drink.... Look at the birds in the sky*—I thought of the storks that had built their nests atop the church—*they do not sow or reap, they gather nothing into barns, yet your heavenly Father feeds them. Are not you more important than they?*

Perhaps so, I thought, but those storks are luckier than I, well fed and snuggled down in their nests. Soup's fine, but where's the food?

The meal finally arrived, a plate of green beans, boiled onions and carrots, and the pork and chicken that had been boiled in the soup. In my famished state, it seemed like ambrosia. For nectar, we each got a half-cup of red wine and as much water as we wanted from large clay ewers. We were meant to mix the wine and the water as in the ritual of the Eucharist, and as the ancient Romans did, to make sure the wine supply lasted through the year.

I observed the brothers' eating habits. Some ate with their cowls over their heads, preferring absolute privacy as they ate. While I was watching them, they were watching me, some peering from the depths of those cowls. I felt no hostility in the air, only intense curiosity. Still, such concentrated scrutiny made me uncomfortable. At the end of the meal after the closing blessing, the abbot stood and addressed his monks.

"My brothers, you have of course been curious about this stranger in the midst of our company. This is don Ygnacio Pferkon, an ex-Jesuit, who is a prisoner of the Crown for a variety of reasons of state I am not privy to. Our friend, your former abbot Dom Gerónimo Gómez Flores has written that the Crown believes don Ygnacio has valuable knowledge he has not yet divulged. He will be sequestered here for an indefinite time. I ask you all to be considerate of him in your daily contacts, and to pray for him, that he may soon be inspired to impart to His Majesty the information he so much desires. You may go in peace now."

There was a rustling of cloth, scraping of shoes on stone, and some murmured exchanges among the monks. Eugenio came to me as I stood by my bench amid the bustle of their departure, and offered to light my candle. I followed him as we again climbed the wide stone staircase to my cell. He spoke the whole time.

"The rest of us will be singing compline, and then we snuff the candles. We say matins at four; you'll hear us, since your cell's wall is also the wall of the church's transept. But no need for you to get up at that hour. You must be exhausted from all your travels." He continued giving me useful information and I glanced at him, suppressing a smile at a monk this talkative. In the cell, he took my candle outside to the nearest lamp and lit it.

"That's easier than striking a light with flint and steel. Here's a bit of steel and a bundle with punk kindling...and a few slivers of wood. If you need a light during the night, you can start one with this. I usually prefer to grope my way in the dark, but then I know the plan of this building.... Enough idle chatter. I must go sing compline. May the Lord bless you with a good night's sleep."

I thanked him and remained standing until I heard his footsteps descending the stairs. Then I knelt beside the cot and devoted myself to prayer. I spoke my prayer inwardly, composing it as elegantly as I could. In this way, too, I sought to honor God.

Oh, my Lord and my God, what am I to do? How can I use my talents to glorify you in such a situation? I gave myself without reserve to our mission endeavor in New Spain and would willingly have died for you there. Even in my worst troubles—lonely, homesick, frightened, in mortal danger—even then I knew I was doing good work...for you. And now, so many dark years have come between. Here in Spain, two short weeks' march away from the Rhineland, my homesickness is much worse. I long for the sight of my sister Isabella and I would weep at all the separations, all the pain, the losses and the deaths, but tears no longer come. I have wept too often.

My mind wandered, remembering. For a time, I had the consolation of being imprisoned at the Port of Santa María with Jakob, who became a dear friend. We could speak German together; we could compare our memories of the stark beauty of the Sonora with its deserts and their giant saguaros, the mountains and their majestic pines. He could add his knowledge of the tribes and the medicinal plants of New Spain to my own lore. He was helping me complete my notes....

I brought my mind back to focus on my prayer. *But now, Oh Lord, I am isolated: a finger severed from its hand, and the hand itself cut off from the brain that directed it, for our Society is suppressed, our Father General imprisoned. I cannot grasp the extent of the tragedy—not only for our Society with its missions and their converts, its schools, their pupils and students, but also for your Church as a whole. What faithful and fruitful servants have been wasted! Give me the courage to endure and be patient, Oh Lord Christ, to wait for a sign from you. There will be, I can feel it, there must be some way in which I can glorify you here. Only keep me from despair, I beg, long enough for me to discover what that service might be.*

After a moment, I added a few final words. *Lord, please help me regain my health. I'm wasting away with malaria, 'repeating sickness' as my Indians called it so long ago, at Misión Ati...that's fourteen years now, Lord. Is there no way to stop this disease?* I feared that any help for it would be a true miracle, since I had been unable for nearly eight years to get my hands on 'quinine,' that New World medicine, the one so ironically called 'the Jesuits' powder.' I was again suffering, as in the beginning, from periods of nausea, fever, and all the rest. *Have pity, Lord. Give me some relief!* I ended my prayer with a little formula of thanks—after all, I was still very much alive—and an Our Father.

As I blew out the candle and stretched full length on my cot, pulling the blanket over my body, I noticed the chill in the room. It wouldn't seem chilly to someone with more meat on his bones. I'd never been thinner. I reached out and touched cold stone. These walls seemed to breathe out winter, and it was mid-July. I shivered. The pain in my ankles had subsided to a distant throbbing, and my wrists only hurt when I fingered them. In the darkness, new sounds came to me, surrounding me. My own stillness made them seem loud: the patter of continuing rain on the tiled roof of the cloister above my head and upon the leaves of the trees in the garden below, accompanied by the high chirping of crickets. And yes, Eugenio was quite right; I could also hear the voices of the monks singing Gregorian chant on the other side of the wall. I closed my eyes in exhaustion, and before long I slept.

ℰℭ

After morning Mass, the abbot summoned me to his quarters. He seated himself behind his worktable, eyes raking me beneath his heavy brows, his expression alternating between concern and mild suspicion, the latter evidenced by a squinting of one eye more than its mate. I waited, standing before him, until he spoke.

"You look better than you did last night, don Ygnacio. You were able to sleep, I hope?"

"Yes, thank you, Dom Gregorio; I woke a few times, but managed to rest well. I've had enough food for the first time in days—also this morning. I appreciate your generosity."

He nodded, acknowledging my thanks, gesturing toward a leather-seated oak chair next to a long credenza.

"Sit down, please."

On the credenza were a pair of thick candles in brass holders, a number of calf and vellum-bound books, a handsome silver chalice, a small monstrance and a statuette of the Blessed Virgin. Glancing at his books, I could see a Bible, St. Thomas Aquinas' *Summa theologica*, and a Duns Scotus.

I sat facing him, but sunlight streaming through the large mullioned windows dazzled me, leaving him a dark silhouette. With his permission, I stood again and lifted the heavy oak chair, with more effort than it should have cost me, moving it a few feet until I was out of the direct light.

For the first time, I noticed a violin with its bow lying on a shelf near the window. It must have been in deep shadow the previous night. I sat waiting for him to speak first, as he was my superior now, all the while contemplating that violin with a powerful yearning. I had not played, had not even seen an instrument, for many years. I suddenly realized my left hand was making fingering movements.

He was not watching me, but seemed to be thinking something through with head inclined. At last, he spoke.

"I must apologize for my discourtesy last night. I'm under extreme pressure right now, and the fate of the monastery is in question...." His voice tapered off.

"It's quite all right, Domine. After all, I was thrust upon you here. I should be the one to apologize." I could only hope my words would find a receptive heart.

He nodded. "I won't ask why you're still being held prisoner, don Ygnacio, but I can tell you I'm deeply sorry for your plight. Your Society did a lot of good during its short life. Much good. Future generations will bless you for the reforms you Jesuits introduced. On the other hand, there must have been good reasons for your suppression...you became arrogant, I'm told, and perhaps lax as well. At least that's what I hear...but I don't entirely trust all I've heard. There are envious detractors out there who are saying much worse than that. I heard about your brothers' suffering during the expulsion." He paused, looking at my face. "I see the scars of abuse you wear. I hope none of that was done by any of our people...in the Church, I mean...the Holy Office, the Inquisition?"

"No, Dom Gregorio. Those are my gifts from secular authorities. My worst beatings were at the hands of an army officer who tried to force me to tell him where the gold of Sonora was hidden."

"Is that why you're here, the king's prisoner still?"

"Yes, Domine, I believe it's the real reason behind the official excuses. No one can believe those of us of the Society of Jesus, serving as we did in an area where gold was discovered, hadn't helped ourselves to it, or that we simply didn't know locations of the richest lodes."

Dom Gregorio's eyes bored into mine, and the room grew suddenly colder. "Well? What *do* you know about that gold?"

"Next to nothing, Domine. Our Father Visitors...the ones who inspected the missions and kept us all in touch with the rules and practices of the others...forbade us to have anything to do with gold. We were not allowed to touch it. For instance, we were even forbidden to wear gold buttons on our robes. I know that a few were tempted by that sort of thing—"

Dom Gregorio raised one eyebrow as he looked at me, his voice heavy with irony, "But of course you were above such temptations."

I shook my head with a faint smile. "It's just that I was never in a position to be tempted."

"Hmmm." He stroked his chin with thumb and two fingers. "I can see why His Majesty's interrogators never made any headway with you. I wonder...perhaps you Jesuits will all get away with fortunes, despite the hardships they've put you through...and you, don Ygnacio, might well be typical of the rest of the members of your Society."

I drew my breath in sharply, held it, then let it out in a rush. My gaze fell away from him, focusing on the cold tile floor. His reaction was so typical. On the one hand, he understood the fate of the Society and empathized with its loss. He pitied me and held me as an example of the sufferings of the whole. At the same time, he could not believe any of us innocent. The members of a group so severely punished *had* to be guilty. I felt a momentary jab of anxiety. What would be his reaction when he found out that I was guilty...of quite another 'crime?'

As for the gold, not one of our interrogators, and now not even this abbot, could believe that we had no golden secrets to hide. Greed blinded them all.

I expected to be dismissed at once, but was surprised. The abbot's next words lifted my spirit; my eyes met his once again.

"Be that all as it may, it's none of my business. You are, of course, confined to this monastery, don Ygnacio. There may be opportunities for escape, but your condition is weakened enough that you probably won't get far, even if you try. Our dogs will track you down. We'll expect you to help with our daily labor to earn your meals, and you'll be closely supervised. Join us for Masses, and I'll see how best to use your talents."

"Very well, Dom Gregorio, I'll do my utmost."

ౠ౦ౘ

Having nothing pressing as yet to occupy my time, and no place to go but the church or my cell, I chose instead to stroll out into the cloister garden, to sit on a bench under an apple tree and enjoy the morning sunlight. Dom Gerónimo Gomez Flores, the Royal Inspector from Madrid, had been right. The fresh country air, the scent of the green and newly-scythed grass, the various flowering plants and trees, were already doing me and my morale a world of good. I leaned back against the trunk of the tree, closed my eyes and let the sun flood my face.

My reverie was interrupted by angry voices, raised to one side of the cloister, coming from an area screened from me by shrubbery.

"You're the scum of the earth, Tomás, you, your beloved friend and all the others in your circle. Traitors! You're destroying us all by betraying La Caridad!" The voice was brassy, bullying. I was amazed that any monk could speak so to a brother.

The porter's quieter, timid voice answered, becoming more assured as one word followed another.

"You just can't understand it, can you, Metodio? There can't be another opinion beyond your own...and those from within *your* circle. At least we have a grip on reality; we see the handwriting on the wall, you know. This place has been decaying away for some time, already."

"Decaying away because brothers of your ilk have been undermining it. La Caridad is our mother! You're giving in to the bishop's grab for the land and its produce, and you're killing the mother that fed and clothed you all these years. Not to mention the spiritual food she supplies. Matricide!"

The brassy voice had become suffused with emotion, maudlin but sincere. A breathing space, and then a furious snarl, "Just you go on with your plans and

I'll kill you, you and that special friend of yours."

"You're irrational, Metodio...maybe even insane.... Stop! STOP THAT! GET YOUR HANDS OFF ME!" The quieter voice rose in tone and volume, accompanied by the sound of a scuffle. I was rising to intervene when a third voice rang out, a voice I recognized as Eugenio's.

"Brothers! Brothers! Have you forgotten who and what we are? This is a house of prayer. Of contemplation. Christ's house. Our Lady's."

"Brother Eugenio, this man..." the brassy voice began.

"Remember Christ's words, Metodio. Even if you feel that Tomás is your enemy, you must love him."

ൠ൚

The exchange continued in lower tones, a more civilized give-and-take, Metodio's voice dropping toward a normal level. The trio began to move away. I waited, unmoving, not wanting the monks to know I'd overheard the entire quarrel. Once their footsteps faded, I climbed the stairs and took refuge in my cell, where Metodio's words repeated themselves over and over: "I'll kill you, you and that special friend of yours."

I had just witnessed a striking example of the division within La Caridad, and Brother Eugenio's earlier words came back to me, now as a warning as well as a mystery: "We're at each other's throats. But then there's the charter...."

Chapter III

I'll Kill You

Brother Eugenio came to fetch me in the afternoon, saying the abbot wanted him to be my guide through the monastery. Not a word about the violent argument that morning.

The fracas must have been overheard by everyone on either level of the cloister, not to mention nearby halls and rooms. Where had Dom Gregorio been? And why was Eugenio so nonchalant? I'd been in a position to overhear the argument from my cell. Surely he must have wondered about my reaction, if I had.

"I'll show you the areas where you might be put to work," was all he said. We began with the large kitchen, festooned with an array of cooking vessels of all types hanging on the walls. An olla of red terracotta about three feet tall stood in a niche, containing gallons of pure spring water for drinking, cooking, and washing up in the neighboring sink carved out of limestone. I was impressed by the vast chimney, which passed through the second story and attic, ending in a small, bright aperture against the sky far above my head. Its lower opening formed the 'ceiling' of half the room, allowing several different fires at one time. An inspired cook must have designed it. Against one wall, sheathed with a metal plate, were chains for hanging huge cauldrons or perhaps setting up a spit to roast a whole cow or pig.

We went next to the section of the monastery that had been destroyed by the earthquake twenty years before, the one that devastated Lisbon. There was not much of the original structure left standing, just rubble.

"That earthquake shook this area, too," he explained. "Portugal is only a few miles away, you know. It also damaged parts of Ciudad Rodrigo, including the cathedral, though thank God not too severely."

"Aren't you going to repair the damage?"

"We haven't the money or manpower. Part of the problem I told you about."

Eugenio warmed to his role as guide with each new stop, but when we toured the wine cellar he could scarcely contain his pride. The huge room with its earthen floor was filled with casks of white wine and red, source of our dinner wine the night before. Wooden racks against the walls were lined with corked bottles of green and brown glass, their necks all slanted down.

"Do you cultivate your own vineyards?"

"Oh, yes. It's quite a tradition around here. We produce passable wines, though there are far better ones. From Robledillo, for example. Still, ours are good enough to serve as the blood of Our Savior. I think the main reason the bishop wants to annex Robledillo is for its wines. They're worth a king's ransom, you know."

I was startled at what seemed to me a gross exaggeration. "You're using a figure of speech, of course."

"No, no, don Ygnacio. I'm speaking of Emperor Carlos V, who preferred those wines to any others in his realm. And that included the wines from your home region. Robledillo's wines are famous because of it."

He continued his explanations, but my thoughts dwelt momentarily on that last statement. This obscure village was producing wines superior to those of the Mosel or the Rhine, of Switzerland or Austria? No wonder there was a life-and-death struggle going on over the town.

As we left the wine cellar, Eugenio was still talking away, shaking his head with a doleful air. We were approaching the vegetable garden.

"…and we're having trouble keeping the weeds out of our vineyards and cultivated fields. Too much land, too few hands. We need to hire more workers, but there is no money. Just look at those weeds."

The garden seemed to cover at least two acres. Peas at their peak, lettuce, celery, beans beginning, beets, turnips, spinach—every European vegetable one could imagine.

Eugenio was pointing to some healthy-looking weeds crowding the vegetables in their rows. They did not look all that threatening to me, but I knew he was bothered by their presence.

I looked in vain for corn and tomatoes and potatoes, musing on the inconstancy of mankind. When I was in the Sonora, I'd longed for home cooking. Here, I sighed for frijol or tepary beans, camote, yucca root, and a drink of atole. And corn tortillas.

"Do you have any experience with farming, don Ygnacio?"

His question brought a smile. "I taught my mission Indians how to cultivate their crops, European style, and in the process did plenty of planting, cultivating, watering, hoeing and weeding myself...not to mention harvesting and storage. Yes, I'd say I've had some experience."

"Then here's probably where you'll be working." Eugenio then pointed out the limits of monastery property to the north and west, where I could see wheat fields. We turned then to re-enter the buildings. It seemed odd that I would be working outside the monastery walls.

"What makes you think I won't try to escape, once I get outside these walls, Brother Eugenio? Or will you be using one of your few precious workers to keep an eye on me?"

"Escape?" He looked me up and down with a lopsided grin. "I can see you're a highly educated man. I can tell from your speech, and that certain refinement you have about you, despite those scars on your face. I hope you don't mind me speaking this way. Men such as you do not violate their vow of obedience. You're still a priest, even though you no longer belong to any order. I suspect you feel you owe obedience to the king and even to our abbot. And then, to be quite frank, you don't look strong enough to run far, even if you did hit me over the head and bolt for freedom." He chuckled. "But never fear, someone will be watching, even though you may not see him."

That afternoon I began my duties in the garden, labor that would last throughout my stay. I was tested to the limit of my strength at first, but wholesome food and adequate rest fortified me, and I began to regain the weight and muscle I'd lost through prolonged close confinement and repeated malaria attacks.

☙CB

My many years of exile taught me the folly of counting days, or should have. I fell into the earlier habit without quite realizing it, calculating the time of my trial as some 2,920 days—8 x 365—to which I added 220 more, for a total well over 3,000. Counting them as they passed would have been an absurdity. Nonetheless, I was counting the days since my arrival at La Caridad. A little over a month had passed since then, and August had sent her warmth into the darkest corners of the monastery, even my own cell. I'd come to know all the monks by sight and name. Those who'd troubled to talk with me from time to time, I knew even better. The number of convinced partisans of the bishop's point of view continued to surprise me. They believed the bishop was Dom Gregorio's superior, and were honoring their vow of obedience by supporting him. Fanatics of obedience, I called them.

I reflected on my own negative reaction to their position. I, as a Jesuit, was bound by my vow to obey *perinde ac cadaver*, like a corpse. I'd often pondered the ambiguity of that metaphor. After all, when did a corpse ever obey a command?

While most of Dom Gregorio's men seemed quiet and dutiful, nodding to me as they went about their choir duty, scribal, farming or maintenance tasks, there were others who represented extremes. Brother Eulogio was a loner, always eating with his cowl over his head, face down to his plate, rarely speaking unless forced to do so, a chronically timid or frightened man. Oddly enough, he did much of the scriptural reading at meals. He had a gentle, almost silky voice, accented as he read the words of Jesus.

The other extreme was Brother Metodio who, as I'd already observed, was an angry man, ready to quarrel with and attack anyone who expressed an opinion on just about anything. I suspected the current controversy kept him permanently on edge.

Caught in the middle of the controversy was Dom Gregorio.

He'd been listening to me during Masses. "You have a decent voice, don Ygnacio. Would you care to join the choir monks during Mass, and sing the responses? Father Plácido is always looking for talent."

Flattered, I agreed. "Thank you, Domine, it would be a privilege."

Father Plácido, the choirmaster, a rotund fellow with a thick fringe of brown hair around his skull, had already shown a strong interest in me. For two weeks at least he'd watched me from his place before the choir, or from the ambo when it was his turn to officiate at Mass. I'd noticed, but hadn't realized his purpose.

"Ah, don Ygnacio, *you* can *sing!*" he exclaimed with evident pleasure when Dom Gregorio presented me.

"I carry a tune, Father Plácido."

"Plácido, he's a baritone, and you're short of baritones since you've only Gelasio, Metodio, and Leopoldo. Don Ygnacio would make a fourth. Tomás could crank his chin back up where it belongs and go back to being an honest tenor. I'm exempting Ygnacio from singing matins with you, though, until he has begun to recover his health."

"Excellent! Excellent! Welcome, don Ygnacio...even without matins. Do you know the responses already?" Father Plácido towed me along by the sleeve and pointed to a place between Brother Metodio and a handsome man with a mop of curly, copper-colored hair. That would be Leopoldo, but was his title Father or Brother?

We tried out a *Gloria*. I could hear the tenors struggling with their lowest notes.

"Father Plácido," I said in the pause after the first run-through, "Couldn't this be keyed a fraction higher? The tenors are having trouble with those B-flats."

Metodio turned on me. "Who are you to make changes in our music? What business is it of yours? We've been singing the *Gloria* this way ever since I can remember, and here you come in, sing for three minutes and you're already a greater authority than any of us. I—"

Plácido cut him short. "Brother Metodio, calm yourself. The suggestion's a good one. At least, let's give it a try," He blew the new note.

The tenors were relieved, but not Metodio. After rehearsal he pulled me aside and, without pausing for breath, began his attack.

"You Jesuits are troublemakers. I've read about how you come into a place with your fancy new ideas and disrupt our ancient rituals the way you just did. You're greedy for power, that's what they say. You've already made an impression on our abbot, and now even on Father Plácido. Pretty soon you'll be running the place." His upper lip lifted in one spot, like a dog snarling. "By then, you'll have a free hand to teach your heresy. I hear you Jesuits have indulged in that, too."

My retort was sharp, but controlled. "Brother Metodio, I'll not argue this with you, not on the grounds you've established. Your premises are false, as well as vicious. I wish you a good day."

I strode from the church to begin my day's work in the garden. The labor was all too familiar by then, but I went at it with such emotion I was drenched in perspiration, muddy and exhausted.

Metodio's words weighed heavily on my mind, and his vehemence upon my soul.

৪৩৫৪

When I was not needed for labor in the garden or vineyards, I was allowed some free time to explore the monastery. A narrow door along the upper cloister walk had often intrigued me, and on opening it I found a small chamber deep in dust and bird droppings. To one side, a ladder passed through a hole in the ceiling. Out of curiosity, I climbed it and discovered the bell-ringer's loft, an airy space under the bell tower. Three window-like rectangles had been left open in the tower, looking north, east, and west. The north opening, directly over the front entrance, seemed at least three stories above the cobblestone courtyard. I could look out over the valley and the winding road of that first rainy night, leading in the direction of my far-away German homeland.

A bench in the loft was covered with pigeon droppings and thick with dust, like the chamber below. Otherwise the loft was bare, except for the bell ropes attached to the bank of bells above, threaded through holes in the floor so the monk announcing Mass could ring the bells from ground floor. The loft allowed access in case a rope broke or if the bells needed repair or replacement.

I scraped off the bird droppings with a short piece of wood I found on the stone floor nearby, and dusted the rest of the bench with my ragged handkerchief. Then I sat there, or on a windowsill, to catch more of a breeze, alternately reading my breviary and gazing at the sunlit landscape. I could hear the squawks and quarrels of fledged young storks, bickering over their status either as babies needing food or adults ready for flight to far-off places. A few times I leaned from a window to watch the adults fly in, long legs dangling, to land on the roomy nests or on ledges above me. Flapping away again, they became graceful as they picked up speed. They were big, impressive birds, and they were free. *"Look at the birds in the sky; they do not sow or reap...."* I envied them.

The loft became my place of meditation. I'd take books up there: the poems of Fray Luís de León or of San Juan de la Cruz, borrowed from Dom Gregorio. I enjoyed Fray Luís's brilliantly intellectual poems evoking the 'harmony of the spheres,' which for him expressed God's harmonious purpose. San Juan's reduction of his very feminine *alma*, his soul, to nothingness, *nada*, in the presence of Christ the 'bridegroom' seemed to me to complement rather than contradict Saint Ignatius of Loyola's 'God in all things.' Both men believed the best way to unite with God was to cease to center one's consciousness on self.

The words of Saint Augustine, as he addressed God, could apply to both saints as well: "Late have I loved thee, O Beauty so ancient and so new, late have I loved thee.... You called and cried to me to break open my deafness and you did send forth your beams and shine upon me and chase away my blindness: you breathed fragrance upon me, and I drew in my breath and I do now pant for you: I tasted you, and now hunger and thirst for you: you touched me, and I have burned for your peace."

ಶಿಂದ

One Sunday afternoon I climbed to the bell loft and crossed to the east window. A coach was standing just outside that huge, stone gate with the overhead iron fan, my entry point that first rainy night. How different the horses looked from above, broader of back than I'd realized, with necks and manes tossing and tails swishing at flies. The coachman was helping a woman down the steps.

I was spellbound, not having seen a well-dressed European woman in nearly six years. She wore a sky-blue dress that shone in the sunlight, with sleeves and collar of white, and her hair was caught behind her head with a blue ribbon. It cascaded down her back in auburn waves as shiny as the billowing skirt. Though her coloring was different, something in her stance and movements reminded me of my Beatriz. From my perch, this woman looked altogether lovely.

She was waiting for someone, or something. I followed the direction of her gaze. Turning to the north window, I saw the door standing at right angles to the church entrance. It opened, and one of the monks emerged. I could not guess who, as he wore his cowl. I watched him cross the courtyard below, the *Plaza de las Cadenas*, then unbar and open the heavy gate a crack, slipping out. Was he Tomás, our porter? If so, why had he not thrown open the gate so the coach could drive inside?

To my amazement, the figure in the black robe embraced the lady.

A flush of embarrassment heated my face as I realized I might be intruding on an intimate love-tryst, yet I continued to stare. The two separated, and then, linking arms, walked up and down the road, earnestly talking. After a few minutes, she handed the monk what I could only guess was a stack of letters, tied with string. He'd pushed his cowl back. Copper-colored curly hair! It was Father Leopoldo, my fellow baritone and the monastery's instructor of boys. He and the lady embraced once again, and she pulled away, giving him a last peck on the cheek. He helped her mount the steps and waved as the coach drew away.

Father Leopoldo, of all people! He pulled his cowl back over his head, re-entered the Plaza and hurried to the door. Was he hiding his identity? Did

Dom Gregorio know about this? I was not about to tell him.

༄༅

I began to have an occasional visitor in my lofty refuge, Brother Gelasio, the bell ringer. He was 'in charge' of the space I'd invaded, and swarmed up the ladder one day to find out what I was up to, swinging himself over the last two rungs and landing well inside the chamber in a swirl of skirts.

"Don Ygnacio, we've been curious to know what you've been doing up here," he said, not needing to catch his breath. "Since this is my area, I thought I'd just come up and ask."

"I hope I'm not disturbing anything by meditating up here. I like to read here, and think, and enjoy the view. That's all."

"Oh." He paused, considering, clear green eyes unfocussed, his triangular face still. Then a pixyish smile quirked the corners of his small mouth. "I don't think anyone will see any harm in that, so long as you're finished doing the job Dom Gregorio assigned you for the day."

"Always, before I come up here. But, Brother Gelasio, being here gives me a momentary sense of lightness...of joy, and freedom. I look northward toward home and dream. It's balm to the soul of this prisoner, you see."

He favored me with a look of sympathy. "I understand. I come up here too...it's sort of my secret hiding place. Not so secret, now, but you're welcome to use it, too. As far as I'm concerned, you can come up here any time you like."

"Thanks, Brother Gelasio. I'll ask Dom Gregorio's permission before I invade your space again, though. Tell me about yourself. Where are you from?"

He'd come from Robledillo de Gata, the eldest of a prosperous peasant's sons, brought all the way to La Caridad for Sunday Masses when he was a boy. He had been fascinated by the brotherhood and longed to join the Norbertines, rather than follow in his father's footsteps as owner of the *estancia* and tender of vines and olive trees. There were three younger sons who could do that labor, even though it meant Gelasio would lose the family inheritance to the next oldest brother. He'd been steadfast in his desire, and his father, who'd recognized him as the most talented of his boys, at last gave in.

Gelasio owed everything he knew about God and the world at large to the training he'd received from the brothers.

He began appearing more often in the loft, and we briefly passed the time of day before he applied himself to his task of ringing the bells from there, rather than from the ground floor. All four bells had different pitches and were rung in a patterned sequence. The sound was overwhelming; I covered my ears to ease the pain. Afterward, we'd go down to join the choir.

Father Plácido often gave Gelasio solo parts. He'd meet us and escort the 'bell ringer' to his place in the baritone section, an arm around Gelasio's shoulders. The contrast between them was striking. Bear-like Plácido waddled along, escorting the younger monk, hampering his normally quick and fluid gait. Plácido's special attention was merited, for Gelasio had a distinguished voice, true and mellow, carrying the rest of us.

Shortly after that first meeting in the loft, he began arriving earlier, first by ten minutes, then fifteen and finally twenty minutes. We'd talk while he invariably sat on the north windowsill, never holding on, sometimes with his feet dangling over the outside. He assured me with a grin that he had been doing this for years, with never a mishap.

"One mishap would be one too many, Gelasio," I kept telling him, but he ignored me.

His main concern was to find out what I believed about the vow of obedience, especially the vow I'd taken. I quoted St. Ignatius's *Letter On Obedience* to him: "In all things *except sin* I ought to do the will of my superior, and not my own."

Gelasio was intrigued. "Do you think that obeying our bishop in Ciudad Rodrigo could possibly be a sin? He's clearly our superior."

"Your abbot, Dom Gregorio, is your absolute superior, and his word is law here in the monastery. This is his fiefdom." I hesitated, proceeding uncertainly. "I'm not sure the bishop has any real jurisdiction over him...or you, for that matter...but he believes he does have jurisdiction over the parish of Robledillo."

"Well, don Ygnacio, I think he does, too. And I think we have no business trying to hold on to something that belongs to the diocese. I say we turn all the rights and privileges over to don Cayetano and be done with it."

My surprise must have shown, as he was watching me closely. "But I understand that your monastery's welfare depends heavily on Robledillo, and without its voluntary labor, its donations and the young men like you who come here as postulants, you might go out of existence."

Gelasio frowned and thrust out his narrow jaw, looking like a stubborn imp, a far cry from his usually benign expression. "God will provide. I think it is sin to resist the desires of the bishop."

"Has he issued an order to your abbot, I wonder?"

"I don't think so…."

"In that case, there is still room to maneuver."

His green eyes flashed with sudden exasperation. "Don Ygnacio, I must ring the bells now."

I waited for him at the bottom of the ladder this time. Clearly I'd said something he had taken to heart, but in the wrong way. Maneuvering and compromise did not fit his vision of things as they should be.

But with that thought came another. Gelasio was reluctant to consider compromise for a reason. He must have decided on a course of action already. But what?

ဆဝငြ

As I was mounting the stone staircase to the upper cloister one day around mid-morning, a familiar voice called my name. Father Plácido was standing at the base of the stairs, smiling and holding up a linen-covered basket. He beckoned to me, so I turned about and went down to join him. He nodded at the basket.

"Our baker, Brother Francisco, always bakes *pan dulce* on this day. These are fresh from the oven. I'd like to share them with you."

"With me?"

"I've been wanting to talk with you for days, but couldn't think of a good excuse. These are delicious. Try one! You're much too thin anyway."

I followed him into the garden, to a stone bench under an apple tree, where he uncovered his hoard of six large pastries. They were a cross between cookie and bun, still hot and fragrant, sweetened with honey from the monastery's bees. Irresistible! I chose one and ate it slowly, savoring every bite. He ate two.

"Why did you want to talk to me?"

"Tell me about the savages in the New World, don Ygnacio. Do they really have their faces in the middle of their chests, as Pliny the Elder says?"

I laughed. "Pliny had a wild imagination, Father Plácido. He pretended to know many things he had no inkling of. No, those people are men, just like you and me. Their skin color is darker and they have black, straight hair and black eyes as well...or nearly so...but they're a handsome people, on the whole, often much better made than we are."

"But how can that be? Surely, Christians are better made than anyone else?"

"God has shown them great favor, Plácido. They are strong and healthy—or they were, until we brought them our European diseases—very athletic, and they have tremendous endurance. Physically, they outdo us. We are too civilized, too soft, you see."

I accepted and ate another *pan dulce*, while Plácido wolfed down the last one in the basket.

"Did they always accept your teaching of the Gospel, don Ygnacio?"

"Not always. In one mission, Guevavi, I failed in one of my best efforts, to convert a powerful medicine man and his tribe. That's a long story, perhaps for another day. But in the two other missions where I served, I had good success."

His expression turned to that of a small child listening to tall tales. "Were you ever in mortal danger?"

"Oh, yes, quite a few times." I told of a moonlight ambush in a narrow canyon by ranch hands, hired by a murderer.

Plácido's eyes grew even wider. "You were ready to defend your mission and your flock with your life, weren't you?"

I paused, remembering my feelings of long ago. "I suppose I was. Yes, I would have died for them."

"And I'd die to preserve Our Lady of Charity, too, don Ygnacio."

Father Plácido was truly a gentle soul. I wondered if he could have endured the savage torment handed us Jesuits, concluding that he'd have numbered among those who'd fallen. I smiled sadly at the rotund figure next to me, with his soft, pudgy fists clenched in his lap.

ଚୈଓଃ

I was strolling in the garden one morning after Mass, reading my breviary, when my baritone choir mate, Father Leopoldo, joined me and walked silently by my side for a while. Leopoldo seemed to be in his early thirties. I'd finally found the right description for his unique hair color—that of new-fallen ripe chestnuts, a shade darker than the lady's hair. The coincidence was interesting. I wondered if it could have been a reason for their attraction to each other.

Shorter than I, he glanced up at my face and broke the silence at last.

"There are strange plants in the New World, don Ygnacio. I know about some of them from my investigations and correspondence, but you lived there. Your presence here...well...it's a wonderful gift for someone like myself. Please, tell me what you know of those plants. You must have worked with them first hand.

I was flattered. He considered me an authority. "Yes, Father Leopoldo, I used many of them, especially the healing herbs. There are plants growing in the Sonora Desert that are found nowhere in Europe, and we'd do well to import them. Perhaps we already do...I have no way of knowing."

His eyes sparkled with curiosity. I'd always made a study of eyes, and his were lavender-blue, not that unusual this far north. In fact, I'd begun listing the various colors in my mind—hazel for Eugenio, brown for Dom Gregorio and green for Gelasio. Several monks had very dark, almost black eyes, but I'd not quite seen lavender-blue anywhere in my travels.

Leopoldo continued. "What were they, these healing herbs?"

"My knowledge comes entirely from my Indian converts, so credit for the information must go to them. There's the mescal, for example. It's a cousin of the aloe plant, but a giant by comparison, five to seven feet tall, and it puts up a flower stalk that can be as much as seven yards high when it's about thirty years old, not much younger than you are. I've used its boiled juices to heal all kinds of internal disorders, from heartburn to diarrhea, and the juices extracted from its root will heal wounds, even infected ones in a few days."

"I must write down what you're telling me. Could you come with me to my cell, please? I can do it best there."

We spent a pleasant morning as I recalled other remarkable plants and animals, then, in answer to his continuing requests for more information, I evoked for him the feeling of limitless space of the Sonora, the purity of its air, its moonless nights when millions of stars were visible in crisp clarity. I described the various tribes I'd gathered in one or another of the three missions where I served.

Leopoldo's graceful gestures, the range of his vocabulary and his refined manners soon told me he was not from a village or a nearby farm, like Gelasio and Plácido. Finally, my curiosity got the better of me. I had to ask him.

"Your speech and mannerisms tell me that you come from a noble family, Father Leopoldo. Am I right?"

He chuckled. "For a foreigner, you have a good eye, don Ygnacio. My father, the marqués Andrés Vicente Cerralbo y Villafuerte, is still living, though a very old man of eighty. My name, by the way, is Leopoldo María Cerralbo y Yeltes. My mother, the marquesa, died when my sister, Clara Eugenia, was born. I hope you can meet Clara one of these days soon. She's the dearest person on this earth to me."

I began to suspect the lady I'd seen was his sister. "I understand completely. I dearly love my sister, Isabella, too. I'd write to her if I could, but I've never been allowed to send letters outside Spain since my captivity here. And where is your family?"

"We're still living mainly in the Casa de Cerralbo on the Plaza Mayor in Ciudad Rodrigo. It's the old family home, built in the sixteenth century. I'll show it to you one day. And then, we have other properties outside the city as well."

"But who's running all these properties? Surely, you can't do all that from here, from La Caridad?"

"I have a brother, Arturo, the first-born, about ten years older. He's the one who'll inherit and who already has the burden of keeping the properties up. I do dabble in collecting. Not of 'worldly goods,' exactly...but plants, as I've hinted to you already. That's why I'm so interested in what you can tell me. I write letters all over the world, and my correspondents send me specimens from exotic lands that I plant...or have planted...in the family's gardens. But, I'm fulfilled here at La Caridad as a religious. And I love teaching."

I left him with the promise that I'd give him more information on Sonoran plants, as much as I could recall. About three days later, when he joined me as I walked the cloister and its garden, we had a different sort of conversation.

"I suppose you must all be familiar with the habits I've developed since I came here to La Caridad, Father Leopoldo. The cut of this robe of mine and my northern appearance must make me stand out."

"True, don Ygnacio. And?"

"And I spend a good deal of time up in the bell-ringer's loft, so I've become acquainted with Brother Gelasio."

"Yes, we do know that. Gelasio's a simple and honest fellow. And?"

"And Gelasio has been talking to me about the problem of Robledillo. His main concern is his vow of obedience. He seems convinced that you all owe obedience to the bishop and shouldn't be resisting His Grace's move to annex

Robledillo de Gata parish to the diocese. He even asked me about my own vow of obedience—"

"I suppose you regaled him with talk about you Jesuits and your blind obedience to whatever orders you receive!"

I turned, startled by such a retort, to see Leopoldo's face flushed with red. He was angry and his voice rose with his next words, delivered before I had even a moment to answer.

"Well, let me tell you, it's people like you who should know better, who're egging on simple monks like Gelasio to undercut Nuestra Señora de la Caridad. Our lives would be easier without interference from the likes of you!"

"Just a minute, Father Leopoldo. I did nothing of the kind. I—"

A hand was laid on my arm, and on Leopoldo's as well. I turned to see my choir director, Father Plácido, who'd heard Leopoldo's words. He now walked on between us, still holding each of our arms.

"When I first heard a voice raised in anger," he said, "I thought this stranger, here, was a sinister troublemaker arguing with my angelic brother. But it sounds like it's the other way around. The angel's the troublemaker. What's so important, Leopoldo, that you have to yell at don Ygnacio?"

"It's that fool Gelasio. If he had his way, he'd sell all of us out to the highest bidder...I mean to the city and the diocese."

"Peace, my brother! You may be sure of this: that I also hate, and to the death, anyone who would trade the welfare of our mother, Our Lady of Charity, for favors from the bishop. But surely not our Gelasio...not him. I know Gelasio's a bit extreme, but he's selling none of us, I assure you. Let's not get so upset about this."

Plácido's face had momentarily hardened and his eyes flashed as he spoke of the monastery's welfare. His feeling seemed to run as deep as Leopoldo's, perhaps deeper, but his voice and manner soon resumed their usual sweetness.

He continued. "And then, there's the charter...." He stopped in mid-sentence. "Anyway, Leopoldo, did you know that Brother Eulogio is ill and you're his replacement this evening to do the readings at dinner? You'd better look them over so you don't stumble too badly."

When Leopoldo left us, I asked the question burning on my mind these many weeks. "Father Plácido, what's all this about a charter?"

"Ah...that's something you should ask Dom Gregorio about. He seems to think it might save us, but he surely knows nothing's certain in this day and age."

As Plácido walked away, I watched him from the garden path. He knew about the charter and he knew enough to answer my question, but the very same man who'd offered me *panes dulces* and talked of dying for his love of Our Lady of Charity was protecting his knowledge from me. They all were.

And I wondered to myself, why?

ᗏ)Ᏸ

A month passed, and then another. I'd devoted my farming talents and labor to helping with the harvest.

Onions were arranged on racks in the cellar, turnips and carrots buried in earth up to their tops, lying in slanting rows in bins along the cellar wall. Apples, too, were carefully stored, enough to last through the cold months. Fruit had been pared, dried, and strung on cords, ready for winter use; the wheat was threshed and packed away, waiting to be taken once each week to the mill on the Río Águeda just outside Ciudad Rodrigo. Honey had been gathered and stored in clay pots while the bees hibernated. Smoked and air-dried hams and goat meat hung from the rafters. There would be abundant winter food to feed the thirty-odd people who inhabited the monastery.

My acquaintance with the various monks had become deeper, my liking for some of them stronger, and, I believed, theirs for me. I continued to study and meditate on Biblical passages, as I had done most of my life, and read any books I could lay my hands on. Dom Gregorio was generous with his collection. Whenever he went to Ciudad Rodrigo or Salamanca, he'd invariably bring back the latest books, or controversial ones—such as a Spanish translation of Montesquieu's *Lettres persanes*—that were causing comment or scandal in the world at large. He and I discussed them, and he often bowed to my greater depth of learning while I admired the sharpness of his mind and chuckled at his dry wit. I only grieved that I was not able to exercise my calling, for I was *a priest forever, according to the order of Melchizedek.* Nothing could take that from me, not even death.

I pleaded several times with Dom Gregorio to allow me to celebrate Mass, but he put me off with a shake of his head or a remark. "We have plenty of celebrants, don Ygnacio. Perhaps...sometime later. We'll see." This state of affairs lasted until mid-November.

ᗏ)Ᏸ

I awoke from troubled dreams in the chill, cave-like blackness of my cell, not knowing what time it was. I could no longer remember my dreams, but something somewhere in the monastery was profoundly wrong. Had it indeed been a dream so vivid it left me with that feeling?

I rose and groped my way out of the cell and to the paler square that marked the open air of the balcony. There I leaned out over the railing, listening and even sniffing the air, catching only the scent of wet and rotting leaves. Nothing more. Not a breath of air stirred, not a bare branch creaked. I began to hear snores and other sleepy noises from neighboring cells. That was all.

After standing there shivering for some minutes in the blank darkness and silence, I turned back, assured my alarm was caused by my dreams. Years before, out in the desert, I perceived trouble by some mysterious means, and usually at night. Perhaps this was something similar, but it was just as likely I'd lost the talent. I went back to my cot and, after half an hour or so, fell asleep again.

I next awoke to shouts, hurrying feet and cries of distress in the gray dawn. The whole monastery seemed to be astir. I leaped out of bed and pulled on my robe, stepping out onto the walkway still unbuttoned. Monks were rushing out of their cells and down the stairs. I followed as fast as I could until I saw them squeezing through the door perpendicular to the entrance to the church, the door I'd first used to enter La Caridad. As I left the building, I could hear sobbing and someone praying, another repeating, *"Agnus Dei qui tollis peccata mundi, miserere nobis,"* taken up and chanted by the entire group.

I skirted the crush of monks standing in a tight semicircle around something black on the cobblestones. Managing to get a glimpse between their packed and shifting bodies, I saw that it was one of the brothers. Then I realized what must have happened. Above me, nearly forty feet up, was the square window I used so often to taste the breezes and admire the countryside.

I edged closer, aghast at the thought of such a devastating plunge, and was finally able to see what the others saw. The form on the cobblestones lay on his back, his skull crushed from the fall and the front of his habit splashed with blood.

My new friend and brother, Gelasio!

Chapter IV

Storks Make Poor Witnesses

Father Plácido comforted Tomás, whose sobs and groans were muffled against the larger man's shoulder. Others around me were silent, fighting their tears as I fought my own. I had begun to love Gelasio, this man who had chosen to befriend me. His face, turned skyward, wore a calm, almost peaceful expression, despite smears of blood and a congealed rivulet from his nose. I prayed for the peace of his soul, making the sign of the cross. When I finished, I looked up at that window where he always insisted on sitting.   A stork, one of the first arrivals from up north to over-winter here, stood poised at the peak of the belfry, surveying the scene below as if preparing a report for some magistrate. What would he say in his report, I wondered? That Gelasio had finally become too careless, like a fledgling that played too close to the edge? Or, that another bird had pushed him?

I returned to the chaotic scene before me and, without pausing to think of my precarious status as a prisoner at La Caridad, did the very thing I would have done while a missionary in the Sonora Desert. I reached down to close Gelasio's half-open eyes, realizing I was the last to glimpse those green irises. Then I laid the more sensitive back of my hand against his chest. He was cool. Dead for at least two hours, it seemed to me, perhaps three.

My actions provoked an angry rumble from the others. Surprised, I straightened to meet a sea of outrage. I had somehow committed an unforgivable breach of protocol!

One monk elbowed his way forward, tossing back his cowl. It was Brother Metodio, his face distorted with grief and fury.

He jabbed a finger at me. "YOU! It was YOU, minion of the Devil, blackbird. YOU threw our brother down!"

His accusation shocked and confused me. I glanced over both shoulders, but there was no one else he could have meant.

"Me? Oh, no, no...you...why? Why me? What on earth have I done? I...." I stopped, stricken by the enormity of the accusation. There was a spontaneous ripple among the brothers. They were backing away, distancing themselves, leaving me isolated next to Gelasio's pathetic remains.

Metodio continued, no longer shouting but with a tone equally deadly. "*You* were the one that spent hours up there in the loft. Our poor brother went up there to talk to *you*. You knew his habits and you had ample opportunity."

"Why should I commit such a hideous act? Why are you so sure it wasn't an accident? Gelasio was reckless up there. He might have slipped and fallen."

"Bah! Gelasio has been ringing our bells for years. He knew what was safe and what wasn't. *You* are the new element here, the unsafe element, you...you plotting Jesuit, *pájaro de mal agüero*, bird of ill omen! Someone paid you to do this."

Metodio's charge was absurd, but I began fearing its result. Great slanders had been heaped upon our Society of Jesus, eagerly accepted by the public. Consumed by their raw grief, these brothers' unreasoning fears could drive them to irreparable violence.

My back was to Gelasio' body. As I faced them, Metodio, still the fiery agitator, moved a step closer. I felt cornered. My voice quavered with emotion, but I ignored it.

"Gelasio was my *friend*! He was one of the few who's been good to me. I do not—I would never—repay kindness with evil. You, all of you, have worked beside me in the fields...for months, now. Don't you know me better than that?"

The knot of monks loosened a bit as Brother Eugenio jostled his way forward to stand by my side, followed by Father Plácido. Eugenio put his hand on my shoulder, while Plácido stood between Metodio and me, pressing his bulk against my side. I felt a surge of gratitude that at least two of them would take the part of an outcast like me, ragged and defenseless remnant of a once-great Company.

Plácido confronted the glowering Metodio. "Don Ygnacio didn't do this. He would never—"

"PEACE, METODIO, FOR THE LOVE OF GOD!" bellowed the abbot, drowning out Plácido's words. Dom Gregorio had come through the side door in time to witness most of the scene. He strode around to stand before and a little above us, on the steps to the main entrance to the church. "Peace, all of you, I say! It is I, not you, Metodio, or any of the rest of you, who'll determine what we'll do next, and I say our first task is to give our brother the proper rites." His voice turned gentler. "Tomás?"

The porter raised a red and tearstained face at the mention of his name. "Yes, Domine?"

"Open the doors to the church, my son. Then toll the bells for our brother, your friend Gelasio. Toll them well, in memory of him."

The abbot paused just long enough to see Tomás gulp and move away, head drooping, then resumed his peremptory tone.

"Porfirio! Tadéo! Go get the bier. It's behind the side altar on the left. We'll carry him in and lay him before the altar, as is right and proper. When you've done that, take a couple of the horses or mules and get out to Robledillo to notify his family and friends, and take the bad news to Bishop Cuadrillero in Ciudad Rodrigo. Tell anyone else you think of who has a reason to come. The news will spread fast enough. Tell them the requiem Mass will be...will be early morning...8:00 o'clock...day after tomorrow. That should give the Robledillo mourners time to get here." He scowled at Metodio, then said through stiff lips, "Examine your conscience and hold yourself in readiness, my son. I'll speak to you after the burial."

Finally, he turned to me. "And you, don Ygnacio, I'll also speak with you. Directly."

Was he being hostile? I couldn't tell.

Tomás was already opening the heavy church doors, and in the short pause before they swung open I spoke to the abbot *sotto voce*, across the body of the dead man,

"Please, Domine, we must lock the door to the bell loft as soon as possible. No one should have access to that loft; it needs to stay as undisturbed as possible. Someone must search it to see if anything up there can help us understand what happened."

He gave me a sharp, stern look and nodded, one eyebrow slightly raised.

Once the doors were open, we sang Psalm 130. We began in unison, for I knew the psalm quite as well as they did: *De profundis clamo ad te, Domine, Domine audi vocem meam! Fiant aures tuæ intentæ ad vocem obsecrationis meæ.... Spero in Dominum, sperat anima mea in verbum ejus....* "Out of the depths I call to you, Lord; Lord hear my cry!"

The abbot was soon back, wearing a black stole and carrying a basin of holy water. He sprinkled both the corpse and his assembled monks, including me, and I blinked as holy water spattered my face. How long had it been since I'd been on the receiving end? Or the dispensing, for that matter.

Just as the bells above us began to toll, Porfirio and Tadéo reappeared with an elegant walnut stretcher, covered with a blanket to protect the brocade, and set it down on its folding legs. They lifted Gelasio's stiffening body and laid him on it. Two more monks stepped up to grasp the rear handles of the bier.

Father Leopoldo appeared at the door of the church with the cross, and led us all as we processed, two abreast, into the sanctuary. Plácido insisted on walking by my side. We sang again as we accompanied the body.

Miserere mei Deus, secundum misericordiam tuam; ...Penitus lava me a culpa mea, et a peccato meo munda me.... "Have mercy on me, God, in your goodness.... Wash away all my guilt; from my sin cleanse me...."

Gelasio's body would lie in state as we waited for the mourners to arrive from Robledillo, the abbot said. The weather was cool enough that the body should keep until then. Meanwhile, his grave would be dug in the nearby cemetery and a humble coffin made. We'd all devote ourselves to fasting and prayer. The following morning, we'd celebrate the solemn requiem Mass and carry him with due ceremony to his last resting-place.

Dom Gregorio stopped one of the younger monks, Mateo, and told him to watch over the body. He'd be the first to keep vigil. I was preparing to leave the church, but the abbot made eye contact that could only mean I should not. I sat in the nearest pew and waited while he ascended to the sacristy and hung up his stole. He returned and sat with me.

"We must talk straightaway," he said, "before you forget something vital. Metodio is right about one thing: you saw more of Gelasio than the rest of us, these past few weeks."

"I'll tell you everything I know, Domine, but, if I may, there's something even more pressing. Someone must first look at the chamber up there, before any traces of what happened disappear. Forgive me for being so forward, but there were mysterious deaths in the New World that I helped to investigate. My experience might be helpful in discovering the reason for Brother Gelasio's death. May I accompany you to the loft to aid in your investigation?

The abbot stared for a moment. "Yes, very well. I'll go up there, and you with me. If there's anything to find, we'll find it together."

He motioned for me to precede him and we climbed the stone staircase to the upper cloister, squeezing through the narrow wooden door. I started up the ladder first, Dom Gregorio close on my heels. We both began to shiver, even though bright, yellow sunlight filled the loft. Its warm glow was deceptive, thanks to chilling breezes up there. I stopped on the top rung, hoping to see something before we trampled over it.

"Too bad storks don't speak our language, Dom Gregorio," I said, as I swept my gaze across the floor. "They might have told us exactly what happened here." Gingerly, I stepped aside to make way for him. He smiled faintly, eyebrows raised at my levity.

"My experience over many years of observing them, don Ygnacio, has taught me that storks make notoriously bad witnesses."

"Ah, look here!" I pointed to an area about the middle of the chamber, where dark splashes stained the stone. I stooped and scraped at one of them with my thumbnail. The scraping was soft enough to smear on my nail as I touched it. The blood was fresh, for I could smell the faint odor of iron filings. A ragged spattering of blood drops led to the square opening above the plaza, some of them smeared as if they'd been stepped on.

"He must have been killed here, or at least stunned. Someone came up the ladder and struck him. It had to be someone he knew; someone he expected."

I got down on hands and knees and peered along the stones from the splashes to the opening. By moving my head back and forth to catch the light just right, I was able to see scuff marks in the dust between me and the window. They seemed to show signs of a struggle, quite different from footprints elsewhere, caused by normal traffic.

"Look, Dom Gregorio," I said, "If you crouch down as I have just done, you'll see scuff marks on the stones. There was a struggle after Gelasio was struck, and then he must have been pushed out the window."

Wordlessly, the abbot knelt as indicated, turning his head so his cheek was an inch above the floor. "Ah! Yes, I see the jumble of marks in the dust. I don't suppose you can tell who made those tracks?"

"No, Domine. But I'm puzzled that no one heard anything. This was a fight to the death. There must have been a great deal of noise." I went to the window. There, on the sill, was a smear of blood, partially effaced. "He was still bleeding when his attacker pushed him over the edge. His habit could have wiped part of the blood off. I pray to God he was unconscious. My poor friend Gelasio!"

My voice broke. I took deep breaths to stifle my emotion, and we continued searching the chamber. Other than a congealed puddle of wax with burned wick in the center—the remains of a candle stuck on the corner of the bench either by Gelasio or by his murderer—there was nothing else.

I thought for a few moments. Blood in evidence here meant a wound, or wounds, prior to the fall. "We should look at his body, Dom Gregorio," I said. "We must learn the source of this smear, and those splashes of blood on the floor. Anything, even the tiniest detail, may be crucial in finding the killer." The abbot nodded and followed me as I turned to the ladder. I wondered at my shift in roles, a promotion from suspect to investigator.

We came back down and approached the altar, where Brother Gelasio was lying on the bier, feet toward the tabernacle. Mateo had not yet returned to begin the vigil, and the overcast day made the church too dark for our purposes. We lit two candles from the tiny vigil lamp, flickering day and night by the tabernacle.

"We'll need to turn Brother Gelasio's body on its side, Domine, if I'm to see if there are any wounds, but I'll need someone to help me. Should we wait for Mateo, or...?"

Loathing the very thought of disturbing my dead friend, I met the abbot's eyes. He hesitated, his expression sympathetic, but like me, he seemed reluctant. Finally, he drew in his breath and sighed. "I'll help you turn him, don Ygnacio."

We rolled up our sleeves and turned the corpse on its side. The body was inert, stiff, and yet rubbery. Gelasio was no longer there, I reminded myself. The temple was empty. The upper part of the robe and the sash were stiff with the blood I'd already seen as he lay on the cobblestones. Other than that, he had bled very little. I pulled the cloth aside enough to examine my friend's chest and back.

"I feel many broken bones...ribs, collarbone and upper arm, but he was not stabbed," I said.

"So he must have been struck on the head, stunned, and then thrown down."

"It would seem so. That way, we could have taken his death to be accidental, since damage to the head would be seen as a result of the fall. If Metodio hadn't accused me of murder, the idea of a killer might never have come to mind."

Dom Gregorio's lips widened in a brief, ironic smile. "Perhaps I should thank him, not reprimand him."

We settled Gelasio on his back once again.

When Mateo arrived minutes later, ready to take up his vigil, Dom Gregorio and I left the sanctuary to wash up at the spring-fed tank outside, the universal water supply. There I noticed a fragment of fine white cloth, snagged between two irregular stones at the corner of the retaining wall around the tank. It had been torn from something, a handkerchief, perhaps? Any other time I might never have noticed it, but my mind was receptive to anything unusual, anything new. I'd not seen that scrap of white before.

I bent lower to look closely.

It was roughly an inch wide by two inches long, drawn tight by some force and stained with blood at one end. I first showed it to Dom Gregorio, then carefully picked it out of the crevice and put it in my pocket. We went directly to his quarters.

Relations between us had grown warmer over the weeks. Our long discussions about the books he'd lent me, our mutual respect for each other's views and talents had led to greater trust. He'd twice alluded to the gold supposedly waiting for me in Sonora, but in a half-bantering tone, making me wonder if he'd ever taken the accusation seriously. Now, he sat behind his writing table, waving a graceful hand towards the chair facing him.

Not thinking who should make the suggestion, I blurted out my thoughts. "Should we pray for Gelasio, Dom Gregorio?"

"Quite right." He folded his hands on the table, closed his eyes and thought his prayer through for several moments. When it came, I admired its simple elegance.

"Lord God, our heavenly father, we pray that you have mercy on the soul of our brother Gelasio, and may your bright angels escort him to his place in the heavenly choir. May his glorious baritone fill the celestial realm, soaring in praise of your majesty. Remember the humble and fervent service of a man who devoted his entire life to you, and forgive any sins he may have committed. Give us the strength to bear his loss, guide us in discovering who committed this dreadful deed, and give us the wisdom to bring that person to justice and return him to your righteous ways. Amen."

For a while we simply sat there, thinking our personal thoughts. My concentration faltered from time to time. Human frailty asserted itself, allowing my mind to wander, and my gaze fell upon the violin. Dom Gregorio caught me looking at it.

"You can't keep your eyes off that violin, can you? I've noticed that before. Do you play, don Ygnacio?"

"Forgive my distraction, Domine. Yes, but it has been years...since my arrest in 1767. I don't know if I still could."

"Well, I'll be glad to let you try the instrument sometime later, when we get a moment of leisure—depending on how you answer my questions. But first, I need to find out anything I can about your relations with Gelasio. You spoke with him almost every day, yes?"

"That's right, Domine."

"You gained each other's confidence?"

"I felt so, Domine."

"Did you share any Jesuitical secrets with him that you later regretted?"

I paused, shocked, wondering just what he had in mind. "No, nothing that I regret."

He sat staring at me for a time and then blurted out, "I must put this to you directly. Did you kill Brother Gelasio?"

I was staggered by the rapid shift of topics, from violin to a friend, then to murder. Yes, I had a secret, and I considered it a noble one. But here, as in the prison near Cádiz, it would be considered a crime. And now I was being asked if I were a murderer. *"Did you kill Brother Gelasio?"*

He'd be asking everyone the same question, but he was correct about my seeing more of Gelasio than any of the others had, much more in recent weeks. The implications of his adjective 'Jesuitical' were not lost upon me, either.

"Yes, Domine, I saw a good deal of Brother Gelasio, but I must repeat that I shared no secrets with him, nor did I kill him. Gelasio became my friend, and I have precious few of those. Why should I return evil for good?"

I'd known, before the Expulsion and suppression of the Company of Jesus, that detractors had been spreading slander against us. We were too successful, too prosperous not to excite envy. Some of the criticism was justified, for we had admitted men who proved unfit to serve among us, but still it hurt me, disappointed me, to see the abbot echoing such prejudices. I'd come to like Dom Gregorio.

He stood, and our eyes locked. Finally, he nodded. "Yes...I cannot believe that you killed our brother. Your behavior up to now seems to confirm your innocence. When did you see him last?"

I unclenched my fingers from the skirt of my robe, greatly relieved.

"We talked about a week ago, on that warm day we had. I was up there in the loft, reading and meditating, as usual. Brother Gelasio came about twenty minutes before he rang the bells for Mass."

"What did you talk about?"

"He seemed uneasy to me. Tense. We talked about trivial matters mostly, but then he returned to a subject that had been plaguing him for months, the matter of your monastery losing control over the parish of Robledillo. He'd questioned me some time ago about my vow of obedience, my 'Jesuitical' vow, as *you* would no doubt call it."

My bitter tone sounded more biting than I intended. The abbot's chin firmed, and his mouth became a line.

"I'm sorry I used that word. It was offensive. But go on."

"Very well, Domine. I explained the vow to him. Gelasio then told me that he was certain that the monastery—including its abbot—owed obedience to the bishop and should not resist the takeover. But it was the end of our conversation that left me thinking. There was good deal I simply did not understand."

"Such as?"

"I must paraphrase him, of course...I'll do my best. He said he thought the bishop was close to moving ahead on the matter of Robledillo Parish, but it would be so much simpler if he had the charter in his possession."

Dom Gregorio stirred uneasily. "The charter?"

"Yes, I asked him then what he meant by 'the charter,' as I've asked others who mentioned it...Eugenio and Plácido...but I was given no explana—"

"The charter! So they all know about that. Just a moment."

He strode to the credenza and fished a small brass key from his pocket. Behind a side door was a row of drawers, one of them locked. He inserted the key, opened the drawer and began rummaging through the documents stacked inside. I rose from my chair to watch. Was he about to show me the document?

But something was wrong! He began muttering under his breath as he leafed through the papers for a second time. Finally he lifted them all out and went through them one by one. When he straightened and turned to me, I saw sweat beading his forehead and upper lip. His face was ashen.

"It's gone! Ygnacio...the charter's gone!"

Suddenly he staggered. I rushed forward and caught him, led him to a chair and urged him to sit. "Is there something I can get for you, Domine? A strong drink?"

"In the credenza. The right-hand door, the shelf. Brandy." He covered his face with one hand. "No, no, no, no," he moaned, each word coming forth almost as a sob. "Oh, no!"

I found a decanter and glass, removed the crystal stopper and poured the glass about a third full. "Domine?"

He took a gulp, then another, coughing briefly after the first. The liquor seemed to calm him, though his breathing remained ragged. I waited as he wiped his mouth with the back of his hand. He stared straight ahead, eyes unfocussed, as if no one else were in the room. I felt pangs of sympathy, wishing to help him by keeping his mind busy. An explanation might help us both.

"This charter is obviously of extreme importance, Domine, but I have no idea what it is or why anyone would steal it. Please help me understand its significance."

He took a third swallow of the brandy, closed his eyes and rocked back and forth, grieving without a sound. After many moments he wiped his face with his handkerchief, then leaned back in the chair and heaved a great sigh, finally composed enough to speak.

"I'll give you a little history lesson, Ygnacio. The charter is a Latin document, penned on vellum by a scribe and signed by His Majesty King Fernando III, the father of Alfonso X, 'el Sabio, the Learned.' It is dated 1234, exactly sixty-nine years after this monastery was founded."

I nodded. "At least I've heard of Alfonso el Sabio, Domine."

"Good. Well, his father, Fernando III, was called 'the Saint' because of his amazing exploits. Not only did he unite Castilla and León, two separate kingdoms until then, but he also conquered Córdoba, Sevilla, Murcia and Jaén, which had been held by the Moslems for centuries, and he forced the king of Granada to become his vassal. He was a passionate Christian in a land still very much divided among the three religions, and he did all he could to increase the power of Christian establishments, such as this monastery."

"So...what is in the document, Domine?"

"Patience, Ygnacio, I'm getting there. It gives our monastery jurisdiction in perpetuity, the right to tithes and tributes from any person settling on or farming lands belonging to the monastery and from any villages, present or future, that should be settled in its vicinity. Robledillo de Gata is an ancient settlement, and existed as far back as Roman times and beyond. It is mentioned, as an example of a village tributary to the monastery, in that very document."

"Dear God, Domine. Losing the charter is a mortal blow."

"Absolutely. Without it, our possessions can be whittled away. It anchors our claim against the bishop's in something more than a petty power struggle. God help me, Ygnacio, we may be doomed without it." He tossed down the rest of the brandy with a single gulp and held the glass out to me, gesturing for more.

I rose at once to fill it again, surprised at my own acute anxiety over the loss of the charter. Granted, I was attuned to the abbot's feelings in the matter, and both of us were still in shock from Gelasio's death, but that wasn't it. My uneasiness was deeper; selfish, perhaps. I feared for my own future.

If the bishop were to annex Robledillo, if this monastery were to cease to exist, what would become of me? I'd almost despaired of ever breathing free air again, but here, at least, thanks to Dom Gregorio, my prison was tolerable. I was well housed and fed; a few of the monks were kind to me, there had been no beatings, no interrogations. If La Caridad were to collapse, I'd be shipped to another prison. Where? Under what conditions? The next jailer would doubtless be informed of my 'crime.'

The abbot arrested my thoughts. "Well, Ygnacio, are you going to hand me that brandy or stand there forever?"

"Forgive me, I was working out the implications." I turned my mind to practical considerations of the moment. "Are there any copies of the document? At the Vatican? Who knows of its existence? The bishop?" I volleyed questions at him until he held up a hand to stop me.

"There should be a copy at the Vatican...but who can tell? There've been so many upheavals in Church history since 1234. The popes were in Avignon during most of the fourteenth century, and who knows what was happening to archives left behind in Rome? As to who knew about the document, more people right here in the monastery knew about it than should have. With the tension as high as it has been, with my monks taking sides, with so much anger and violence, knowledge like that is extremely dangerous. Gelasio was killed over this very document, you may be sure. The question is, who stole the charter and how? Who has it now?"

"Hmmm. Has Brother Gelasio been in your quarters recently, Dom Gregorio?"

"Not for months...at least not to my knowledge. And no one knew where the charter was kept...unless—"

"Unless what?"

"I'll have to think more about that. We'll talk later, Ygnacio, but I need some peace and quiet now. After Gelasio's people from Robledillo have gathered and properly mourned him overnight, I must conduct a solemn requiem Mass, and give thought to a eulogy and the many other problems this death will bring to a head. Would you excuse me?"

"Certainly, Dom Gregorio." I rose to leave the room, wondering about his switch from 'don Ygnacio' to plain Ygnacio. Was that a sign he'd put his trust in me? Why? And what would be his reaction, should he find out about that 'crime' back at the prison? At the fringe of my consciousness, just out of reach, lived the perpetual fear of a return to the beatings.

As I left the room, I lingered outside for a moment, my hand on the latch, my bowed head pressed against the carving of a lamb upon the half-open door. Other visions from the past crowded my mind.

The light of evening is waning in the prison cell at Santa Maria. Jakob is back from his latest session with the Royal Interrogators. He still holds himself upright, maintaining his dignity, but as soon as the cell door closes behind him, he slips to his knees and falls prostrate on the floor, moaning. The beating has been severe. I kneel and slip my hand under his chest, unbuttoning his robe so I can pull the bloody cloth away from his back. I rise again and find one of the few clean rags we have left, tear it in half and soak that in water. All I can do is clean the wounds. I have no medicine, nothing to ease his pain.

They've demanded of him what they've so often demanded of me: What have you done with the gold of Sonora? *Where is it hidden?* They've been brutal *this time. His back and shoulders are laced with crisscrossing whip cuts, and my own back smarts in sympathy. My own flesh is engraved with scars of countless interrogations, whip cuts from the week before, and before that, and before, and over and over, stretching back through those eight years.*

Images flow from further back. The heat of that July night in 1767 stifles me, a typical summer night in New Spain. We obey the summons of the bell and enter the church for the meeting, expectant, talking excitedly, speculating. Letters signed by our superior order us to congregate at Mátape to consider 'an important matter,' but now the bolts shoot home on the church doors and we are told we are arrested for crimes against His Majesty. Trapped, we mill around like animals as the hours pass, fifty-one of us, all Jesuit missionaries from Sinaloa and Sonora Provinces. We are lined up next day and marched, with no more than our breviaries and the clothes on our backs, across the miles of desert to Guaymas. Heat rises in wavering, suffocating bands from the sand. The older man next to me falls and cannot rise again. Others fall as well.

Starving on the beach at Guaymas, I dig for clams with shaking hands. I find one, smash the shell and swallow the sandy, salt-bitter, leather-tough body nearly whole. My brothers die of malaria in the swampy camp near San Blas. They die on the death march across New Spain to Vera Cruz, one after another, stumbling, falling, sick and exhausted, grateful to lie there forever, no longer responding to the whip.

The hold of the prison ship sailing for Spain is dark; we are crammed near the bilge where slaves bound for New World markets died just as we are dying now. I gasp, the stench of my dead brothers' bodies suffocating and ever present, lingering in my nostrils to this day.

സ෬

As I quietly closed the door behind me, I saw Dom Gregorio pour himself a third glass of brandy, full this time. I was amazed that he still appeared quite sober, but I knew better.

Chapter V

A Wider Perspective

Brother Eugenio and Father Leopoldo were both waiting for me outside the abbot's chamber. As I closed the door behind me, they fell into step on either side, like bodyguards, and escorted me out into the cloister. There we paced in somber silence around the colonnade, struggling with our shock and grief.

Leopoldo was the first to speak. "I apologize for Brother Metodio's outburst, don Ygnacio. I'm afraid there's a lot of suspicion and hostility against you here at La Caridad, just because you're *different*. You're not one of us, but I wanted you to know that many of us sympathize with your situation. Eugenio and I both wanted you to know that. We support you."

"Thank you, Father Leopoldo."

"You've probably noticed Metodio's quick temper," Eugenio added. "He's a spokesman—unofficial, of course—for the ones who resent you and your presence here among us."

"I'm afraid there's nothing I can do about my presence here among you. Believe me, if I could get back to my homeland, I'd leave at once. That's not to say I'm not grateful for the kindness many of you have shown me, but we all agree on one point: La Caridad is *not* my place." My tone was sharper than I'd intended, but my focus was on Gelasio. Even though Dom Gregorio had not made it my duty, I felt an inner compulsion to find out whatever I could about my friend's death. "We'll talk about such things later, if we must. Right now we need to think of Brother Gelasio. Do either of you know what he was doing late yesterday or last night? Why would he go up into the bell loft in the dead of the night?"

There was such a prolonged silence I began thinking they intended to ignore my question, but Leopoldo spoke at last.

"We've been wondering about that, and we simply don't know. Everything we saw him doing was his normal routine. And last night...you know my cell's on your side of the cloister; Gelasio's opposite to mine across the patio...I slept right through the night. Saw and heard nothing. Eugenio says he didn't hear anything from Gelasio, either."

I turned to Eugenio for confirmation.

"That's right. Gelasio sleeps...uh...slept three cells down from me. I'm a light sleeper, but I wasn't disturbed last night."

I decided not to mention my sudden awakening in the darkest hour of the night, feeling something was profoundly wrong. "Well, someone should question everyone. It should be Dom Gregorio, since he has the authority." Both monks glanced at me with questioning looks, their expressions as effective as words.

I was certain they were asking how I could presume to plan the abbot's next move, even in theory.

⁎⁎⁎

I was surprised to see the number of people who'd come to pay their last respects to Brother Gelasio. Many more villagers from Robledillo joined the group of family and friends keeping vigil since the previous afternoon, and a large group had come from Ciudad Rodrigo. I joined the choir monks, and we entered the church in solemn procession, to the sound of the tolling bells. Tomás had succeeded Gelasio as bell ringer, doing honor to his friend and, if he could keep from breaking down, would join us in the choir. Those brothers who were not part of the choir were assembled in a small group in one of the forward pews, the best seats reserved for the chief mourners. I was in an excellent position to observe, since I was at the extreme left of the choir.

Eugenio whispered to me, "That's Gelasio's mother, the big, bony woman. Those are his brothers and sisters in the first pew."

I followed his cue and saw a dignified woman in a simple black dress, her face heavily veiled. She clung to her husband, who bowed his head against hers in grief. Gelasio's numerous siblings sat with their husbands and wives, many of the women in various stages of pregnancy. Their husbands, uncomfortable in their best black breeches and jackets, sat with knees wide apart and work-coarsened hands splayed on their thighs.

Eugenio next pointed out the group from Ciudad Rodrigo. "There are the shopkeepers his family deals with. Most of them have known Gelasio since he was a little boy. That bunch over there are mill workers. And look...the bishop has sent his emissary, Father Miguel Ybarra. He's the one over there speaking to Dom Gregorio. He must have a special interest in this funeral, anyway. His family lives in Robledillo and his younger brother works for the Cerralbos – an expert winegrower, if I'm not wrong."

I nodded. Ybarra was a short, slender man, a severe black cassock molding his figure like a chess piece. His balding head, round skull and beak of a nose reminded me of paintings I'd seen of Saint Ignatius. I could also look down on Gelasio's body, laid out in the new coffin. Ritually washed and clothed in a new black robe, his hands were clasped around a large wooden crucifix lying on his chest. Decay had begun to soften the tissues of his face and gravity dragged his flesh down, sharpening his nose and pulling the corners of his mouth into a smile.

A pain knifed through me, so sharp I feared I'd lose control and be unable to sing. The enormity of this death engulfed me, adding to my untold losses. Family, fellow seminarians, friends—scattered, dead, dismembered. Now these few new friends were being torn away as well. I chided myself for self-pity and compared my paltry pain to that of his family, especially his mother, the *mater dolorosa*.

My Lord God, keep me from dwelling too much on self.

The Mass began. After scriptural readings, Dom Gregorio preached a moving eulogy, and I wondered how much of his inspiration had come to him while he was under the influence of brandy. I was still in awe of his ability to hold his liquor. After the service, all of us accompanied the coffin to the cemetery, where the abbot intoned graveside prayers. According to Dom Gregorio, I was not allowed, as a prisoner, to mingle with the Mangas family, but the words were delivered without conviction. I disobeyed them and approached Gelasio's parents.

"Señor Mangas...Señora...forgive the intrusion of an outsider, but I must tell you that your son, Gelasio, had the goodness to reach out to this stranger over the past months. He was one of the few here who had enough compassion...and I feel his loss like a deep wound. Please accept my condolences." My voice was rough with emotion.

Gelasio's father, whose face provided the model for his son's, looked me up and down without replying. His eyes were green, like Gelasio's, but cold and steely. He said nothing, but his wife laid a gentle hand on my arm.

"I can see that you loved him," she said. "Thank you for that."

Her husband pulled her away, turning to speak to one of his other sons, but she looked back at me with a kind smile and I bowed my head. If I'd been less moved, I might have followed, might have mingled with the family and learned something of value: a hint of any motive for the killing, or some shred of information about the charter. But such behavior was not only forbidden, it was unbearably crass.

Gloom and stillness settled over the monastery for the rest of the day, since the abbot had decreed fasting and meditation until the following morning. I was told that he was questioning all monks who occupied cells above the patio garden, to learn if anyone had heard or seen anything during the night. I could only hope that he'd share any knowledge he might glean with me.

I was restless and uneasy, pacing the cloister and garden, trying to see a pattern in the events so far so as to begin unraveling the riddle of Gelasio's murder. A futile effort, I knew, and it was neither my responsibility nor my place to investigate the killing, but my mind churned on, nevertheless.

Around four the following morning, I awoke briefly to the sound of the chant coming through the church wall. The monks were singing matins and lauds. Their routine had begun again. Breakfast that morning was subdued, but welcome nonetheless. I'd taken my last mouthful of steaming oatmeal porridge, sweetened with honey, and was wiping my lips when Eugenio tapped me on the shoulder and whispered, "You're wanted in the abbot's quarters, don Ygnacio."

I thanked him and left the refectory. Shortly afterward, I was knocking on the abbot's carved door. It was open, as usual.

"Sit down, Ygnacio," he commanded, without preliminaries. "I'll be taking you into Ciudad Rodrigo with me today. I wrote to Madrid months ago for further instructions on how I'm supposed to treat you, and since I've received none as yet I'll use my own discretion."

"If that means I can see something of the city, I'd be most grateful, Domine! But of what possible use will I be to you?"

"I'll be visiting the bishop, don Cayetano Antonio Cuadrillero y Mota, to report about Brother Gelasio's murder and also to find out, from his point of view, how far he's gotten in this business of annexing Robledillo Parish. I want you to observe everything. His reactions, what he says, who are his trusted associates, anything, everything. I'm sure he wouldn't tell me if he had the charter, but his manner might give him away."

"But, Domine, I know next to nothing about the protocols of a situation like this. I'm a total outsider."

"Precisely, Ygnacio. An outsider, therefore a cool and objective witness. Your observations won't be colored by any preconceptions, and I've already seen that you're a keen observer, unlike our storks."

I bowed in obedience. "If you need me, of course I'm at your disposal, Domine."

෨෬

The road swept in a wide curve to the left, and up the slope, toward an imposing medieval gate looking as if it had once housed a portcullis. The hilltop wore its walled city like a crown. Beyond the ancient and weathered fortifications loomed the great cathedral, its bell tower facing north. The road ran along the city wall for a time, where I saw the fresh masonry of star-pointed fortifications still under construction outside the medieval walls.

Leopoldo was with us, since the abbot had granted him a dispensation to leave the cloister to see his sister and take care of 'some family business.' He explained the new construction to the abbot and, indirectly, to me. The extra fortifications were to double the city's defenses against the Portuguese and French. The Portuguese had attacked and looted both city and monastery in the recent past.

Light was cut off for the time it took the coach to dive into the short tunnel through the wall that housed the city gate, jolting and rattling over cobblestones and thoroughly jouncing the three of us. We all grabbed hold of whatever we could, just to stay in our seats.

The coach slowed to a walk at the Plaza Mayor, but I maintained a grip on my seat nonetheless. A handsome building at the end of the Plaza was the Casa Consistorial, the Town Hall. Three houses down, near the mouth of the Rúa del Sol, was a three-story mansion with an ornamental stone frieze running across its façade, displaying the family arms, fantastical images of plants, animals and people, their precise images blurred by time and weather. In Italy, I reflected, this would be called a *palazzo*; here it was merely a *casa*, a house.

The coach stopped in front, and Leopoldo got down. "Dom Gregorio, please, on the way back, may I introduce don Ygnacio to my sister and show him the house?"

"Of course," the abbot nodded. "I'd like to see doña Clara myself."

We left Leopoldo there, then were taken from the Plaza Mayor down a narrow street that came out near a large and imposing church. Named for the first marqués de Cerralbo, La Capilla Cerralbo, or Cerralbo Chapel, was so-called to distinguish it from the cathedral, I guessed, but it seemed far grander than a mere chapel. I longed to look inside, but we were soon past and heading to a small park near our destination, the Episcopal Palace.

The building's façade, centuries-old, was half dismantled and hidden by scaffolding. Still intact was a modest entranceway with a weathered, wooden door.

At the abbot's request, I clanged the little bell beside the door. After a short wait, a priest in a black cassock admitted us. It was Father Ybarra, the bishop's emissary at the funeral.

"Ah, Dom Gregorio. His Grace thought you might be coming in, given the grievous circumstances. Let me go find out if the bishop can see you right away."

Bishop Cuadrillero, a corpulent man in his mid-sixties, received us cordially, although he appeared puzzled Dom Gregorio had brought me along. He waved at a tall servant standing nearby, calling, "Ricardo, bring us some refreshments. My favorite white wine."

Then he led us into the flagstoned inner courtyard, a quiet garden whose elegance contrasted with the rundown exterior of the building. It was adorned with late-flowering shrubs, fully mature trees and a well, its pulley mounted on an arch surmounted by an ornate cross.

"Forgive the chaotic state of the entrance and the façade. I'm having the front half of the palace rebuilt." His words seemed directed at me, although he was speaking to Dom Gregorio.

A second servant met us. He gestured at a table and chairs, screened from the rest of the patio by tall plants. "Will this do, Your Grace?"

The bishop stared at bird droppings, leaves and twigs littering the surfaces.

"Clean it up for us, and it will do admirably," he rumbled, rolling his eyes to the sky.

There was a short wait. The servant whisked away the debris and spread a linen cloth on the table. Ricardo reappeared with a bottle and three glasses in one hand, a dish of dried fruits and nuts in the other. He set down the dish with a flourish, arranged the footed glasses and poured each full of white wine.

"That's the wine from Robledillo?" the bishop asked.

"Yes, Your Grace, still cool from the cellar."

Satisfied, the bishop raised his glass to the two of us and expressed his condolences on the death of Brother Gelasio. He fixed the abbot with a questioning stare, his bushy white eyebrows forming double arcs over hooded eyes. "Do I understand correctly that your man was murdered?"

"That seems to be true, Your Grace. Don Ygnacio and I searched the bell loft where poor Gelasio was attacked, and found evidence that he was struck on the head in the middle of the chamber, dragged to the window and thrown down. Truly shocking, the worst of sins, a grievous breach of the tranquility of our monastery and profoundly disturbing to all of us, since we all believe the murderer is living among us."

The bishop's face was grave. "And what are you doing about it, Dom Gregorio?"

The abbot placed his hand on my sleeve. "I'm putting a good deal of faith in my ex-Jesuit friend, here. He tells me he solved two murders while he was out in the mission field in northwestern New Spain."

"Ah, indeed!" His Grace eyed me with fresh interest, inspecting my patched and threadbare robe. He lingered on my left cheek, and I put my fingertips to the scar quite by reflex. It was the first time he'd looked directly at me.

"I suspect this case may be more complex than murder among the savages," he said. I started as I realized he was talking directly to me. I bristled a bit.

"Those murders, Your Grace, involved Europeans and not the 'savages,' as you call them. The Indians in my three missions were well behaved...at least during my years among them."

"I don't know if you were aware of it, don Cayetano," the abbot broke in, "but Brother Gelasio was convinced the diocese should annex Robledillo Parish, and that the monastery should not be resisting the move. Did he, by any chance, visit you? Or did anyone else bring anything here from the monastery in the last few days or weeks?"

Was the abbot's question a form of bait? Was he hoping to provoke a reaction for my benefit? I could think of no other reasons for such a direct approach, but I couldn't imagine His Grace ever admitting the charter was in his possession.

Don Cayetano again arched his brows. He seemed to be choosing his words quite carefully. "I'm only aware that opinions at La Caridad are strongly divided on the issue, Dom Gregorio. Brother Gelasio was certainly not alone in backing the diocese. And, the matter is far from settled; discussion could take months, still, or it could all be resolved in an instant by higher Church authorities. As for me, I have no wish to move hastily. As far as I know, neither Gelasio nor anyone else came here from the monastery recently. I'd be happy to enquire further and let you know, of course."

I watched the bishop's every nuance. He spoke with a vague smile on his lips, and stared over the abbot's head instead of looking him in the eye, gesturing with palms outward as if blocking any further inquiry. There was an almost imperceptible squirm as he shifted his feet. He was not being candid. Had the abbot noticed? Apparently not, as he continued in the same line.

"Please do let me know if you find anything out about either issue: annexation of Robledillo or a clandestine visit from Gelasio. I'd be most grateful, Your Grace. And, please, let me know if any of my monks make contact with you here...perhaps one of them might do so one of these days soon, without my permission or knowledge."

The bishop's lips twitched as he broke into a benevolent smile. "Naturally, Dom Gregorio."

The abbot's requests seemed strangely idle. After all, this was a tug of war where the stakes were high enough to motivate another man's murder. Neither of these two combatants was being candid with the other.

I'd bowed my head, rubbing my brow and thinking about the exchange, when the bishop addressed me. I snapped to attention.

"Don Ygnacio, is it? When and where were you arrested? I must warn you that I've made a hobby of finding out everything I can about the expulsion and suppression of your order. After all, the destruction of the Society of Jesus is the ecclesiastical Event of the Century, par excellence."

His choice of words rankled me; a note of sarcasm crept into my reply, though I tried to suppress it. "Yes, odd though it may seem to you, I think so, too...Your Grace. As to when and where, I was arrested at our College of Mátape, in Sonora Province, New Spain. That was July of 1767. Afterwards, many of us died of disease, exhaustion, and brutal treatment...only twenty-seven of the fifty-one priests who began the trip in Sonora arrived at Vera Cruz. I've been a prisoner here in Spain since 1769."

The bishop sighed. "And you are still, to the *secular* authorities at any rate, a prisoner here in Spain." Here he stopped to give Dom Gregorio an ambiguous, hooded glance either to express his disapproval of the abbot's laxity or his fraternal complicity. I remained impassive, presuming I was not to understand. "But at least you are alive. Thousands of your brothers were deported from this country, arrested in their houses and schools, herded with only their breviaries and the clothes on their backs onto ships of all types and descriptions, and forced to sail to Civitavecchia, in Italy. Did you know about that?"

"I heard the rumors, Your Grace."

"And you knew they were refused permission to land by your own Father General, Lorenzo Ricci, and by His Holiness, Clement III?"

"Yes—"

"And then the ships sailed here and there, around the Mediterranean, for a month or two before they were allowed to land on Corsica, which had insufficient resources to feed and house so many men. They died by hundreds, maybe thousands, at sea and on land, of scurvy, thirst, starvation, disease...perhaps beatings as well. So, perhaps you are lucky, don Ygnacio." His eyes drifted back over the scars on my face.

I was immediately burning with curiosity. My confinement kept me from the truth about the calamity that had so utterly destroyed us Jesuits. I knew no more than sketchy and unreliable facts.

"I'm most grateful to you for telling me about our Company's fate. I must admit that much of this is new to me...being in prison, as you know. Can you tell me more? Why did His Majesty Carlos III decide to destroy the Company?"

I'd drained my glass. The bishop reached across and refilled it to the brim, leaned back in his chair and took a sip of his own.

"His advisors persuaded him, of course, in particular the President of the Council of Castilla, the Conde de Aranda...a disciple of the French 'philosophers' and Encyclopedists. I'll share a bit of juicy gossip I heard when I was last in Rome. It appears someone—perhaps the Duc de Choiseul, Aranda's French counterpart—forged a letter supposedly from your Father General. In that letter, 'Father Ricci' claims to have documents proving beyond a doubt that our king was an illegitimate child. The letter was immediately shown to the king, who was shocked beyond measure at such a dastardly attempt to dishonor him and the royal family. He became the Jesuits' implacable enemy overnight. If this was a conspiracy between Choiseul and Aranda, they succeeded beyond their wildest dreams and snuffed out thousands of brilliant minds...teachers, philosophers, scientists, theologians, explorers.... The world is poorer for it, and I, for one—God forgive me—hope those two roast in Hell."

I was seized by conflicting emotions. My eyes brimmed with tears: tears of grief for my dead brothers, some of whom doubtless were in seminary with me; tears of gratitude to the bishop for his understanding and sympathy for our suffering. I felt myself blushing at my own emotion and my vulnerability.

At the same time, I judged the bishop a cunning old fox, hiding something vital from Dom Gregorio. To cover my confused feelings, I seized my brimming glass and drank off the wine. Unaccustomed to so much alcohol all at once, I was catapulted into a strange state of giddiness. While my memory seemed enhanced, it was combined with a maudlin sense of my Company's situation that caused me to burst out with a mini-homily.

"Your Grace, I thank you for your generosity as well as for your information. Only these lines from Luke's Beatitudes can be a consolation now: 'Blessed are you when people hate you, and when they exclude and insult you, and denounce your name as evil on account of the Son of Man.... Behold, your reward will be great in heaven.' That's the only reward we Jesuits will receive; of that I'm certain."

I fell silent then, aware of my blunder in preaching to my superiors, aware that my tongue had seemed to thicken by the second, and that both men had noticed. The bishop appeared amused, but not Dom Gregorio. He stood, looking at me with a mixture of pity and impatience.

"Thank you, Your Grace, for your kind hospitality. I must tell you—you know this already—that La Caridad believes it has a valid claim to Robledillo de Gata Parish, and to give up that claim would be to revoke centuries-old precedent and rights, which we can substantiate with documents if forced to do so." He gave the bishop a broad, confident smile as if he were congratulating him on a promotion to the Archbishopric. "In other words, Your Grace, we will not relinquish our claim without a fight."

The bishop's vague smile hinted at his amusement, and his narrowed eyes and drooping eyelids gave him a self-satisfied but guarded air.

"Of course, Dom Gregorio, I'd expect nothing less. It's none of my business, of course," he continued, glancing at me, "but why don't you spend a modest sum on a few yards of black cloth? Don Ygnacio shouldn't have to go around in rags."

The abbot nodded. "Perhaps. Presently."

We took our leave, and the abbot ordered Brother Tomás to drive the carriage back to the Casa Cerralbo and wait for us there. He wanted to walk back, through the streets. While showing me the city, there'd be ample time to think about and discuss the preceding meeting, with little chance of being overheard.

The cooler air and brisk physical activity cleared my head as we walked. We proceeded downhill along the Calle Díaz Taravilla, turned right on the Calle Colada and passed through the forbidding city gate, a structure made no less unfriendly by the saints' statues occupying niches above and to either side of the opening. Once outside, we paused, enjoying a lovely view of the Río Águeda and the ancient Roman bridge crossing it.

Finally, Dom Gregorio turned our conversations back to the meeting. "Well, Ygnacio, what did you think of that interview?"

I focused on the question, realizing that the walk had sharpened my perceptions while it cleared my head.

"The only *substantial* news exchanged in the meeting were the facts, or in the king's case, the gossip, about us Jesuits. As for the rest, no real information was given or received...except that you'll continue to fight the annexation. But, I did watch His Grace closely."

"As I noticed. And your impressions?"

"I think he was lying, or at least bending the truth, when he said no one from the monastery had visited him. Also, when he claimed not to be in any hurry to annex Robledillo, and that discussion could go on for weeks or months. I think he expects to win the battle fairly soon, either by intervention from higher authorities, or by pulling your teeth, getting possession of the charter. His facial expressions, gestures, posture—everything, in fact, told me he was not being straightforward with you, Dom Gregorio."

"Possibly. I had the same impression, but couldn't be certain. Perhaps he already has the charter. What do you think, Ygnacio?"

"Not yet, or he'd have been more smug. Yet he was self-satisfied enough to convince me he thinks he'll get his hands on it soon."

"You give me hope, Ygnacio. If he doesn't have the document yet, there's still some chance I might recover it. We must think of a way to do that. Any ideas you might have are more than welcome."

By now, we'd reached the vast stone pile of the fifteenth-century castle with its crenellated fortifications, impressive for its sheer solidity and mass. From there, we walked eastward along the battlements atop the medieval city wall, around the perimeter of the city. Dom Gregorio pointed out a mill on the river below us, where our wheat was ground every week, and various landmarks in the valley spread out beyond.

We descended a stair at the Calle Velayos, leading us back inside the old city, and passed beside the Iglesia de San Agustín on our way back to the Casa Cerralbo. Along the way, I mused on this universal obsession with the charter, this force so powerful it seemed to push the horror of Gelasio's murder into the background.

Obsession or not, it was logical after all. The murder, Robledillo's fate, prospects for the city, the monastery and even my own future were inextricably bound up with that missing piece of vellum.

Chapter VI

The Damsel and Don Quijote

Leopoldo was standing in the open door of his ancestral home, waiting to welcome us inside. My promised 'tour' consisted of a quick walk through the hall to the walled patio behind the house. As he hurried us along, he waved at the stairs, mentioning the bedrooms above, and pointed out the drawing room filled with heavy, ornate, and uncomfortable-looking furniture. I glimpsed a row of dark family portraits along the walls as we passed. The reason for the haste shone through in Leopoldo's smile.

Giant lily pads rocked gently in a cascade of water from the marble fish that surmounted the patio's fountain. Various exotic plant species were still in bloom, their names and backgrounds recited for us with more than a touch of pride. Leopoldo's 'plant hobby' was in evidence everywhere.

As we turned to re-enter the house, a handsome woman in her mid thirties swept through the door.

"Poldo! Why didn't you tell me you were coming?" She ran to him and flung her arms around his neck, kissing him and kicking one heel in the air. I recognized her as the woman at the monastery gate and my earlier suspicions were confirmed. She was, indeed, the sister so dear to him, Clara. I stood by, my mood lightened by this woman with her sprightly, outgoing presence. Still, her manner again reminded me of my lost Beatriz, and I felt a pang of longing.

She turned to Dom Gregorio, who seemed to be a familiar guest. "Good afternoon, Domine, and welcome once again. Are you staying for supper? Please do! I'm sure the cook can accommodate all of you."

"Sorry to disappoint you, my dear, but we must be getting back to La Caridad. Of course, we couldn't leave before taking a moment to talk."

Leopoldo put his arm around his sister and turned to me. "Clara, I'd like you to meet don Ygnacio. He's an ex-Jesuit who's staying at the monastery for a while...we don't know how long. An intriguing fellow. He knows all about the New World."

I protested. "Hardly, Father Leopoldo. I was only in New Spain, and most of the time in one area, at that."

Doña Clara greeted me with pert charm. She then took Dom Gregorio's hand to lead him, and with him the rest of us, back inside, where she turned to me.

"Oh, do let's all sit down together right away so you can tell me about New Spain, don Ygnacio. Where were you, and what did you do there?"

I began to describe Sonora and its missions as she guided us into the family sitting room, cozier and more inviting than the formal drawing room. We gathered at a round table and, since the afternoon was becoming chilly, Clara called the maid to light the charcoal-burning heater.

An elderly woman bustled in, dressed in blue with a crisp, white apron and a white kerchief on gray hair mingled with blond. She glanced at me and at Dom Gregorio. Then, with a start, she turned her faded-blue eyes back to me. Her lips parted.

Leopoldo noticed. "Josefina, this is don Ygnacio Pferkon, a priest from your homeland, I believe."

The woman curtsied and looked down at her hands. "I'm very pleased to meet you, Father, I'm sure."

I detected her accent. "*Woher kommst du, Josefina?* Where are you from? I'm from Mannheim."

"I was born in Wiesbaden, Father," she replied in German. "My name is really Gertrud...but no one here can pronounce that. I went to work at Bremerhaven and married a Spanish sailor, and that's how I ended up in Spain. It's a long story, Father."

"And mine, too. My name, in its proper German form, is Ignaz Pfefferkorn. I'd like to talk with you one day when there's time. It's such a blessing to hear my own dialect."

I nodded to Gertrud/Josefina and turned back to my hosts, apologizing for speaking in a foreign language. Its cadences, along with the ease I felt in expressing myself, flooded me with nostalgia for my home. Meanwhile, Josefina lit the heater and in a matter of minutes we were toasting our feet and sipping cups of thick, steaming-hot chocolate served with tiny, crisp cakes.

"How did we ever live without chocolate from the New World? It's so exquisite!" Clara exclaimed, taking a sip. "But, don Ygnacio, you were a Jesuit, you say. Tell me more about your own country. You and Josefina seem to share a common background. Where are you from?"

"We're both from the same area, the Rhineland. My own city, Mannheim, was built where the Neckar, another river, flows into the Rhine. It's a beautiful place, doña Clara. I wish you could see it. I wish I could see it again, too…."

My tone, which I'd intended to be light, nonetheless betrayed me. Clara took my hand in both of hers. "You poor man. How long has it been since you saw your home?"

"I joined the Jesuits when I was seventeen. That makes it…thirty-one…no, thirty-two years ago. I doubt you were born then, doña Clara."

"Now, don't flatter me, don Ygnacio. Do you have family left there?"

"I have no idea. You see, I've been a prisoner for the past eight years, and I've been unable to write or receive letters—"

"Oh, how terrible!" She looked stricken as she interrupted. "What did you do to make our king so angry with you?"

"I wish I could answer that question. I've heard rumors, gossip, but neither I nor anyone I know committed any crime sufficient to merit such punishment. But, please, let's speak of something more cheerful. Tell me about your own life here in this beautiful city."

The conversation took a lighter turn, and we finished our chocolate and the crisp cakes. When we were ready to go, Clara took both my hands in hers to say goodbye. Her directness amazed and pleased me—flattered me as well—and her parting words were poetic.

"Your eyes, don Ygnacio, tell your story. They're beautiful eyes, you know, but so sad. You'd make a perfect knight of the sorrowful countenance, *un caballero de la triste figura*. Please come back, I'd love to hear more about Sonora."

୫୦୯୫

Conversation was next to impossible on the trip back to La Caridad, so jolting was the ride. I sat alone on one seat, facing Dom Gregorio and Father Leopoldo, pondering Clara's words.

Was I a don Quijote? He'd gone out on a mission to rid the world of monsters, to rescue maidens in distress, bring back the Golden Age of chivalry and do good to all. My age, forty-nine last birthday, and my dilapidated physical condition were about the same as his, but I'd begun my mission when I was twenty-eight. The monsters I fought were ignorance, false gods and the bizarre and sometimes-violent illusions the worship of those gods entailed. Add to that my struggles with my own inner demons—my doubts, fears, and temptations. My rescue efforts were not limited to maidens, but included whole populations in distress.

Had I been tilting at windmills? In my most depressed states, I sometimes believed so. Our endeavor to educate the native populations of New Spain was brutally frustrated. I was certain most of those Indians, by now, were back to their ancestral practices. Even if the Franciscans could muster the manpower to resume the mission effort in Sonora, they'd never match our concern about educating the people.

Ours was a Herculean effort aimed at bringing them up to the level of the European settlers, to enable them to compete on an equal footing, to save them—easy victims because of their ignorance—from being enslaved by rich landowners and mining operations. The effort required tireless dedication. But a succession of real giants, not mere windmills, defeated us: the Portuguese, the French and the Spanish Crowns. The Spanish expulsion and now the utter suppression of our Society crushed me, dashing me down, shattered and bleeding, as surely as the windmill hurled don Quijote to the ground.

At the end of his adventures, Quijote returned to his home a broken man, shorn of his chivalric illusions. What fate awaited me, I wondered? The one consolation that buoyed me up was my faith. Surely, I would not follow Quijote in losing that, too...or would I? God have mercy!

છાજ

In a gloomy mood, I stepped from the coach and re-entered the monastery. We joined the monks coming from singing Vespers and filed into the refectory, fragrant with savory odors. They whetted my appetite, but about halfway through the meal I began to feel distant warning signs of a fierce headache. I excused myself and made my way upstairs.

Squeezing my temples with my left hand, I paced the upper cloister walkway for a while, hoping to stave off the inevitable, but the headache grew worse, blooming inside my skull like a noxious flower. I lay on my cot with a groan, and curled up in a ball, wrapping my arms around my head. A wave of nausea struck me. By then I was certain my malaria had returned to torment me once again.

Fever and diarrhea appeared within the hour. I'd been free of the disease for months, and now it seemed to want to make up for lost time. If only I had that bitter white powder called quinine, or 'Jesuits' powder.' The Indians first treated us with it. Then we distributed it to Spanish physicians in the New World, and shipped it back to Ours – our fellow Jesuits – in Europe. Physicians in Spain seemed to ignore our revolutionary treatment for malaria, though. They had little access to such novelties from the New World and, often enough, even less incentive to try anything new.

Whenever I could concentrate I prayed this would be a short relapse, but all too often I'd drift away into delirium with my prayer unfinished. I lay on my cot, alternately burning with fever and shivering with chills, too ill to go down for meals. When I awoke it was dark outside. A figure huddled in my chair, barely recognizable in the feeble light of a single candle: Brother Eugenio.

"We were worried when you didn't come to meals," he said. "Father Plácido will be back soon with something to eat. He's convinced you won't last long without sustenance."

My voice sounded weak and strangely distant as I thanked him. "I don't know if I can hold anything down yet other than water, Brother Eugenio, but don't be too worried. I've survived worse relapses. It's malaria...I've had it for years. Without the medicine called quinine it follows its own path. Eventually it'll leave me in peace for a month or two, but it always comes back."

Plácido came puffing in, a bowl of soup balanced in one hand and one of the small loaves clamped under an arm. "Damnable stairs! They'll be the death of me yet! This is chicken soup, don Ygnacio. I know you'll get better if you take some nourishment." He held out the bowl, and the odor overwhelmed me. Nauseated, I turned my head to the wall, trying to avoid gagging. "I'm...sorry, Father Plácido, but I won't...be able to eat anything for a while. Just...take it away for now, please. I'll try...again in the morning."

Plácido stared, his round face registering disbelief and immense disappointment. "Oh, but don Ygnacio—"

Eugenio took his arm and jerked his head toward the door. The two stepped just outside my cell and began a conversation *sotto voce*, which, by a trick of the echo in my room, I could hear quite well.

"Eugenio, he'll die if he doesn't *eat*!"

"He's a tough old bird, Plácido. He'll live through the night, but we've got to get him out of this cell and into a more convenient place. Here he's farthest away from everything—the refectory, kitchen, water supply, latrines—everything."

"Yes, but where?"

"You have seniority, Plácido. Go ask Dom Gregorio what to do. The *Sala Capitular*, the chapter room, is empty and we're not due for a meeting. We could move him in there until he's over this. Set up his cot there."

"Good idea. Very well, I'll ask. It would be good to move him tonight...less work for us in the long run. I'm sick of running up those stairs every few minutes. Always stairs and more stairs."

"Go quickly. It's getting late. Dom Gregorio reads at night, but even he goes to bed well before dawn."

Plácido's heavy footsteps receded down the walkway, and Eugenio reappeared in my cell. "Better, now that the odor of soup isn't so strong?" he asked.

"How did you know?"

"I've lived a few years, too. Once or twice sick like that, and I remember how it is." He had a dampened rag, and sponged my forehead with it. Then he felt my face and neck. "Still feverish, but a little cooler than earlier in the day. You were delirious, you know, crying out and talking. Fascinating things. You talked with someone called Wolf...something."

"Wolfgang?"

"That's it. And someone else, someone with a name like *Llevjo*."

"Djevho was a medicine man who saved my life when I was dying of this very disease. A fine man and a worthy adversary. Had a strange power, a sort of aura about him. I could never convert him."

"Yes, Llevjo was the name. Exactly. Anyway, you asked him for quinine—that medicine. But even more interesting was a woman's name. 'Beatriz! Stay by me...please! Beatriz!' and then you moaned. You stretched out your hands. Who is this Beatriz?"

Eugenio's rendition and pantomime of my outcry was so heart-rending, I blurted out the truth without thinking.

"I loved her, Eugenio. But we never...." I stopped myself. "I don't know why I tell you even that much, but since I have, I'll tell you more, perhaps, when I'm stronger."

His curiosity produced a stare, but he didn't press for more. Instead, he sat once again. The short exchange tired me, but I'd barely closed my eyes when I heard movement, then a complaint.

"Cursed stairs! Bane of my life!"

It was Plácido with a pitcher of water and a clay mug. This time I accepted the offer, drinking at least a quart while he and Eugenio again exchanged whispers outside the cell.

"Well? What did the abbot say?"

"We're to bring him down to the chapter room and make him comfortable. He *likes* don Ygnacio. He's worried about him enough to talk of sending for a surgeon tomorrow."

That last part frightened me. I'd seen too much of Spanish surgeons. I called out to them. "Plácido! Eugenio!"

The two stuck their heads back into my room, looking surprised. "Yes, don Ygnacio?"

"For the love of God, and if you have any regard for me—as I believe you do—let me talk to the abbot before he sends for a surgeon. They always want to bleed a man, and they've done me enormous harm over the past few years. I was bled every time I had one of these attacks back in that prison near Cádiz. I got sicker, much sicker, every time. Weaker. Took me forever to get over it, and I'm not over it yet. Promise me, please! Beg the abbot not to do anything before talking to me." I struggled to a sitting position and strained to stand up to confront them. My knees buckled and I fell back. Eugenio helped me to stretch out again.

"It's all right, don Ygnacio. We'll see to it. Now, you just rest. I'll go find some help. We'll carry you down, cot and all."

Plácido gave me a reassuring nod, and their voices receded down the walkway. I lay quietly and listened. The rest of the monastery was silent, but before long the two reappeared with Tomás and Mateo.

They picked me up as announced, cot and all and, after a precarious ride down the stairs, placed me in the dark chapter room while Plácido went for a candle. The feeble light showed me an audience hall furnished with the abbot's carved walnut chair on a dais, and rows of benches for the monks. They placed me parallel to a side table, where Plácido set the candle.

He felt my forehead, speaking gently. "You're feverish. Do you need anything before we go, don Ygnacio?"

"Thank you, Plácido. Yes, more water...and another blanket. It's cold in here." Plácido gestured to Tomás, who left the room. He returned shortly with the pitcher and mug, and a ragged blanket he spread over the two warm ones I already had to keep out winter cold. I thanked them, and promised to sleep.

"We'll leave the candle," Eugenio said. "It should give you light and keep you company until you fall asleep."

Once I was alone, chills overtook me. I shook uncontrollably, clenching my teeth, until I fell into an exhausted stupor. I was almost asleep when I became aware of a still, black figure, a monk, standing over me. I felt intense hostility surrounding me like smoke. He stood immobile, fully cowled, no features visible in the flickering candlelight.

My eyes went to his hands. A dagger! My heart pounded as I tensed every muscle. I knew I couldn't get away, and was too weak to defend myself. Thoughts flashed before me, a jumble. Who was this enemy? Why had he chosen the moment of my greatest weakness to attack me? What had I done, that he'd want to kill me? Which one of them was it?

I am a priest. I am a Jesuit. God help me!

I closed my eyes, crossed myself and recited my favorite prayer aloud. "Soul of Christ, sanctify me. Body of Christ, save me. Blood of Christ, inebriate me. Water from the side of Christ, wash me…. From the malevolent enemy defend me. In the hour of my death call me, and bid me come to you, that with your saints I may praise you forever and ever. Amen." I'd reached the end, and still no deathblow. When I opened my eyes, the figure was gone. Why hadn't he killed me? Was it Gelasio's murderer? Had my prayer somehow deflected him? Or was it all a figment of my delirium?

I thanked God for sparing me and considered what I might do now. There was no way to lock or to block the door to this chapter room, so I resolved at last to commend myself to God once again, and to try to sleep. In any case, He would take me when it was my time to go.

ಬಂಚ

Next morning, Dom Gregorio tried persuading me to accept a surgeon's visit. I explained my fears and, though skeptical, he finally agreed, seeing my terror at the thought of more blood loss. I was still pale and shaky from the last assault on my body, back in Santa María.

I was well enough to talk at length by the third morning. Eugenio waited until then to coax me into telling of Beatriz. He sat by my side, a man much my senior anticipating my story like a child. I told him what I felt I could.

"I was investigating the murder of an army officer, a captain killed when he came on government orders to inspect financial records at Ures, one of our missions in Sonora. Beatriz was the widow of a lieutenant. She'd come in the company of soldiers, from Durango, hundreds of miles away, to visit her husband's gravesite. On her way, she stopped at the mission, where I first caught a glimpse of her late one night.

"I didn't know who she was. She was dressed in filmy white—probably her nightdress—standing in the plaza before the church with her long, wavy black hair unbound, hanging to her waist and rippling a little in the breeze. She stood there in the moonlight, slender, graceful, her hands joined in prayer. From that moment to this, her face and form have been imprinted on my mind."

"Are you sure she wasn't a succubus, sent by the Devil to tempt you, don Ygnacio?" Eugenio's eyes widened.

I smiled. "No, she was solid flesh and blood, devout as well, and quite unaware of her effect upon a poor mission priest. I saw her the next day at the captain's funeral, in elegant mourning dress. It's true, her beauty was almost more than I could bear, a temptress in spite of herself."

Eugenio leaned forward, whispering though there were no others to hear. "Did you two...?"

"No, no. The closest we ever came was during the following three days, when I escorted her to the Jesuit college at Mátape, where her husband was buried."

I paused in my tale as memories flooded me. *Her foot slipped that first morning, as she mounted her horse. I caught her and lifted her to the saddle, feeling her soft body pressed against mine, her fingertips gliding across the back of my neck....*

"Yes, don Ygnacio? Go on, go on!" Eugenio's impatience broke my trance.

"The ride there was a hard one, since we had to make it in a single day. There was only wild country and possible Indian attack in between, you see. As we rode, we talked and came to know a little about each other, as is only natural.

"She had a pistol in her saddlebag and knew how to use it; her husband had taught her how. She was protecting me, not the other way around."

Eugenio hitched his chair a few inches closer.

"And? And?"

"And there was an Apache raid on Mátape Mission that night. The danger we shared cemented our friendship. The day after the raid, I went with her to visit her husband's gravesite and the battlefield where he'd fallen. We prayed together. When Father Jakob saw us leaving the mission church, my arm around her, he was very disapproving. *He* knew what was going on. It was written all over him."

"Was he right? Did you do more than pray together, don Ygnacio?"

"Just prayer, Eugenio, just prayer. And then, on the third day, in the company of two novices and a priest from Mátape, she and I returned to Ures. From there, the two novices took her back to Durango."

And I couldn't stop daydreaming about her; she haunted my midnight dreams.

"That's all there was?" Eugenio looked disappointed.

"Not quite. I saw her again later, after I'd solved the army captain's murder, as I hope to solve Gelasio's killing."

I paused, thinking how little I'd learned so far, fearing my limited freedom would make discovery of the killer impossible. Eugenio cleared his throat, impatient once more, and I resumed my story.

"Yes, I saw her one last time, after our arrests. We spoke just before I embarked on the prison ship, chained much as you saw me when I arrived here. She had married the governor of Sonora Province, but I could tell she felt more than friendship for me, even then, as I did for her."

So much passed between us at that meeting, so much was left unsaid. We'd both felt the powerful bond that united us, a spiritual, emotional bond that remains unbroken to this day.

Eugenio's exasperated sigh ended my reverie. He wanted me to continue, of course.

"Before I left the prison in Cádiz, I received a diary from her. She'd kept a record of that whole episode. Once I'd read it through several times, I gave it to Father Rafael Mendoza, who was imprisoned with me at the time."

How I wept over that diary as I read it, much to Rafael's amazement and concern. When I gave it to him, it was like peeling a fingernail from the flesh.

"Father Rafael wanted to be my biographer, you see, or at least to write something about that time in my life, and perhaps he did. I have no way of knowing. That's all there was to it, Eugenio."

My conscience pricked me. After all, in telling Eugenio only what an objective observer would have seen pass between Beatriz and me, I'd lied to him. He rose, then, and thanked me for my honesty. His words belied his frustration with my story, however. Plainly, it was not as lurid as he'd hoped.

ഇരുൽ

Two days later, Dom Gregorio came in, grinning with self-satisfaction, bearing a folded piece of black cloth. He'd taken the bishop's advice and bought cloth enough for two new robes. I sat up and he laid the cloth across my outstretched arms.

Once I was well enough, I could make the robes myself. I couldn't thank him enough. The ones I had were made from half-rotten cloth, soon after I got to Cádiz, at least six years back, and couldn't have lasted much longer. The patches were already tearing out of the cloth. If a major seam split...well, a near-naked prisoner would be, at best, an embarrassment.

But I did not have to get well before the tailoring began. Father Plácido offered himself as an expert at cutting and sewing, having made quite a few habits for himself and his brothers. With meticulous care, he took apart one of my robes and laid it out on the new cloth, cutting it to match. He was not only a perfectionist, but a rapid worker as well. In a few days I had two elegant and well-fitted garments to adorn my 'newly resurrected' self.

Since no ghostly figure had returned with its long knife, I almost convinced myself that I'd been hallucinating. Almost, but not quite. There was a murderer among us at La Caridad, and it was well known that Dom Gregorio and I were in that loft soon after the murder, looking for clues. I told no one of my dagger-wielding visitor. After all, even if the murderous monk was indeed standing over me that night, what could anyone do about it? My delirium would be blamed, and the event ignored.

While my illness lasted, Eugenio, Leopoldo, and Plácido took turns sitting with me. Leopoldo, more scholarly than the others, read scripture to me, my breviary, or one or another of the books lent by Dom Gregorio. The abbot often sat and talked with me as well. I was amazed at their kindness, and needed to say so.

"Dom Gregorio, I can't begin to express my gratitude for what you've done for me. I can't imagine why the four of you have taken me under your wing like this, but I thank God for each one of you. I fear I'll never be able to repay you. Perhaps, as the saying goes, you'll receive your reward in heaven."

"It's our Christian duty, don Ygnacio. Besides," he lowered his voice, "we like you. You're an intriguing person and we're all learning from you about the New World. You break the monotony around here." We both smiled at that.

I thanked the other three, and received similar replies. I praised God, too, for their kindness, which kept me from falling into bleak depressions that would make me even sicker.

About ten days passed, and I sensed that my system was rallying. The end of the malaria attack was signaled by a return of appetite, to Plácido's great delight. He and Eugenio saved special tidbits for me, and plied me with hot chocolate made with milk, and *panes dulces*. When I got out of bed, they supported me, walking with me on the first day, around the cloister and into the garden until I regained enough strength to walk without them.

੪つℭଷ

Dom Gregorio visited me one morning after Mass, with his old violin under his arm. "Ygnacio, you've been devouring this instrument with your eyes for weeks. I'm sorry I didn't offer to let you play it sooner. Tell me more about your music."

"My family was musical, Domine. I come by my violin playing honestly."

"You should have insisted long ago. I'm sure the old fiddle's in miserable shape, but take it and try it out." He thrust the violin into my hands.

"It's been eight years since I played, Dom Gregorio. Not since my arrest in 1767. I may have told you that, weeks ago. This old fiddle and I will be a perfect match, both in miserable shape." I took the instrument and used my old robe to wipe it with care. The instrument was still laden with accumulated dust from months, maybe years, on the shelf. I examined the strings, badly in need of wax. A beeswax candle solved that problem.

After waxing the strings and bow, and with some trepidation, I began to tune. None of the strings snapped, so I drew the bow across them experimentally. The sound was neither good nor abominable, so I played a simple nursery tune from my childhood, then adjusted the tuning once more. I then attempted an excerpt from a religious cantata composed by a fellow priest, Antonio Vivaldi.

I was rusty, of course, and made any number of blunders and lapses of memory; the neglected violin voiced its protest with a shrill and colorless tone. Despite those flaws, the abbot enjoyed the interlude.

"You must play something every night, Ygnacio. I enjoy it, and when you're practiced enough, you can play during some of the Masses. Did you say you played the violin in the New World?"

"Yes, Domine. I took my violin with me from Germany. We Jesuits all knew the universal language of music was a proven aid to conversion. In Atí, my first mission, I began playing to console myself, to fill the void of my loneliness. I soon realized that my Pima Indians were powerfully attracted by my playing."

"Then it was true what they reported—that those savages had an affinity for music."

"Domine, I'd never call those people savages. Some individuals earned the name, but most were people like us, only lacking any education and, of course, ignorant of the Good News."

&ଠଓ

Once I was strong enough to mingle with others in the monastery, I noticed their increased tension and unrest. I overheard enough to know they were discussing Gelasio's murder in whispering groups of three or four. Sometimes they included me, but not often. We missed Gelasio and mourned his violent death, but were also fearful the murderer would strike again. Everyone knew where Gelasio stood on the matter of the diocese and Robledillo. Most everyone assumed he'd been killed over it. As a result, feelings of any sort about the potential loss of the parish were expressed guardedly when in public, or not at all. Those who, like Gelasio, were in favor of obeying the bishop kept total silence on the issue. Ironically, their silence branded them supporters of the bishop, singling them out as potential victims as well.

As soon as I could, I returned to my choir duties. On my first appearance, Plácido stopped his directing immediately and bustled to my side, supporting me with an arm around my waist. I felt it a sign of his favor, remembering how he escorted Gelasio when he'd been star of the baritone section.

He gave me a little pat on the shoulder, then took his station before us as I once more stood between Leopoldo and Metodio. "Give praises to God for the return of a third baritone voice, and a good one at that," he said, smiling at me.

I was deeply in Father Plácido's debt. Thanks to him, I'd been transformed from ragamuffin to respectable priest, clothed in keeping with my dignity. He'd provided me with two new robes and nearly new shoes.

My shoes always bothered him, as much as the condition of my robes. They were scuffed and discolored, torn about the uppers, with holes in the soles and non-existent heels. While I was still bedridden, he'd taken them to the monastery's cobbler, Brother Fernando, who'd patched the leather uppers, added new soles and heels, then oiled the leather and polished it with soot and a strap of wool felt. I not only felt taller wearing them, I felt renewed. There was a spring to my step.

∞∞

On my way up the stairs after choir practice, I met Brother Metodio on his way down. Since that violent scene over Gelasio's dead body, I'd seen the man only in the choir. He was forced to stand next to me there, but kept his back turned as much as possible. I assumed he was avoiding me, not only out of dislike but also of prudence, after the abbot reprimanded him for his outburst.

I was lost in thought when we nearly collided. He halted on the stair above mine, glaring down, his face a mask of the purest hatred. "Jesuit!" he hissed. "Conniving, plotting Jesuit! You've wormed your way into our abbot's favor with your sweet hypocrisy, and have him now at your beck and call. I know how you operate; I've read about you. You plot and scheme, despoil and murder, and you pour your cloying corruption into the ears of those in power until you have them in your thrall."

His vehemence amazed me. I broke in, even though I was convinced I could say nothing that would make the slightest impression.

"Stop right there, Metodio! What you've read is libel. I have no connections, no power, no reason to plot or corrupt. Where do these ideas come from?"

"Not all us Norbertines are fools. You Jesuits plot and assassinate. King José of Portugal...you tried that and failed, but you've succeeded other times. You! We know about you, a hireling of the bishop. He sent you here to destroy this monastery. You'll dupe Dom Gregorio into making a fatal move that'll put us all in the bishop's hands."

His voice dropped to the merest whisper as he leaned forward, speaking so close to me that drops of saliva spattered my face.

"Beware, *Jesuit*," he said, spitting out the words, "we know about your criminal ways. We have news about your activities from our friends in Cádiz. Some also believe you killed our brother Gelasio. The abbot may tolerate you, but *we all know*. Many pairs of eyes are watching you, watching everything you do, listening to everything you say." With that, he swerved around me and ran down the rest of the stairs.

I wiped my face on my sleeve and stood for a long moment, feeling a cold chill down my back. Was Metodio the apparition at my bedside? Or was that one of the other "pairs of eyes" wishing me dead? He somehow had knowledge of my 'crime,' knowledge his abbot did not yet possess, and it gave him potential power over me. How would he use it?

His loathing was fed by the anti-Jesuit tracts that must have been circulating, spreading the most absurd drivel. Like all hate literature, at least some of its charges were believed. The assassination attempt on the life of the Portuguese king had been blamed on us, the Company, by his Prime Minister, the Marqués de Pombal, and we'd been expelled from Portugal as a result. Throw enough filth and part of it will stick.

At length I continued up the stairs, returning to my cell. What did Dom Gregorio know by now? How many monks knew my secret? How many were plotting my death? Metodio's hatred would not, could not be kept from the others. He was compelled to spread it, such was its insidious nature.

I crossed my arms, shivering as I clutched my own body, feeling exposed and vulnerable. The conditions of my imprisonment might soon be changed for the worse, and the hostility building against me might make one Ignaz Pfefferkorn, S.J., the next murder victim at La Caridad.

Chapter VII

Christmastide

I told no one of my encounter with Metodio, for I feared I might inadvertently reveal too much about my 'history' in Santa María. I worried daily, since, if Metodio revealed what he knew of it, God only knew what would come of that. Nor did I mention the sinister figure at my bedside. Even though I felt myself in danger, there was little I could do but place my trust in God.

Advent passed, week by week, with no further disturbances as the monastery prepared to celebrate the Birth of Christ. Father Plácido exceeded his own high standards in training the choir in the special chants of the season, and I reveled in the music.

Christmas Eve Mass was his triumph. Our voices wove glorious harmonies that uplifted our souls and carried me back on a wave of nostalgia to masses sung during my years as a novice. The sanctuary was fragrant with evergreens decorating the ambo and railings. Clusters of holly with glowing red berries adorned the saints' statues as well. Hundreds of worshippers came from Ciudad Rodrigo, the nearby farms and villages, many coming all the way from Robledillo. They filled the vast nave. We fasted all day, then sang the Midnight Mass. After intoning the closing words, *Ite, missa est; Deo gratias*, we gathered in the refectory sometime after one in the morning. At last we were about to enjoy the banquet whose tantalizing aromas wafting from the kitchen had distracted us from our pious thoughts over the previous two days. Wine flowed freely from the very onset of the feast.

A *caldo*, a soup of chopped root vegetables, was served, hot and steaming, and we could choose from a selection of breads in many shapes, including complex braids. The centerpiece was a whole roast pig, the traditional apple in its mouth, stuffed with breadcrumbs, herbs and several kinds of sausages. Nearby villagers had contributed four geese, now roasted to perfection, their skins crisp and brown. These were flanked by bowls heaped with the seasoned late fall greens we'd gathered for a quick boil. At meal's end, a sweet liqueur made from apricots grown at La Caridad accompanied a huge Christmas cake.

Not content with this prodigious display of talent, the baker presented *turrónes de almendra y de yema*, confections of egg yolk and almond paste, and another almond-paste favorite, *mazapán*, which I knew back home as *Marzipan*.

I sat isolated, as always, an empty seat either side of me. On this night of all nights, it made me feel an outsider, an interloper. At last, wineglass in hand, Brother Eugenio came to sit next to me. "Are you enjoying yourself, don Ygnacio? You look a bit sad."

"I'm remembering Christmas Eve dinners with my family in Mannheim, Eugenio. I'm being set apart here as a foreigner and prisoner. I understand that, but it does make a contrast."

"I guessed as much." He sat quietly, watching the others. "At least I can get a better look at all of us from here," he said. "We're noisier than usual this Nochebuena, this Christmas Eve. We're usually joyful, yes, but not drunk."

He gestured toward a pair of monks, one laughing open-mouthed with an arm draped over his brother's shoulder. The other man slumped in his seat, pounding the table with a fist and making his plate jump.

"Plácido's lost all sense of proportion," Eugenio continued. "I could swear he's eaten a whole goose and all the stuffing by himself. Look at him."

My friend, the choir director, was drowsing at his place, one chubby fist propping up his left jowl. His massive belly drooped over one thigh, stretching the seams of his habit. A half-eaten goose drumstick was slipping, forgotten for the moment, from his greasy right hand.

"If I were a painter, he'd make a perfect model for the Sin of Gluttony. But it seems to me you all have excellent excuses to eat and drink too much, Eugenio. What do you think?"

"We're worried, don Ygnacio. Perhaps it's that."

"Of course. Gelasio's death."

"That...and the fate of the entire monastery...and our fear the killer will strike again. You may well be in danger, yourself. I'm sure you're aware of that."

"Very much aware, Eugenio."

I had no illusions that a majority of the monks here approved of me, or even half of them. I felt it a privilege to be liked by Dom Gregorio, Plácido, Leopoldo, and Eugenio, perhaps tolerated by a few others, but that left a large number who would not befriend me. I knew their names, but little more.

I rose, shook Eugenio's hand, wished him all the blessings of the season and went over to wish Leopoldo and Plácido a happy Christmas. Plácido heaved himself to his feet and gave me a half-drunken embrace, the goose drumstick still clutched in his fist. Then I made a special detour to greet Dom Gregorio. He looked up, chin on fist, apparently sober. I could never tell, in his case. I'd seen him fill his wineglass six times, and I may have missed a few.

"Ygnacio, I have a new French brandy, imported through Lisbon. Come have a nightcap in my rooms?" His command took on the intonation of a question.

"I'm sorry, Dom Gregorio, but I'm really tired. Please excuse me this once."

He stared up at me, disappointment written on his face, then motioned toward the door with one graceful hand, dismissing me. I gave him a friendly wave, left the refectory and made my way up the stone stairway to my cell. The sounds of revelry floated up to me long after I had stretched out on my cot, and then they echoed in my dreams.

ഇൗ

Christmas Day was drowsy and quiet at the monastery. The choir monks, along with cooks, janitors, scribes and nearly everyone else had been given a day of rest. Mass was said, rather than sung. Many of the brothers were sleeping off the night's excesses, and I walked alone reading my breviary in the garden and barren orchard. I became chilled and found a warm spot near the fireplace in the refectory. There were still embers, so I built up a small fire and sat there to continue my reading.

Only a few men appeared for dinner that night, and we all ate sparingly. I retired early to my cell, lit my candle and began to read my Bible. I re-read the Creation stories in Genesis, began to visualize the Garden, and meditated on it.

Did God *intend* for man to fall? The question disturbed me. I'd never considered the Fall this way before, and I stood, taking a few paces in my small space. Without that Fall, we'd have remained without a moral sense, if we now defined it as that ability to distinguish good from evil...for there was no evil in the Garden until Satan entered there. But surely my definition was correct: moral sense was, and is, the ability and freedom to choose between those two opposites.

My mind tugged at the problem, and I became so deeply engrossed the world around me receded.

Since God's creation was perfect from the beginning, were not Adam and Eve given the ability to choose between the two, before the Fall? But then, how could they possibly know evil, unless its understanding were imbued in them? Perhaps they understood it in a different sense, merely as a matter of obedience or disobedience. The first pair was free to obey God's command, or not. If they'd resisted the Serpent, they'd have become immortal, but static as at the moment of their creation, *perfected* in the etymological sense: finished off; done.

I took a few more paces along the walkway and back again to my cell. God, I thought, who is omniscient, must have placed the Serpent in the Garden for His purpose. The Serpent—the very principle of evil—then set a choice before God's favorite creatures: to remain *perfect* as they had been created, or, as the Serpent put it, to "become like gods, knowing good from evil." He was holding out the possibility there was something *better* than perfect. Eve was the more ambitious of the two, committing a sin of pride in trying to better their condition, as if that were possible, by rivaling 'the gods.'

What a horrendous trap! There was no other word for it. I struck my palm with my fist, grimacing as I did. Poor Adam and Eve had no inkling of the degradation that would follow their simple act of disobedience.

Instead of living on in bliss, not knowing the full extent of the dark side of reality, their eyes were opened. The knowledge they gained had an immediate corrupting power. I imagined their revulsion as such knowledge washed over them. It must have felt like a moral wound, a deep nausea similar to one's feeling when he suffers a serious, potentially mortal, physical injury.

I took another turn inside and outside my cell, pitying our universal ancestors. Their innocent nakedness became besmirched with diabolical awareness. God alone, who'd separated darkness from the light, was able to withstand full knowledge of the pit, in all its depth and depravity, without corruption. Not so Adam and Eve. Once they'd discerned evil, they all too often chose it. It clung to them like hot tar. Their very flesh became corruptible, and they felt pain; they died.

I was so deep in my meditation that sweat broke out on my brow. I wiped my forehead with my sleeve. Of course, I told myself, all of it was part of an over-arching Plan. From that time to the Incarnation, mankind struggled and fell, then perhaps rose a bit higher than before the struggle. I nodded in relief. God had a remedy for the sad consequences of that original fatal choice.

Through the coming of the Savior, their fall became a Fortunate Fall, leading to the Redemption of those who believe in him. Though we still struggled in the same way, we now had hope that, through Christ, in the end all these struggles would lead to true perfection through Him, with Him, in Him.

I knew there were wildly heretical elements in all this—for I had questioned God's purpose in my heart. I'd be burned at the stake if anyone ever read the mystical diary where I recorded my thoughts, but—God willing—no other *person* would ever know them. The situation at La Caridad was a perfect example of the corrupting power that original sin brought into the world of mankind. Here, before my eyes, a controversy in Church politics had led to hatred and enmity—and to murder.

I applied the meditation to my own experience as a missionary. We Jesuits built, we taught, we spread the Word among ignorant unbelievers. Then earthly powers destroyed all those fragile structures, the physical, the intellectual and spiritual, and threw our converts back upon their own resources, forcing them back into their ancient customs and beliefs. Still, I mused, a few might have learned something lasting from our efforts, and those few might remain on a higher plane. We Jesuits, too, were destroyed along with all our endeavors. Would we come back stronger one day? More spiritual?

Again, I wiped my brow, sinking onto my cot, exhausted by my own intensity. Crack! A sharp sound broke the stillness of the night. What was it? Again crack! Something struck the outside wall of my cell and skittered across the walkway. A pebble! I sat still, holding my breath. A third one followed. I rose and slipped outside the door, pressing myself against my wall, blinking to adjust my eyes to the dark. Another pebble struck, on the other side of the door.

I stepped to the railing and made out a hooded figure in the garden below, saw it beckon to me, heard the hoarse whisper.

"Don Ygnacio! Come down!"

I hesitated. Who was he? The voice was vaguely familiar—but it could be any of those who remained strangers. Was this the confrontation I feared? Would I receive a knife between my ribs?

Self-confidence overcame my caution. Surely, I could defend myself, since I was very much on my guard. Perhaps I'd learn something of value, since so far I'd made no progress in discovering Gelasio's murderer. I turned away from the railing, moved quietly along the walkway and descended the stairs.

The robed figure accosted me at the bottom step. "Follow me," he whispered. "We can talk normally outside. In here, sounds carry."

His whispered voice did sound familiar, but I still couldn't place it. We took the quickest route to the outer courtyard, the Plaza de las Cadenas. I shivered as I stepped outside, and it wasn't just the chilly breeze penetrating my robe.

"Who are you?" I pressed.

"It's me, Metodio."

He pulled back his cowl, and I could make out his face in the frosty light of the half moon. I froze in my tracks, stepped back with one foot, and prepared to defend myself.

"Brother Metodio, this is an unexpected pleasure."

"Forget the sarcasm, Ygnacio. It's unsuitable for a priest, even a *Jesuit.*"

"You speak as if you'd rather spit out that word, Metodio," I replied in kind. "Perhaps I detect a bit of sarcasm in you as well?"

"All right. Truce. I called you down here to strike a bargain, not trade insults. I know things you need to know, and I'll tell you if you'll tell us what you've learned so far." His voice was calmer, but there was a steely edge to it.

"Who are 'us,' Metodio?"

"We who want to save this monastery. If the bishop wins and annexes Robledillo, it'll only take a few years before our beloved motherhouse withers away and dies. I weep when I think of it."

His voice grew hoarse with the words, as if he were on the verge of tears. I could well understand such emotion.

I began to relax. It seemed obvious I was not in mortal danger. "Why do you think this...*Jesuit*...would tell you the truth? The last time we met, you all but accused me of murder, as well as of some mysterious criminal act back at the prison in Santa María."

"We've been watching you, Ygnacio, and you *seem* to be trying to help our cause and to find the murderer. You wouldn't be doing that if you'd killed Gelasio, unless you're cleverer and more devious than the Devil himself. We've seen how Dom Gregorio trusts you, and we have years of proof that he's a good judge of character. He couldn't be that wrong. Your success couldn't be due entirely to your deviousness and your wiles."

I was tempted to object to his statement that I was devious and wily, but took another tack. "A few more of your brothers have befriended me, too, you know. All of them couldn't be wrong about me, all the time."

"That's what we decided. We'll trust what you tell us, but of course we'll put it to the test."

"So, what do you want me to tell you, Brother Metodio?" I asked, restoring his title.

"A simple quid pro quo. You reveal everything you and Brother Gelasio discussed up there in the bell ringer's loft, and I'll tell you what we've seen. Perhaps we can cooperate in catching the murderer if we don't work at cross-purposes. Gelasio started out very much on the bishop's side of the controversy, but he may have reconsidered. That might have been enough to get him murdered."

I paused, thinking through my words before I spoke. "The real issue for Gelasio was the vow of obedience, Brother Metodio. He observed all his vows, but that one seemed to be his main focus. He knew Jesuits are supposed to obey their superiors *perinde ac cadaver*, like cadavers, as people never tire of repeating, so he questioned me on the subject."

"And who did Gelasio think his superior was? Bishop Cuadrillero?" Metodio's voice rose with each word, a crescendo in musical terms, but tinged with anger.

"Apparently. I told him the case was murky. In my opinion, his true superior was Dom Gregorio. Abbots have been absolute superiors over monasteries for centuries. In any case, I quoted St. Ignatius's *Letter on Obedience*, where Ignatius says, 'In all things *except sin* I ought to do the will of my superior.'"

"Aha! That could be the key. You told him the ultra-obedient Jesuits could disobey a command if they thought it sinful. Perhaps he thought the bishop's will was sinful and he switched sides in the last minute." Metodio's enthusiasm swept aside his hostility for the moment.

"It's possible." I went on to outline less significant exchanges between Gelasio and me. Metodio questioned me further, and at last, despite his reservations about me, seemed satisfied I'd told him all I knew.

"Then here's what we have for you, Ygnacio. Perhaps you're not aware certain brothers have been whispering about the charter...that it's lost or stolen."

I stared. No one beside Dom Gregorio and I knew the charter was missing. It could only mean the abbot had confided in someone he trusted, one who'd betrayed that trust. I answered truthfully. "I knew it was gone, Metodio, but that fact was still a secret."

"It still is, officially. But some of us have put the rumor together with...well, let me tell you what we've seen. You know Brother Tomás, I suppose?"

"The porter, yes."

"Exactly. He's also a part-time janitor and has keys to most of the rooms in the monastery. Now, this is what I saw. About a month before the murder...must have been sometime in October...I was on the upper walkway in the cloister and happened to glance out at the garden below. I caught sight of someone hovering at the abbot's door, apparently seeing if any key on his ring would fit. I stopped and moved to a point where I could see the brother at an angle and make out his face. I also recognized his build, of course. It was Tomás."

"How did you know he was not merely going in there to do some routine cleaning?"

"Because of the stealthy way he was moving and the way he kept looking over his shoulders. Anyway, he found a key that fit, and in he went."

"What did you do?"

"Nothing. He came out almost at once, and had nothing in his hands. At the time, I thought maybe his visit was legitimate after all. Since then, I've come to think that something disturbed him in there. Maybe Dom Gregorio was taking a nap in his bedroom. Who knows?"

"Did you tell Dom Gregorio?"

"No, I thought the incident was too trivial—at the time."

"But you did know that Tomás could now come and go in the abbot's quarters, whenever he had the opportunity. Surely that was not a trivial matter."

"True. In hindsight, I should have reported it, but that's not all. Brother Mateo saw him about a week later, leaving the abbot's rooms. He thought Tomás looked guilty about something, since he stopped right outside the door and stared in all directions to see if anyone had seen him. Mateo thought he could see a bulge at Tomás' waist as if he had hidden something under his habit. You know how thin he is. Anything like that would show. But Mateo remembered Tomás was a janitor, and thought he'd just finished a job for Dom Gregorio. Maybe he'd confessed privately to him, had been chastised, and that's why he was looking so guilty."

"So, we think we know Tomás stole the charter?"

"Yes."

I nodded. "It seems logical, but Dom Gregorio showed me the locked drawer where the charter was kept. How would Tomás have found it, without having a key?"

"He was an amateur locksmith, but a good one. If he had to, he could open anything. He must have tried every locked coffer and drawer in the abbot's quarters, until he found the one that contained the charter."

"But we *don't* know if he gave it to Gelasio."

"That's what you must find out for us, Ygnacio."

A touch of irony colored my answer. "I'll try to follow your command, Brother Metodio, but what makes you think he'll talk to me?"

"He was on Gelasio's side—the bishop's side, I mean. And, he was Gelasio's shadow, whenever, wherever he could be. He loved that man. He knows you and Gelasio were getting along well. You're not involved in this tug of war—at least as far as we know." His eyes narrowed. "So, he might be more willing to confide in you. Try, Ygnacio...*don* Ygnacio. *Please try!*" Metodio's plea slithered out between locked teeth. He was finding it hard to beg a favor of this *Jesuit*.

"I'll try at the first good opportunity. Naturally I'll let you know anything I find out."

"Good. I hope to God we can trust you in this. We thought we had nothing to lose. I'll go back now, by another way. Two of us coming and going together could wake someone up."

"Understood. Goodnight, Brother Metodio."

ဆင်္ကြ

I carefully opened the side door and stepped from the courtyard into the blackness inside, closing the door behind me without a sound. The space served both as antechamber to the chapter room and opening onto the cloister. While I paused to allow my eyes to adjust, I sensed a rustling quite close to me. The hair on the nape of my neck bristled while I listened, not breathing. Someone was quietly feeling his way along the wall, in the direction of the cloister. It could only mean one thing: we'd been overheard! I could by now make out the lighter space that marked the archway into the cloister, and moved in that direction. I thought I glimpsed a dark blotch, a monk's habit perhaps, flapping as with rapid movement. It blended with the deeper shadows, receding in the direction of the side door to the church. Was it my imagination? I couldn't tell. I began to run, cursing as I tripped over something soft. I fell heavily to my knees on the threshold under the archway. What had tripped me? My foot was tangled in it, whatever it was. I felt quickly, touching what appeared to be a monk's cloak. Dropped there on purpose, to trip me? With my bruised knees protesting, I hobbled in pursuit, but the eavesdropper had disappeared inside the church. The door was standing open and I followed him in.

There was but one light in that cavernous space, the red vigil lamp next to the tabernacle. It produced more shadows than light. I stopped dead still and listened, trying to quiet my own ragged breathing. Nothing. The shadows were so black they became shapes, with form and substance. I stood there, just inside the door, for long minutes, hoping to hear the slightest sound—even the noise of breathing—anything that would echo in the vast nave.

Still nothing.

I made my way around the walls, still hoping to see or hear something as my position and perspective shifted, but after a complete circuit I realized I'd lost him. Perhaps there was another exit to the church and he'd gone straight out.

At last I returned to my cell to toss sleeplessly for the rest of the night.

ಬಿಂ

Next morning, I hurried to catch up with Tomás after Mass, trying to ignore my bruised knees from the night before. "Tomás! Brother Tomás!"

He turned at the front door of the church to see who'd called. When he saw me he became the very picture of fear: open mouth, eyes wide. He shook his head and raised a hand, as if fending me off, then twisted away and dove through a group of his brothers standing near the door. Why such fear? Surely he knew, as did all the monks at La Caridad, I was helping Dom Gregorio solve Gelasio's murder. Was it the guilt of his theft weighing on his mind? Did he suspect someone had betrayed him? I pitied the man, but my desire to question him outweighed my concern. I couldn't show compassion for his fear, since he'd succeed in evading me if I did. I rushed after him.

"Slow down, Tomás, I need to talk to you."

He was in the Plaza de las Cadenas, in front of the church, looking around furtively as if for some place to hide. He crossed to the porter's cubicle where he spent a good part of each day. There he whirled to face me, his back against the doorjamb. His tone was defiant, not that of a panicked man.

"I'm on porter duty, don Ygnacio. I can't talk to you now."

"If not now, when? I must ask you about Gelasio, and about the charter."

He gulped, drawing back slightly and staring like a mesmerized bird when threatened by a snake. Suddenly his words were more a wheeze than spoken. "The charter?"

"Yes. Now listen to me...your friend was murdered because of it, and you know how it disappeared. Two brothers saw you going in and out of the abbot's quarters when Dom Gregorio wasn't there. They think you took it, but I'm here only to find out who killed Gelasio, not to get you in trouble. The charter's the key. Help me!"

When I stepped closer, he shoved me back. "I can't be seen talking to you, don Ygnacio. Leave me alone! Go away!"

Were his violent gestures for the benefit of someone watching from a distance, I wondered, perhaps from the church doorway? I moved closer once more, and he shrank back, stammering.

"The ch-charter? What if I did know something?" He rallied, drawing himself up as if challenging me, fists clenched. "What I know won't help you!"

"For Gelasio's sake, Brother Tomás! Please!" I put as much bite into my near-whisper as possible, emphasizing the urgency. If, indeed, someone were watching, he'd see only gestures. He'd not have the benefit of hearing my words as well. I shrugged and threw up my hands, indicating I'd learned nothing, that Tomás refused to talk. Tomás appeared to understand what I was doing. He whispered back.

"All right, Gelasio begged me to get it for him. I did it for him. Now go! Leave me!" He gave me a second shove, but without much force. Was it also a gesture?

I backed away two steps. "Will you talk with me later?"

"Maybe. Maybe tonight. Now go!" He shook his fist.

I swung around and stalked away, frowning as a final gesture. Then I headed for the same side door where Metodio and I were overheard. I glanced quickly at the open doorway of the church, but the brothers were already dispersed.

There was no one there.

෨ങ

During dinner, while Brother Eulogio read the scriptures, I mused, distracted. Tomás gave the charter to his friend, Gelasio, and the murderer took it from him. I'd supposed all along that it had somehow fallen into Gelasio's hands. Now I knew how, but no more. Tomás was apparently giving all his attention to the scriptural passages, though his occasional quick glances told me he was thinking of our impending meeting.

We ate in silence: bread and soup, then a thick stew with extra bread; the daily half-cup of red wine and water. There was the usual movement, a few monks leaving the room and returning, but I paid scant attention. Later I recalled Metodio and Porfirio leaving, as well as Leopoldo, Eugenio and Plácido, but at the time, I attached no significance to that. My attention was on Tomás, only wavering for a moment or two when I leaned back to pick up the saltceller the novice next to me had knocked to the floor.

Some twenty minutes later, Tomás rose with a look of mild confusion. He stepped backward across his bench, a bit unsteadily it seemed to me, then went over to Dom Gregorio and whispered something. The abbot nodded and made the same graceful dismissing wave with his hand he'd given me on Christmas Eve night. Tomás moved toward the door, and just before he crossed the threshold, he yawned, shielding his mouth with one hand. With the other hand on the doorjamb, he turned in my direction, shaking his head.

What did it mean? He appeared as one suddenly aroused from deep sleep; the head shaking was that of someone clearing away the remnants of a dream.

Why had he become sleepy so suddenly, in the middle of the meal? Had he been up all night, perhaps worrying about his role in the twisted mess of Gelasio's murder? He'd be vulnerable right now in such a drowsy state. My anxiety grew. If his sudden grogginess was a ruse to put others off the track, perhaps he was waiting for me in his cell. If not, perhaps he was ill. I left the table, thinking to talk to him, or at least assure myself he was safe.

His door was wide open and he was stretched out on his cot. His blankets were still in their usual place, folded.

"Tomás!" There was no movement, only a prolonged snore. I stood there for a moment, irresolute, looking down at his relaxed and peaceful face. I must have guessed right—he'd been up all night, extremely bothered by my knowledge. I decided to let him sleep. Our talk could wait a few more hours.

Before closing his cell door, I spread his blankets over him.

ಬಂಆ

I awoke in good time for early Mass, but was surprised not to hear the bells. Tomás was never late. His was a labor of love; he rang them in memory of his friend, Gelasio. Was he truly ill? Was that the reason for his strange drowsiness?

As I considered this with increasing alarm, I heard a shout, then the same rush of scurrying feet and raised voices as the time Gelasio's body was discovered. Everyone was rushing to the same cell, across the Cloister, the one belonging to Tomás.

I followed, dreading what my senses were shouting. Father Plácido emerged from the cell, his face twisted in grief and fear. "Someone get Dom Gregorio. Brother Tomás is dead."

Father Leopoldo started down to inform the abbot. Plácido made his way toward me, tears wetting his rounded cheeks, through the press of his brothers crowding into the tiny space inside Tomás' cell.

"Why, don Ygnacio?" Why did he have to die? I loved him!"

Guilt sat like a vulture on my shoulders. I had a very good idea why Tomás had died. He'd been murdered because he'd been seen talking to me. My stomach twisted into a knot and I felt nauseated. Why had I been so indiscreet in chasing him? My quest for information outweighed my humanity, my good judgment, including my Jesuit training in logical procedure. Worse, I'd failed to protect him. I'd left him sweetly sleeping, still vulnerable to attack. I should have kept watch over my brother, been his keeper!

I opened my mouth, but no words came. Instead, I reached out to the big man, who came into my arms like a child, pressing his face against my chest and sobbing. Many other brothers were weeping, too, for themselves as well as for Tomás. I felt their fear.

Eugenio came over, placed his hand on Plácido's shoulder and spoke gently, trying to comfort him. Plácido detached himself from me then, leaning instead on Eugenio. I stayed close, listening as Eugenio supplied the words I'd not found the strength to say: that God's mercy compensates for the cruelty of mankind; that Tomás was with the saints and was happy now.

More footsteps echoed on the stairs. Dom Gregorio was taking them two at a time, followed by Leopoldo. The abbot's face was drawn and white. "EVERYONE OUT OF THE CELL!" the abbot barked. "Who found him?"

Plácido raised his head. His eyes were red and puffy and his voice was ragged. "I did. Death is loose among us, Domine. It's Divine Will, I feel it is. Divine Will has decreed that some of us must die violently, one by one—" His voice broke. "—those of us who side with Bishop Cuadrillero against our Motherhouse. Who'll be next among us?"

"Don't make a bad situation worse, Plácido," Dom Gregorio scolded.

"You...and don Ygnacio...come in with me. The rest of you wait outside."

He waited until the cluster around the door moved away, then went inside. We followed. There, he made the sign of the cross over the still body.

"May you rest in peace, Brother Tomás, and may Christ receive your soul."

Tomás was lying much as I'd left him, though his head was twisted to the side, one arm dangling. His mouth was open, as if he had fought to breathe. There was no other sign of a struggle. "Did you touch him, Plácido?" the abbot asked.

"Yes, Domine, I felt his hand. It was cold and stiff. I could see he was dead." Plácido sniffed and wiped his eyes on his sleeve. "But otherwise I didn't touch him."

The abbot turned to me. "Examine him, Ygnacio. Tell me what you think. What caused this man, my brother, to die?" His voice broke on the words 'my brother,' and he whispered the last two syllables.

I bent over Tomás, looking for anything that could account for this death. "What did he say when he left the table last night, Domine?"

"Only that he was suddenly very sleepy, and needed permission to go to his cell. He looked a bit unsteady, and I did wonder why he was so tired at such an early hour. But I didn't think anything so serious as this could be wrong."

"I watched him leave, Domine, and he looked terribly sleepy to me, as well. I wondered then what could have caused such sudden drowsiness."

Plácido had regained some composure, even though he was now standing within inches of Brother Tomás' body. "He didn't come to choir duty this morning for matins and lauds, Domine. I was about to reprimand him for oversleeping. That's the reason I came to his cell."

"But instead you found him in a sleep that will now be eternal," I said, continuing to examine the body as best I could. I found no mark, no signs of violence. "Either he died from a sudden apoplexy, or he was poisoned." I spoke in a near-whisper, not to be overheard by the monks I imagined were straining to hear our words through the cell door. "We need to talk about this in private, Domine."

The abbot stepped outside the cell, where he ordered that the stretcher be brought up, the same one that had borne Gelasio's broken body to the altar. Then he spoke to the assembled group of monks.

"Be patient for a few minutes and stay here until we return. We'll all follow

Brother Tomás' body in solemn procession into the church. Father Plácido will lead the chant. Ygnacio, you and Plácido come with me. Leopoldo, you come too." As we left, I heard the word 'murder' in the undercurrent of whispers.

ജൗ

Once we were away from the others, I spoke of my own needs. "Domine, I must talk with you privately, confess to you." He gave me an oblique glance, with a slightly puzzled frown. It was all about my role in Brother Tomás' death. Perhaps I'd not been directly responsible for his murder, but I had certainly hastened it through my lack of discretion and my failure to watch over him.

No sooner were we four alone than the abbot began, turning first to me. "So, you think Tomás was murdered, Ygnacio?"

"I fear so. And your monks think so, too, from what I just heard. You see, back in mid-October he was seen picking the lock to your quarters—or rather, finding a key that would open your lock. Then, about a week later, he was also seen coming out of here, looking very guilty. The witness spoke of a bulge under his habit at that time. Then Brother Tomás admitted to me, yesterday morning after Mass, when I questioned him, that he'd taken the charter 'for Gelasio.' Sad to say, that was all he was willing to tell me at that moment. He'd have told me more later, but that was not to be. Clearly, the murderer took the charter when he killed Brother Gelasio, and the same man must have killed Brother Tomás after he was seen talking to me. The murderer feared I'd learn something from poor Tomás that would give away his identity."

"I see. At least I know now how the charter disappeared, but how did he get into that locked drawer?"

"He picked the lock, Domine. I'm told he was an expert with locks."

"And yet there was no mark on him. How, then, was he killed?"

Leopoldo spoke for the first time. "I was one of the first to see him, right after Father Plácido found him. I think Tomás was smothered. His mouth was open as if he had been gasping for air. Probably given something to make him sleep, and then someone held a pillow over his face."

Dom Gregorio nodded. "Yes, I saw his open mouth too. But...."

As the matter was discussed, my mind drifted to something unusual I'd sensed as I bent over Tomás, a peculiar odor about him. It was vaguely familiar, yet something I could not place. Perhaps belladonna? The physical aspects of the murder pointed to poison, but I had no means to discover for sure what it was, and now there'd be no further chance. Whatever the odor might have been, it would be diffused by all the activity when they brought Tomás down.

But it was something familiar, something I'd smelled some other time, perhaps as I worked with poisonous herbs out in the desert of New Spain, and the chill of fear mingled with my guilt.

I was more than ever convinced I'd be the murderer's next victim.

Chapter VIII

The Bishop and the Lady

Two new graves now marred the well-scythed grass in the monastery graveyard, and a gloom of resignation pervaded La Caridad, a strange combination of boredom and unspoken dread that I could almost smell. Anyone who'd once argued in favor of the bishop's annexation of Robledillo now feared for his life. His fears spoke silently, through his actions and expressions, through his spiritless movements and the sag of shoulders.

My own foreboding, tied to my involvement with the murders, kept me on my guard. Before retiring each night, I tipped my chair up against the cell door, which unfortunately opened out. I couldn't brace it, but by placing the chair as I did, the slightest movement would send it down in a clatter. It would wake me, create an obstacle for any attacker and give me a few seconds to react. My frontier experiences made me confident I could fend off a murderer, and I'd all but recovered from my malaria attack. If the malaria returned? I didn't want to think about that. Certainly I'd be sick enough, almost, to welcome Brother Death.

La Caridad itself seemed frozen in time. Nothing seemed to change, no news from Ciudad Rodrigo, nothing from Robledillo.

Dom Gregorio consumed ever-increasing amounts of brandy, though his keen awareness of the monastery's problems appeared unaffected. He often invited me to drink with him late into the evening hours. I accepted those invitations, partly out of real friendship and delight in our intellectual give-and-take, and partly out of concern. I became protective. He'd fall suddenly and profoundly asleep, almost in the middle of a sentence. I'd then stand him up and walk him to his bed, remove his shoes, cover him and say a little prayer over him before leaving for my own cell. I feared that his abuse of drink would lead to apoplexy or some other severe illness, and tried admonishing him, but he merely waved away my warnings with a smile.

"Ygnacio, the sooner God takes me, the sooner some other poor devil will shoulder the impossible task of maintaining this monastery. I'll be happy to leave it all behind, believe me."

෫ဎၒ3

It was mid-January—now 1776—when Dom Gregorio's invitation took on an air of mystery. He had news, he said, but would tell me no more at the table. Unable to resist the bait, I knocked on his door shortly after he'd left the refectory. As I entered, he waved a folded document on which I could see the remnants of a wax seal.

"From His Grace, don Cayetano Cuadrillero y Mota," he announced.

"A letter?"

"A summons, Ygnacio. Here, read it."

It began with the bishop's expression of profound sorrow over the death of yet another of La Caridad's monks, noting that the murderer had now done away with a fraction less than a tenth the population of the monastery. He went on: "I recall your stating you had documentary proof that the monastery should retain the parish of Robledillo de Gata. A number of weeks have passed, and you should have been able to marshal any legitimate proofs of your claim to the parish—other than time-honored tradition. Please call upon me to discuss the matter of the jurisdiction over Robledillo at your earliest convenience. Bring your prisoner, the ex-Jesuit don Ygnacio Pferkon, who might add his own insights to our deliberations. Besides, I find him amusing company."

"What does he mean by 'amusing company,' I wonder? That I was drunk and revealed my deeper feelings?" That I should be deemed 'amusing' seemed unfair, as my spoken thoughts in the bishop's presence were earnestly sincere. I clenched my jaw.

The corners of the abbot's mouth twitched, and he arched one eyebrow. "If the shoe fits, Ygnacio…." He waited. When I didn't reply, the other eyebrow rose to join its mate. "Well?"

"Of course I'll go," I finally answered. "I could use some time away from these walls. At least we should be able to tell if the bishop has the charter. If he does, he won't be able to hide his satisfaction."

"And if he doesn't have it?"

"Then either it's been destroyed, which I doubt, or someone's playing a deeper game. That's what I suspect."

He peered at me. "But *what* deeper game, and why, Ygnacio?"

"You know the situation here far better than I, Dom Gregorio. You tell me."

༄༅

Porfirio, now the carriage driver in place of Tomás, was a dour man, tall and thin, whose only acknowledgement of my presence was a frown and a buck-toothed grimace. Otherwise, it was the same group I'd traveled with the previous visit to the bishop. I was enjoying the outing, an escape from the stifling miasma of fear within the monastery—I felt safer outside—when Leopoldo broke into my thoughts, speaking above the rumbling of the wheels.

"I'm trying an experiment that might interest you, don Ygnacio. I'll be planting maize from the New World as soon as the weather warms a bit more. I've heard it's good cattle fodder."

"How will you oversee the planting, Father?" I asked.

"When I've outlined my plans for the year's crops, my sister will send the plantation foreman to the monastery to consult and get complete details."

We were passing partly plowed fields at that moment. I visualized them standing tall with maize as I knew it. "Have you thought of planting other New World vegetables like tomatoes and potatoes? They're both fine foods, delicious and nourishing. My Indians grew and ate them more readily than the European vegetables we introduced. They thrived on them, and they made their bread with corn—or maize, as you call it."

"I've heard something about tomatoes, don Ygnacio," he answered. "My correspondents in Italian monasteries are having good luck with them, and I've been considering planting them, but I'll have to think more about potatoes. Both plants are relatives of deadly nightshade, as you probably know. It's always wise to be cautious when introducing new foods that might harm the very people we want to feed."

I felt he'd missed my point that the Indians thrived on both 'poisonous foods.' Had Tomás' death made him that aware of poisons? My thoughts were diverted by sudden darkness as we passed through the gate and the short, dark tunnel in the fortified city wall to the rear of the cathedral. As before, the coach's wheels jolted and echoed noisily on the cobblestones. Seconds later, we drew up next to the Episcopal Palace.

"Ygnacio, you and I will get down here," Dom Gregorio said, "and Leopoldo, you take the coach to your house. We'll see you there later."

The abbot and I swung down from the high door, and I watched the coach as it circled the little plaza and moved off at a trot towards the Plaza Mayor. When I turned about, Father Ybarra was already greeting Dom Gregorio at the open door of the palace.

"Come in! Come in, Dom Gregorio, don Ygnacio! His Grace don Cayetano is expecting you. Terrible news from La Caridad. The whole city is upset, especially since we're told this second death is also a murder. Our deepest sympathies."

"Thank you, don Miguel," Dom Gregorio acknowledged, "but I daresay we're a bit more upset than the city, wondering which one of us will be next. And yes, we're almost certain Brother Tomás was murdered." Ybarra shook his head, but said nothing more as he led us into the bishop's reception hall. A large room, its domed ceiling was painted with a scene of the Assumption, the floor was covered with Portuguese tiles in a blue, yellow, and white floral design and heavy blue and gold brocade drapes hung at the windows. In a word, the room was imposing.

"Please, make yourselves comfortable," Ybarra said as he left. "The bishop will be with you directly."

Don Cayetano entered the room like a broad and majestic ship approaching its mooring. His protruding stomach was swathed in a wide band of purple watered silk, and he leaned slightly backward as he moved, shoulders turning a bit left and right with each step. We stood when we saw him, and he gestured for us to sit again as he lowered himself heavily into a high-backed armchair. Then he glanced over his shoulder and raised a hand, signaling to the same servant who had served us the first time we visited. The man responded in an instant.

"The usual, Your Grace?"

"Yes, Ricardo, white wine from Robledillo and something light to eat. Thank you." He paused only long enough to see the servant nod, then turned to the abbot with a mournful shake of his head.

"Dom Gregorio, I cannot adequately express my sorrow at your continuing misfortunes at La Caridad. Your situation seems to be going from bad to worse. I pray that these killings may end—I'm assuming the news we have is accurate and the second death is a murder—and that your ex-Jesuit helper, here," he bowed slightly in my direction, "may quickly solve the enigma of these assassinations."

I was watching Dom Gregorio's expressions, not surprised to see his facial muscles tense as he answered.

"Thank you, Your Grace. We're all under severe stress at the monastery, fearing another attack. Yes, your assumption is correct; we believe Brother Tomás died an unnatural death, and so far don Ygnacio has done no better than the rest of us in solving these crimes. But you summoned us here, don Cayetano, for reasons other than commiserating with our unhappy situation, I believe."

The bishop's bushy white eyebrows drew together at the abbot's cold formality, a frown that disappeared when he turned to me. "You're looking considerably more respectable today, don Ygnacio. I think our friend Dom Gregorio, here, must have taken my suggestion to heart and furnished you with material for a new robe." He glanced at the abbot with a mischievous twinkle under half-closed eyelids.

"Yes, Your Grace, Dom Gregorio has been most generous. Not one, but two new robes." I made my answer as neutral as possible, while watching him as closely as I could. Which of the two men was the better at his game, I wondered.

He nodded, as if admiring my robe, then turned back to the abbot. The hooded eyes were wide open and his head was thrust forward, giving him the aspect of a bird of prey about to strike. Even his hair, wavy and iron-gray, resembled a bird's crest. He needed only a hooked beak to complete the image.

"I trust you brought your documentary proof allowing you to block transfer of Robledillo parish to this diocese?"

The bishop appeared to know Dom Gregorio was defenseless. He watched the abbot's rather obvious discomfort; watched him lick his lips before replying.

"I'm afraid not, Your Grace. You see—"

"You didn't bring it *because* the charter is lost. Is that not so?"

The abbot flinched, but rejoined with a demand. "Tell me how in heaven's name you know that!" He left off the bishop's honorific.

"Most of the diocese is informed there was a charter, Dom Gregorio. How many of your monks knew about its existence before Brother Gelasio's death?"

"I thought only two, possibly three. Trusted confidants."

"Wait," I interjected. "Brother Eugenio mentioned it to me, early on, before the first murder, and Father Plácido spoke of it in Father Leopoldo's presence, also back then. Among those, only Leopoldo is a close confidant of yours, Dom Gregorio, so the existence of the document was widely talked about within the monastery."

Bishop Cuadrillero waited just long enough for me to finish, then cut in again.

"Too many people knew of its existence early on, as don Ygnacio said, and just as many people found out about its disappearance. Certainly enough to bring the news to this palace."

I considered his statement, chin in hand. Metodio knew the charter had been stolen, and so did Brother Mateo. How many others they had told? Eugenio, Leopoldo, Plácido, and of course Gelasio and Tomás all knew about its existence, had deduced or been told that the thing had disappeared, or had stolen it themselves. Any one of them, even Tomás or Gelasio, could have talked to someone outside the monastery about it, a visitor most likely, and the news spread from there.

The bishop was right. Many must have known of its disappearance.

Dom Gregorio's face flushed with frustration and anger. His knuckles showed white as he gripped the arms of his chair, but his voice reflected none of his emotion.

"Yes, Your Grace, but the charter has been *stolen*, not lost. It's possible don Ygnacio might discover who the murderer is *and* recover the document at the same time. In any case, once it turns up it will take months for ecclesiastical legal experts to decide on its validity. You may be assured that I will make every effort to uphold the rights of Nuestra Señora de la Caridad in the face of the threat from Ciudad Rodrigo until such a decision is made."

The bishop's lower lip protruded as he stared down at his plate, one beefy hand toying with a bit of bread and manchego cheese. Without raising his head, he peered through his eyebrows at his adversary.

"Am I to understand the charter is the only document you have that would bear on our controversy?"

"Well...yes. I can, of course, document centuries of contracts and records of trade between Robledillo and ourselves, centuries of Masses and sacraments, of bequests—"

"Quite." Cuadrillero heaved a sigh as if a weight had lifted off his chest. He'd found out what he needed to know...and so had I. His expression as he turned in my direction was benevolent and mildly curious. "Have you made any progress in your attempt to discover the murderer?"

"Not as much as I'd like, Your Grace. I have a few ideas, many hints, threats and coincidences. But I need something more. A capstone, if you see what I mean, don Cayetano." *That answer should be sufficiently imprecise.*

"Vaguely, don Ygnacio, since your statement is vague in the first place. But I can understand why you can't speak of suspicions at this point. On the other hand, I have news for you."

"Oh?" I sat forward on the edge of my chair. What news could this be? Had my sister Isabella discovered my whereabouts? He tipped a bottle to refill my wineglass, but I waved him away with a smile and shake of my head. Instead, he refilled his own.

"Yes, news. A colleague of yours, also a former missionary in the Sonora area of New Spain, is due to be released before too long, and he might be coming through here. I received word from the archbishop in Madrid, who knows of my interest in the fate of all you ex-Jesuits."

My voice betrayed my eagerness. "His name, Your Grace?"

"Bernardo Middendorff. The archbishop thinks all you missionaries from Sonora probably knew each other."

"We did, don Cayetano, we did. Some of us were close friends. Bernhard Middendorff was one of the men I sailed with when we left Cádiz for the New World, on Christmas Day, twenty-two years ago. Christmas Day, 1755, it was. Bernhard is dear to me. You wouldn't have heard anything about Michael Gerstner?"

I can see us still as the ship is towed away from the dock at Cádiz, beginning to rock gently on the tide as we approach the 'bar.' We've waited so long, some of us for two years, for this sailing, and we burst out singing at the top of our lungs, praising God that we are at last on our way. Michael links arms with Bernhard and pulls him into a dance on the deck. I'm shyer and hesitate a minute or two before grabbing Joseph Och's arm and pulling him out on deck, too. The four of us polka to our own singing until Bernhard slips and drags Michael down, and Joseph and I run into them, and we all land in a heap, howling with laughter.

The sailors think we're crazy, forgetting proper decorum and dignity, but then, surely they've seen other Jesuits ship out, other men expressing their joy that they'll soon be doing God's work at last. At least, that's what we think.

Memories continued flashing through my mind. We stayed together as long as possible after we finally landed at Vera Cruz in New Spain, and even after that, when we were assigned to missions hundreds of miles apart, we'd ride to see each other whenever we could. One of my most treasured possessions had been the folding knife Joseph once gave me, which served me in all sorts of difficulties until the Apaches finally captured me and stole it.

The bishop broke into my reverie, smiling. "Don't ask too much, don Ygnacio. I'm speaking of a possibility, not a certainty. Was Gerstner one of your companions too?"

I blinked, a bit out of focus. "Yes, Your Grace. He was taken into the prison in Cádiz at the same time Bernhard and I were. I thought maybe the two of them would be released together."

"Not to my knowledge. Of course, even though I have excellent informants, I can't know everything about you former Jesuits." He paused for a moment before continuing, "I did hear some amusing gossip about your activities in the prison at the Port of Santa María...." The corners of the bishop's mouth curled a bit and he shot quick glances at me, then at Dom Gregorio.

The abbot sat up straight, eyebrows raised. "Activities?"

I held my breath. I'd been wondering all along if the abbot knew. It seemed obvious now that, for some reason, Dom Gerónimo had never told his counterpart about my 'crime.' An oversight? Because he was truly my friend and wished to protect me? I would never know.

The bishop then provided me with a surprise beyond anything I could have imagined, in the form of a partial and misleading answer to the abbot's question.

"Yes. Don Ygnacio was imprisoned with another ex-Jesuit, Jacobo Sedelmeyer, who was adding information to don Ygnacio's notes describing Sonora Province. They would tell the guards and the royal inspectors during their visits amusing stories about their experiences."

Relieved, I drew a long breath. Don Cayetano had quickly deduced, as I had, that Dom Gregorio knew nothing about my true 'crime,' and his words were meant to calm the abbot's suspicions. Why he was shielding me? Planning to use his knowledge of my past in some way? My sudden new fears were shelved for the moment when he steered the conversation in another direction, a clever ploy.

"I'm told you were very ill shortly after I saw you last."

I quickly followed his lead. "Yes, Your Grace. I suffer from malaria I contracted in New Spain. The only thing that controls it is a medicine called 'quinine,' shown to us Jesuits by the Indians. We tried to inform European doctors about it, but I've seen none of it here in Spain. That's why my bouts of the disease are so severe."

"Quinine...hmm. Yes, I think I've heard of it." He inclined his head and gave me a sympathetic look. Then, as if his interlude with me was part of some strategy, he turned back to the abbot with quite a different expression. I would have called it false benevolence.

"If nothing is forthcoming regarding that lost or stolen charter after fourteen days, Dom Gregorio, I shall proceed with the annexation of Robledillo de Gata Parish."

"Understood, Your Grace. I will fight you with any means at my disposal."

"Which appear to be very limited, my friend."

As the bishop escorted us to the door, he squeezed my shoulder with a gentle smile. "Good night, don Ygnacio, *vaya con Dios.*"

ഇരു

We trudged back in silence towards the Casa Cerralbo, through the winding city streets and past the massive church named for the same family, the so-called Cerralbo Chapel. The sun had set by then, and twilight was fast darkening to night. Our moods darkened with it. Dom Gregorio's drooping shoulders bespoke his frame of mind.

At last, he gave voice to his thoughts. "It's just as I feared, Ygnacio. He's going to proceed against us, whether or not the charter turns up. I've known that for weeks. Tried to drown my worries about that, and my fears about the murders, in cognac. Doesn't work, Ygnacio. You know that. God has decreed that the era of the monastery is over, and I'm just a piece of flotsam left over from a bygone time."

"Domine, at least we know he doesn't have the charter himself. He's counting on it never turning up. It would make his task of annexing Robledillo much simpler. But, facing facts, tell me...would the return of the charter really make that much difference if the Church hierarchy is determined to shift power from the monasteries to the dioceses?"

"The Church moves like a glacier, Ygnacio, you know that. Tradition is of utmost importance. Given its fierce stand against innovation, a man would think a document from the early thirteenth century would carry a lot of weight. You haven't had much to go on in your search, I know, but—damn it to hell, Ygnacio!—I do wish you'd get on with it and solve these murders and this robbery."

We'd arrived at Leopoldo's ancestral home, and the abbot rapped on the door with the heavy doorknocker. Josefina responded. "Come in, Dom Gregorio, Reverend Father Ignaz. Father Leopoldo and doña Clara are waiting for you in the great room."

I replied in German. "*Guten Abend, Gertrud, wie geht's?*"

"*Ganz gut, Pater. Bitte, Bitte, kommen Sie herein! Folgen Sie mir!*" "Fine, Father, please come in! Follow me!"

There was no need to apologize to Dom Gregorio for using my native language, as Gertrud's brief reply in kind was accompanied by gestures and a smile.

She led the way into the familiar room, where two scions of the Cerralbo family stood to greet us: Leopoldo in his monk's habit, cowl thrown back so his mop of copper-hued ringlets glinted in the light of many candles; Clara in a low-cut gown of pale green satin, her shapely bosom half exposed. Bright chestnut hair cascaded over her shoulders in waves and curls, tied behind her head with a ribbon of deep green velvet. I confess my eyes lingered longer on her than on Leopoldo. It was clear they adored each other, her face raised to his, her eyes aglow, his arm encircling her waist.

Their affection was so marked as to be unnatural. I wondered if ever the love between my sister and me could have become that intense?

Leopoldo spoke first. "Welcome to our home once again, both of you. How was the visit to don Cayetano?"

The abbot's troubled voice underscored his words. "Difficult and discouraging, Leopoldo,"

"Yes, I thought you looked gloomy. The bishop must have given you a difficult time."

"He pressed me hard. Wanted to know if I had any defense other than the charter, and of course he already knew that Nuestra Señora de la Caridad had none, other than six hundred years of tradition."

"Well, Domine, I have a wonderful remedy for melancholy." With theatrical flair, Leopoldo opened a walnut sideboard, where stood several bottles and an array of glasses. Without another word, he poured amber liquid into a large balloon snifter. I winced at the size of the glass, and at the quantity he was decanting, which defeated the very purpose of a snifter. It was a third full – more than a cup – when he held it out.

"Try this one, Domine. It will certainly improve your frame of mind."

Dom Gregorio clutched at the offering like a man in high seas clinging to a piece of flotsam. I drew a hissing breath between my teeth as he swirled the brandy and drank off at least half.

"Whooooh! *Excellent* cognac, Leopoldo; I feel better already." His voice was breathy from the vapors.

"Would you care for hot chocolate?" Clara asked, speaking especially to me.

"That would be a fine treat, doña Clara." As I answered, the abbot shook his head.

"I'll just nurse this miraculous cognac, thanks." He held the snifter with both hands against his chest to warm the liquor within. "It has an unusual aroma, Leopoldo. Where's it from?"

"It's not really cognac, Domine, but brandy. It's grown not too far from here. I think they add wild thyme to the grapes while they're fermenting. That gives it spiciness and warmth, don't you find?"

While my attention was on Clara, Dom Gregorio nearly drained his glass. She left the room while Leopoldo, glancing at me with an impish expression, returned to the sideboard again. I raised a warning hand, but he ignored me, held up the bottle against the light to check its level, then filled the snifter a third full again.

Dom Gregorio had settled himself in the most comfortable seat in the room, as if the wing chair were reserved for him. As he swirled the snifter, he smiled distractedly.

"Leopoldo, the bishop thinks taking over Robledillo will be a simple matter. He seems cocky; thinks the charter won't turn up. Ygnacio believes he doesn't have it, but Cuadrillero seems to be telling us that, even if it should turn up, he can discount it."

Leopoldo spun away from the sideboard. "How can he do that? Surely, a document at least five hundred years old, written by a king, can't be counted as trivial!"

I cut in. "Don Cayetano seems to believe the Church is changing, that the era of monasteries is over and the diocese will be the center of power from now on. If he has the backing of the hierarchy, he has all but won the battle. I do think, though, that at the very least, lip service will have to be paid to the document before it can be dismissed, if it can be found. And that lip service could last for months or years."

"I'm just a relic of a bygone era," Dom Gregorio said in a self-pitying tone, his words slurred. Alarmed, I saw that he'd already drunk two thirds of the brandy.

Leopoldo interrupted our intense exchange with an abrupt shift of focus. He began on an apologetic note. "Reverend Fathers, I must excuse myself for an hour or two, to go see my foreman. He's going to show me the seed corn that just arrived from the New World. He tells me it's moldy and may not germinate. We must decide what to do...whether to risk planting it anyway, or revert to a more traditional crop. I'll need to see just how bad it is before I can make any decision. I'll be back before dinnertime."

How odd, I thought; he behaved almost as if he were on a prearranged timetable.

He'd barely closed the door when Clara and the maid reappeared. Josephina carried a tray with steaming cups of hot chocolate, and a plate of delicate, crisp pastries. I was surprised to see there were only two cups. Doña Clara began arranging them and the pastries on a low table in front of me.

"Doña Clara, did you know your brother was going out before you asked about the hot chocolate?"

"Yes, he'd told me. That's why he came into Ciudad Rodrigo, you know, to talk about the spring planting with the foreman. Certainly not to see me."

"Ah, doña Clara, I know him better than that. He'd take advantage of any excuse to see such a lovely sister." I surprised myself by my own gallantry, realizing with a start that my unconscious mind was merging Clara and my Beatriz, a dangerous development.

Clara ignored my compliment to hover over the abbot, who was still holding the nearly empty brandy snifter against his chest. "Dom Gregorio, would you care for a pan dulce? They're not too sweet to go with that brandy, I think."

"No...no thanks, doña Clara...I'll just sit here...an...and enjoy the glow from this c...cognac." His speech was markedly impaired by now as he waved the glass, asking for more. Doña Clara moved at once to refill it. She'd turned, with the glass once again a third filled, when she caught me shaking my head violently and mouthing the word NO. I was disturbed, since I'd never seen the abbot so intoxicated, even after drinking more than an equivalent amount back at La Caridad.

She must have known what my warning meant, but she went ahead, helping Dom Gregorio to grasp the glass.

Then she leaned over me and whispered into my ear. "Let's indulge him for once, don Ygnacio. He's depressed by the visit with the bishop. He needs a little relaxation."

Confident that she'd set my mind at rest, she sat next to me and picked up her cup of chocolate. "A toast, don Ygnacio!"

"To what?" I was surprised, my attention distracted from the unfortunate abbot.

"To you, don Ygnacio. To your service, saving souls in that New World desert, to your survival up to now, to your loyalty to the Church and to your Society, and to you as a fine Christian man."

"Thank you, doña Clara, but I can hardly drink to your praises of me." I dropped my eyes to the cup and saucer in my left hand, desperate for an appropriate counter-toast. Finally the words came to me.

"To the liveliest and most charming lady I've met in many a weary year."

It was true, literally, since I'd met no ladies of any description since boarding the prison ship at Vera Cruz harbor in—how long ago was it?—in eight years. When the flutter of Clara's eyelashes suggested my words were well received, I sipped the hot, sweet drink, thickened with a sprinkling of flour. Essences of vanilla and cinnamon rode on the chocolate flavor.

Then she proffered the plate of delicacies. "Have a pastry, don Ygnacio. They're my favorites."

I selected one and was savoring its buttery flavor when I was distracted by a movement from Dom Gregorio. He'd abruptly slumped in his chair, sloshing some of the brandy on his robe. We both went to his assistance.

When I took the snifter from his hands, half the contents were gone. He'd drunk nearly a quart of brandy in a short time. How could his system survive such an onslaught? Obviously, not too well. He was deeply asleep, emitting gentle snores, his slack features looking worn and old.

I lifted him by the shoulders and settled him more securely in the chair, so his head was resting in the corner between the back and wing. Then I stood beside him, pity and regret washing over me along with a sense of kinship.

Here was a talented, intelligent man, a faithful servant of the Church, being destroyed by the very institution to which he had given his life.

Even so, why had he lost his self-control so readily? Become intoxicated so quickly? Such lack of resistance was not typical of him. In my experience, he could drink indefinitely and still show no symptoms. Something mysterious was at work here. The thought nagged at me.

Clara's tugging at my sleeve broke concentration. "Don Ygnacio, please sit down and finish your chocolate before it gets cold. He'll be just fine where he is; don't worry. Anyway, when my brother gets back, he'll see to him—he's known our abbot for years."

I smiled at her use of the possessive—our abbot—and, despite my concern for Dom Gregorio, returned to the sofa and sat beside her. I took a long sip of the chocolate, still warm, and another of the pastries she offered. She was smiling as she contemplated my face and clothing.

"Such an improvement since last time, don Ygnacio. I must tell you," here she turned aside with a coquettish smile, "that I was the one who chose the cloth. Your robes—and I made sure Dom Gregorio bought enough material for two—are as fine as they are because I contributed my time and expertise, not to mention a small monetary supplement. And I see that an excellent tailor sewed the final product. You look very elegant, Father." She used my title for the first time, at the same time pressing her thigh lightly against my leg.

I felt something like a tingling, reminding me of a feeling I had told Eugenio about—hadn't I?—long ago in Sonora. I edged slightly away, trying to concentrate on a coherent answer.

"I don't know how to thank you, doña Clara! These robes have made me feel almost myself for the first time since the Expulsion. The tailor, by the way, is Father Plácido, the choirmaster. I suppose you know him?"

"Oh, yes, the fat one. Yes, he's quite amusing...quite nice. He's a very talented musician. I didn't know he had other talents as well."

"He's one of the few...besides your brother, Dom Gregorio, poor Brother Gelasio and Brother Eugenio...who've really befriended me at La Caridad. Plácido stepped between me and some of the brothers—one in particular— who were ready to attack me when Gelasio was murdered. He smoothed my relations with the choir monks, too."

She touched my arm. "Let's not get lost in trivia about today's problems, don Ygnacio. Please tell me about the Sonora Desert, about your Indians, your missions and your adventures. I've been waiting for months to learn about all that, and now's my opportunity to hear an uninterrupted version!"

I was flattered by her intense interest, but disturbed by my own reactions to her closeness. The press of her leg and that tug on my sleeve, and now her touch—all amounted to insistent physical contact. A seduction attempt, but why? What was her motive?

Nevertheless, I began, albeit with some discomfort, telling of our landing and how we rode up from Vera Cruz to México, the capital city.

"From México we struck out on mule back for the far northwest, the Sonora-Sinaloa region, where all the Jesuit missions were located. We went through tropical forests, doña Clara, with ferns as big as many trees here in Spain. And there were acres of nothing but palmetto palms, low growing on swampy ground, so thick we could hardly push through—and with sword-like leaves that often cut like knives. Insects swarmed about us so we had to wear white cloths, draped like veils over our heads and faces, with our hats jammed on top. We tucked the cloths into our shirts to keep the gnats out of our eyes and noses, and off our bodies, and especially to discourage mosquitoes. Still, many managed to sneak under the protection."

Doña Clara hugged herself and shivered. "I *hate* insects. They're bad enough here in Europe. They're the Devil's own brood, I must say. Don't they call the Devil Lord of the Flies?"

"That's right, but not all insects are carnivorous and blood-sucking. There are many useful and benevolent ones as well. It's impossible to generalize about any part of God's creation."

When I paused, thinking I was being didactic and boring, she shifted her position so her thigh and knee were again touching mine. "Do go on, don Ygnacio. I think all this is fascinating."

I moved a fraction of an inch away, breaking the direct contact, but there wasn't much room left on the couch. Now I was certain of her intentions, but uncertain how to handle them. I'd not yet eaten the second pastry, choosing this time to take a bite. It gave me reason to shift my position once again. To my dismay, there was no more room to move.

Doña Clara pressed closer, waiting with the rapt expression of a child for my story to continue.

"The terrain was extremely rugged there, with a high central mountain chain formed unlike anything we see here in Europe. Travel grew more difficult the further we went to the north. I happened to have been assigned the mission farthest north of all, so I ended up riding on alone, with a couple of Indian guides and a small military escort."

"Weren't you afraid, don Ygnacio?" She squeezed my arm, her eyes wide with apprehension. I couldn't help but respond to her nearness, against my will. She was deliberately trying to seduce me, even though I found that hard to believe.

I paused for another bite of the pastry, analyzing my feelings, for my mood was darkening. It was not only out of concern for Dom Gregorio, but because of her brazen behavior. My disillusionment with her conduct, so unlike my memories of Beatriz, was clouding any pleasure I might be taking in our conversation.

I'd thought better of her from our previous encounter. Yes, she might feel some real attraction for me, but this...this *onslaught* seemed to be an assault in the service of some other cause. What cause, I wondered? Whose cause?

I answered her question. "Yes, of course I was afraid. And with good reason. A group within the Pima tribe had just staged a violent revolt shortly before. They martyred Father Enrique Ruhen, a priest from my own region of the Rhineland, and slaughtered a number of Indian converts as well. When I got to San Miguel de Sonóita, where my mission was supposed to be, the Indians had already torn down the church and the priest's house. We all feared a deadly attack, and so we returned south to Atí, which became my first mission."

"I would have been terrified, don Ygnacio. You were very brave to go on under such a threat." She gazed into my eyes.

"I was young, inexperienced and very scared, doña Clara. Although we had no way of knowing it at first, the Pápago Indians at Atí were frightened, too— of our reprisals. They went into hiding at our approach and refused to come out until I finally understood that they were afraid of the soldiers. I made what I considered a life-or-death decision and sent my military protection away."

"And were you attacked there, all alone?" I had her entire breathless attention, both hands on my arm.

"No, not at all. The Pápagos finally came out from hiding. They made me welcome. They turned out to be one of the most generous and kindly groups of converts I taught."

"Oh, don Ygnacio!"

She released my arm and fanned her face in an exaggerated gesture of relief, "Now I can breathe. But do go on!"

As I continued my story, she plied me with more pastries and then wine. I was aware my words were more halting, as I concentrated on two things at once. True, she'd been forthright when I first met her, both bold and intimate in her observations. She'd complimented me then, but this was something much different. She not only wanted to come closer, she'd already done so—her flank pressed against mine. I could feel the swell of her bosom against my arm.

I'd just finished telling her about my narrow escape from being sacrificed by the Apaches, thanks to a Christian convert, the chief's wife, when she shattered whatever was left of my reservations.

"Ah! God saved you, Ygnacio, through that Indian woman. I thank God you're still alive and that He brought you here to me!" She threw her arms around my neck and planted a passionate kiss on my mouth, one hand traveling like a butterfly over my hair.

I was affected by her advances, of course. If I'd been younger or in better health, I might have had real trouble controlling myself, but my arousal was dampened by the speed with which she moved from a cup of hot chocolate to a passionate kiss.

Obviously, hers was a calculated seduction attempt, and my weaker self stabbed me with a pang of regret. I'd have been flattered, were she to have found me personally irresistible, not merely a pawn in some political game she and her brother were playing. But what game?

I was forced to stand and disengage myself, since she had cornered me on the sofa. "My dear doña Clara, you're an attractive woman indeed, but this assault on me and my self control seems contrived. Why are you doing this? Surely, a lovely woman like you can find younger and handsomer men, not to mention legitimately available men."

She stood, twisting her hands and blushing all the way down to her low-cut bodice.

"Oh, but I *do* find you handsome, don Ygnacio, despite your scars, maybe because of them. And age has nothing to do with a man's attractiveness. You're mysterious, exotic, and...and vulnerable. For me, that's an irresistible combination. The Church has repudiated you. Why should you remain loyal to its dictates when they no longer affect you?"

"Doña Clara, I—"

She put an index finger to her lips, then raised both hands, palms toward me. She wanted to have her say, and I let her continue.

"Why not allow yourself to love? I'm certain you feel something for me, if you'd only open yourself to your desires. And of course you're right. I was deliberately trying to entice you, and my reasons have just as much to do with the heart as with the head. Can you forgive me for moving too fast?"

Her words echoed genuine passion, and I was beginning to doubt my cynical thoughts.

"You shouldn't be moving in that direction at all, fast or slow, doña Clara. The one thing the Church has not taken from me, cannot take from me without a lengthy and complicated procedure, is my priesthood. As a priest, I must and I do honor my vows." I stopped.

Her eyes were pleading, filling with tears, and her lips parted, but it was her hands that drew my attention. They were open and outstretched as if she were about to receive a gift I could never give. She was beautiful. Her image blended with that of Beatriz, obscuring reality for a moment before fading.

My voice sounded strange in my head as I continued, constricted, almost disincarnate, such was my emotion.

"I...I'm fond of you.... I like you, doña Clara, very much...and I hope there's some other way we can continue to be friends."

It was at that moment I sensed another person in the room.

Chapter IX

A Drunken Abbot

Father Leopoldo was standing just inside the door. He'd entered the room unnoticed, and his worried glances were shifting back and forth between Clara and me. How long had he been standing there? He was to have been gone an hour or two, yet here he was back. Surely he'd been gone less than an hour, adding to my earlier suspicions about his unusual departure.

His appraisal concluded with Dom Gregorio, slouched in the chair. "I won't comment on what I just heard, or hazard a guess on what's been going on here," he said, "but I hardly think it would stand scrutiny in the light of day." He moved to Dom Gregorio's side and pressed his fingers against the abbot's neck, just under his jaw, shaking his head as if worried. "Clara, did you?...."

Leaving the question unfinished, he turned to the sideboard, picked up the brandy bottle and held it to the light. I saw the level, as well. The bottle was practically empty.

"Gone! He drank nearly a quart. You could've killed him, Clara Eugenia. But lucky for you, for all of us, his heart is still beating."

She looked chastened, and her voice was small. "I knew how he drank and how he could hold it, so I didn't think it would hurt him. Is he really ill?"

"Only time will tell us that." He turned to me with a scowl. "Meanwhile, don Ygnacio—"

I interrupted, anxious to cut off his angry diatribe before he began. He'd blame me as the assailant of his sister's virtue, of course, despite what his ears must have told him.

I turned to her. "Doña Clara, I know you were planning to serve us dinner in a few minutes, but it would be best if we were to take our poor Dom Gregorio back to La Caridad and eat a bite there. I'm certain you didn't realize how much he'd drunk. Please apologize to your cook. Father Leopoldo, we can discuss this whole matter further in the coach. Please!"

Leopoldo's reply was cold and formal. "Yes, I agree. The coach is right outside. We'd better take him back."

Clearly, I was to be blamed for his sister's behavior. I said nothing. We lifted the abbot's limp body out of the chair, each draping one arm around our necks. His feet dragged on the way out, but we managed to get him through the door. Porfirio jumped down off the coachman's seat to help us, but just as we prepared to hoist the abbot into the cab, he was suddenly and violently sick. I signaled to Leopoldo, and we bent him at the waist so he could finish vomiting without soiling himself or us any further.

"Porfirio! Get cloths and water from the house!" Leopoldo ordered, as I began to wipe the abbot's mouth with my handkerchief. It occurred to me that I should clear the inside of his mouth and throat also, so he would not inhale any vomit, but by now my own handkerchief was useless. I borrowed Leopoldo's, twisting the cloth into a spiral and clearing the abbot's nostrils as best I could with a corner. His handkerchief was torn, which made the task a bit easier.

Leopoldo issued another order. "Drop those soiled handkerchiefs on the pavement! I'll tell the gardener to wash the street with buckets of water. He can pick them up then." His tone was unusually harsh, but I was more than happy to obey.

"This is a miserable mess, Father Leopoldo, but Dom Gregorio will be much better off now that he's rid of some of that brandy. If he hadn't thrown it up, he still could have died from intoxication."

Leopoldo merely grunted.

When Porfirio returned, we finished cleaning up as best we could, wiping our shoes and brushing down our robes where they'd been spattered. Finally, we were able to lift the abbot into the coach and make him comfortable. One of us would have to hold him in his seat on the way back. It turned out I was to be the one. Leopoldo perched on the opposite seat, locking eyes with me as if he expected me to look away.

"Don Ygnacio, I won't be coming back with you, not now. I must speak to my sister to hear her side of this – once you've told me yours. If Dom Gregorio is in any state to notice my absence, tell him...tell him I'm detained on family business. I'll be back early tomorrow, in the family coach."

I spread my hands. "Do as you must, Father Leopoldo. I have no say in it."

"I want to know exactly what happened between the two of you in there while I was gone." His tone was that of an interrogator, icy but laced with authority.

"Your sister first invited us to have a cup of hot chocolate and Dom

Gregorio refused, preferring the brandy you supplied him.

"That was before I left."

"Yes. Then, when the chocolate and pastries arrived, she offered the abbot a pan dulce, but he refused, requesting more brandy instead. She replenished the snifter, as you must have guessed, and it is quite large."

"Go on."

I summarized the chain of events, ending with doña Clara's admission that her heart was engaged as much as her head. "That's all that happened, Father Leopoldo. You surely heard that last exchange yourself."

"If that's all you did, don Ygnacio, then most of the fault is on her side. She's a lonely woman and very emotional, very...shall I say...responsive. Her husband was killed in a skirmish with the Portuguese. You couldn't know that, of course.

I felt a pang of sympathy. "Widowed so soon! But why can't she remarry?"

"She's too old to marry again at thirty-four, and she refuses to enter a convent. No children, either. If she'd had one, she'd be too busy with him to indulge her idle fantasies. If she's the one to blame for this evening's...uh, indiscretions, I'll not hold this against you. But before I can say that for certain, I must talk with her." His voice remained cold and angry, but I felt that his anger reflected disappointment and frustration with the situation. It seemed directed more at Clara than me.

I'd returned his steady gaze all this time, never wavering. "That sounds sensible to me, Father Leopoldo. Will I see you in the morning? I do want to clear up this unfortunate turn of affairs."

"Most likely. Take care of our abbot."

He swung down and left the coach, and shortly afterward the abbot and I were off to La Caridad. Since the windows were fixed in place, the air became stuffier by the minute, saturated with the cloying odor of vomit. It was easier to cradle Dom Gregorio than brace him in his seat, so I held him in my arms the whole way. Was this the way a mother holding her hurt child might feel, I wondered? I shifted my position so he rested more comfortably, straightened his crumpled robe and loosened his collar.

At times during the ride my tears welled up. I couldn't help comparing the abbot's habitual dignity to his present abject condition. He'd become my friend, and now he was lying here in my arms, unconscious, slack-faced and soiled, like a homeless drunk. He'd come to this because he couldn't bear his helplessness in carrying out his duty as guardian of Nuestra Señora de la Caridad. The charter was in hostile hands, and he was not only incapable of fending off the bishop's designs on Robledillo parish, but powerless to defend his monks from the stealthy killer who struck by night.

His frustration had driven him close to suicide. I remembered his outcry as we were walking to the Casa Cerralbo. "Damn it to Hell, Ygnacio!—I do wish you'd get on with it and solve these murders and this robbery!" It was a plea for help, directed at me. His words meant I should redouble my efforts, concentrate as never before. Anything and everything could be relevant, including what I'd just experienced in the Casa Cerralbo. The whole evening disturbed me. There were false notes everywhere. Certainly I needed to think it through, but later. My deepest concern at the moment was to care for this man in my arms, watching over him through the night in case he vomited again and, in his stupor, suffocate.

When we returned, Porfirio lost no time in spreading the word of Dom Gregorio's overindulgence. Several of the monks offered to help, but I refused them. It takes only one person at a time to watch over another, and I elected to be that person. Sleepless, I spent the night hours hauling water, stripping him to his under drawers, bathing him and putting him to bed. I bathed as well, changed my own robe, then walked the floor, keeping watch. I fasted, rather than think of dinner.

There in the abbot's quarters, I strode up and down, hands clasped behind me, my breathing quick and shallow, barely conscious of my continual motion. The events played themselves over and over, like theatrical scenes before my mind's eye. I recreated Dom Gregorio's slide into drunkenness. So rapid! Yes, even his drinking had been rapid. He must have wanted urgently to forget. Or, had I been so enthralled with doña Clara's closeness I'd lost all track of time? I winced inwardly at his slurred speech and uncoordinated gestures as he waved the glass asking for more brandy, there on the stage of my memory.

My convictions fed upon themselves. He must have been drugged, what else? Hadn't he said the 'cognac' had an unusual perfume, like thyme? Or was that Leopoldo, explaining the aroma?

I recalled Leopoldo's face as he entered the room later, by turns frightened and angry. He'd crossed from the door to Dom Gregorio's chair in a rush, and placed his fingers on the abbot's neck, feeling the pulse at the artery just under the jawbone. Of course! Why would he do that unless he needed to find out if the abbot were dead? Why would he have been thinking in such dire terms, since Dom Gregorio appeared simply to be asleep? He knew it was the abbot's habit to drink heavily, and at that point, he hadn't yet seen the quantity left in the bottle, so why had it entered Leopoldo's head to check the pulse? And, too, Doña Clara said she didn't think the amount he drank would harm him, that he usually could drink anyone under the table. If the brandy were drugged, at least she didn't know about it.

I went to Dom Gregorio and felt his clammy forehead, peering at his puffy, closed eyes and sunken gray cheeks. There was no response. I was now convinced he had been given a mild poison, yet even though his condition hadn't improved, it hadn't seemed to worsen.

Would he recover?

I resumed my pacing, now thinking of doña Clara's advances. Far too hasty, as if she had wagered with someone—her brother, probably—that she could seduce me within an hour. I relived the telling of my stories while she posed and responded in her artificial way. That was not the Clara I thought I knew. The first time we'd met, she already seemed to feel something for me, as I did for her. That admission was difficult for me. Even so, her behavior this time seemed forced.

Was she doing a favor for her brother? After all, the two of them were standing together like lovers as Dom Gregorio and I walked into the family room. Leopoldo said earlier that he loved her above all things. That admission struck me then, and still did, but if he loved her as I loved my own sister Isabella, how could he possibly ask her to prostitute herself in such a way? And if she were the honest woman she seemed at first to be, how could she possibly consent to approach me the way she did? The whole thing was preposterous, and deeply disturbing.

Also, Leopoldo returned much earlier than he'd announced. That thought kept returning. He'd never said why the time with his foreman had been so short. He'd never even mentioned the foreman, or the maize.

Clara's blush convinced me she knew she'd disgraced herself. She was genuinely embarrassed in the end, but she had me believing in her affection for me. That much shone through all the artificiality.

I paused in mid-stride. What were my feelings for her at that very moment? A pang of disappointment, yes, or disillusionment, but underlying that? A ghost from a faraway desert, a ghost with long, flowing hair, her filmy nightdress rippling around her in the midnight breeze? I shook my head and, frowning, turned my thoughts back to Clara's words. They, too, might have reflected her true feelings, in spite of a failed attempt to further her brother's schemes.

Her brother's schemes? Yes, I'd admitted to myself that's what they were, nothing less. He'd never intended to be away for an hour or two, nor did it seem possible he could have spoken with his foreman in such a short time. And when he returned, his anger was genuine. Why? Was it aimed at me for an imagined seduction attempt? The jealousy of a brother, too close to his sister? Or was it because he'd seen that his plans had gone wrong?

Dom Gregorio looked as if he might be dead, and there I stood, preaching morals to Clara, far from bedded. I clenched my fist and struck my palm. *Father* Leopoldo, indeed! What sort of priest would play pimp for his sister, to entrap another priest in some nefarious political scheme? None of it was believable, and yet all of it was true. No other conclusion could be drawn.

If it were true, what in God's name could be his motive?

Something else now came to mind, a detail that had been nagging at me, and I cursed myself for not having paid more attention at the time. I relived the miserable scene in all its ugliness. My unfortunate friend, the abbot, was contorted in the throes of vomiting next to the coach. I waited, then wiped his mouth with my handkerchief, and then with Leopoldo's. His was torn! A rectangular piece was missing—was I remembering correctly? Surely I was, because it was narrowed at the tear, making my task of cleaning Dom Gregorio's nostrils easier. I was able to form that part into a tight twist.

My mind's eye saw the rectangular fragment of bloody handkerchief caught at the edge of the water tank. Were the two a match? Why hadn't I made that link when it counted?

Instead, on Leopoldo's orders, I threw the handkerchief to the ground.

By morning, my incessant walking and strenuous efforts to recall every detail had me exhausted. First light dawned upon a conscious but thoroughly miserable abbot, racked by vertigo, nausea, and a violent headache. I was delighted to see that he had, however wretchedly, regained his senses. I was better off, but not by much. As the sun rose, I found that I, too, was afflicted with a headache. The fact was not surprising. I'd heard that headaches could be caused by prolonged intense mental activity, tension, hunger, and lack of sleep. I'd embraced all four.

I tried meditating the headache away, but was startled out of my inner world by Dom Gregorio's pathetic croak through cracked lips.

"Water! Give me water, Ygnacio!"

I poured a glassful, and pulled him up to a semi-sitting position against the pillows while I supported him. I had to brace the glass, since his shaking hands were spilling the water on the bedclothes. He drank, licked his crusty lips, then groaned as he lay back against the pillows.

"I'd be better off if I'd died last night. It's my damnable pride that's done this, Ygnacio." He sat up abruptly, dry retching as a wave of nausea hit him. I held a pan ready, fearing his stomach would reject the water, and thanked God when he became calmer and lay down again.

"Why do you say your pride did it, Domine?"

He gathered strength before replying, pressing his long fingers to his temples to ease what was obviously a painful headache. "I thought I could hold any amount of liquor and not pay the penalty, but I've been taught a lesson, Ygnacio. I've never been sicker, certainly never because of drinking. I don't understand—"

"You drank nearly a quart of brandy, Domine."

"I remember...I think. But still...it affected me so quickly! That's never happened before." He rolled his head against the pillow with a fleeting frown, closed his eyes and was soon asleep. That he was equally puzzled over the effects of that brandy added to my suspicions. He knew the effects were unusual, and he was more than accustomed to heavy drinking.

He seemed to be out of immediate danger, and my tired mind told me I'd digested all there was of that remarkable night. I pulled his comfortable armchair closer to the bed, sprawled in it and relaxed. I felt myself drifting. Before long, I fell asleep.

I awoke before dinner hour, inadvertently waking the abbot when I replaced his chair. He was pale and shaky, still complaining of a slight headache and raging thirst, but otherwise much improved. I brought him glass after glass of cold water.

"Go ahead and eat with the others, Ygnacio," he said. "Just see that someone brings me a tray with some soup and bread. That's all I dare eat for the moment. But, God be praised, I'm actually hungry!"

"So am I, Domine, downright ravenous."

ℰℭℰℭ

As I entered the refectory, I found Leopoldo talking with a group of monks about to seat themselves. He saw me and left them to come speak to me. His face was grave, but with a hint of friendly smile.

"Don Ygnacio, I must apologize for last evening. Clara explained everything. She told me, and I believe her, that she was entirely to blame for the whole incident. And now, I only hope we can put all of it behind us." He paused, earnestly searching my eyes. I nodded, but he continued before I could reply. "And how is Dom Gregorio? I knew you were taking good care of him, so didn't want to disturb you before dinner."

"He's recovering, but still too weak to come out to eat. I'll take him some food. But tell me, when did you get back?"

"About noon. As I said, I thought it better not to disturb you."

"Well done. Both of us slept through the day. I stayed awake all night watching over him. But, before dinner begins, is there anyone to say the blessing in Dom Gregorio's place? You have seniority, I believe."

"I got here in time to say it at noon. I assume I should do that again?" It was a question.

"That's how it seems to me. Now I must find someone to fix a tray. He asked for soup and bread."

"I could take care of that, don Ygnacio. You need to get some rest."

My inner recoil was so intense I quickly sought to disguise it. "Oh, no thanks, Father Leopoldo. I began this care-taking task and I'll stay...until Dom Gregorio is totally himself again."

As I made my way toward the kitchen, I was possessed by fears, the product of my visceral reaction. Was it possible that Dom Gregorio could have been the intended victim of a third murder?

Might Leopoldo the schemer be Leopoldo the murderer as well?

Chapter X

Robledillo

My suspicions festered all through the following day, and the next, but Dom Gregorio's recovery was steady, suggesting the poisoning was not as serious as I'd thought, if it had occurred at all. And yet, the incident churned away in my mind, eating at my spirit while sharpening more than ever my desire to identify the murderer of La Caridad. To those rankling suspicions, I added remorse. I'd let a possibly valuable clue slip through my fingers, in the form of a torn handkerchief. In its stead were Leopoldo's less than adequate explanation and apology: *Clara explained everything. She told me, and I believe her, that she was entirely to blame for the whole incident. And now, I only hope we can put all of it behind us.* He'd not mentioned the incident thereafter.

Two days after his bout with the brandy, Dom Gregorio was the abbot once again, making preparations for The Presentation of the Lord, to be celebrated 2nd February. He put Father Plácido in charge of celebrating Mass in the monastery church that morning. I would not be there for that Mass. I'd be once again traveling with the abbot, starting at dawn for Robledillo de Gata. A Mass and procession in the village were to be followed by a festival and a Town Council meeting, all arranged by him.

Father Leopoldo would be with us once again, this time as an important landowner and member of the council. I was a bit uneasy, yet was pleased I'd be seeing more of the countryside outside the monastery walls. I was curious to see the village celebration, so I thanked the abbot warmly.

The council meeting, to be held at Leopoldo's own *casa* in Robledillo, would measure the villagers' feelings about possible annexation by the diocese. Gelasio's family and boyhood friends lived there. Perhaps one of them would supply useful information to help solve one or both of the murders. Brother Gabriel woke me at 4:30 that morning, and we were underway by 5:00, in total darkness. He rode outside as brakeman, on the back of the coach, while Porfirio drove the four-horse team.

If I'd been puzzled by our early start, my questions were soon answered, since Robledillo lay eight leagues away. We arrived first at a village called Pastores, after trotting past wheat fields bounded by networks of four-foot stone walls. Over the centuries, hundreds of thousands of tiny stones had been fitted together into coherent structures that stretched for miles.

The team was fresh and the morning pleasant, not too cold. All seemed normal until we came to an abrupt halt at the top of a yawning gorge. I was suddenly looking down the nearly vertical side of a canyon to a silver ribbon of water far below.

I pressed my face against the coach window. "This reminds me of river gorges in New Spain, Domine. What river is this?"

Leopoldo answered, a little too quickly. He seemed overanxious to resume normal relations. "It's still the Águeda. We have to work our way down to the bottom, where there's a Roman bridge. I'll get down here and help Gabriel slow the coach down. I'll be operating the brake lever on the cliff side. Pray that those brakes don't fail!"

The road narrowed abruptly just as our coach plunged over the lip of the gorge, barely clinging to the canyon wall on a portion as steep as any I'd ever seen, snaking around hairpin curves. The brakes shrieked and complained repeatedly as the two monks threw their combined body weight against the levers. They succeeded in keeping the coach from riding up on the horses, but barely.

We came to a near halt as Porfirio steered the horses around a switchback, slowly maneuvering the coach behind them. Any number of times, I found myself gripping my seat and holding my breath, as we seemed to hang over the abyss with nothing between the outside wheels and the river below. I heaved a sigh of relief when we reached the ancient narrow bridge at the bottom, only to begin the climb on the other side. Three of us got down and walked behind the coach to lighten the horses' load as the harrowing trip repeated itself in reverse. At least we'd still be among the living, even if the coach should slip off the road.

I prayed for the safety of our two brothers who had to ride, Porfirio the driver and Gabriel, still manning the brakes, now to keep the coach from rolling backwards on the steepest inclines.

"How much farther, Father Leopoldo?" I gasped, winded when we reached the top.

"Oh, we've only come about a third of the way, don Ygnacio. There's more rugged road up ahead."

Gently rising plains resumed, and we were again running through pastureland crisscrossed with those millennia-old stone fences when we passed through Martiago. We stopped there, in front of the medieval church, to water the horses.

"This village once belonged to La Caridad, too," the abbot said, "but it has been tithing the city for some time already. Our resources are being whittled away bit by bit. Martiago's a good wheat producer, but nowhere near as rich as Robledillo."

"How far have we come, Dom Gregorio?" The sun was already well above the horizon. "Not quite half way, and the worst is yet to come." He smiled at me indulgently. "This is the Sierra de Gata, the mountains on the frontier between Estremadura and Portugal. But surely, don Ygnacio, you've seen more spectacular mountains than these. The Alps? And those in New Spain?"

"Briefly, many years ago, Domine, I saw the Alps when I was still a scholastic. I crossed over into Italy, but on foot and by easy stages. The world was a different place for me then."

I remembered my joy, my naive anticipation of high adventure, my certainty of the great service to God I would surely render. Yes, I'd served God and experienced high adventure, but how different it all seemed now.

The beauty of the landscape made further introspection impossible. We were climbing through a mixed forest of oaks and chestnut trees, leafless now, offset by pines and holly with its polished evergreen leaves. Dry and yellowed skeletons of frost-killed bracken ferns brushed the sides of the coach. When the climb became truly steep, we got out to walk once again, which afforded me a better view of details such as rushing streamlets of purest spring water, bordered in ice, that came tumbling down the mountainside. The cold was biting at this altitude, and we could see our breath. We paused again at one of the springs to drink, slowly because of the water's icy chill, and to rest the horses. Then, once more, we faced another precipitous descent.

This one was at least as harrowing as the river gorge had been, but more imposing. We could see for miles in the sparkling winter sunshine. Far below us, I made out a huddle of miniature white houses with red tile roofs and the church's bell tower rising above them, but the clarity was deceptive. The approach, tortuous and difficult, took another hour, with the precarious road often hanging over chasms that looked to be hundreds of feet deep.

We arrived at last at Robledillo a little past 10:00 that morning, after a five-hour journey. The little mountain streamlets, joined together, formed a sizeable torrent here, called the Árrago. I guessed that trout fishing was a favorite occupation of the villagers when they weren't tending their olive groves, or wheat fields, or the vineyards on the well-maintained terraces covering the south-facing slopes. We were met at once by young men who took charge of the coach and horses. The mayor, or *alcalde*, greeted us officially with a delegation of city officials, and the parish priest, don Alfonso, then escorted us up steep streets to the little plaza in front of the church. Then the celebration began.

The population of the town was large enough to have formed two *cofradías*, fraternities of devout laymen who carried out good works in their everyday lives. In festive processions, these men wore robes and pointed, satin hoods with eyeholes, one *cofradía* in gold satin, the other in intense midnight blue. Now they came singing up the street, the foremost quartet of the gold brotherhood bearing a platform on their shoulders, with a massive carved wooden cross from the village church. The midnight blue quartet followed, carrying the statue of the Virgin, and the remaining members of each group carried lit candles that would later illuminate the church. Banners and garlands festooned the street, and the women and children of the village strewed fern fronds in front of the marchers.

Leopoldo said that, in warmer seasons, wild flowers were scattered in the path of processions. He'd become more congenial during the trip, acting as though the events in Ciudad Rodrigo were ancient history. I held my doubts, as neither his early reappearance, nor the amount of brandy he first poured, were a part of his explanation later.

The marchers halted in the little square before the church where we were waiting. Father Alfonso, Dom Gregorio, and Leopoldo led the *cofradías* and the villagers into the church, singing verses from Isaiah 35: "*Confortamini, et nolite timere, ecce Deus vester...*" "Be strong, fear not! Here is your God, he comes with absolution; With divine reward he comes to save you. Then will the eyes of the blind be cleared, the ears of the deaf be opened; Then will the lame leap like a stag, and the tongue of the dumb will sing, Alleluia!"

Father Alfonso then began the Mass, speaking to the congregation, "Forty days ago, we celebrated the birth of our Savior...."

After the ceremony, the members of the *cofradías*, still in their satin robes, mingled with the crowd in a colorful pattern at the foot of the dais outside the church, as musicians began to play. I was astonished to see a bagpiper among them. The instrument was not as complicated as the Scottish bagpipe I'd once heard, but wheezed and squeezed forth a similar sound. The dancing and singing was still in full swing when Dom Gregorio and Father Leopoldo started down the sloping street toward Leopoldo's house. A group of some twenty men broke away from the festivities and followed, don Josef Vicente Sierra, the mayor, at their head. I was walking beside Leopoldo.

"Clara will be at the house, don Ygnacio." He eyed me. "She promises there'll be no repetition of what occurred during your last visit. I'm sure you'll be...uh, discreet. You'll do nothing to...ah...draw her attention."

I took four more steps downhill, amused at his ability to be imperious and wheedling at the same time. He seemed to be protecting his sister from me, a possible predator. If so, what became of my theory that he'd planned Clara's seduction attempt?

The Cerralbo house, taking the space of two normal houses on the main street, resembled a Swiss chalet more than anything I'd seen in Spain to this point. A carved wooden balcony ran the full length of the upper floor, under a pitched roof.

The stairway to the upper floors began ony a few feet in front of the entrance. Leopoldo led the way upward, and I could only glimpse a large room on the ground level, its floor tiled in regal red, set up as a banquet room. On the upper floor we entered a room big enough to hold the crowd of dignitaries. Chairs were arranged like an audience hall, two chairs on a low platform in front and the rest in rows. Window-doors opened onto the balcony.

The party of men filed in after us and took their seats, chair legs squeaking on the wooden floor. Leopoldo pointed to a chair halfway down the rows.

"Sit here, don Ygnacio," he said. "You can watch things from here. I'll be on the side opposite you, closer to the door in case I need to give instructions."

I took my seat while Dom Gregorio and the *alcalde* approached their places on the raised platform.

Leopoldo had made an excellent choice for me. If I turned my chair a bit with my back to the windows, I could see everyone in the assembly. I realized that my presence was causing a stir among the dignitaries, something Dom

Gregorio noticed as well. As soon as everyone was seated, he stood and addressed them.

"You've all noticed the stranger in our midst. I would like to introduce to you don Ygnacio Pferkon." He turned to me. "Could you stand, please, don Ygnacio?"

I obeyed at once and bowed, meeting their curious stares, now no longer covert but piercing and direct. Dom Gregorio continued. "As you can see from the cut of his robe, he is an ex-Jesuit priest and missionary who served in New Spain for eleven years before the Expulsion. He has come to La Caridad and will remain with us for a while—we don't know how long—at the pleasure of His Majesty, King Carlos III. While he is here he has placed himself at my service, and is attending this meeting at my invitation."

The abbot paused and looked around to see if there were any questions. Seeing none, he continued.

"I wish to express to all of you at this time my profound condolences on the death of our beloved Brother Gelasio. Our especial sympathy goes to the Mangas family, which has lost a fine son, as well as to the parish of Robledillo at large, for all of you have lost a friend and neighbor, a young man you have known from babyhood and watched with pride as he grew into an admirable man, a productive brother monk at Nuestra Señora de la Caridad. I wish to note our sorrow also at the death of his friend and fellow monk, Brother Tomás of Béjar, murdered less than forty days ago. Please include him as we pray. At this time, let us stand and pray for the peace of both their souls."

With much scraping of chairs, the group stood while the abbot led us all in the Lord's Prayer and then a short prayer for our poor brothers, Gelasio and his friend Tomás, ending with "*et lux perpetua luceat eis,* may eternal light shine upon them." After a respectful pause, the group resumed their seats and the abbot continued.

"We have two matters to discuss here today: the murder of two of our own and the annexation of the parish by Ciudad Rodrigo."

Here, the *alcalde,* a short man with abundant, wavy black hair, dark eyes and a head too large for his body, spoke up for the first time.

"Domine, it would seem appropriate, since we've just prayed for the peace of two souls, that we deal with the problem of the murders first. That would seem to me more urgent and certainly more respectful of the dead than to plunge headlong into politics."

There was a murmur of general consent.

Don Josef continued. "I regret to say, Dom Gregorio, that since the murders took place at the monastery, the assassins, or more likely, the assassin is no doubt one of your own monks. It had to be someone who knew the two monks' habits, their schedules and the plan of the monastery. What steps have you taken to discover his identity?"

The abbot squirmed a bit on his chair before replying. "I've questioned everyone in the monastery, don Josef. So far, my inquiries have revealed nothing. Every one of my monks claimed to be sound asleep at the time the murders must have been committed, and no one heard or saw anything unusual. I am, of course, continuing my inquiry, but have no real progress to report."

An elderly man now spoke up. I'd already noticed more than half the group was made up of men well into their years. "We'll expect you to find these men or this man and bring him to the secular authorities for just punishment, Dom Gregorio, no matter who he is, how important his function, and no matter how fully you've trusted him in the past."

"I'm doing my best, don Alejandro. All of you have a responsibility in this matter, too, since Brother Gelasio was your own friend and neighbor. I would ask all of you, please, to report to me anything suspicious you may see or any information you may hear in Robledillo, about him or Brother Tomás, that might help me discover the truth. Someone knows what happened in each case, and that person might be sitting right here in this room. Please, keep your eyes and ears open. Let me know the slightest thing you suspect would help." More murmurs swept the assemblage. A short, stocky man stood to be recognized.

"Have you discovered motives for the murders, Dom Gregorio? Any ideas?"

"We think it had to do with their stand on the annexation of Robledillo by the diocese of Ciudad Rodrigo. Brother Gelasio was in favor of the change, and his friend backed him."

Amidst more chatter, the same man stood again. "This is getting us into the politics of the situation, I fear, but if that's truly the cause, don't you think still more killings might take place? It would seem the monastery is as divided on the issue of annexation as the village is."

The abbot winced. "Let us pray to God that we can control our passions, not resort to any more violence, even if the very existence of the monastery is at stake."

Another man stood, speaking out before being recognized, "And this ex-Jesuit here, what is his function in all of this, Dom Gregorio? Why did you invite him here for this meeting?"

The abbot glanced at me, then back to the speaker. "He's had considerable experience in solving murders. He unmasked two murderers while serving as a missionary in New Spain. His talents might help us all. As for this meeting, he is here, as I've said, as an observer."

An undercurrent of whispers followed his answer. The looks directed my way were not entirely benevolent. Dom Gregorio leaned toward the *alcalde* and whispered in his ear. Don Josef nodded, then spoke up.

"Is there anything more to be said about the murders of Brother Gelasio and Brother Tomás at this moment?" Silence followed. "In that case, since we've already broached the subject, let us turn to the matter of Robledillo and the diocese of Ciudad Rodrigo."

Several men rose to their feet, anxious to speak. Don Josef recognized the oldest person among them, don Pedro Antonio. I saw annoyance among younger men in the group.

The speaker began with a voice somewhat strained, but steady. "Don Josef, Dom Gregorio, I'm here to defend the rights of the monastery over those of the city. We've been a unit, this parish and La Caridad, for more than six centuries. We are here to sustain and help each other. Dividing us would be like splitting a body in half and expecting each separated half to continue to function. The situation of the monastery would be even worse than ours. In gratitude for loving service over more than six hundred years, I say let Robledillo remain united to Nuestra Señora de la Caridad."

His remarks won applause and supporting cries among older council members, with prolonged applause by Father Alfonso, whose clapping continued well after others stopped. No one could doubt where the priest's sympathies lay.

I was closely watching one of the younger men, perhaps in his mid thirties, who'd seemed more agitated each second of the speech. He'd not applauded, and now he was granted recognition.

Don Pedro Justo was tall and deep-chested. His commanding presence was enhanced by a heavy, square face and deep voice, which he employed with a note of sarcasm.

"I'm sure we're all moved by don Pedro Antonio's touching plea for fidelity to tradition...." Here he stopped for a condescending smile at the elder man. "...but we live in a world of reality. Ciudad Rodrigo is a center of commerce, and our lives these days depend upon trade, no longer upon barter, nor are our days any longer centered upon the ecclesiastical calendar. Now I ask you, where do we sell our exquisite wines, our olive oil and other produce at a profit? In Ciudad Rodrigo. Who grinds our wheat? The mill in Ciudad Rodrigo. Where do we buy the commodities we can't raise ourselves? In Ciudad Rodrigo. Does the monastery contribute in any way to our physical well being? No. La Caridad drains our resources, siphons off some of our best wine. The city sustains us, not the monastery, and always has.

"As for our spiritual well being, our own church here, our own Father Alfonso, along with the cathedral in Ciudad Rodrigo can serve us quite as well as the monastery. Most of us have already recognized where our true interests lie. Many of us are no longer tithing the monastery with a tenth of all we grow. We no longer send our sons to the monks to follow in their footsteps. This is true even among some of you elders in the community, so why pay lip service to La Caridad when you aren't really supporting it?

"I say we should accept the new order. Robledillo de Gata Parish should belong to Ciudad Rodrigo."

A sinking feeling fell upon me. Youth would certainly prevail over age in this issue; the monastery was doomed. And, however irrational it might have been, I felt that my own lot was tied to the fate of the monastery.

Silence followed Pedro Justo's speech for a few seconds before pandemonium erupted. Elders and younger men stood at once, all demanding to be recognized. Both the *alcalde* and Dom Gregorio were on their feet as well. Dom Gregorio's powerful voice at last prevailed over the chaos.

"SIT DOWN!" he roared, "and you'll be recognized one by one. This is an issue that must be decided rationally."

A few recalcitrant men lingered on their feet, but one after another they obeyed the abbot's command. He raised his voice again.

"I must reveal to you a secret that has preserved the relationship between the monastery and Robledillo Parish over the past five centuries, and it is this: a charter was drawn up by King Fernando III in 1234, around seventy years after the monastery was founded. The document guarantees Nuestra Señora de la Caridad's rights to tithes and tributes from any villages, present or future, settled in its vicinity. Robledillo is specifically mentioned as one of the oldest settled towns in the region. The diocese would have to abrogate that charter before it could annex Robledillo, and it is my opinion that the Vatican itself would have to abrogate it. As far as I am concerned, until the matter of the charter is dealt with, this discussion is closed."

I was astonished. Why had Dom Gregorio allowed himself such a risk, since someone in the assembly might be aware that the document had been stolen? His demeanor impressed me, but while I took note of my own mixed feelings, I scanned the assembly, monitoring the reactions there.

As adept as I was at interpreting facial expressions, I saw only spontaneous surprise and shock. There was a rumble of discussion among the twenty men. Finally, one of the younger men blurted out what could only be considered a challenge.

"If you had this charter all along, why haven't you confronted the bishop with it?"

"Ah. That," the abbot answered, "is a matter of Church politics."

The man looked baffled, but he said nothing more. At this point the *alcalde*, apparently fearing the session could degenerate into something uncontrollable, banged his gavel and declared the meeting adjourned. Most of the men stood, a few stayed seated, all in intense and passionate conversation with those nearest them.

I caught Dom Gregorio's eye. He raised his eyebrows and I shrugged in reply, signaling that I'd learned nothing of any use. There was only my gut feeling, based on the spontaneous surprise on all faces when the existence of the charter was revealed. The intensity of the ongoing conversations and arguments assured me the document was not to be found in Robledillo, at least not among these council members.

"Come now, gentlemen, let us set weightier matters aside for the moment." Leopoldo projected his powerful baritone to the full. "We have excellent wines, and delicacies to tempt your palates."

The council members began moving toward the stairs. We were descending three abreast when the young man beside me laid his hand on my shoulder and began to speak into my ear in low, rapid tones.

"So, don Ygnacio...that's your name, isn't it? You're the abbot's spy, informant, and sneak. Am I right? I understand you Jesuits are experts in such matters. I hear murder would not be an unthinkable act for you...and that you had opportunities as well. What was *your* motive?"

We'd reached the bottom of the stairs. The young man faced me with a malicious smirk, turned away, then edged his way among a group near Leopoldo. Our host was gesturing towards a long table, loaded with delicacies, where a number of servants stood by with wine bottles and glasses. The dignitaries were beginning to serve themselves.

The church bells had just rung 3:00 o'clock, and I'd not eaten all day, but I held back, angry and anxious at the same time, a sudden nausea suppressing my appetite for the wealth of food displayed. The young man's verbal attack had hit me like a blow to the stomach, and an intense cloud of feeling overwhelmed me. I was moving, dreamlike, in a world so foreign that no communication with others was taking place, no understanding possible. The young fellow was right to an extent: I surely was the abbot's spy and informant. Why bring me otherwise?

At last, I shook off the feeling and approached Leopoldo.

"Who is that young fellow over there next to don Josef, shoving bread and pâté into his mouth? Just now, he all but accused me of murdering Gelasio—maybe Tomás too."

"Ah, pay no attention to him. That's a cousin of mine, don Beltrán Cerralbo y Villegas. He's a student at the University of Salamanca, and thinks he can solve the world's problems. A bit of a troublemaker, I fear. He's still too young to know when to hold his tongue. But he's probably voicing his—"

Clara cut him short. "Don Ygnacio! What a pleasure to see you here." There was no trace of awkwardness in her manner, only self-confidence. She took my hand and led me closer to the table. "Let me choose the best delicacies for you. And then let's talk."

Surprised, I felt my tensions melting away in her presence. My muscles, tensed as they were in rigid knots, began to relax, and the world was coming into focus. She caught me contemplating her face with gratitude, and rewarded me with a smile. For the first time, I noticed the dimple in her right cheek.

"I'm really not very hungry, doña Clara. The hostility of some of the guests has taken my appetite."

Her expression was one of sympathy. "I know it must be hard, don Ygnacio. I heard you tell Leopoldo what my cousin said to you, but if you'll let me take care of you for the moment, you won't have to put up with any more innuendos and snide remarks. Besides, Dom Gregorio tells me he has a task for you."

I covered my surprise. Why, of all people, would Dom Gregorio be delivering such a message to me in this manner? And when had he found time, since our arrival in Robledillo, to speak privately with doña Clara? Until we'd arrived in this room, he'd been with the town dignitaries every moment.

Chapter XI

Mountain Road

I was about to question doña Clara further, when I saw her eyes flick to one side, past me. A sly smile had turned up the corners of her mouth. Hesitating, I turned in time to see the abbot materializing from the group. To my astonishment, I saw he was carrying his violin and bow. He addressed me in a voice meant to carry above the hubbub of conversations around us.

"Don Ygnacio, passions were running high in the room upstairs, and they haven't calmed down yet. I wonder, could you play something soothing for us, to help us begin the convivial part of the meeting?"

A hush descended on the room, as those nearest to us quieted others. He thrust the instrument at me. I could do no less than accept it, although he'd put me in a position of having to play without rehearsal or even a moment to reflect. I quieted my rush of thoughts, gently plucking the strings to assure myself they were in tune, and yielded to my calling. The Holy Spirit was with me.

An air from Monteverdi's "Jephtha" drifted into my mind: the warrior-king's daughter, who had been condemned to die *"in holocaustum,"* laments her coming sacrifice, her lost youth and the fact that she will die a virgin. It was a simple enough piece for voice, and I knew I could adapt it. Embellish it, too, if I felt confident enough.

I raised the violin to my chin and corrected the tuning a bit. Then, from my central position in front of the main table, I spoke to the assembly. "You may know this piece already. It's a lament by Monteverdi, intended to express the feelings of someone condemned to die. It was originally a soprano aria, which I'm attempting to transform on the spot into a violin solo. Please bear with me. I dedicate it to the memory of my friends, Brothers Gelasio and Tomás."

My heartbeat and breathing were rapid, and sweat was breaking out on my brow and upper lip. "Dear God, Blessed Mother," I prayed silently, "grant that I am not so possessed by stage fright that I betray my purpose and spoil my tribute."

I closed my eyes and launched into the lament with a dramatic opening chord. After a few bars, I dared add a few more embellishments, and despite the mediocre instrument, I played the piece well. When I finished, I wondered if somehow the number of guests had tripled, such was their response and approval. The shouts rising above their applause were heartwarming, and my cheeks were equally warm with my blush of pleasure.

"Play something else, don Ygnacio."

It was Leopoldo! I could hardly refuse my host, so I played a simple but lively polka, a dance melody from my childhood, to end on a happy note.

Doña Clara, hovering near me during the performance, waited only until the applause abated and guests turned again to the table. She was glowing.

"That was moving, don Ygnacio. You're a remarkable man. But even remarkable people need food, and in your case especially so. You're still far too thin!"

At the same time, Dom Gregorio squeezed my shoulder. "Thank you, Ygnacio. I'm glad I thought of asking you to play. If you look around, you'll see that the guests are a lot calmer. You worked your magic. Now, let me put that violin away."

We were standing before the long table. Arrayed on white linen were a *serrano* ham, various pâtés, numerous cheeses, several varieties of breads, cold dishes I couldn't identify, *panes dulces,* confections made of dried fruit, a selection of wedges from a fresh melon—heaven knows how it had been preserved since harvest time—and a basket of apples.

Clara gave orders to the servant standing behind the table. "Two plates, Jorge." She turned to me. "For you, don Ygnacio, we'll start with a pâté. Most people choose that finely ground one with the bits of olives mixed in, because it looks so good. But the best of them all is this coarsely ground one here. It's a country pâté, and its flavor is exquisite."

She directed the servant to cut a good wedge of it, and a big piece of white bread she said was special. Left to my own selections, I'd not have chosen it, but it did have an intriguing crust.

She continued making choices for me, until my plate was heaped with bread, the best of the cheeses, ham, pâté, dabs of two of the casserole-like dishes, a slice of melon and an apple that Clara insisted tasted 'just like a pear.'

"I doubt I can even begin to eat all that, doña Clara."

"Ah, we'll see, we'll see."

Her plate, in comparison, seemed almost empty: a slice of bread, one little wedge of cheese and a slice of melon, but she assured me it was all she wanted or needed. I moved in the direction of empty tables where we could sit, but she boldly looped her arm in mine and steered me toward a side door. Was this to be another frontal attack? If so, I'd be safer mingling with others there, even with Leopoldo's cousin. I could not afford to be found alone with her again.

I protested. "Doña Clara, I'm supposed to be observing everything here, watching faces and talking to people, to find out anything I can for Dom Gregorio's investigation. Where are you taking me?"

"You know what they think and how they look already, don Ygnacio," she retorted. "You don't need any more controversy tonight, that's clear. You'll learn far more from me."

I gave in with a sigh, secretly relieved that I might escape more stares and remarks from the likes of young don Beltrán. She led me through the side door that opened onto a miniature terrace with a small table and two chairs. We set our plates down, and Clara beckoned to a servant through the open door, making a pouring motion. He soon appeared with two bottles of wine. We chose the red, which he expertly decanted into two glasses. Eagerly, I began sipping mine, pausing to enjoy its character. The wine of Robledillo was indeed excellent, but was any wine worth two murders and the potential destruction of a monastery?

We were silent for a few minutes while we ate. To my great surprise, my nausea was gone. Clara's presence, despite my previous experience with her, had me feeling sheltered and secure. I was ravenous, and the food was delicious. I finished my entire plateful before she started on her melon.

When I'd finished the last scrap, she half-rose and signaled the same servant.

"Juanito, more wine—the white, this time—and bring us an assortment of *panes dulces*, please."

I used the opportunity to think of my next words. "Tell me, doña Clara, your brother mentioned that your family owns several places outside Ciudad Rodrigo, but I never imagined anything as charming as this. So are there still other properties?"

"Oh, yes, don Ygnacio, and our *casa de campo* nearest the city is the nicest one. But come, let's not stay here. I want to show you around Robledillo."

With wine glass in one hand, *pan dulce* in the other and me in her wake, she pushed open a side gate with her hip. We began our way up the steep, narrow street.

"What were we talking about?" she asked. "Oh, yes, our country property. That's where Poldo's planted most of his exotic herbs, flowers, and all. He specializes in tulips. You should see them in spring. Some of those bulbs cost hundreds of pesos for a single one. We quarrel over the extravagance sometimes. The other places are farms and vineyards, with small houses mainly for the workers."

We walked under a charming wooden structure that spanned the street, connecting two houses. It was covered with vines that would flower in season. "That's actually a room," she said. "It's been there as long as I can remember. The buildings on either side belong to the same person, who prefers to sit up there and watch everything that goes on in town. Worst gossip imaginable."

My laughter was genuine. "It's a good idea for a narrow street like this, especially since there's not that much entertainment otherwise."

We strolled on up the street, Clara pointing out features of the local architecture.

Houses with continuous balconies were set closely, one above the other on the steep hillside, their walls a mixture of slate, wood, and clay. Level nooks contained wooden balustrades, enclosing areas for drying fruit.

"This building style is very ancient, don Ygnacio. There are Roman structures all over this region and things even older...standing stones, caves with paintings going back to the beginnings of time."

"It's beautiful, doña Clara, and mysterious." I drank in the details, wishing I were a free man. What, I wondered, would my life be like as, say, the pastor of the village church, Nuestra Señora de la Asunción?

It would be good to spend more time getting to know this valley and its people. But its peace was an illusion, I knew. After all, it was inhabited by my fellow human beings. Clara and I walked on in easy companionship, the only sounds the noise of our footsteps and the muffled rushing of the nearby stream. I broke the silence first.

"To get back to the subject of your properties, does your eldest brother administer all of them?"

"Well...yes, Arturo keeps track of things, but Poldo does more than even he knows. It's Poldo who knows what we're growing and when we should grow it. He's keeping the family fortune going with our produce—or at least that's what he tells me. Arturo is good with figures, maybe property management too, but he knows nothing of plants."

"And Dom Gregorio allows your brother so much freedom?" I was not as surprised as I sounded, given the latitude the abbot was allowing me.

"He doesn't need much freedom to take care of planting schedules. Arturo or I—or Carlos, our foreman—visit him once a week and tell him what's happening, and he advises us on what needs to be done next. If he needs to take care of something in person, he gets permission to leave the monastery for a very short time. Like those times he came with you and Dom Gregorio into Ciudad Rodrigo."

"Ah. I see. An ideal arrangement, it seems."

Clara took an abrupt turn onto a stone platform jutting out from the street. The Árrago was rushing down its rocky bed just below us. I had a good view of the backs of houses facing the street.

The opposite bank was covered with steeply terraced vineyards, olive groves, garden and wheat plots, some of them bounded with those wooden balustrades. How glorious it must be in spring and summer.

Clara continued speaking of her brother's privileges. "Yes, don Ygnacio. Because Poldo is very devout and likes the cloistered life, he can teach, which he loves. He can supervise his plantings without the petty concerns he'd probably have if he were not semi-cloistered, and he can keep up with a worldwide correspondence about his beloved plant specimens."

We turned back and walked farther up the street, Clara leaning on my arm, past a miniature tavern and under another structure built over the street. Then we turned back. I glanced down at the lovely woman by my side, at her shining, coppery curls, regretting that the interlude was over so soon.

When we let ourselves back in through the gate, I saw that little inside the Cerralbo house had changed. Men engaged in heated discussions were seated around tables or standing near the food. There was still no consensus among them. The priest, don Alfonso, with Dom Gregorio and don Josef, were conferring together off to one side.

"Tell me, doña Clara, did you know before this afternoon about the charter giving the monastery jurisdiction over all the surrounding lands?"

"Yes. Poldo mentioned it to me quite a while ago. Dom Gregorio confides in him a lot, so I imagine he knew about it months ago."

"It seems not to have been a closely kept secret at the monastery," I said. "But I see that Dom Gregorio's looking around, probably for me. I'd better join him. Thank you, doña Clara, for your delightful companionship."

"But we didn't have time for you to tell me more about Sonora."

"Soon, I hope. Soon."

Dom Gregorio beckoned as soon as he saw me. "We must get back, Ygnacio. It's getting late. We've decided to ride horses back to the monastery. I assume you know how. If not, you'll go back with the coach in the morning, under Porfirio and Gabriel's supervision. It's too late now to drive a coach over these roads; nightfall will catch us still in these mountains. But Leopoldo and I must get back tonight."

"Of course I can ride, Domine. I'm still shaky from my illness, but I'll manage. I rode constantly in New Spain, horses and mules."

☙ℭ☙

The late afternoon sun minted the Cerralbo house all gold, and chill was in the air as Dom Gregorio, Leopoldo and I stood in the small courtyard. I reflected that I could have stayed in this beautiful village overnight and ridden back at my ease in the morning. Too late now; I'd already spoken. The Cerralbo stable hands had a third horse tacked and ready for me in case I wanted to ride. All three animals were led into the street in front of the house, where we mounted. The abbot waited until Leopoldo and I were both mounted, then took my horse's bridle.

"I hate to do this, Ygnacio, but I'm going to tether your horse to Leopoldo's. I'm reasonably sure you wouldn't make a break for freedom, but on the other hand, should temptation overcome you, I'd have lost the king's prisoner! You wouldn't get far in this cold, since you don't know these mountains, but you'd cause us unnecessary trouble. I'm truly sorry, Ygnacio." The abbot's voice, a bit husky and hesitant, convinced me more of his regret than his words did.

I flushed, hurt and angry. "For God's sake, Domine, I thought you knew me better than that! I...." I turned my face away, knowing the futility of words, hunching my shoulders and taking a breath through my teeth. Such treatment was demeaning, even humiliating, but there was nothing I could do about it.

I realized, with a jolt, that I'd almost forgotten my status as prisoner because of the kindness of those few monks who favored me. True, I recalled few if any times when I was not being watched from somewhere, by someone, but still I was surprised the abbot's behavior could wound me so deeply. Suspicion lay just beneath the surface of these limited friendships.

I thought of another possibility, that 'crime' of mine back in Cádiz. If Dom Gregorio had learned of it by now, of course he'd treat me like a man not to be trusted.

The grooms made quick work of tying my horse's bridle to Leopoldo's horse's girth. When we left Robledillo, we first headed south, crossed the river and turned east. Only then did we finally begin the journey north. Dom Gregorio rode in the lead, Leopoldo next and I brought up the rear like baggage on a mule.

Wherever we found level areas, we were obliged to move as fast as we could, as it was getting cold quickly. The abbot had business in the city next day; he had to return to La Caridad no matter what.

Twilight lasted longer than I expected, and we were well up the mountain when darkness came. Our horses were surefooted and mountain-wise, and the night was bright. The road before us was a ghostly white streak, steadily rising, curves and switchbacks seeming less onerous and dangerous now that we were single file. We climbed at a brisk walk and trotted when the terrain was more level, and the horses had no difficulty.

I recalled one of the most dangerous curves as we approached it, a jackknife with a steep drop on the outside. In the gloom, I recognized the single scrub pine that grew on the brink of the abyss. Dom Gregorio trotted around the bend and disappeared from sight.

It was at that moment I saw something move in the darkness. It flickered on the side of the upward slope for a split second before it disappeared into deeper shadow, and I thought for the briefest of moments it was a human head and shoulders, silhouetted against the night sky. It most certainly was not an animal.

"Leopoldo, watch out!" I called, but too late. His horse barreled into a rope stretched across the road, fell to its knees and rolled, throwing Leopoldo clear. He landed, it seemed to me in the darkness and confusion, on his shoulders and back, somersaulting and disappearing over the edge. My own horse was harshly jerked to his knees as well, tethered as he was, and I, too, was nearly thrown.

As both animals struggled to their feet, I scrambled off, one step away from the precipice, my blood pounding in my ears. Gasping for breath, I peered down, at first seeing nothing.

Finally, about twenty feet below, I could make out Leopoldo's form looped over a rocky outcropping.

"Leopoldo!" I shouted down, but there was no answer.

As Dom Gregorio came charging back, I called out a warning. "Watch out, Domine, there's a trip rope across here."

My warning was in time. The abbot halted his horse and dismounted.

"Someone tightened it right after you passed by, Domine. God only knows where he went. It tripped the horse, and Leopoldo's down there. I don't know if dead or alive. He isn't answering."

The abbot shuffled toward me, stopping when his shins came in contact with the rope. He fished in the pocket of his robe and pulled out a knife, bending to cut the cord in the center.

"Don't, Domine! We need that rope. If we can get down to Leopoldo before his body slips off that ledge, and we can tie the rope onto him." I ran my hands along the rope, toward the scrub pine.

"Good thinking, Ygnacio. But you may not be able to get the knot loose; it's had plenty of tension against it."

I found the knot and began to work at it as fast as I could with fingers stiff from the cold. Time and temperature were against us. "I think it's beginning to loosen, Dom Gregorio. Perhaps you can finish untying this end while I go see about the other."

The abbot began pulling at the knot while I traced the rope to a tree on the other side. That knot was easier, a hastily looped structure that gave way as soon as the abbot had worked his side free. Thanks be to God, the rest of the rope was a long coil lying next to the tree, the entire length enough to reach all the way down to Leopoldo, I judged. I swept it all up and carried it back.

"Which of us goes down for Leopoldo?" the abbot asked.

"Domine, since I'm the lighter of us, you should be the anchor up here. You're also stronger than I. Logical?"

"Quite. Let me tie one end around your waist, Ygnacio. Then I'll hitch the rope around this tree and pay it out as you go down."

"Perfect. Just be sure you tie a good knot."

When we were both satisfied with his knot, he tied the other end around the tree as a precaution, and I went over the edge backward, grabbing at anything I could find with my feet and hands. The slope was not completely vertical, so the descent was quicker than I'd expected. There was barely enough rope!

I reached Leopoldo just as he was beginning to come back to consciousness, relieved when I heard his groan. "Be still, Leopoldo. Don't move," I ordered. "I'm going to tie a rope around you so Dom Gregorio can pull you up. You've fallen over the edge of a cliff."

A moan, then a faint murmur. "What happened? God, it hurts!"

I finished untying the rope around my waist and began working it under and around his body, bracing myself as best I could. If I fell now from the ledge, nothing would break my fall. I glanced downward once, but could see nothing, thank God. My imagination filled in the details. If Leopoldo moved before I got the rope secured around him, we could both plunge to our deaths. Despite my repeated orders, he moved an inch or two, but he actually helped me; I was able to loop my leg over the rock. More balanced now, I worked faster. At last I was able to knot the rope and adjust it under Leopoldo's arms.

I called up to the abbot. "The rope is tied, Dom Gregorio. You can begin pulling now."

"God and the Blessed Virgin come to our aid!" came the abbot's booming voice from above.

The rope tightened. Leopoldo was raised a bit off the ledge. He was becoming fully conscious of his situation by now. As soon as he'd been hauled a foot or so upward, he began trying to help himself. He crouched on the ledge and moved his hands up the rope while I slipped under him and pushed. His tremors had the rope vibrating, and he was gasping.

"I'm hurt, Ygnacio. Can't do much. How did I get down here?"

"Horse tripped."

It was evident that Leopoldo was too injured to help much. Somewhere I found the strength to push him from below, all the while scrambling and clawing at anything I could find. At one point a small bush I was holding gave way, and Leopoldo's robe was the only thing keeping me from the chasm. Dom Gregorio couldn't hold our combined weight, and we slipped back a foot, both of us crying out in panic. I found a toehold, and again we strained. I began kicking new depressions in the hardened soil with either foot, making toeholds while Dom Gregorio held us steady. That seemed to work better.

When we finally were hauled over the top, we all flopped down on the road, exhausted but thanking God.

We took stock of our injuries. The abbot's hands were rope-burned and bleeding, and my knees, arms and face were skinned and bruised, but these were superficial.

As soon as we'd both caught our breaths, we examined Leopoldo, who was injured far worse. He complained of pain in his upper back and neck – not surprising, since I'd seen him fall on them first. I could feel nothing broken there, nor could Dom Gregorio, although the skin was scraped and bleeding. His breathing was shallow because of pain, and I found two broken ribs where he'd landed on the rocky outcrop that saved his life.

"We need to pray our thanks to God for saving our lives, despite our injuries, don't you think, Domine?" I said.

"Go ahead, Ygnacio."

I said aloud whatever was coming into my head. "Oh God, our merciful Father, we thank you for Leopoldo's life, and for giving us the strength and resources to bring him back safe from what could have been a fatal plunge. Give us, we pray, the means to find the killer who caused it before it is too late, and help all of us to heal in body and in spirit. Amen."

Dom Gregorio broke the brief silence. His words mirrored my thoughts.

"We can't go on tonight, Ygnacio, we'll have to go back. It's only a little more than half an hour's ride down to Robledillo. We'll go back and spend the night, and I'll send a messenger to Ciudad Rodrigo to tell them what happened. But, how are the horses?"

I stood with a groan to check on them. They were grazing in placid contentment a few yards down, cropping withered grass on the safe side of the road. I marveled at their calm indifference to human drama, oblivious of our dire situation.

Leopoldo's horse had skinned knees. I felt his front legs with care, and found swelling only around the knee joints, but he was limping badly. A pulled muscle, perhaps. The saddle was scraped and damaged, but thanks to it, he'd suffered few injuries to his side and withers.

My horse had bruised knees, too, and a scraped area was bleeding down his leg, but he seemed sound enough. I led Dom Gregorio's horse back to him. "Since this one's completely sound, Domine, I'd suggest that you and Leopoldo ride double. I'll ride my own horse and let Leopoldo's follow at will. I don't think he'll want to stay up here alone."

We picked our way back down the mountain, trying to hold our horses down to a slow walk, particularly where the road was uneven. They tended always to shift their rumps left or right at these places, adding a quick step or two. Leopoldo gritted his teeth against the pain, for with every uneven step, his broken ribs jabbed raw flesh.

It took more than an hour to return to the village.

ΣΟΩ

I woke by the church bell at three in the morning. The first thing I saw upon opening my eyes was light wavering through the crack under my door. Who, at that hour, could be lingering by my door? I tensed, waiting for a possible attack. A killer was very much still at large, although I knew now it could not possibly be Leopoldo.

The door opened a tiny bit at first. Then another few inches. Not a sound came from the hinges, not one squeak or other hint to tell me someone was there.

Then, slowly, my 'assailant' stepped into the opening. It was Clara, a candleholder held high in one hand!

She spoke without hesitating. "Ah, you're awake. I came to see if you were all right. We've just finished working on Poldo, making him comfortable enough so he can rest. I waited until he finally fell asleep." She leaned over me, holding up the candle. "You've got some scrapes on your face...the bridge of your nose is skinned. What else?" She brushed my nose with one gentle fingertip.

Her touch had reminded me of my mother. "Nothing more serious than what you see, doña Clara. More scrapes and bruises, that's all."

She continued, but in a voice now laced with emotion. "Dom Gregorio told how you risked your life to save my brother. Poldo knows he would have died without your help, and he's very grateful, very much in your debt. Thank you, my dear...my kind friend...F-Father. And as for me, I'll never forget what you did tonight, either."

She paused. "Please forgive me for the other night—I'm still blushing, even though I've been trying to act casual about it. And I haven't forgotten your last words that night. You said, 'I hope there's some other way we can still be friends.' Of course! I'll always be your friend. I know you must be exhausted, so sleep again now, my dear Father Ygnacio."

She turned to leave.

I couldn't let her go like that. I sat up and, with a surge of tenderness, reached out and caught her wrist. Gently, I took the candle, placed it on the nightstand and pulled her down beside me on the bed. My back was braced against the bedstead.

"Doña Clara, I need to tell you how it happened. Please, I need someone to hear this story. Maybe you can help me figure out who'd do a thing like that." In reality, finding a culprit was far less important than telling my story to someone kind and sympathetic, someone I liked very much.

"All right, I'll stay. Dom Gregorio told me you were magnificent, that you never lost your head. He admitted he lost his, though, or at least he wasn't using it properly a few times."

"I don't know about that. Your brother wouldn't have survived without Dom Gregorio. But let me tell you from the beginning." She listened intently until I reached the part where the abbot was about to cut the rope with his knife.

"There! That's where he wasn't using his head. The rescue might not have worked if he'd made that one little move. A cut rope tied together could have come apart, or it might not have reached. And you stopped him."

"True." I continued the story.

"...and then I slipped just as I was pushing your brother upward. I grabbed his robe to keep myself from falling, but Dom Gregorio wasn't prepared for my added weight. We slipped down at least a foot, but of course I thought the end had come. I was terrified. I must say, I'd rather die of an Indian arrow than by a fall into that fathomless abyss."

"A slip like that was bound to happen at least once. Dom Gregorio wasn't prepared, another instance of him not using his head."

"Perhaps, but thanks to him we landed on the road, safe if battered, and we praised God then and there. Tell me, doña Clara, why and how an attempt like that could be made on your brother?"

"You're sure it wasn't meant for the abbot?"

"How could it be? The dark figure I saw waited until the abbot had ridden past, then he tightened the rope. He probably didn't know my horse was tied to Leopoldo's, so I might have been killed, too, or else he didn't care."

"Thank God neither of you were killed! I care...about both of you...so very much." Her voice trembled and her eyes were wide in the flickering light, like pools into which I was falling, plunging to an infinite, dizzying depth. Somehow I managed to continue speaking while our eyes remained locked.

"But...the killer has to be someone here in Robledillo. It's somebody who knows every blade of grass, every pebble on that road, and knows it in the dark. Who'd want to kill your brother? That's certainly what happened."

"I love Poldo dearly...but...he's up to something, Ygnacio...Father Ygnacio. Whatever it is, I'm afraid it's not right...not very pretty. Someone here must want him dead over it, yes, but who? I don't know. What I do know is that my brother begged me to entice you into compromising yourself the other night. It was deliberate. I went along because I love him, even though I knew it was wrong. I'm afraid for him. He's deep in trouble of some sort, and he needed to have a hold over you because you could be useful. I think he put something in Dom Gregorio's brandy, so he'd pass out and I'd have a better chance—"

"You're confirming what I'd worked out for myself, but what is he planning? It's big, or he wouldn't be imposing like that on your love for him. It's deadly serious, since someone nearly murdered him for it."

"I don't know yet. I do know that in doing whatever it is, he not only put his life at risk, he endangered yours, too. I'm so sorry, Ygnacio."

We both fell silent for a long moment while I pondered what to say next. She took my hand and began playing with my fingers, head bowed. I did not withdraw. When she spoke again, her voice was strained and hesitant. "Tell me...Ygnacio...what should a woman do when she's in love with a priest?"

I wasn't prepared for her question. I drew in my breath with a gasp, choking on my first word. "I...I...." Her question was mine, only in reverse. What should a *priest* do...?

"Oh, I know all the usual clichés," she said, at last. "Don't give me any of those trite formulas; I know them all." In the semi-darkness, she pressed her trembling fingers to my lips to keep me silent. "You 'sacrifice' your love— whatever that means—as if such a thing were even possible. You dedicate it to the Blessed Virgin or to Jesus Christ or to God. You rush to confess it all to the nearest priest, who will admonish you. You enter a convent. You surrender the deepest, most sincere, most beautiful feeling you've ever had to a theory. A dogma. A principle. An iron creed. My God, Ygnacio, I cannot be that false to myself. I know what I'm feeling is not from the Devil."

The sensation of unreality I'd experienced the previous day possessed me again. Time was suspended, my exhaustion and hurts receding into the background. Nothing counted but the present moment, this urgent, overwhelming moment.

I was next aware only that I was holding her in my arms, not knowing how this had happened. I was murmuring with my face buried in her hair. "God created man in his image...male and female He created them." For me, at that moment, she was Clara, Beatriz, the Eternal Woman all in one, and my mouth found hers in a prolonged explosion of lightness and joy. My mind echoed her words, 'I know what I'm feeling is not from the Devil.'

I was ready for her, ached for her. Her body pressed against mine, her arms were around me, her quick breath against my neck spoke of matching passion. But, as I held her, my mind began to function; I began to think. Timely hesitation. I knew I was crossing an invisible line, abandoning a lifetime of discipline and training, breaking a barrier that must not be broken.

She must have felt the subtle change come over me. My voice was muffled, as if I were hearing it from a distance.

"Doña Clara, this is my fault. I should never have detained you. And I...I've gone too far. Forgive me, Clara! But, you see, I'm still a *priest*, a priest about to break a vow. I can't...we mustn't...." I straightened and pulled away from her, dropping my arms.

"Ygnacio," she whispered, her forehead pressed against my cheek, "I understand. I know your principles and I know you'd be completely honorable if we did this, no matter what the consequences, but we *can't*. I don't want those consequences for you, my dear, my beloved. You must remain who you are, without guilt or blemish. Dear God! Do you see us, God? The only reason I give this man up is for *his* sake. For *him*, for his well being, for love of *him*! Not for you!"

She rose from the bed. I made no move to stop her, even though I was still shaking with desire. She took up the candleholder. "I'll always be grateful, don Ygnacio, dearly beloved. I thank you for all you are, thank you for saving my brother, thank you for returning my love. And I'll forever be your friend."

In the darkness, I wept into the bedclothes. God forgive me, my strength might have failed, but for hers.

&OCR

I lay awake listening to the succession of church bells until I heard five followed after a long interval by two strokes. Five-thirty. Gray light began to filter through my window. My inner turmoil was receding by now, mingling with thoughts about my brush with death. The persistent question plagued me, now shared by Clara: who had attempted Leopoldo's murder?

Who knew without doubt that we three would be riding after dark, on that road, in that way, so that he could set up a trip rope? Was he the same one who'd murdered Gelasio and Tomás? Or, was more than one person involved? Could someone who knew the details of our trip to Robledillo have set up an attack even before we'd left La Caridad that morning? Who'd helped him plan that attack?

The idea was unthinkable, loathsome to me, given my respect and affection for the man, but could Dom Gregorio himself be behind the murders?

Chapter XII

Letters and Quinine

We arrived at La Caridad after dark the following day. The night after, Dom Gregorio invited me into his quarters after dinner. "Sit with me, Ygnacio, and tell me what you learned in Robledillo."

To my surprise, he brought out the bottle of brandy instead of wine, pouring a third of a glass for each of us. The bitter lesson of the thyme-scented 'cognac' seemed to have lost its sting.

"Well? What did you notice?"

I chose my words carefully. "We had a powerful lesson up there on the mountain, Domine, but it's still open to conjecture. Either there are two murderers, or the one who killed Gelasio is amazingly evenhanded, killing indiscriminately. If the motive is to kill off monks who favor the bishop's side of the quarrel, he made a grave mistake in attacking Leopoldo, who's on the monastery's side. At least, I think he is. The attack simply doesn't make sense—not with the information we have now."

"Agreed, Ygnacio. There's surely something here we don't understand. We do need more information. But the charter? Is it or is it not in Robledillo?"

"It's my feeling—*only* a feeling, mind you—that it's not in Robledillo, and that your revelation of its existence came as a complete surprise to everyone there. Why did you do it, when the thing is lost, Domine?"

"I wanted to see, and for you to see, the reactions. If any of them had had it, his reticence, his lack of spontaneity—something—would have betrayed him. Either you or I would have noticed it. Too many people here at La Caridad and in Ciudad Rodrigo know that the charter exists, but that it's now lost, stolen. That news would have leaked out soon in any case. So, are we any farther ahead?"

I considered the question as he asked it. Leopoldo's fall was terrible, of course, and it most certainly looked like an attempt on his life, but it might well have been planned as something less, perhaps a scare. By choosing a priest who'd sided with the monastery, the murderer could spread confusion as to the real motive behind the previous deaths.

"No, Domine. We only know that the first murder, Brother Gelasio's, was committed by someone inside the monastery who knew its layout, all its nooks and crannies. He was probably someone Gelasio knew and trusted, since he'd gone to meet the murderer at two or three in the morning. It was some sort of underhanded plot between the two of them. Whoever murdered Gelasio has a cool head and tried to make the death look like an accidental fall. Under normal circumstances, the body might not have been discovered until time for early Mass, since only then would the bells have failed to ring at the customary time. Unless someone had the presence of mind to feel the body's temperature, all of you might have thought Gelasio had slipped and fallen just before ringing the bells. That he seldom rang them from the loft might have been overlooked.

"As for Tomás, he was murdered under our very noses, in the refectory, I think. Someone poured enough poison into his wine to stun him, and then later, perhaps, if he thought necessary, gave him a lethal dose sometime during the night. Or, he might have smothered him with a pillow, as Father Leopoldo suggested."

"Again agreed, Ygnacio. What about the bishop in all this?"

"The bishop knows more than he was telling, Dom Gregorio. Someone from the monastery is probably meeting with him somewhere, corresponding with him perhaps. You asked him during the first meeting if anyone from here had visited him *there*, in the Episcopal Palace, a question he could have taken literally. He could say 'no' and not be lying...technically at least...if the contact was made elsewhere. He may have his hands on the charter by now. Add all this together and it leads us nowhere, I fear, Domine."

"But you seem to have gotten somewhere...with doña Clara, Ygnacio," he observed with a knowing glance.

I shook my head and finished my brandy in silence. I was not anxious to discuss my feelings about doña Clara with the abbot, and he did not press the matter.

"Pour me another, Ygnacio. I'll see you in the morning."

I left him sipping slowly, staring at the floor between sips and tapping his teeth with his left thumbnail. His questions did not support my latest worry about his possible involvement in Leopoldo's 'accident,' but the main premise was still there in my mind. Someone knew we'd be returning at night, on horseback, from Robledillo. That same someone could have sent an accomplice to make the attempt.

৪১০৪

During the days following, I exhausted all my physical energies in my gardening duties, while my mental energies were divided between thoughts of doña Clara and the murders. Out after early morning Mass until dark, I planted seeds in rows in the newly plowed and harrowed garden, for spring was fast approaching. A week went by, and then another, as I planted the hardiest of the bulbs and seedlings in their disciplined and geometrical furrows. The more delicate flora would wait for the earth to warm further.

Gardening was backbreaking but joyful labor, I thought, a time to dig with one's bare hands and toes in the stuff of God's creation. Working the soil might even be the most blessed of activities, since it surely resembled God's own work with the universe, planting races of plants and animals: lions here, apes there, sowing seeds of whales in the ocean and planting an experimental race of humans in a garden called Eden. Like my plants, they'd be cultivated and would grow and thrive, or else, falling out of harmony with their surroundings, would wither and die. And yet, it was Abel, not Cain the planter, who'd been chosen by God.

As I bent over the soil, placing another onion in its bed, I noticed a whitish stone resembling a seashell. I picked it up and wiped the loam off on the skirt of my work robe. It was, to all appearances, a clamshell, yet unquestionably a stone. I dropped it into my pocket for further study later, in my cell.

Another source of joy had come on the wings of springtime: the storks were mating and repairing their nests on the church tower. The sight of their industry filled me with hope, for all of us believed that storks bring good luck. One day soon, I'd climb back up into the bell ringer's loft, despite my reluctance to return to the site of Gelasio's death, to watch them as I had before.

I was in the midst of thoughts like these when Brother Mateo tapped me on the shoulder. "Don Ygnacio, the abbot wants to see you. There's a letter, he tells me, and it's important."

"Very well, thank you, Brother Mateo. I'll clean up and see him directly." I straightened my back with a groan. Nearly fifty years old. Not getting any younger. I went to the water tank and washed my arms, hands and bare feet. It was still early, so I wasn't yet sweating heavily. I only splashed my face, since I'd not yet wiped my brow with the back of my wrist, a habit of mine that inevitably left a track of mud across my face.

The inside of the ragged old robe I was wearing served as my towel. After drying my hands and feet, I shook it and brushed off all remnants of my work in the field, then put on my shoes. I was presentable enough to speak to the abbot, I felt, since urgency was inferred.

Seconds later I knocked on his door and was admitted at once. Dom Gregorio was eager and excited. His face was glowing and his back was arched, with one foot forward, head thrown back, as if preparing to give an inspired oration.

"Ygnacio! Do you remember Don Josef, the alcalde of Robledillo?"

"Yes, Domine, I met him after the Council meeting. A short man with dark hair and eyes. He had a head large enough for a man twice his height, as I recall."

"Precisely. Good memory, Ygnacio. Well, he has always been on the monastery's side against the diocese, and has continued to press the villagers to produce any evidence that could help solve Brother Gelasio's murder, even though the killer might be one of the monks on the side of La Caridad."

"And he brought something? A letter, Mateo said?"

"Exactly! From Gelasio to his father. A voice from the dead. Here, Ygnacio, read this."

I took the letter, dated 2nd November, 1775.

> *Querido Padre y Señor,*
> I have wanted to write to you for some time about my situation here at the monastery. It is no longer the refuge for meditation and prayer I joined ten years ago, but a place of continual debate, conflict and controversy. I know you are more current than I on the efforts of Bishop Cayetano Antonio Cuadrillero y Mota, to annex our parish of Robledillo to Ciudad Rodrigo. You also know my feelings in the matter. I regret that my understanding of the Rules of Obedience set me at cross purposes with your own views, for I know you want the parish to stay with the monastery as it always has been.
> Division on this question goes deep here at the monastery. A majority, as is only natural, is for keeping

the status quo. One of the monks in good standing here is playing a double game, pretending to be on Dom Gregorio's side while reporting the abbot's every move to those of us on the bishop's side and even to the bishop himself.

I have just found out that this man is betraying us as well. He is doubly a traitor. He has only his own interests in mind, and will negotiate with the bishop, selling what he knows to His Grace in return for certain favors. I once believed in this monk's integrity and have risked everything to help him; I will now risk everything to stop him, and to expose him to our abbot for the traitor he is. I am writing this to you, my dear father, in case something should happen to me.

Your loving son, Gelasio.

I read the letter through twice. "Why didn't Gelasio's father bring us the letter sooner, or at least give it to you during that meeting? It clearly bears very much on his son's death. It provides the motive."

"Don Joseph said Señor Mangas feared it would blacken his son's name and memory, so he preferred to keep the letter secret, even though the information about the double-dealing monk would remain hidden. He thought we'd catch the murderer long before this."

"We've had too little to go on, Domine. But at least we now have a reason for both murders."

"Exactly! This is the first progress in weeks, months, Ygnacio. Perhaps now you can see clearly who the killer is?"

I looked at the abbot's hopeful face, and felt guilty. "I'm closer to a solution, but so are you, Domine. I'm no miracle worker. How many monks have taken La Caridad's side in the controversy?"

"At least fifteen of our twenty-four, Ygnacio."

"Then we've narrowed our suspects down to fifteen, Domine."

೭೦೦೮

Daylight came much earlier by the last week in March. Pre-dawn twilight found me climbing the ladder to the bell ringer's loft, for I wanted to watch the storks, to see what progress they were making with their nesting. But the moment I climbed far enough to rise above the level of the stone floor I shuddered with a sudden chill. Brother Mateo, who'd taken over the task of bell ringer from Tomás, had been up here a time or two, so much I knew. The loft was thoroughly trampled, and any trace of Gelasio's brutal murder had been obliterated, but those absent splashes of blood in the center of the chamber were so ingrained in my memory that I thought I saw them—the blood of a man who was trying to right a wrong, trying to prevent a calamity, the blood of my friend. I stood there in the cold morning air, gasping for breath, not for the exertion but from emotion. Nothing was more important than finding a solution to this first killing. It would lead, I was certain, to a solution for the second one, plus clarification of the attempt on Leopoldo. And, I prayed fervently, in time to prevent a third murder.

My somber thoughts were interrupted by scratching noises and the sound of wings being stretched and flapped. I went to the north window and leaned out, looking up. There were two nesting stork pairs on the ledges either side of the bell tower. The larger bird of the pair on my left was preparing to fly. I sat on the ledge, hands hooked around the window frame on both sides, and leaned out backward, looking up.

The large bird, the male, I supposed, eyed me and discounted me as trivial. He stretched his neck, pointing his beak to the sky, flapped his wings again, and then leapt from the ledge. He glided for an interminable moment, descending almost to my level before he began moving his wings in majestic sweeps, gaining altitude once more.

The female, meanwhile, seemed to be weaving, as if she were sitting at a loom, her head and neck moving in a steady rhythm back and forth. She was attaching a stick to the old nest the pair was cleaning and repairing, transforming it stick by stick into the sturdy nest of the previous season. The second pair imitated the movements of the first. By the time the second female had woven her stick into the dilapidated pile she was restoring, the first male was back with yet another stick.

I envied their beauty and freedom. How I longed to spread such wings and glide back to my homeland. And yet, I realized, their lives were bound in an iron-clad pattern, year after year, the same departures and returns, nest building, egg laying, rearing of young. God gave his creatures the skill and wisdom to live their lives as he planned them, and they never deviated from His plan.

Just as their lives were determined, so was mine. Other men were free to act as they pleased, to choose the good or revolt against God's will and do evil, to make selfish choices working against the benefit of the Whole.

And yet, prisoner though I was, could I not also work evil? Could I not also choose the good? Were we—any of us—free in any other sense? Did the storks also believe they were freely choosing the course of their lives? Perhaps it was all a matter of horizons, I thought, theirs more restricted, ours a bit broader, but if we could see far enough perhaps we'd find that we, like them, were doing no more than treading God's treadmill.

The gray sky was turning gold; dawn was approaching. I contemplated the growing splendor of sunrise, saying a prayer of thanksgiving, when the corner of my eye caught a surreptitious movement out there, along the highroad, the Carretera de Cerradilla. Two figures were hurrying along, both muffled in dark cloaks. When the bottom of one cloak flapped open, I saw a habit worn beneath. Monks! Two of our own brothers, outside the gates, showing obvious guilt at violating the Rules! Their furtive movements told the story.

The light was growing stronger. I thought I recognized them as Eugenio and Metodio. Yes, I was right. They avoided the gate, crossing the field to reach the wall facing the bell tower, there in front of me, and after a few moments of invisibility Metodio's head appeared above the wall. He pulled himself up and straddled the stones, reaching down to pull Eugenio up after him. The pair dropped inside the courtyard and scurried across, to slip into the side door next to the church. Neither looked up, but Eugenio's words drifted up to me.

"Next time we leave the city half an hour earlier. Mateo's due to ring the bells any minute."

He was right. Hardly had the door closed behind them when the bells above me began to swing. Mateo was pulling the bell rope from the narthex, just behind the closed church doors.

&OCB

I sat that night in my cell, long after I should have been asleep, considering what I'd seen at dawn and trying to find some logic in the haphazard information accumulated so far. I knew that puzzles often presented themselves in a different light when facts were rearranged, so I began itemizing my facts as a start. Perhaps with repetition, I'd see something obvious.

What did I know?

First, that a monk well acquainted with both the monastery and Gelasio had murdered him, a monk for whom Gelasio had risked everything, but whom he confronted in circumstances unknown. He'd gone to meet his murderer, presumably hoping to prevent Robledillo being handed over to the diocese for the wrong reasons. What were those reasons? What else did I know?

I knew the chain stretched farther, since Tomás had risked everything for Gelasio by stealing the charter for him. The charter was not yet in Bishop Cuadrillero's hands—that much I'd learned at our last meeting—but the bishop probably knew who had it. He was confident he could annex Robledillo without effective resistance from Dom Gregorio.

Did I know anything more? Only questions.

I began pacing the cloister walkway in my bare feet, hoping my footsteps would be soundless as most of the monks would be asleep at that hour. I leaned over the railing, listening to the night breeze as it rustled the cedar below me. I held my breath for a moment, but there was no other sound in my universe. Without moonlight, I saw only shades of black.

More questions crowded my mind.

Would the piece of bloody cloth I found caught between stones at the water tank match Leopoldo's torn handkerchief? Who was the monk standing over me with a dagger as I lay helpless in the grip of fever? Who eavesdropped on Metodio and me? Who saw me speaking to Tomás in the courtyard, and resolved to murder him because of it? What was the strange odor emanating from Brother Tomás' gaping mouth as he lay dead on his cot? Could it truly have been belladonna?

Who tried to murder Leopoldo, and why? The spot chosen for the attempt was close to Robledillo, far from La Caridad. Had someone from La Caridad traveled all that way, unseen and unnoticed by others here, or was the assailant from the village? That seemed more logical, since the timing of our return might have been chosen even before the council meeting. Again, I could not dismiss the possibility, however abhorrent, that the abbot himself could be involved in some way. He was an intelligent man, extremely so, therefore quite capable of manipulating chessmen in the battle game over La Caridad. Game, indeed! It seemed an appropriate word, used in a macabre sense. What game, therefore, could have induced Leopoldo to drug the abbot and involve his sister with me? And, finally, what were Metodio and Eugenio doing in Ciudad Rodrigo? Why those two monks together? One of my closest friends in the monastery skulking across the courtyard with my 'enemy?' Was Metodio my enemy still, or was he, too, playing a game? Try as I might, these questions refused to resolve themselves into any intelligible pattern.

As I sat at my table in the cell, pressure against my thigh reminded me of the stone from the garden. I fished it from my pocket and began studying it, glad for the distraction. Earlier, I'd thought it was a clam.

I was closely acquainted with the shape, size, and conformation of clams, having survived for nine months in our prison camp at Guaymas, in New Spain by digging and eating clams that looked very much like this stone. Now I examined it from all sides in the light of my candle.

It was intact, both sides of its shell present, the smooth and elongated lump of its hinge clearly visible. The slight fluting of the shell at the edges, and some of the uneven bands that followed the shell's contour, had been preserved as well. I noted how clumps of wet sand, now also turned to stone, had clung to one side. The whole thing was about two inches thick by nearly three in length, smaller and dumpier than the tough and rubbery Pacific clams we dug on Guaymas beach. I remembered how they tasted raw, and how we thanked God for them.

Some had theorized that that stones like this one, so closely resembling living animals in the sea, were special creations of God. Why, then, I wondered, was it not equally possible that the conformation of sea and land had changed? That many thousands of years ago, the garden out there had been a beach? Maybe an earthquake had destroyed a sand bar, the seawater trapped behind it drained away and the animals killed by such a sudden change somehow turned to stone in a slow process over those eons. To my mind, such a happening would be more logical than that God should trouble himself making replicas of living clams, complete with haphazard clumps of imitation wet sand.

Pleased with my own theory, which might never be proved or disproved, I laid the rock aside and returned to the murders. Doña Clara said Leopoldo was involved in some dangerous scheme. Did it include murder?

೮೦಄

Two nights later I sat up with Dom Gregorio, played the violin for him and discussed Miguel de Montaigne's essay called 'On the Cannibals.' I returned to my cell long after the monks were asleep. Nothing about the small room suggested anyone had visited it in my absence, but as I knelt to pray I noticed a small bulge under the blanket near the head of the bed. I laid a hand on it and felt the outlines of a bottle.

I pulled back the blanket and found a small vial wrapped in a folded paper tied on with a thread. I quickly slipped out the paper and read it. It was dated four days earlier.

> To: don Ygnacio Pfefferkorn
> I find your situation as prisoner of the crown for the past eight years incomprehensible and intolerable to any thinking person. Your difficulties are compounded since you suffer from a disease contracted in the course of doing God's and the Church's work. It is ironic that there is a drug your order discovered and tried to disseminate, but that you have lacked due to the ignorance of our physicians. I hope symbolically to repay your Society through you, a Jesuit and representative of your order, for having discovered this medicine to control malaria, a scourge for millions world-wide. I am therefore happy to enclose a supply of this drug you called 'quinine.' I was able to find it in Salamanca after intense inquiry. I pray that it will last you through the next six months or so, *Deo volente.* I am sending this to you by special messenger, in the hope that it will reach you before you suffer another attack.
> In Christ, Cayetano.

I was stunned. I read and re-read the letter, unable to believe in the bishop's goodness and charity. The man might well have saved my life, and he even spelled my name correctly. I shook the vial and saw that a tiny spoon, carved from bone, was inside, probably to be used to measure doses. I uncorked the little bottle and drew out the spoon, careful not to waste a single grain of the medicine. To my further surprise, a very thin sheet of paper was wound around the spoon's handle, also tied with a string. I painstakingly untied it and smoothed out the crumpled note. This one was dated three days earlier, the same day I climbed to the bell loft to observe the storks:

Don Ygnacio,

This medicine that the bishop gave me yesterday will be brought to you secretly by special messenger, but this note must be even more secret. You are in great danger. This is what I overheard this morning. Bishop Cuadrillero heard confessions today. Someone, who however was not confessing, as I could tell from his words, was in the booth. I could not see him nor did I hear everything. This, though, I did hear: "The charter is yours if you will pledge to save my family honor." The bishop replied something I could not hear. Then, "I'll only give up the charter if you make a firm commitment." Another mumble from the bishop. Then this: "Pferkon knows more than any of them. He apparently hasn't put everything together yet, but, given his Jesuit logic, he soon will." I strained to hear the bishop, but still could not. The last words I heard were addressed to the bishop: "Don't worry, I'll take care of things. Think only of the charter, and how you can easily lay your hands on it." At this point, the curtain of the booth moved. I slipped into a neighboring confessional and waited half an hour until all was still. Use this information as best you can, but look to yourself. Above all, beware of your closest associates.

Miguel Ybarra y León, O.F.M.

So! Here was evidence the murderer had contacted the bishop directly. *The charter is yours if you will pledge to save my family honor.* What an odd exchange that would be. But I reminded myself that I was in Spain, where honor meant more than life itself. I'd known all along that I was in mortal danger, but Father Ybarra's warning brought the threat breathtakingly near.

I reread Ybarra's letter. It was carefully worded, and I had the impression he knew more than he was revealing. *Above all, beware of your closest associates.* He surely knew which one was a danger to me, so why not simply tell me?

I moistened a finger and tasted a few grains of the powder. Its familiar intense bitterness spread over my tongue, but there was no additional flavor. It was pure. The bishop had given the vial to Ybarra the day before hearing the 'confession.' I wondered if he'd have been so kind if he'd heard the 'penitent' first.

But I was being uncharitable.

I sat holding the vial for a moment, then tucked it in the pocket of one of my good robes. I said my prayers and reviewed my options. I lived in a cell that could not be locked, spent my days cultivating the soil, oftentimes in some isolated nook of a garden bed or the graveyard. I was also cut off from the monks by many barriers. As an ex-Jesuit, I had an entirely different background and training, and a different religious experience from theirs. I dressed differently, spoke differently, was from a foreign culture and had worked in an unimaginably foreign environment. Those who had befriended me were few indeed, and saw me mostly at meals or during Mass. The rest were either hostile or indifferent. A murderer could easily pounce on me in the dead of the night, sneak up on me and crush my skull in some blind corner or stab me after making a supposedly friendly approach. All I could do was to commend myself to God and steel myself to cope with whatever He had in store for me.

೫೦೮

I awoke at daybreak feeling ill, as if the arrival of the quinine had brought the curse of malaria with it. I refused to believe it. I was merely indisposed, I told myself. A slight cold. There was nothing specific, only a general sense of uneasiness and a distant headache. Perhaps it was only an effect brought on by the anxious, restless night. Every slight hurt I'd suffered over the past week was making itself felt—a bruise here, a sprain there—as if they were major injuries. I thought of the cold, clean air of the bell ringer's loft and, after pulling on the old and ragged robe now reserved for my gardening work, I made my way to the little room off the upper cloister and dragged myself up the ladder, to what I now thought of as the 'death chamber.' Once there, I breathed in great gasps of dawn air, detecting scents of newly turned earth, and apricot blossoms from the orchard, wondering at the keenness of my sense of smell. Illness heightens it, I recalled, at least for me. I moved to the window and sat, leaning out backwards, bracing myself as I'd done before. The storks were just beginning to awaken and stretch their wings.

The large male stork who'd built his nest almost overhead swooped past me, making eye contact as before. He looked self-satisfied. Perhaps he was the one who witnessed the first killing, and now was gloating that he knew who the murderer was and I did not. As I watched, I again considered Leopoldo's role.

He had the abbot's trust and could come and go almost at will, therefore could make easy contact with the bishop, but it seemed unthinkable he could be the murderer. He'd been one of the killer's intended victims. The thought of my friend Leopoldo as a double murderer was too horrible to be entertained further. I shrank from the idea, thinking it a whisper from the Devil.

And yet another incongruity tugged at my mind, something at odds with everything I knew. Eugenio was my friend, yet he and Metodio had been sneaking back into the monastery from Ciudad Rodrigo. Why those two together? How had they gone to the city, how had they returned? What had they been doing there?

At least they had one common cause: to save the monastery. But why go to the city? I stopped my thinking and, as if movement would interrupt the churning of my thoughts, climbed down the ladder and descended the stairs to hear Mass, my head throbbing in rhythm with my steps.

I had no appetite for breakfast after Mass, and had to force myself to do my work in the garden. I did not want to face the possibility that another malaria attack was coming on, no matter how forcefully I willed it away. Further, I was unable to continue dwelling on the possible solution to the murders, or I should say, on the embryonic, partial solution. I simply could not concentrate, so ill was I feeling.

I did thank God, however, for moving the heart of the bishop, and for the supply of quinine now hidden in the pocket of one of my good robes. Perhaps this time I could shorten or at least diminish the attack.

I struggled all day at my labors, accomplishing little. By nightfall, blinded by the headache, I was also feeling queasy. I washed up at the water tank and considered climbing all those stairs to my cell to get the quinine, then decided not to expend the energy. I'd eat dinner first. Perhaps I'd feel better afterwards, and could dose myself well before retiring.

We took our places in the refectory, rose as the abbot entered, and remained standing for the blessing and initial prayers. Vertigo was setting in. I resolved to get upstairs right after supper, as soon as I could, and take the first dose of that precious medicine.

We resumed our seats and Brother Eulogio began reading the Scriptures. The soup arrived, and my unnaturally sharp sense of smell detected a faint but unmistakable stench. Either the soup was too old, and was beginning to turn bad, or something half-rotten had been cooked into it. Perhaps I was merely imagining it. Nevertheless, I was overwhelmed by a rising tide of nausea, and it seemed to bear me up with it as I rose from my bench to escape the smell. I became dizzy and I staggered, reeling where I stood, pressing one hand over my mouth, the other to my forehead. A circle of blackness was closing in, restricting my field of vision. The last thing I heard was Dom Gregorio's voice, calling me from a great distance.

"Ygnacio! Ygnacio!"

ഇൻ⁊

I'd apparently clipped my chin on the corner of the table as I collapsed, for I awoke much later with a sore jaw and a bitten tongue. From much experience, I knew that my fever was high and I was half-delirious. It seemed I'd been plunged into a fevered fantasy, lying in a bed surrounded by maroon velvet curtains tied back with braided silken cords. Heavy gold tassels swung from each tie.

I was lying between satin sheets, not rough blankets, and my head rested on a satin-cased, down pillow. Light came from several candelabra in the room, one on the ebony bedside table, one on the mantle of an ornately carved marble fireplace, one on a chest in front of the window, almost out of sight, and at least one more. The matching window drapes of maroon velvet were closed, and a small fire was crackling in the fireplace.

Various gloomy portraits from the previous two centuries hung on the walls in ornate gold frames, along with a large ebony and ivory crucifix and a painting of the Pietà. I had never, not even during my childhood in a moderately well off burgher family, been surrounded by such luxury.

"Where in God's name am I?" I mumbled aloud. A stab of pain revealed the extent of injuries to my tongue and jaw. I started in surprise as Clara appeared, carrying a tray on which were a cut glass pitcher and water tumbler.

"Ah! Awake at last, Ygnacio. Forgive me; I just went out to get you some water. You were saying?"

"But...but am I insane? The last things I remember were being swamped by nausea as I sat at the refectory table, standing up and beginning to faint."

"Yes. And you crashed into the table before anyone could catch you. You have a bruised jaw and you bit your tongue so badly that the blood flowing from your mouth had Dom Gregorio thinking you'd had a seizure. He certainly showed how much he cares about you. Fortunately, my brother was right there, too, and understood what had happened."

"But why am I here? And where is this?"

"Poldo and the abbot made you as comfortable as possible in the abbot's own bed. Dom Gregorio insisted. But then my brother persuaded the abbot to let him bring you here, to the Casa de Cerralbo, so our own physician could see to you. Dom Gregorio didn't resist the idea for long. He said he owed you more than he could repay, and you were to get the best of care. They carried you out to the coach and brought you here about an hour ago."

Despite my fever, a feeling of icy cold flashed through me. Leopoldo could now dispose of me in any way he pleased. I saw that I was wearing a silk nightshirt. I had no idea where my own clothing was, nor whether I'd have the strength to leave this place even if I could find a robe. Another chilling thought struck me. "Did they bring any of my things?" I asked.

"Of course, Ygnacio! They were very few: your two good robes, your shaving equipment—"

"Oh, good. Thank you, Clara." I closed my eyes, exhausted by the effort to remain rational, to ask the questions that needed asking. The fever was gaining on me, yet I had to remain lucid long enough to find out if the small vial had come with the rest of my things. *Please, God, be merciful! Dear Jesus, please! Blessed Mother, come to my aid! I need that quinine more than anything else on earth right now."* My prayer was said in desperation.

I vaguely heard Clara—or was it Beatriz?—speaking to me again. "Do you want water, Ygnacio? You look so flushed."

"Yes please, Bea...Clara. I'm thirsty and hot...very hot...the climate must have been warm like this at one time, and it would seem logical that there were salt seas in this area eons ago, with normal marine life. Then perhaps there was an earthquake, and an estuary suddenly drained of water, leaving the marine life high and dry. They all gradually turned to stone. That's why one turns up stone clams in the garden—"

"Ygnacio!"

The alarm in her voice brought me back. I'd been raving, despite my bitten tongue. "Forgive me...Clara. Yes, I'm thirsty."

She helped me sit up, holding the glass to my lips, and I drank awkwardly and noisily, each swallow accompanied by a stab of pain. I was getting worse, and still had no idea if my medicine had come to Ciudad Rodrigo, along with me. I lay back and, before I could ask about it, fell asleep, my parched throat and body relieved by the much-needed moisture.

೮つಛ

I awoke sometime during the very early hours of morning, recoiling from a dream about Metodio and Eugenio, in which they were plotting my murder with a shadowy third person, this time not Leopoldo. The dream seemed so real that, when I looked around me, I was amazed to find myself in the luxurious Cerralbo bedroom. Clara was sitting asleep in the comfortable chair at my bedside. She was simply Clara this time, without the ghost of Beatriz. She'd been keeping watch over me all night. I raised myself on one elbow, and that slight movement was enough to wake her.

She reached out to touch my hand, and then my forehead. "Are you all right, Ygnacio?"

I brushed away the cobwebs of my feverish dream. "I think I'm better, Clara." My tongue was still terribly sore, so I continued carefully. "I can't tell you how grateful I am that you've stayed with me this way. Please go now and get some real rest."

Her willingness to care for me despite our strained and ambiguous bond generated an intense, almost painful surge of gratitude and love. However, suspicion began to seep into my warm feelings, darkening them like so much smoke. How guilty was her brother, and just how much did she truly know about his dangerous game? Would my refusal to make love to her, that night in Robledillo, create resentment? Would she fall in with his plans over it? By her own admission, she 'adored Poldo.' The adoration between them showed. My thoughts came sweeping over me in a rush, even as she answered me.

"I'll be just fine, Ygnacio. I did rest while you were sleeping. Is there something I can get for you?"

"Yes." I forced myself to lick my lips, though the action proved painful, in order to be understood. "I wonder...could you look into the pockets of my robes and see if you find a small bottle there? It contains a white powder, quinine, the only medicine that's effective against malaria."

She rose stiffly, staggering a bit, and went to a wardrobe almost out of my line of sight, against the wall. There was much rustling, but she came back empty handed. "No, there's nothing in your pockets. Should I look through your other things?"

Sudden fear cut through me like a whiplash! Someone now had my precious bottle of medicine, and both notes. I could only pray the note from Father Ybarra had not been discovered, that it was still buried in the powder, wrapped and tied around the miniature spoon, but entertaining such a hope was absurd.

"Ygnacio? Did you hear me?"

I tore myself away from my shock and answered her question. "Yes, I'm sorry. Please look, Clara." My tongue barely allowed intelligible speech. "If the medicine is there, I must take it."

I held my breath while she ransacked my belongings.

"I'm sorry, Ygnacio, there's nothing of the sort here. But never mind. As soon as it's light, our own physician will come to see you."

"No!" I blurted out the word without thought, as I hadn't the energy to frame a diplomatic reply. Her promise was far from soothing, since most Spanish physicians would recommend a bloodletting. In my condition, such treatment would bring me to the point of collapse, or worse. If it were to last longer than usual, what then?

I stared into the maroon darkness inside the bed curtains and tried to think. Clara hadn't answered my exclamation. She watched me with compassion. Perhaps she thought me delirious.

I had to avoid losing blood at all costs. And where was the vial? Anyone could have gone through my pockets while I was unconscious. It could have been any of the monks sent to my cell to fetch my belongings; it could have been Dom Gregorio or even Clara. But most likely it was Leopoldo. It had obviously fallen into hostile hands, for a person harboring no ill will would have left my possessions where they were. Unless it had fallen out in the coach during the trip from La Caridad to Ciudad Rodrigo. Why would such a thing have happened, if it did? Why would the one thing I needed most be the item to be lost?

After several moments of silence, Clara touched my arm. "Please, Ygnacio, try to relax and go back to sleep. It'll be just fine in the morning. Would you like another sip of water?"

"Oh, yes! Please!"

She again braced me in a sitting position and held the glass. I drank greedily, ignoring the shock to my bitten tongue, then lay back and closed my eyes. I could hear her setting the tray down on the ebony table, then sounds of her hitching the chair closer. Her cool hand rested lightly on my forehead as she cooed a little sound of sympathy.

"Poor Ygnacio. Poor, lonely man," she said, a catch in her voice. She smoothed my hair in place. Surely, such sentiments could not be false.

I reached up and found her hand, pressing its soft coolness to my cheek. Willing her to be as innocent and pure as she appeared, I opened my eyes and smiled. Her gaze removed all doubts. I'd been wrong. Never could such a wonderful person become entangled in the dangerous game her brother played, whatever it was. Never could she be untrue in that way. She loved Poldo, but in the end she admitted that her role-playing for him, her ambivalent role-playing, was distasteful, shameful.

I'd not distrust her again.

My hand relaxed and dropped, releasing hers. I sighed, and fell asleep.

Chapter XIII

Gertrud and the Bishop

I was startled awake by the clacking of shoe heels on tile. Someone came bustling in. "Doña Clara! Have you been here all night? How is Father Ygnacio?"

I knew that voice! It was Josefina, Gertrud to me. I opened my eyes, nodding to reassure her, but her worried look remained.

"Father Ygnacio is as well as can be expected. He drank quite a bit of water during the night, and that's all to the good. Poldo should be here before long with the physician. Knowing Doctor Santoro, though, it won't be until after he's had a substantial breakfast." When Gertrud swept up the night tray, the glass pitcher was empty. I must have drunk more than I remembered. It meant I'd been delirious some of the time.

The day had just dawned. I guessed the time to be around six thirty. If Clara was right, the doctor could be up, contemplating his breakfast at that very moment.

My heart started pounding. There might be time to save the situation, if only I could think of a way. The last thing I needed was a physician. I held my breath, waiting. Finally, Gertrud spoke, sounding unusually stern.

"Please, doña Clara, you must get some rest. Leave him to me, at least until Father Leopoldo gets here with the physician. Nothing can happen to him in an hour or two."

"You're right, Josefina, I'm completely exhausted. I'll go lie down. I'm sure you'll take good care of him." She turned towards me and I gave her a farewell wave. She backed out of the room, keeping her eyes on me until she closed the door.

"Do you need anything, Father?" Gertrud asked, again picking up the tray.

"Yes. Urgently." With my bitten tongue, the word slurred to 'urzendly.' "Come closer." She sat down in Clara's chair and leaned over me. I continued in German. "I was brought here last night unconscious, as you probably know."

"Yes, Pater." Her answer, also in German, used my German title.

"The bishop sent me a small bottle filled with a substance called 'quinine,' the only medicine known to lessen the symptoms of my disease. I must have that medicine, for nothing else will help me."

I paused to give my tongue a moment's recovery.

"Please, Gertrud, go quickly to the Episcopal Palace and ask for Father Miguel Ybarra. He's the bishop's secretary. Tell him where I am, that I fainted during supper at the monastery and that I was brought here unconscious." Another pause while Gertrude gave me the last remaining sip of water. "Most important of all is that the quinine was taken from my possessions when I was brought here. Tell him that, please, and that Father Leopoldo's physician will be coming soon to bleed me. Another bloodletting will weaken me, maybe fatally. Don't forget any of this, Gertrud. Now, repeat what I just told you, please."

She repeated faithfully everything I'd said, then, "But Pater, doña Clara will be very angry if I'm not here when she returns. She could come back at any moment. I could lose my position."

"I understand, but this is a matter of life or death for me." I pointed to the door with one hand and made shooing motions with the other. "Go now, while there's still time, while doña Clara is still asleep and before Pater Leopoldo gets back with the doctor."

"I'll do my best, Pater Ignaz."

The door closed and I was alone, fully awake and finally rational for the first time since my fall. I racked my brain to come up with some plan to prevent the doctor from bleeding me. Unless Gertrud could persuade Father Ybarra to intercede, I feared there was no hope.

I would, of course, refuse to be bled, but I'd be overruled on the grounds that I was delirious and therefore not responsible for my own welfare. I struggled out of bed and staggered to the wardrobe, groping through the pockets of my robes. Nothing was there beyond my rag of a handkerchief. The effort exhausted me, and I collapsed on the bed, panting. Perhaps once I'd regained a little more strength, I could find and search my valise. I struggled to sit up, looked for the water pitcher before realizing Gertrude had taken it, and lost consciousness.

ॐ

A hearty laugh and the noise of two men tramping up the stairway brought me back. The door was thrown open to admit a welcome gust of fresh air, and Father Leopoldo stood just inside, his auburn curls glinting in the mid-morning light. When he saw I was fully awake, an exaggerated smile broadened his face.

"Don Ygnacio! I'm so glad you've regained your senses. Your lower face is swollen; that was a bad fall you had. How are you feeling?"

"Thank you, Father Leopoldo. For now, at least, my fever seems lower." My unconscious hours had intensified problems with my painful tongue, and still there was no water at my bedside.

"I'd like you to meet our family physician, Doctor Horacio Santoro. He's seen our family through thick and thin, don Ygnacio. Probably saved our lives countless times. He'll take good care of you."

The stout figure behind Leopoldo wore a full-length cape over his black suit. An untidy, white-powdered wig perched rather crookedly atop his gray hair, which was tied behind his neck with a black ribbon.

I wondered at Santoro's casual and modern attire, since most Spanish physicians I'd encountered had worn traditional black robes. They concealed the blood better, I thought, clamping my teeth together in distaste and anguished anticipation of the ordeal to come.

The doctor set a black leather valise on the floor beside the bed and bowed to me with a flourish. "Don Ygnacio, it's a pleasure to meet you, Father. A pity it has to be under such unfortunate circumstances. Ah, well, I have a few tricks up my sleeve."

"Indeed, I expect you do, doctor." The irony I added was lost on both men. "I'm happy to hear you've been such a help to the Cerralbo family."

Leopoldo broke in. "Where's Josefina? She's supposed to be here taking care of you."

"She went downstairs, Father Leopoldo," I said, a valid statement. "She should be back up here any minute." *I hope and pray with reinforcements of some sort from—of all places—the Episcopal Palace.*

Doctor Santoro unclipped his cloak and swirled it across the chair next to the bed. One corner of his mouth lifted into a jovial curl that accentuated the tilt of his wig.

"Well, let's get on with this. The first step in any treatment of an illness like this, don Ygnacio, is to get the poisons out of the body. Let's have that left arm! After that, we can talk about further treatment. Happily, we don't have too many cases of malaria up this way."

He hummed a few tuneless notes as he rummaged in his valise, pulling out a tin basin, a length of cord already spotted with the blood of some other unfortunate, and a wickedly gleaming little scalpel. He squinted at the scalpel, making a moue with his lips, and laid it on the ebony table, then rummaged further, managing to come up with nothing else.

I shuddered involuntarily. "Doctor Santoro, I've been bled white for this same ailment back in the prison at the Port of Santa María and it never helped me in the slightest. Rather, it made the condition much worse. It weakened me so much I had no strength to fight the malaria off. Do you think we could skip this step and go on to 'further treatment' without delay?"

The only way I could hope to convince these men I was not in the grip of delirium was by using a coldly rational tone. All the confidence and authority I could muster went into those few words.

Santoro's reply was immediate, nearly interrupting me. "Nonsense, man! Bleeding is a tried and true remedy. Been used for centuries." He grasped my arm. I resisted with all my might, tightening it against my ribs with strength born of desperation.

"Just relax, don Ygnacio, it won't take more than a few minutes and you'll see how much better you feel." He was hovering over me, pushing and pulling the silken sleeve of the nightshirt up my arm, working it above my elbow despite my panicked resistance. He managed to work the cord between my body and arm, drawing it in a circle around the biceps. He began tying a slipknot, literally sitting on me.

"Do I have no say in this matter?" I roared. "This is *my* body! *My* life!" I shoved him away and sat up on the edge of the bed, unwinding the cord and placing it on the table. I couldn't defend myself for long. I knew it; they knew it. They stepped outside and conferred in the hall outside. I caught the word 'sedative' then, and heard Leopoldo running down the stairs.

The physician returned to my bedside. I shrank back, forming myself into a ball at the upper end, with arms around my knees.

"There, there, don Ygnacio, your worry is misplaced. We're not here to harm you, not at all, not at all. I know what I'm doing, unlike those heavy-handed surgeons down there in Cádiz. I assure you, you're in much better hands here. Father Leopoldo is mixing a soothing drink for you. He's an expert herbalist, you know. He and I confer together often. It will soothe you and take away your fears."

I waited, my heart hammering in my throat, praying Gertrud would return in time, but no. Leopoldo reappeared in the doorway, with an elegant crystal glass of lavender liquid. Normally I'd have admired the beauty of its color, as the glitter of refracted sunlight shone through prisms cut in the glass. Drinking the contents was another matter, one that filled me with dread. Leopoldo held out the glass to Santoro, who turned back to me wearing that same insidious smile.

"Here we are, don Ygnacio. This will make you feel better. You won't even feel the knife."

I was frantic to say something—anything—that would stave off the inevitable when I heard a loud noise, a pounding, from downstairs. It was the front door knocker, wielded with authority and considerable force, followed by voices—Gertrude's first, thank God!

"Your Grace! What a surprise!"

Then came the bishop's unmistakable rumble. "Good morning, Josefina. Do I understand correctly that Father Leopoldo has taken the ex-Jesuit, don Ygnacio Pfefferkorn, under his wing? That he's here in this house?"

"That's true, Your Grace. Father Leopoldo and Doctor Santoro are with him right now. Would you like to see don Ygnacio?"

"Indeed. That's what I came for. Lead on, please." I could hear his heavy tread on the steps.

Leopoldo and the doctor both had stopped to listen to the exchanges below. With the bishop's first words, Leopoldo was at the doctor's side. "Help don Ygnacio to drink, doctor. I doubt he can manage alone."

The physician knelt on the bed, bracing himself against the headboard, and pressed the glass to my lips, tipping it for me. Leopoldo started around the other side of the bed.

"Noooo!" I bubbled into the liquid, shaking my head at the same time and turning my face away. I pulled on his arm, feeling helpless as a child, and the drink spilled. None had entered my mouth, thank God! I wiped my wet lips with a sleeve, not daring to speak beyond that single, desperate word.

Suddenly the doctor and Leopoldo both stopped as if frozen in space. Bishop Cuadrillero's impressive bulk filled the doorway. He scanned the room and its inhabitants, his glances flicking over the basin, cord and knife. His narrowed eyes and thunderous frown gave Doctor Santoro pause. The glass, now half empty, remained in the doctor's hand, inches from my face. Slowly, it was withdrawn.

"Just what is in that glass, Santoro?" The bishop spoke gruffly. "Don Ygnacio clearly doesn't want it, whatever it is."

I could no more than stare up at him with gratitude and surprise. Why had don Cayetano come himself? What could Gertrud have said to bring this about?

The physician's reply was defensive, hardly matching his earlier tone. "It's only a sedative, Your Grace, to calm don Ygnacio so we can get on with the bloodletting. He seems to have an unreasoning fear of the procedure." The doctor stood, drawing himself up with dignity to face the bishop. He set the glass aside.

Don Cayetano cocked his head. "Fear? Hmmm, yes. Perhaps not so unreasoning."

Behind the bishop, Clara appeared in the doorway, very simply dressed, her eyes puffy from insufficient sleep. "What's going on in here? Ah! Your Grace! Forgive the intrusion!" Confused, she took a step backwards.

The bishop favored her with a well-practiced but emotionless ecclesiastical smile, no doubt reserved for female parishioners. "No need to excuse yourself, dear lady. It's a simple matter. My coach and four will be arriving here within minutes to take don Ygnacio to the Palace. I walked here while the horses were being harnessed; it takes less time. You see, I have access to the medicine he requires. Quinine." He then turned to Doctor Santoro. "My personal physician will take over his treatment from now on. No reflection on your own fine skills, of course."

Finally he turned to Leopoldo. "I'm most grateful to you for your generosity in caring for this destitute man. You are certainly carrying out Christ's injunctions."

"Thank you, Your Grace," Leopoldo replied, dryly. "But, how did you know don Ygnacio was here? We got here from La Caridad after dark."

The bishop's eyelids drooped, a habit I'd noticed whenever he was being evasive. "You know what a small city this is, Father Leopoldo, you grew up here. Now, then, let's get don Ygnacio ready for the transfer. Would you excuse us, please, doña Clara? Josefina?"

Clara was at my side. "I'm so happy you'll be getting the proper medicine, don Ygnacio, but I'm sorry to see you go. Please get well very soon." She took my hand in both of hers and pressed it. I returned the gesture, my love and gratitude flowing out through my palms.

"I'm sure I'll see you before long, doña Clara. I'm touched and in your debt for your care all through the night." *But what will I do about my feelings for you if you're an accomplice to murder?*

With a lingering look and a gentle, dimpled smile, she hurried from the room, followed by Gertrud. I was helped to my feet while Leopoldo, who'd wordlessly bowed to the inevitable, pulled one of my robes over the silk nightshirt and drew on my shoes. It seemed the nightshirt would come with me as an unsolicited farewell 'gift.' He fetched my spare robe and the valise as the bishop stood at the window, looking down. A clatter of hooves explained his interest. He turned.

"Yes, the coach is here. Don Ygnacio, put your arms over my shoulders and Father Leopoldo's, and we'll get you safely downstairs."

ഇൽ

The two men virtually lifted me into the bishop's luxurious coach. Before he closed the door, Leopoldo, by all appearances deeply concerned, shook my hand. "I'm so sorry my efforts to help you got interrupted this way, don Ygnacio. I know Doctor Santoro well, and I'm sure he'd never harm you."

"It's all right, Father Leopoldo, I know you thought you were doing your best for me. I only thank God that I've been spared another loss of blood. Just tell Dom Gregorio what happened, please." My words belied my thoughts. If this man were a murderer, he was slyer than the Serpent.

"Of course. God go with you, don Ygnacio, and may he bring you quickly back to good health." He blessed me more formally in the name of the Father, of the Son and of the Holy Spirit, and closed the coach door with a final wave.

I sank back against the cushioned seat, a semblance of calm returning. Don Cayetano rapped on the roof and the coach began to roll. I turned to look at his heavy, jowled face, unable to suppress my gratitude another moment. I mumbled around my sore tongue.

"Your Grace, thank God you came in time. It was a matter of life or death."

His bushy white eyebrows rose in mock surprise. "Do you really think so, don Ygnacio?"

"Yes, Your Grace. I knew that without quinine, as weak as I am, a blood-letting would make an end of me. That together with a sedative, who knows how strong."

"And what *else* do you know?" He peered at me, eyes wide, head thrust toward me. I'd seen such looks before, the hawk contemplating its prey. Again, I pictured the beak as I considered his question for a moment. Father Ybarra would be in trouble if I revealed too much, and there could be other unintended consequences. What could I have known or deduced, had I not received Ybarra's note? I remembered Gelasio's last letter to his father. I took a deep breath. Perhaps I could limit the extent of his questions.

"Only my suspicions, Your Grace. I suspect that by now you either have the charter, or will soon have it in your possession. My impression is that someone may be using it to extort some favor from you. I'd guess the negotia-tion has been going on for some months. It may even have begun before I first met you."

Don Cayetano smiled, his eyes narrowed to slits. "You Jesuits are clever. And what else do you think you know?"

"I feel strongly that the same person may be guilty of two murders, may have attempted another and could be contemplating a fourth—me. My life is in danger, Your Grace, and has been for months, but lately more than ever. The person who has the charter—or who had it, if you've already accepted the bargain—has always thought I was dangerous, and by now thinks I must have deduced too much. I've had death threats, both direct and indirect, Your Grace. I believe they originated with this same person, no matter how they reached me."

"Indeed." The bishop leaned forward and peered out the window. "But your theory still doesn't explain all the facts, don Ygnacio. Well, it seems we've arrived at the Palace. Wait in the coach, and I'll get Miguel—Father Ybarra—to help. We'll get you upstairs and comfortable. I've sent my valet to the physician in Salamanca for more quinine, and he'll be back tomorrow. Your messenger this morning did a splendid job of convincing first Miguel, and then me, of the urgency of your case. The person who stole that quinine must surely want you dead, and it would be a simple matter to murder a man as sick as you are by bribing a physician, for example, to allow your blood to flow a little too long. No one would think your death strange; no one would investigate."

"Yes, Your Grace, the thought did occur to me."

He patted my shoulder, then heaved himself out of the coach, which creaked and tipped on its springs as he climbed down.

I waited, relaxed for the first time since I'd regained consciousness in the plush bed in the Casa Cerralbo. For a precious few seconds I felt no tension. No one, directly or indirectly, was trying to force something on me, nor was I trying to resist anything. How different from the preceding stressful hours.

I started a mental review, beginning with Clara's tension as she hovered over me, straining against the barrier of my priesthood, struggling with her self-restraint, tempted but hesitating to violate the simple friendship we'd agreed upon that night in Robledillo. Added to that was my own tension, not knowing whether or not she was involved in her brother's schemes, whatever those might be. Then the constant stress of my visceral attraction to her; then my anxiety over the theft of my quinine and my fear at the loss of Father Ybarra's dangerous message.

The quinine would soon be replaced, but I continued to worry about Ybarra's note falling into the wrong hands. I did not doubt that it had.

I'd feared for my life when Leopoldo, ostensibly trying to help me, had forced his trusted family physician on me with his set and antiquated ideas on how to treat my illness, even to insisting I drink that ever-so-harmless sedative, the crystal glass full of lavender liquid.

And all of it had taken place while I was weak from illness, literally help-less.

Ironic as it seemed, my life seemed less threatened here, sheltered by the bishop, than at the monastery under the protection of my friend Dom Gregorio. Until Bishop Cuadrillero returned with Father Ybarra, when I would again be under some sort of pressure, I could call these moments my own. I yawned, heaved a great sigh and stretched out my legs.

My respite lasted ten or fifteen minutes longer. Don Cayetano loomed in the coach's open door accompanied by Ybarra and Ricardo, the servant of my two previous visits.

"Don Ygnacio," Father Ybarra began, sticking his head into the cab, "thank God that maid came in time. An intelligent woman. She came first to me and told me exactly what had happened. Despite her accent, she expresses herself clearly. She certainly convinced me!"

I nodded, wondering about my own accent. "I thank God for Josefina far more fervently than you do, don Miguel."

They busied themselves helping me climb down from the coach. The bishop gave me a worried glance. "When was the last time you ate?"

"Your Grace, not since the midday meal yesterday. And yes, I'm feeling quite weak."

"Do you have any appetite?" Ybarra asked.

"Some. Perhaps a little soup."

Bishop Cuadrillero turned to Ricardo. "As soon as don Ygnacio is comfortable upstairs, see that he gets some food. Bland things, easy to digest."

"Yes, Your Grace."

Ybarra and the bishop each hooked one of my arms across their shoulders. We crossed a patio, passed under an arcade, then negotiated a staircase three abreast, a clumsy feat at best. Ricardo followed with my valise and extra robe.

The bishop threw open the door to a spacious chamber, paneled in brown wood, with a black-beamed ceiling and large window opening onto a balcony. "This is our best guest room, don Ygnacio," he said, gesturing to a view of geraniums and hibiscus in the patio below. I was helped to the four-poster bed, where Ricardo turned down the covers for me. A basin and pitcher of water were in place on a bedside table. Father Ybarra told me to rest for awhile, that food would be brought to me in a short time, and the bishop gave me a kindly nod.

"Relax, don Ygnacio. You're in good hands."

He turned to leave, followed by the others. When the door had closed softly behind them, I pulled off my robe and shoes, drank two glasses of cool water and splashed more water into the basin. After rinsing my face and hands, I crawled between the sheets—not satin, but fragrant, clean linen—and fell asleep at once despite my feverish cheeks and underlying sickness.

ଈଓଷ

The quinine arrived the next day. I dosed myself with the amount I'd always used before my captivity, and prayed it would work still. Don Cayetano's physician came to see me, but did little more than feel my forehead to gauge my temperature and take my pulse, saying he'd wait to see what effect the quinine had before prescribing anything further. I ate as much as I could tolerate and slept a good deal, and on the third day my fever, along with the other symptoms, had greatly diminished. My sore tongue was nearly normal again. Even my bruised jaw felt better.

At first light that morning I made my way to the desk across the room and looked through the drawer for writing materials. It was well stocked with quill pens, a stoppered pot of ink, sheets of paper and a small pan of sand used to blot wet ink. I sat and began to write:

> *Reverendo Padre y Abad, Dom Gregorio:*
> Father Leopoldo must have told you days ago that I was summarily taken out of his hands by Bishop Cuadrillero and moved to the Episcopal Palace. By some divine miracle, he arrived just as the Cerralbo family physician, Doctor Santoro, was about to bleed me, ignoring my protests and pleas. The bishop, you see, has discovered a source of quinine, and knew that my best chance to recover would be through that medicine, not by bloodletting. I began taking quinine three days ago, and now feel well enough to write this note to you. As soon as I gain sufficient strength, I am sure don Cayetano will return me to the monastery. Meanwhile, I remain, unlike the storks of La Caridad, your alert and obedient servant in Christ,
> Ignaz Pfefferkorn, S. J.

I reread the letter several times, knowing the bishop would read it himself before sending it out. I'd chosen one word most carefully, hoping it would convey the proper message to my friend. That, and my reference to the storks, who owed their loyalties to no one. Only he would understand. *"My experience over many years of observing them has taught me, don Ygnacio, that storks make notoriously bad witnesses."*

Chapter XIV

Violins and Other Seductions

I gave my note to Ricardo when he came with my breakfast. "Please see it's delivered to the monastery, Ricardo. I assume you'll need to show it to Bishop Cuadrillero before it leaves the palace."

"I'll ask, don Ygnacio. I can't say what the procedure will be, but I'd be glad to take your letter."

But once the letter was in Ricardo's hands, I began doubting my wisdom in adding that special word, 'alert' to the standard letter closure, 'your obedient servant in Christ.' While it conveyed exactly what I wanted—the idea that I was watching for anything that would help Dom Gregorio's cause—it might also 'alert' the bishop. Would he not wonder about such a choice of word? But it was too late; Ricardo was gone. If the bishop asked for an explanation, I could make reference to some conversation I'd had with Dom Gregorio about the effects of malaria on me. My personal signal to the abbot that I was back to normal would be my return to an alert state. In fact, it was the truth.

I whiled away the day napping in the afternoon and reading a breviary and a book of the poems and meditations of San Juan de la Cruz that I discovered among several volumes of the Fathers of the Church. At dinnertime, Father Ybarra knocked.

"If you feel well enough, Don Cayetano and I would be pleased if you dined with us downstairs."

"Thank you, I'd be happy to join you. I'm feeling well enough to begin being bored up here alone."

He hesitated in the doorway, fixing me with a compassionate stare. "Thank God we got to you on time. You may have observed, as we have, that Leopoldo is…." His voice trailed off and he beckoned me to follow him, stepping to my side as we descended the stairs.

I prompted him, eager to know what he was about to say, certain he'd been on the brink of a crucial revelation.

"Leopoldo is...what, Father?"

He merely shook his head with a wry expression, clicking his tongue against his front teeth. He allowed me the dignity of walking alone but stayed close enough to catch and assist me if needed. I arrived in the parlor out of breath and shaky, but my attention was not on myself. I was burning to find an opportunity to question Ybarra further.

Don Cayetano rose when we entered, and extended his hand to me. I bent to kiss his ring. "No, no, don Ygnacio. None of that formal nonsense. I simply want to shake hands. I'm delighted to see you well enough to join us this evening. Please sit down."

I was more than happy to do exactly that, as my legs had begun to tremble. "I'm in your debt, Your Grace. Without your timely rescue and the quinine you've supplied, I'd be at death's door by now. If Doctor Santoro had gone ahead with that bloodletting...." The thought made me shudder visibly.

The bishop waved away my thanks as if the rescue had been a trifle.

"Glad to be of service, my friend. By the way, I hear that you play the violin quite well. I have an instrument here...." He turned to Father Ybarra. "Miguel, could you fetch the violin from that cabinet over there?" He pointed at a cabinet with four doors, each decorated with an embossed leather insert. Ybarra opened the third door and took down an instrument case, carrying it to a small table under the central chandelier. "Shall I open it, don Cayetano?"

"Of course!"

The leather case was lined with deep-pile red velvet, and an exquisite violin lay cradled inside. I stood again, and was hanging over Father Ybarra's shoulder, unable to suppress a broad smile. The bishop was watching my reaction.

"May I, Your Grace?"

"Why else would I have brought it out, don Ygnacio? Take it out. Try it. Try it."

I lifted the beautiful instrument, turning it to examine it from all sides in the light of the many candles above my head. It was in perfect condition, its gleaming reddish varnish reminding me of the color of doña Clara's hair. The bow was slack, of course. I first tensioned it, then tucked the instrument under my chin and played a single note, adding a bit of tremolo. The tone was beautiful.

The instrument in its proper position under my sore chin was almost tolerable, but tuning did take longer than usual since I literally had to brace the scroll against the back of a chair while turning the pegs. Nevertheless, the bishop waited patiently, and once I was satisfied, I played a short passage from Jean-Baptiste Lully. The tone was achingly lovely, rich and sonorous, almost bringing tears to my eyes. I lowered the instrument.

"I'd be happy to play more for you tomorrow evening when I'm a bit more recovered, Your Grace."

The bishop's eyes sparkled. "They didn't exaggerate when they said you were an accomplished violinist. And with an excellent musical memory under most difficult circumstances."

I carefully replaced the instrument in its case and sat again. "These present circumstances are not the most difficult, Your Grace; I've faced more frightening situations in the past."

"Ah?" The bishop's eyebrows rose. "Do tell us."

"Well, Your Grace...don Miguel...for instance, my arrival at my first mission. That ranks high among the most frightening experiences of my life." I settled back in the comfortable chair as Ricardo padded silently in, bearing a tray with three glasses of sherry.

"Excuse me for interrupting, don Ygnacio," Father Ybarra put in, "but I want you to know that don Cayetano has opened a bottle of our finest amontillado sherry. All this to celebrate your remarkable improvement."

I took the glass offered me, waited until my companions had theirs, and raised mine in a toast. "To don Miguel Ybarra and Bishop Cuadrillero, rescuers par excellence." I took a sip, drawing my breath in through my parted lips to extract the true essence. "Ah! This *is* a fine sherry, Your Grace."

The bishop sipped his sherry with a satisfied air. "Thank you, don Ygnacio, but please go on with your story."

I continued, in more detail, the story I'd told Clara. "As you know, we Jesuits often used music to attract the Indians, to make first contact and to help us begin to establish our missions. That's the reason they let me take my violin with me to New Spain in the first place. It was one of my most prized possessions, seized, of course, when we were arrested and expelled.

"When we first arrived in the Sonora area, all of us were frightened, since there'd been what has been called the Pima Revolt. A faction in one of the tribes had revolted and attacked several missions. They martyred one of Ours—a grisly death. As much as four years later, the situation was still quite unsettled."

"You had a contingent of soldiers along with you, I assume?" The bishop's eyebrows were nearly touching his hairline.

"True. I arrived with a contingent of soldiers at Atí, my first mission, but the Indians were nowhere to be seen. They were in hiding."

"More afraid of you than you of them. I see."

"Exactly, although at that moment I wasn't so sure. They could have been lying in ambush. In any case, since no Indians appeared in three days, I sent the military escort away."

"Wasn't that rather foolish, Ygnacio?"

"It was extremely risky. I admit I was terrified."

Father Ybarra leaned forward. "What happened?"

"At first, nothing. I went about my housekeeping chores, inspecting and cleaning the church, then cleaning the priest's house and putting my few belongings away. No Indians appeared even then."

"And? And?"

"Then night came. I was white with fear, so I took out my violin and played to console myself. I played all my favorite pieces, and finally, hearing a noise, looked to the window even as I was playing. I stopped when I saw—"

"When you saw what?"

"Indians, many sitting, crowded as close to my window as they could get, some of them still moving to the music I'd just been playing. I hesitate to say they were dancing, since Indian dancing is almost always connected with set religious ritual, but we would call it dancing. They loved music and were fascinated by the new instrument. After that, I had no trouble: they were kind, generous, and pleased to learn the True Religion, anxious to learn to play the violin. A funny thing: they picked up their houses, made of mud and sticks, and grouped them as close to the priest's house as they could get them, practically on top of one another."

The bishop erupted with a hearty laugh. "So they could hear every note you played."

"Exactly, Your Grace."

Ricardo appeared at that moment and announced dinner. Led by His Grace, we entered the dining room where three places were set at one end of a table that would easily seat sixteen. In addition to the central chandelier, there were two candelabra ablaze with candles, set upon a white linen tablecloth. Table settings were of white china edged in gold, with the Episcopal coat of arms emblazoned in the center of each plate. Crystal glasses flanked glittering silver cutlery. A curling wisp of steam rose from a covered silver tureen.

The bishop rubbed his hands and gestured to the side of the table facing the wall. I was to sit there, on his right. Father Ybarra would sit facing us. Was there some significance, I wondered? Was Ybarra to watch me, as I'd earlier watched the bishop for Dom Gregorio?

Prior to sitting, I was asked to say the blessing. I briefly gathered my thoughts, then, crossing myself, I prayed.

"Lord, with all my soul I praise you for the favor you have shown this servant of yours through don Cayetano's timely rescue. I thank you also for the kind attentiveness of Father Ybarra. Through them you have renewed my life and refreshed my spirit. I ask your special blessings on them and that you continue to bless and sustain us all. May this food strengthen and nourish our bodies, our minds, and our spirits, that we may work for your greater glory. Amen."

"Sit! Sit, my friends!" His Grace commanded after a pause. As soon as we were settled, Ricardo poured sparkling white wine the bishop said was one of the best recent vintages from Robledillo. It was to celebrate my recovery.

He removed the cover from the tureen and began dipping steaming soup into gold-bordered bowls. A piquant aroma of creamy chicken with a slightly sour accent awakened my appetite. I used my heightened senses to identify ingredients I knew: sorrel, cinnamon, cream, salt and plenty of freshly ground pepper. It was not too early for sorrel. I imagined tender leaves gathered from sheltered nooks in nearby gardens, puréed and added just before serving.

The bishop finished two bowls in silence while Ybarra and I were occupied with our first.

An artistically arranged platter followed, offering a selection of smoked fish and eel, with hot fresh bread on the side. I picked at a slice of smoked eel, nibbling at my bread and returning in my thoughts to the violin.

"How did you come by that exquisite violin, don Cayetano?"

"One of the priests I came to know well while I was in Rome, don Ygnacio." He helped himself to another piece of fish. "His uncle died, leaving him a number of items of furniture and such—among other things a lute and that violin. He thought they were from a famous maker, Guarnerius, Guarneri, something like that. My friend played the lute and kept it, but insisted I take the violin. I've had it here in that cabinet for a few years now, and at last have found someone to play it."

"I hope I can do it justice tomorrow night, Your Grace, and that I continue to gain more strength."

When Ricardo reappeared to remove the platter, now all but emptied from the repeated visits of my hosts, I felt quite satisfied. The amount I'd eaten was just right, as overeating was something I'd learned not to do after a bout with the dread disease.

But I was wrong in thinking it was the end of the meal. Ricardo then signaled the kitchen that we were ready for the main course. More fish: a grilled trout for each of us, accompanied by white asparagus, butter sauce, and a few sprigs of watercress. It was a Lenten meal, but an elaborate one, and more than I could handle at the moment. The bishop noticed that I'd declined more.

"Try at least to eat the trout, don Ygnacio. It will do you more good than anything else. It was caught just hours ago in the Águeda River."

I felt like a scolded boy, but I could eat only half of the fish and a couple of asparagus spears. I watched the two of them, marveling that Father Ybarra remained so thin. He ate at least as much as the bishop, or was it his first meal in a fortnight?

His Grace sat back at last with a contented sigh, fingers splayed on either side of his belly. He fixed me with a speculative gaze, hooded eyes narrowed.

"You were right about the charter, you know. One of the monks is using it as a means of extracting a number of concessions from me—from the diocese. I haven't yet granted the favors; I'm still bargaining. Don't want to make such large concessions, so I don't yet have possession of the document. But, if Dom Gregorio finds a way to resist me, I may have to make those sacrifices, no matter what the cost to me."

He waited. I met his eyes, narrowing mine a bit in return. "I don't expect you to tell me who this monk is."

The question brought a satyr smile. "Now, telling you *that* would be trusting you too far, don't you think, don Ygnacio?"

"Regrettably, Your Grace. On the other hand, you may be able to tell me about Brothers Metodio and Eugenio. I saw them sneaking back into the monastery, probably coming from Ciudad Rodrigo, one early morning a couple days before your bottle of quinine appeared mysteriously in my cell. Was there any connection?"

"Now that I *am* willing to tell you about." The bishop chuckled. "Yes, those two act as a courier service between here and La Caridad, sometimes singly, sometimes together. A pair of La Caridad laborers who live here in the city...one works in the kitchen and the other in the stable...are trusty enough to let Metodio or Eugenio know when someone here needs to pass an unofficial message. As soon as one or the other can get away, he comes at night and takes back to La Caridad whatever message or package a member of our staff, Miguel or I may have for one of the monks. In this last case, it was medicine for you, don Ygnacio."

"My head is spinning, don Cayetano." I massaged my temples in mock desperation. "On the one hand you're undermining the discipline of the monastery with the help of its own monks. On the other, your two couriers are among those most in opposition to your politics of taking parishes away from Nuestra Señora de la Caridad. The complexities! The contradictions between hearts and heads, between the seductions of practical convenience and political principle! At any rate, thank you for telling me. This means I can eliminate those two from my roster of murder suspects."

"I should certainly hope so! Ah! Ricardo's bringing the flan. Excellent! Would you serve it, please, Ricardo? When I try, it always falls to bits."

"Of course, Your Grace." The moment for revelations had passed as the bishop turned his attention to the dessert. Ricardo set about carving the flan into perfect wedges, pouring a spoonful of syrup over each one. Then, with a flourish, he placed a loaded gilt-edged plate before each one of us in turn. All conversation stopped while we watched his graceful service.

I did manage to eat the flan before I excused myself.

Father Ybarra accompanied me back upstairs. As we paused before my door, I questioned him further.

"Now that His Grace has revealed more about a monk who's trying to extract concessions in exchange for the charter, maybe *you* can tell me more about him. You warned me to beware of my closest associates. You're also aware the vial of quinine that contained your letter was stolen while I was unconscious the other day, probably by Father Leopoldo. In fact, you also might be in danger.

Ybarra nodded, his bony face somber. "Leopoldo is ambitious. Such men are dangerous. Goodnight, don Ygnacio."

"But...."

He would say no more.

As I lay awake after my prayers, I pondered his fragmentary revelations along with the bishop's information. Eugenio once told me Ybarra's family lived in Robledillo, and his younger brother worked closely with Leopoldo's household as one of his winegrowers. If, as the bishop said, the monk negotiating for favors in exchange for the charter were also threatening the bishop's security, Ybarra, devoted to His Grace as he was, would move to protect him. If that monk were Leopoldo, the murder attempt on him could have been conceived here, and be—almost—executed there. The more I thought about it, the more likely the scenario.

The bishop was playing a dangerous game, dangerous perhaps for his own interests, and definitely for me. He knew who had murdered Gelasio and Tomás: the very man who was negotiating with him. He might not be absolutely certain, for the guilty monk was likely not confessing to him, but he knew the man at least had sanctioned both killings. And, knowing the murderer's identity while keeping it a secret meant the bishop was toying with more lives than just mine. Securing Robledillo for the diocese meant more to him than those lives, certainly more than the life of one ex-Jesuit.

And yet he'd saved me from Doctor Santoro's well-meaning ministrations. Why bother?

The last time I had seen him, the bishop said he knew about my 'activities' in my former prison, though he'd concealed his knowledge from Dom Gregorio. Perhaps even then he was planning to blackmail me and use me to spy on Dom Gregorio's next moves.

Of course, in his eyes I'd been nothing short of a trained bear or a clown, entertaining him from the beginning and more so now with my violin playing and my stories of New Spain. My latest performances and stories could only have encouraged him.

I'd be sent back in a day or two to La Caridad, whether I yielded to his unexpressed wishes or not. There, I'd once again be at the mercy of the unknown assailant, who now had even more incentive to do away with me. Don Cayetano knew that as well as I. The quinine that was saving my life, pleasant surroundings, the seductions of the violin and fine food along with the kindness shown me were not disinterested Christian charity. I was being manipulated, about to be exploited, and now more than ever I was alone.

ะ๛ผ

Don Cayetano flattered me with his hearty greeting as I entered the salon the following night.

"Ricardo tells me you ate much better today, don Ygnacio. That's good news. You've lost that pinched look, there's some color in your face and the swelling's down. I trust these are good omens for a violin concert before dinner?"

"Thank you, Your Grace. I'm feeling better in every way, certainly up to playing a couple of violin pieces for you tonight." I inclined my head, smiling at the bishop and his secretary, who returned the smile. The violin case lay open on the table beneath the central chandelier, ready for my 'concert.' I caressed it with my fingertips, conscious of close scrutiny by my audience.

"I'll begin with a lively piece by Marin Marais, popular at the court of Louis XIV of France. Both these pieces were written for a viola da gamba, but I transposed them a long time ago, back when I was a scholastic." I checked the tuning, then launched into the singing, rollicking music. The two men were tapping their toes in time, and applauded me afterwards.

"The next will be for all those men killed in the recent past, their lives wasted. To my brother Jesuits and my new brothers, whose lives were also sacrificed: Gelasio and Tomás."

I played the second Marais, a slow melody, haunting and melancholy, leaving my audience with long and pensive faces. "And now something to cheer you up: 'Spring' from fellow priest Antonio Vivaldi's 'The Seasons.'"

This last piece succeeded in raising spirits all around. I bowed to their applause, and put the violin away just as Ricardo announced dinner.

We sat as before, the bishop at the head of the table, I at his right. Perhaps because the concert had gone so well, I ate with good appetite, rewarded by Don Cayetano's approving nods. Then again, the cook might have had something to do with it. He'd created a main dish of *cigalas*, large, sea dwelling crayfish with a flavor that hesitated between *langouste* and shrimp. They'd been caught the day before and transported overnight across Portugal from the Atlantic coast. A garlicky mayonnaise enhanced their delicate flavor.

The meal was Lenten only in the most technical sense. Any other time of year, it properly would have been called a feast. In my mind, it was another attempt by the bishop to ply me with favors prior to asking his own. It was now just a matter of time.

He did not make me wait long. Once the dinner was finished, he turned to Father Ybarra. "Would you excuse us, please, Miguel?"

"Of course, Your Grace."

"Come, then, don Ygnacio, and follow me. Ybarra exchanged a glance with me as the bishop rose. He seemed to be telling me to be on my guard.

The bishop led the way back into the salon, where we sat facing each other in comfortable chairs. "Now, don Ygnacio," he said without preamble, "I must tell you that I know a good deal about your background and behavior since you were returned to Spain in 1769." The bishop's smile was a trifle too sweet.

I pretended surprise. "Why would you trouble yourself with trivia like that, Your Grace?"

"You're not a stupid man, don Ygnacio. From what I've observed and found out, you're a fair representative of your Company of Jesus. The most important detail of your behavior, and the most useful to me is this: there has been a lapse in communications between Norbertine Abbots, it would seem. Dom Gerónimo of San Norberto in Madrid has never—to my knowledge, at least—informed your friend Dom Gregorio of your crime."

With these words, Don Cayetano once again assumed his bird-of-prey pose, with body tense, head and neck thrust forward. Involuntarily, my own chin came up.

"And what crime is that, Your Grace?"

"You helped a fellow Jesuit, Jacobo Sedelmeyer, to escape the prison at the Port of Santa María. I regret to tell you he's been recaptured and is being held in the Norbertine monastery in Ávila."

I bowed my head, my voice low and husky. "That's terrible news, Your Grace. Yes, I did help him escape and would have gone with him if only I'd been strong enough. Together, we might have made our way home." I exhaled forcefully, a sigh of regret and nostalgia, before hardening my tone. "And so, Your Grace, since you possess this information, I presume you must want something from me. What is it?"

"Not so fast, don Ygnacio. I need to remind you not only that I can make the conditions of your 'imprisonment' at La Caridad much more unpleasant, by informing Dom Gregorio of your exploit in Santa María, but that you owe me your life. You said so yourself. I did go to the trouble of finding that quinine for you, which truly seems to be a miraculous remedy for malaria, and I did rescue you from Doctor Santoro's knife. True or false?"

"All true, don Cayetano. I repeat, what is it you want of me?"

"I want exactly what you probably foresaw, that you keep me informed of Dom Gregorio's every maneuver and of any little move a brother makes that might be of interest to me. Adding to that, you can start insinuating the idea into the abbot's head that his case is hopeless without the charter. I'll not crush him ruthlessly and right away, but I will crush him. Let him know I'll go slowly, allow him time to make a graceful transition."

Midway through his speech, the bishop sat back, lacing his fingers across his belly, his eyes no more than glittering slits under overhanging eyebrows, boring into mine.

I stared back for a long moment, then sighed. "I'm truly sorry to have heard that request, Your Grace. I was praying it would never come to this. I hadn't believed you'd think it necessary to plant a spy in the monastery in addition to other informants you probably have at La Caridad already—and certainly not me. As for pressuring me by threatening to reveal my so-called crime, I run the risk of having that revealed by anyone, at any moment. Some of the monks at La Caridad already know about it...Brother Metodio, for instance. It's only a matter of time before Dom Gregorio finds out. And who knows how he'll react? He might lock me up in solitary confinement even without your intervention."

I paused, thinking back over the past few days, reliving in a flash the little kindnesses and favors don Cayetano and Father Ybarra had done me, as well as their major benefits.

"I hope you won't misunderstand me, don Cayetano. I'm deeply grateful to you for your help and I'm so much in your debt that I don't know how to repay you. Don't ever think I'm not fully aware that I owe you my life twice over, once for the quinine and again for coming in person the other morning to snatch me away from that knife, not to mention the so-called sedative. God only knows what that contained. But, to be quick about this, even so I cannot do what you ask. Dom Gregorio has become a friend as well as a protector. I'll not spy on him. I'll not betray him." I fell silent and waited for an explosion.

I saw a flash of anger on the bishop's face, a tightening of jaw muscles and widening of eyes. He was still leaning back in his chair, though his hands were now clasped tightly together, knuckles white. He turned his face away for a moment, then slowly turned to face me again, leaning forward, heavy brows knit. His eyes cast daggers into mine.

I did not shrink away under his wordless attack, or move, simply gazed back, trying to keep my facial muscles under perfect control.

When the words came, they were steel-edged. "Don Ygnacio, your Company no longer exists, and so you don't have a Provincial to issue orders or to protect you; you have *no one* to protect you. To say Dom Gregorio is your protector is preposterous. He is powerless to do anything of the sort. You're a helpless prisoner of the king, in the abbot's custody. That's all. You're no longer a member of a religious order. In your present circumstances, as the simple priest you now are, you come under my jurisdiction rather than under Dom Gregorio's. In any case, I believe I outrank Dom Gregorio. As your superior, then, I command you to obey me. I know that you, trained as a Jesuit, owe absolute obedience to your superiors." The bishop straightened, raising himself in an imperial pose, the epitome of authority.

I retained my control, remaining immobile. For my retort, I turned to the same phrase I'd repeated on two occasions: to Gelasio when he asked me about our vow of obedience, and to Metodio on the night he revealed that Tomás had stolen the charter.

"Saint Ignatius gave us a way out of this sort of situation, Your Grace. He wrote, 'In all things *except sin* I ought to do the will of my superior.' I fear that I count the actions you ask me to take as sinful. I cannot obey you, and must leave any reprisals for my lack of compliance up to you, don Cayetano. I am, of course, at your mercy."

The bishop continued to stare for a long minute. At last, he shook his head, folding his arms across his chest. "You Germans are an amazingly stubborn bunch. I realized that while I was in Rome. Got to know a few of the German cardinals in key positions. They wouldn't listen to a good argument, wouldn't pay any attention to logic once they'd made up their minds. Well, think it over, don Ygnacio." He paused for a long moment, no doubt allowing me time to consider. Then, he leaned forward again, this time with a paternal smile, his voice dropping to a purring rumble.

"Ygnacio, you know I like you, and I want to become that protector you so badly need. I have the power and the influence to protect you well; I've many connections and many people owe me favors. If you help me, I'll help you. There are ways to get you out of La Caridad and even out of Spain, no matter that you're in the king's custody. And no one the wiser. Portugal's only a few miles from here, then a short boat trip up the coast to Holland, a quick transit across to your homeland. Couldn't be simpler, and it could be done right away. Think about *that*, now. I'll see you at Mass in the morning, don Ygnacio. I'd like to show you the cathedral." He stood without waiting for a reply.

I stood as well, knowing I was being dismissed without the opportunity to comment on this last and most seductive bid, a nearly irresistible offer, as he very well knew. He was a keen judge of men's character, and he'd been observing me. From the beginning of our acquaintance I had displayed my homesickness, my grief and sense of isolation.

I bowed slightly as he swung around and sailed out of the room.

೮ಎೞ

Don Cayetano himself officiated at Mass the next morning, before a nave filled with the faithful. The cathedral choir gave an adequate performance, but in my opinion—quite unprejudiced, of course—they could not match our singing out at La Caridad. As he processed out, the bishop signaled that I was to wait for him. As soon as he was divested, he came to me.

"Let me show you some of the historic treasures we have here in our Catedral de Santa María." He smiled and squeezed my shoulder as if the conversation of the previous evening had never taken place.

The tour was a revelation of the city's history and wealth, past and present. Various side chapels had been built or financed by great families, including the chapel of the Marquises de Cerralbo. I admired the magnificent fifteenth-century choir that dominated the center of the nave, craned my neck at the huge organs whose pipe frames were decorated with carved and gilded angels. I was moved by the beauty of the cloister, combining Romanesque with gothic elements, and even more by clever symbolism expressed by the figures on capitals and in protected nooks: devils, serpents, angels and human beings in a ceaseless and deadly struggle between good and evil. The whole invited prolonged contemplation and prayer.

"The architect's tomb is over there," the bishop pointed. "Benito Sánchez is his name. He began such a magnificent work here, I still say a prayer of thanksgiving when I pass by. The city took two centuries to finish this church. That's why there's such a charming mixture of styles."

He led the way back into the nave and through the main entrance door to the cathedral, laying his hand on my arm in a familiar way while we walked the length of the cobblestoned courtyard as far as the encircling medieval city wall. There we turned to get a better look at the entire building. He pointed upward.

"We completed the bell tower fifty years ago, don Ygnacio, and even though it has no historical significance, it is a graceful structure, as you can see."

"Yes," I agreed, "your architect matched the stone perfectly. The tower harmonizes nicely with the rest of the building."

"One of these days, when you're fully recovered, you must climb up there to view the city," he said. "You can see every detail from up there. You'll need to be careful, though, as you walk from side to side. The earthquake did some damage that we haven't gotten around to repairing yet. There's a six-foot hole in the stone flooring, over close to the southwest corner. I had the gap covered with a wooden frame, but you could still trip and have a bad fall. So, once you're up there, keep your eyes open."

I nodded as I squinted up, comparing the tower's height to the one at La Caridad. This one was taller, more massive.

The bishop continued in a caressing tone. "Have you thought about the last matter I spoke to you about last night?"

"Yes, Your Grace. You very nearly had me. Tempting. All but irresistible. But my answer is still no."

He nodded, eyebrows lifted only a fraction as if he were not really surprised. He continued the tour as if he'd never asked the question, never received my refusal.

"Before we go, you must contemplate the jewel of the cathedral: the Pórtico del Perdón. Come."

We walked back to the main entrance of the church. Despite the pressure I was feeling, my attention shifted to the beauty of the portal. I was awed by the intricate detail of its stone carving portraying the most important incidents from the life of Christ, the twelve apostles, and, as focal point, Christ crowning the Virgin in heaven.

"Exquisite, don Cayetano. Moving. This must be one of the oldest art works in the cathedral; am I right?"

"Yes, quite right. It's thirteenth century. But we'd better be getting back to the palace. Our meal will be waiting, and after that you'll be returning to Nuestra Señora de la Caridad."

And to the murderer, I added in my mind.

Chapter XV

Suspicion

When Don Cayetano rode with me out to the monastery, I assumed he wanted to consult with Dom Gregorio. The gates were flung wide for the bishop's elegant coach, emblazoned with the Episcopal seal on each door, and the four-horse team halted at the same spot where I'd arrived that first night so long ago. This time, though, the church doors were open. Some of my fellow choir members and Father Plácido were visible inside.

The bishop opened the coach door and Brother Mateo moved quickly to the coach in the role of porter, prepared to help His Grace alight, but don Cayetano shook his head.

"Inform Abbot Dom Gregorio that we are here, please."

Why, I wondered, was Dom Gregorio to come to the coach? The reason soon became clear. When the abbot appeared, hurrying as never before in my memory, he wore a puzzled look, a mixture of concern and irritation. Only then did don Cayetano step from the coach, with great dignity and hauteur.

He greeted Dom Gregorio graciously enough, but as a lord would condescend to a servant. Then, as I waited in the coach's doorway, he turned back with a grandiose gesture, reaching up to assist me down.

"I'm returning don Ygnacio to your care, Dom Gregorio," he said. He seemed to be looking down his nose at the abbot, eyelids drooping. "We have many things in common, he and I. Yes, many things...such as our love of good music. I trust you'll keep him safe."

He enveloped me in a cordial embrace, treating me as one of equal rank, and spoke as if we were the best of friends.

"Don't forget what I asked you about this morning, Ygnacio, and don't neglect to come see me as soon as you can. We have much to talk about."

"At Dom Gregorio's pleasure, Your Grace," I replied, my tone sharp. I knew well that he was taking his revenge on me for non-compliance, planting suspicion in the abbot's mind. What else? Dom Gregorio would think I'd already betrayed him, or was planning to do so at my first opportunity. Brother

Mateo and the choir monks witnessed the scene as well, hearing every word. The whole monastery would be told about this fond leave-taking and my probable betrayal in no time.

Bishop Cuadrillero was deliberately making my life difficult. He wanted to make me miserable, enough so I'd seriously consider his offer of escape in exchange for information. What mystified me in all this was just why he'd ever thought I would be such a valuable spy. I was an outsider, with a cloud over my head, and he was darkening that cloud. How could I be effective if he undermined my credibility this way? Or, was revenge sweeter than the prospect of information? It would not surprise me.

He exchanged a few more words with the abbot, all of little significance, and then was handed up into his coach by Brother Mateo. I stood at the abbot's side, neither of us speaking as the carriage left. The abbot then turned.

"Come with me, don Ygnacio. I assume you'll give me a full account of the last few days." His voice was chilly and formal. It was 'don' Ygnacio now. He abruptly spun about, heading back. I was to follow.

I hurried to stay with him. "Of course, Domine. I have a lot to tell you." Lagging as I was, a step behind, my natural answer must have sounded contrived and artificial. He didn't reply, but I noticed the stiff set of his shoulders and the almost military cadence of his stride.

As soon as we were in the privacy of his rooms, he could contain his emotions no longer. An expression of deep hurt mixed with anger accompanied his outburst.

"Ygnacio, Ygnacio! This is a bitter moment for me. Did he break you? Are you an acolyte of Cuadrillero's by now? You looked like 'the disciple whom Jesus loved,' snuggling on his bosom. Perhaps he'll find out you're a Judas Iscariot, instead. Are you?"

His hands went to his head, either side, long fingers curled over his bald pate. "How did he buy you? *Did* he buy you? What have you promised him?"

His usually thoughtful bearing had given way to similes and assumptions, almost accusations. While I understood his reaction, I was no less hurt.

The bishop had to know this man like a brother, I decided. The little charade enacted with me a few minutes earlier had played upon Dom Gregorio's feelings as the bow played upon violin strings, evoking the desired effect with ease born of practice. My hands were up, palms out, almost before he finished his words.

"Wait, Domine! Surely, you can't believe I'd change my character, betray my principles, not to mention betray you and this monastery, in such a short time and with such slight cause. Surely, you're aware that I haven't betrayed my principles and beliefs during these eight, nearly nine, years of imprisonment. Why should I suddenly break now?"

A knowing look crossed his face. "I know Cuadrillero. Have known him for years. His Grace is very persuasive. I've seen many men's resolve collapse in the face of an insidious attack by him, and they were better men than you, stronger men, without serious faults or desires of escape. Cuadrillero uses any tactic he considers useful, from gentle persuasion to violent threats. Leopoldo told me how he snatched you away, just as Doctor Santoro was about to begin a cure. You've been in the bishop's custody for five days. How many pieces of silver did it take, *don* Ygnacio? I fear he owns you by now. The evidence was plain to see as you stepped out of the coach. He practically treated you as an equal."

"That's what he wanted you to think, Domine," I countered. "He surprised me with his actions, but he must have planned them all along. If you know the man as well as you say, then you know he can manipulate *you* as well as me or anyone else. I tell you, what you saw was role-playing to throw suspicion on me and deprive you of an ally. Yes, you're right up to a point. He did try to 'buy' me, or at least to blackmail me into spying and reporting to him every move you make, every 'interesting' thing any one of your monks does. I refused. I steadfastly refused."

"Assuming I could believe anything you're saying, what did he use to blackmail you?"

"My gratitude, Domine. He treated me very well, like a guest instead of a miserable prisoner. Most of all, he did save my life. He supplied me with quinine, and you know what I've had to say about that medicine. I'm back here now, as strong as I am, because of it. And he spared me from the bloodletting that Leopoldo—and you, I fear—think will let the evils out of my system, when I know from experience that it only weakens me. This time it would have weakened me fatally. I'm convinced of it."

In the moment of silence while Dom Gregorio digested my words, I weighed my options. Should I tell the whole truth about my 'crime' back at the prison? That I'd helped Jakob Sedelmeyer to escape? Perhaps it was in my favor to do so. Chances were he'd find out soon enough anyhow, and he would be even angrier with me for suppressing the information.

"There's something else he used to blackmail me, Domine, something Dom Gerónimo didn't tell you about me—for friendship's sake, perhaps. I was sent up here because the king commanded that we German ex-Jesuits all be shipped inland to various monasteries and convents. The chains were added, I think, for the second reason: I'd just helped a fellow Jesuit to escape. He was my cellmate, Domine, a good friend, Jacobo Sedelmeyer, who served God in the Sonora Desert for thirty-one years to my eleven, and who knew three times what I did about the region. I suspect Dom Gerónimo may have recommended that I be sent here not only because of my ill health, but so I would avoid harsh reprisals for my action."

The abbot continued as if I were a stranger. "I'm amazed, don Ygnacio, *amazed* that I should have been kept in the dark about a matter as serious as that one. How was I supposed to know what to do with you if I had no idea of your history? I'll write at once to my friend Gerónimo to find out for myself why he didn't tell me about that crime. And, I still haven't received detailed instructions on how I'm supposed to treat you, so I'll write the Royal Council, too. Whatever it orders with respect to the terms of your imprisonment, I will follow. No more special favors...don Ygnacio."

I sighed. "I repeat, Domine, I refused to act as the bishop's spy in any way. He was angry and called me a 'stubborn German,' and I am. I am loyal to you and to this place that has given me shelter over the months. Don Cayetano went so far as to command me to obey him, and I still refused...on the grounds that obedience to his orders would be a sin. His behavior just now was a ploy to discredit me in your eyes, and it succeeded, Domine; he hoodwinked you. That's all I can say. My story may be less dramatic than the scene you just witnessed, but it's the truth. Think about it, please, Domine."

I waited only long enough to draw a breath, continuing before the abbot could gather his thoughts.

"The bishop did, under my direct questioning of him, tell me that a monk from this monastery is trying to sell him the charter in return for a favor, or favors, but he wouldn't tell me who it is. He's still bargaining, he says, because he thinks the price is too high. But he said he'd pay it if you proved too hardheaded and continued to fight for Robledillo. His exact words were, 'I'll not crush him ruthlessly and right away, but I will crush him. Let him know I'll go slowly, allow him time to make a graceful transition.'

"Domine, if that monk is the same one that engineered the theft of the charter in the first place, he's probably also guilty of two murders. I don't know about the attempt on Father Leopoldo's life—that doesn't fit the pattern—but surely the bishop knows, or at least has strong suspicions of, the monk's guilt. If so, Bishop Cuadrillero is complicit in the murders and we could denounce him for such scandalous behavior. I learned very little else—nothing else—that would be of any use to us, Dom Gregorio, other than the fact that Father Ybarra seems to be, within limitations, an ally."

"Then you learned precious little, don Ygnacio. We knew all of that, or at least guessed it, before you left here. All this time spent, and we're no closer to solving our problems than we were in the first place."

He began pacing the room, hands clasped behind his back, the scowl on his face telling of his frustration, suspicion and impatience with me. I debated inwardly and decided not to share my own suspicions about Leopoldo. I had no desire to drive a wedge between him and his favorite, not until I discovered some key, some damning piece of evidence against his instructor of boys.

I stood waiting, as I could not leave until dismissed, and he continued his pacing as though I weren't there. After five turns around the room, muttering, he finally took notice of me once again.

"Oh, go to your cell, don Ygnacio, and stay there until further notice. I have letters to write."

I closed his door behind me, head bowed with the weight of my depression, and slowly made my way along the cloister toward the stairs. Dom Gregorio's credulity, his quick acceptance of the bishop's playacting, disillusioned me. All this time I'd believed he was my friend, despite my lowly status as ex-Jesuit and prisoner. A friend would not have abandoned me in an instant; he'd have weighed my words and given me the benefit of any doubt.

Two monks approached, but when they saw me they made an abrupt turn into a side corridor. The word had spread already, it seemed. I reached the stairs and began the climb with a heavy heart. Metodio was waiting for me at the top. He looked down at me, giving me the eerie feeling I'd lived this scene before.

"So!" he sneered, "the moment you had the opportunity, you took the side that held the greatest advantage for you, you Judas, *Jesuit*, traitor. So much for your friendship with Dom Gregorio, for your gratitude to those of us who helped you in the past few months. What I've read about your kind is the truth. I should never have been so gullible as to give you information. It only led to another murder. Some of the brothers are still thinking you committed both of them. Now I think they may be right."

"Metodio—"

"Your sins are stronger than you are, and you can't blot them out, traitor," he taunted, parodying a verse from Psalm 65. Then he ran past me, down the stairs. I stared after him for a moment before continuing, even more slowly, to my cell.

Brother Eugenio appeared suddenly on the upper walkway, as if materializing from nowhere. "Don Ygnacio! I heard you were back. How are you? I see your chin is still black and blue. You don't look well to me. Rumors are flying on all sides that you've gone over to the bishop's cause. Can that be true? I can't believe that."

"Eugenio!" I reached for him and embraced him in gratitude. "You're the only person who's doubted the rumors even for a second. Thank God! To answer your last question first, no, it's not true."

"Well, then, tell me what happened. You've been gone nearly a week. It's April already, you know."

"Is it? I've lost all track of time. Dom Gregorio wants me to stay in my cell until he gives me further orders, Brother Eugenio, so come there with me and I'll tell you everything."

We both turned as we heard the rustle and heavy footsteps of someone bustling up behind us. Father Plácido laid a massive arm across my shoulders. "Ygnacio, we've missed you in the choir. I heard what you just said, and I never believed the rumor in the first place. Mind if I come along and hear your side of the story?"

At my door, Plácido gave me a squeeze that ground my shoulder blades together. I looked at him in amazement; he had the strength of a bear. "Come on in. There's only one chair, you know."

Eugenio took the chair, although Plácido outranked him. I sat on the cot, the big man next to me.

"So," Eugenio began, "how did the bishop get you in his clutches in the first place, don Ygnacio?"

"It goes back a few weeks, to when Dom Gregorio and I were summoned to the Episcopal Palace. It was not long after my first malaria attack. Don Cayetano asked me then about my illness, and I told him about quinine. You

remember...the only medicine that would keep the symptoms under control."
The two men nodded.

"The morning after I fainted at dinner and was taken to Father Leopoldo's house in the city, the bishop appeared just in time to save me from a bloodletting at the hands of the Cerralbo family doctor. Doctor Santoro had his knife at the ready, it was that close. Bishop Cuadrillero stopped him and took me with him, because he had access to a supply of quinine."

"But surely Doctor Santoro would've done you some good!" Plácido exclaimed.

"No." I shook my head. "You must remember how violent I was, protesting against being bled the first time I had a bout of malaria. You were both witnesses to that. I told you then that taking my blood had only weakened me so much that I was barely able to function. Another bloodletting would have killed me. So, the bishop saved my life that morning by taking me away just in—"

"And then he gave you that quinine?" Eugenio interrupted. "But everything you're saying proves you owed a great deal to the bishop. He had a right to ask you for a favor, didn't he?"

"He thought so, and he did exactly that. He wanted me to spy on Dom Gregorio, and on you, in return for his favors. I said no, absolutely not."

"Why?" asked Father Plácido. "After all, he saved your life twice, maybe."

"Yes, but you, all of you out here, had done more than that. When I came in rags, and starving, you clothed and fed me. When I was sick, you nursed me back to health. I'm imprisoned here, and you've visited me, helped me. You've befriended me and you are my kind companions. I trust you and I implore God that you trust me. It makes me want to weep to tell you that Dom Gregorio does not. He's ordered me to stay in my cell here until further notice, so I won't be seeing you at mealtimes." I paused, looking at them with gratitude. "I think I'd better pray over all this now, to see if there's any way out."

৩৩੦੪

Noontime passed. I remained in my cell, reading my breviary in the slanting light from the doorway. I occasionally raised my head, listening to the breeze sighing in the branches of the trees in the cloister garden and, from time to time, the footfalls of a monk passing by. I tried to guess his identity from the rhythm of his walk. General silence prevailed otherwise, as most of the monks were engaged in their daily work: scribal, cleaning, teaching, or gardening. I began picking up the muffled voices of the choir monks on the other side of my wall. They seemed to be practicing a new Mass. Father Plácido was busy, too, stopping them every so often. While I couldn't hear actual words, the pattern of our typical practice sessions was clear enough.

Then a different sound mixed with in with the others: a measured tread on the stairway, coming in my direction. I'd been facing my small table. When I turned toward my door, there was a figure silhouetted in my doorway: Dom Gregorio.

"Ygnacio, here, I brought you some food. May I come in?"

I sprang to my feet and offered him my chair, noting with pleasure that he was using my name without the honorific. "By all means, Domine. Please, sit down!"

He first of all set down the tray he carried, containing a bowl of soup, plate of stew, roll and glass of wine. Then he took the chair, inviting me to sit also. "Ygnacio, I need to ask your forgiveness. I've been harsh and unreasonable. Hot headed. Hasty."

"And quick to think the better of it, Dom Gregorio. But what changed your mind?"

"You did, Ygnacio. I began comparing my suspicions with what you said, my fears with your calm. I wasn't listening to you while you were talking to me, but your words echoed in my mind after you left. Before I say another word, Ygnacio, you sit here in this chair and eat this food before it gets cold. There's nothing so loathsome as cold stew." He vacated the chair and hooked an arm under my armpit, lifting me off the cot. I obediently sat facing the tray of food, while he took my former place. "Eat!" he commanded. I said a quick blessing and began with the soup. It was mediocre and lukewarm, but it tasted good nevertheless, and I was hungry. He continued.

"All the time you were gone, while Cuadrillero had you in his power, I was filled with fears and mistrust. I know only too well, you see, how he can corrupt a good man. I've seen it too many times; he destroyed one of my best friends. Then, when he came back here to the monastery with you and put on that act of the great, magnanimous lord who's kind to his servant...me...I went blind with anger. He treated you like someone special, like a crony, a trusted collaborator. I couldn't see you, the real you, any longer. I didn't give you a chance. I'm sorry. Please, Ygnacio, forgive me."

I'd understood all this from the beginning, but I was relieved to hear him say it.

"Of course I forgive you, Domine. I felt the full extent of don Cayetano's power, and he did all he could to corrupt me, too. It's just my native stubbornness that kept me from falling in with his plans. Add to his powers of persuasion the fact that he likes me, I think. It's harder to resist someone who likes you. But I still told him no, no, and no. He was angry, masking his anger with a sweet face and then trying to set you against me. And it worked, until now. I imagine he still thinks I might give in."

"I'm sure he does. And you might. Even you don't know what further pressures you might come under. But the same is true of any one of us. For now, though, Ygnacio, I'm restoring you to your previous status. Once you've finished eating, why don't you join the choir in the church? Father Plácido's rehearsing a new Mass by José de Nebra called *In viam pacis*, 'In the Way of Peace.' It's new to us, at any rate. It seems our choir has been invited to sing it in celebration of Most Holy Trinity Sunday on 16th June in the Cathedral of Santa María in the city."

"What if instructions come in the meantime from Madrid to put me in solitary confinement?"

"Then this Mass could be your farewell appearance. But surely, nothing so dire will happen. Eugenio just pled your case at mealtime with force and eloquence, by the way, and Plácido's been complaining to me about missing your voice. He needs you. Leopoldo and Metodio by themselves are not enough to carry the baritone part. But beyond that, he loves you, Ygnacio, I can tell. And so does Eugenio. He told me flat out that you were not the bishop's man. Plácido's the funny one, though, Ygnacio. He was very concerned about your physical welfare—worried that you'd starve if I didn't bring you some food. He insisted until I promised. He's not one for fasting, is our Plácido."

I smiled. "Far from it. He's been thrusting extra food on me ever since I came. Can't stand to see anyone this skinny. And yes, I'd like to join the other singers down there, Domine. Thanks for the permission."

༄༅

Father Plácido overwhelmed me with affection when I appeared in the nave, stopping the rehearsal and coming to embrace me, then walking me to my place between Leopoldo and Metodio. His arm draped across my shoulders like some heavy animal hitching a ride, soft and warm. I felt embarrassment at his bubbling enthusiasm although, knowing him, it was typical. Choir members exchanged glances, shaking their heads, and whispering quick comments in each other's ears. Plácido ignored them and pointed to the sheet of music on the stand in front of Leopoldo.

"Now, at last, we'll be able to hear the baritone part. Let's take it again from *Agnus Dei*."

Metodio's scowl darkened as I brushed past him to take my place. He leaned backward against his chair as if to avoid contamination, but Leopoldo gave me a warm hug.

"I can see you're much better, don Ygnacio. Maybe you're right: quinine is better than bloodletting. I need to know more about it; you know how interested I am in herbal medicine. Can't believe Cuadrillero pulled in his claws long enough for you to escape so soon—" Although Leopoldo was whispering, Plácido rapped on his music stand with a pointed look at us both. "Let's talk after dinner," Leopoldo said quickly, and I nodded.

We rehearsed until dinnertime.

Leopoldo, that slithering serpent, lost no time in coming to my cell. "I want to know everything at once, don Ygnacio," he said. His tone was breezy as he swung around and sat, uninvited, on my bed. Everything about his attitude proclaimed we were the best of friends; that I had no reason to suspect him. Did he truly believe that, or rather did he think he could put to rest any doubts I might have? I decided it must be the latter.

"Everything at once? Unfortunately, not being God, I can't impart all knowledge to you in one blinding insight, Father Leopoldo, so choose, please. What would you like to hear first?"

"About the bishop. How *did* he know you were at my place?"

"He answered that for you, Leopoldo. Ciudad Rodrigo is a small city. Anyone could have seen the coach arrive and me being carried inside the house."

"Not good enough, don Ygnacio. It was dark, and you're not known in the city. Someone could have reported seeing *a man* being carried into the Casa Cerralbo, but not *which man*. So, how did he know?"

I spread my hands and shrugged. "Beyond what he used as his reason, I can't guess the answer to your question, Father Leopoldo. I accepted his explanation, and therefore didn't press him any further." Although my reply made me *feel 'Jesuitical,'* I truly could not tell him without destroying Josefina's life and livelihood.

Leopoldo fixed me with a speculative stare for a long moment before shifting to his next question. "Well, then, tell me how he treated you. He must have wanted you for some purpose. What was it?"

It was my turn to stare. The presumptive way he posed the question, almost a demand, implied that I was now supposedly to report to him. I thought quickly, and memories of my first meeting with the bishop supplied a way to stifle his pointed questions.

"Let's assume for the moment that the bishop wanted to do 'business' of some kind with me. Let's pretend for the moment that the subject was the gold of Sonora, and that I really do know where it's hidden. You'll remember that this very topic was circulated about La Caridad when I first came here. Ah, the gold of Sonora. Surely the Jesuits must know where it is. Surely, they must have hoarded away treasures for their own uses.

"Further, pretend I actually do have a hoard stashed away, that I might use to buy my freedom. Now let us say the bishop wanted to get his hands on that gold."

I watched Leopoldo's eyes as I spoke, quite certain he hadn't considered gold as a possible reason for the bishop's interest, but he showed no surprise.

"That being the case, Father Leopoldo, would I tell you about it? Would you have a right to ask me what we were negotiating about?"

"I could ask you...but you wouldn't have to answer, of course. As for my having a 'right' to ask, I suppose I'd have no more right than you would in asking me similar questions. Let's drop that subject and return to the earlier question. How did he treat you?"

"I'll tell you that, and I'll even answer your other question, what he wanted of me, in due course. I merely wanted you to know you were going a bit far...presuming too much. Don Cayetano treated me like an honored guest— almost. First of all, he rescued me from your tender mercies, Father. You were forcing Doctor Santoro and his knife on me against my desperate protests, and were urging him to pour your sedative down my throat. God only knows what you'd put into that. I knew another bloodletting would fatally weaken me. The bishop saved my life. What *was* in that sedative?"

"Laudanum. Extract of opium, don Ygnacio."

"Ah. That alone would've knocked me out for a week, more than likely.

To go on, don Cayetano and Father Ybarra hauled me upstairs at the Episcopal Palace and made me comfortable in a guestroom. The following day, a courier came back from Salamanca with quinine, again a life saver. I started dosing myself immediately, and by the third day was able to join them for an exquisite dinner, with superb wines from Robledillo. Those wines probably came from the Cerralbo vineyards, especially since Miguel Ybarra's brother is your winegrower. At least, that's what Eugenio told me. Isn't that right?"

My own words had created an opportunity for me to gain information, and I seized upon it. Leopoldo took the bait.

"The bishop's wines...yes, they're probably from my vineyards, as you say. But Ybarra's family connection is broken now."

"What do you mean, Father Leopoldo?"

"José María Ybarra disappeared. Left the spring labor half done, and just vanished."

I felt an inward surge of triumph. I had the solution to the murder attempt. I kept my face immobile, only raising my eyebrows a fraction.

"How odd. When did he leave?"

"As near as I can make out, sometime in early February. Around the time of that attempt on my life."

"Any connection?"

Leopoldo hesitated before answering, his eyes narrowing slightly. He'd considered the possibility before. "Could be. I really can't say, don Ygnacio. But we're off our subject. You were telling me how the bishop treated you."

"So I was. Yes. Food...wine...and a magical violin. A splendid thing, a Guarnerius—and he let me play it. That was wonderful."

Leopoldo's smile became a sarcastic smirk. "What *wonderful* Christian charity, don Ygnacio. You remember how he complemented me on the same thing—Christian charity—how fine it was that I was caring for 'this destitute man,' namely you. My *imitatio Christi* must have inspired him."

"That must have been it, yes. Of course he was treating me like a celebrity for a purpose. As you said, it's doubtful the bishop ever does anything without expecting a return for it. This time he asked, nay, he *commanded* me to spy on Dom Gregorio and all of the monks here, and report every detail back to him."

"And?"

"And I refused. That's all. He was not pleased. He brought me back here this morning and staged a little farce before an audience consisting of Dom Gregorio, Brother Mateo and some of our choir. In it I was portrayed as Cayetano's beloved crony. The members of the audience believed I'd sold them and the monastery out."

"Hmmm. Yes, so I heard. Meanwhile you've managed to convince Dom Gregorio and a couple of others, notably Father Plácido, that you're loyal and true. Most are unconvinced. I'm afraid I'm still on the fence, but that doesn't mean I'm not glad to see you back. You're still my friend, don Ygnacio."

"Thank you, Father Leopoldo, that's most reassuring." A tinge of irony colored my words. "Now, I have some questions for you, too—"

Brother Porfirio stuck his head into the cell at that moment, pointedly ignoring me. "Father Leopoldo, Dom Gregorio wants to talk to you, right away."

"Well, don Ygnacio, those questions of yours will have to wait for another day, it seems, and so will mine about quinine. Thanks for a most interesting interlude." He turned at the door and gave me an overly cheery wave, leaving me feeling as though I'd just been through another interrogation by the Royal Inquisitors.

One of my questions was answered. Leopoldo and his demands must have posed enough of a threat to the bishop's interests that Miguel Ybarra had moved to protect him. His brother José María could have mingled with the crowd at the reception in Robledillo, or he could have talked to the grooms saddling our horses. The details were easy to imagine. I wondered if his dead body would turn up one day soon somewhere in Portugal. Murder was contagious, it seemed.

୨୦୦୫

Father Plácido worked us hard, correcting every flaw, calling choir members to task individually before their peers for small, habitual mistakes. I was no exception. He insisted our entrances be clean and full-voiced, all *tempi* correct and consistent.

We were crammed into four coaches and transported to Ciudad Rodrigo early on Trinity Sunday evening. The concert was to be held at eight. Members of the congregation expected to enjoy celebratory dinners afterwards in fine restaurants around the Plaza Mayor, or in their homes. We choir members were held in our coaches outside the cathedral until the bishop, priests, and acolytes had begun to process inside. Then we followed them in, avoiding any direct contact with the congregation.

Nonetheless, I noticed many of the monks ahead of me smiling and making near-invisible signs to loved ones in the pews as they approached the choir stall.

As I passed through the door, Brother Eugenio touched me on the arm. "Keep an eye on Father Leopoldo. I overheard something suspicious."

He whispered his message so rapidly it was almost unintelligible, then stepped back so I'd not be seen holding up the procession. I continued walking, craning my neck to see where Eugenio had gone, but he'd melted back among the monks following me, and made no further contact of any sort.

We were nearing the choir stall when I saw Clara. Leopoldo was in his usual place in front of me, with Metodio behind. She gave her brother and me a tiny wave, and I smiled back.

The unfamiliar choir stall surrounded us with carved walnut walls, cutting us off from the many loved ones outside, unlike the open loft at La Caridad. We found our seats and waited for our part to begin. Although this was not the formal Mass for Most Holy Trinity Sunday, already celebrated that morning, Bishop Cuadrillero spoke to the congregation, before our concert began, on the mystery of the triune Godhead and the significance of the Mass we were to sing, *In Viam Pacis*.

Sound quality in the Catedral de Santa María was quite different from Nuestra Señora de la Caridad. Despite the cathedral's greater floor space, our voices sounded fuller, more powerful, and the reverberation—not quite an echo—enhanced rather than detracted from our intertwining harmonies. The massive organ accompaniment was emotionally overwhelming.

We gave the performance every ounce of our effort. Father Plácido received the bishop's congratulations on behalf of us all, and don Cayetano then gave the congregation permission to show its appreciation. Long and loud applause and stamping of feet reverberated throughout the cathedral. I was swept away by the emotion of the moment, but not for long.

I was standing among my fellow singers in the choir stall when, to my embarrassment, the bishop came to the stall gate and beckoned me outside to consult with him.

His narrowed eyes held a mischievous glint. "How are you doing, don Ygnacio? You certainly found the energy to sing like an angel. I could make out your voice above the others in the baritone section." Then, without pausing for breath, "Any new information for me, my friend?"

"Your Grace! How could I possibly have news for you? Nearly everyone in the monastery believes I'm working for you. Do you think they'd trust me with anything worth the telling? What news do you have for me, though? From Bernardo Middendorff, for example?"

The bishop's quizzical look broadened into a smile. "You're a slippery fellow, don Ygnacio, a man after my own heart. No news lately, my friend, but I'll get word to you as soon as I know something. Don't forget, my offer is still open. Now, if you'll excuse me, I need to speak to a mutual friend. You're not my only resource out there at La Caridad, you know."

He made a ponderous turnabout and walked to the side of the sanctuary, where a dark figure was standing in the shadows next to a column. Who was it? I was about to move closer, when someone laid a hand on my arm: Clara.

"Ygnacio! That came close to being the most beautiful singing I've ever heard, certainly from the monks at La Caridad. Did you inspire them?"

"Not at all, Clara, our success is entirely due to Father Plácido's efforts. The man is a genius in the musical realm, and in leading and shaping a choir. Without his iron discipline, we'd never have reached such a stage of proficiency."

"You mean perfection. Is there any way you can get away and come to dinner at our house tonight? My brother will be there and—"

"Speaking of your brother, where did he go? He was here just a moment ago, and now I don't see him in the choir stall."

She made a rapid visual inventory of the monks standing nearby, then began looking around the nave, her expression increasingly grave. Her gaze fell upon Bishop Cuadrillero, and her eyes narrowed. I saw her looking beyond the bishop, to the shadowy figure. Suddenly she withdrew her hand from my arm and launched herself across the nave at a near-run, her skirts gathered in a bunch in one hand.

When she reached the two men, I heard her clear voice across the nave. "Leopoldo! I've known for months you had it, but didn't understand until this moment what you were doing with it. I'm sorry, don Cayetano, but this can't go any further." She reached toward the dark figure and snatched something, turning and running back. I got a glance from her as she passed, teeth locked, with a determined look on her face. A jerk of her head toward the cathedral entrance told me she wanted me to follow. In disbelief, I saw she was clutching a stained and yellowed cylinder of vellum.

Cuadrillero bellowed something unintelligible and clumsily ran after her, hand outstretched, but took only a few lumbering steps before stopping short. Leopoldo collided with him, paused for a word of apology, then sidled past. He snatched up his own skirts in order to run unimpeded, but Clara was already dashing toward the front of the church.

Turning just once in her flight, her taunting expression seemed to say, "Catch me if you can."

Chapter XVI

Dangerous Disentaglement

Leopoldo charged past me without a glance my way. He pelted straight down the center aisle after Clara, trying to overtake her. I, too, began the chase, darting around the choir stall and mumbling apologies as I dodged congregation members blocking the aisle, conversing in knots of three or four.

Clara glanced back once more as she cleared the front entrance. Leopoldo's best efforts were in vain; she was still well ahead. I followed, glancing back to see Don Cayetano trudging after us, shaking his head and mouthing something. From the expression on his face, it was a stream of imprecations, calling down divine wrath upon interfering women.

I gathered my skirts as Leopoldo had done and ran the length of the nave. Outside the entrance, I saw Leopoldo disappear around a corner. I followed. He'd gone through a small door, one requiring me to stoop. In I went, stopping at the base of a dark, tightly wound staircase leading upward. It had to be the way into the tower, to those sights the bishop wanted me to see.

I dashed ahead, hearing noises above, isolated words and the pounding of feet on stone. Not yet fully recovered, I was out of breath and panting. My skirts made the climb even more demanding, forcing me to stop halfway up. I was vaguely aware of an airy chamber there, with three large openings, but I pressed on after a single deep breath.

With pounding heart and searing lungs, I neared the bell loft, the topmost floor. Four steps remaining! Tools were lying about, some on the stairs. A hammer and mallet, then a chisel and crowbar. Torches set in holders lit dark corners, as though the repairman had just left and would soon return. Perhaps he'd listened to the concert.

No time! I vaulted over the final step and rounded the corner, drawing up sharply. There, in the main chamber, brother and sister stood in tense confrontation.

Clara's back was to the tower wall, a guttering torch above her left shoulder. To her right was one of the tall, twin-arched windows with its bell hanging above. A guard railing reached nearly to her waist.

She held the yellowed roll of vellum at arm's length, close to the flame. It was smeared with dark blotches. Gelasio's blood? Leopoldo, poised to leap at her, was snarling his words.

"...it back right now, Clara Eugenia! I won't tolerate your interference. You only *think* you understand, but you don't. It's the only way we can save the farms. Now hand it back!"

Her voice became shrill. "What do you mean, save the farms? What have you *done*, for God's sake?"

Instinctively I took a step toward them, then another. Leopoldo's stance was more than threatening. Would he harm her? He was raging, ready to strike. "Give me that charter, Clara! The bishop agreed. He'll waive the tithes on our property for that trifle you're holding. With that much relief, I can save our lands."

"WHAT HAVE YOU DONE?"

"What have I *done*? How can you be so unaware of our family business? I've spent a king's ransom on my beautiful tulip bulbs and exotic plants, little sister, that's what I've done. Last year's profits, this year's and the next. I've already developed new herbal medicines, remedies that could make a fortune for the family, but that's not all. I plan to propagate and sell tulip bulbs."

"Oh, no. Oh, Poldo, you can't mean that. All this is about *tulips?*"

"You think only that tulips are my weakness, that I collect them for their sheer beauty. No, sister, no. Dutch importers charge up to fifty ducats each or more for the choicest bulbs. I'll sell my own, in competition with them, for another fortune. I'm doing it for us, but it takes time and labor...and money. Now GIVE ME THE CHARTER! I've worked for months to get the bishop to agree to this exchange. Otherwise, I can't even pay our immediate debts. Now do you understand?"

"We'll find a way, Leopoldo."

"I already *found* the way." He lunged at her, but she moved even faster, jumping to the left. She touched the charter to the flame, and the ancient vellum caught at once, burning brighter than any torch. It flared in the twilight, casting light on Leopoldo's fury and disbelief.

I'd almost reached them when he grabbed her wrist and snatched at the blazing document, but too late! She switched it to her other hand and tossed it, blazing and crackling, through the window opening.

Shoulder to shoulder, Leopoldo and I both leaned out the window, each gripping the guard railing. The vellum roll fell faster than parchment, but not like a stone. It seemed to float on the flames, fluttering like some brilliant butterfly. Finally it settled on the cobblestones, burning for a few more seconds before dwindling to a red, twisted remnant.

Then it was gone, a black spot on the lighter stones.

A great burning hand clutched my heart, crushing and twisting it the same way, leaving no more than a blackened, sooty pit where my hopes once lived.

The loss of the charter was a catastrophe for the monastery, whose survival I had identified with my own. Nothing remained to stop Bishop Cuadrillero's seizure of its supporting villages and lands. It might take many months, but the place was doomed, and my friend Dom Gregorio with it. In a way, he could well become the final victim at La Caridad.

I continued staring down, stunned. Leopoldo turned away and stood with his hands over his face. "We're lost!" he moaned between his fingers. He was thinking only of himself.

I snapped about, suddenly angry. "Father Leopoldo!"

Startled, he jerked his hands down. Even though I'd stood beside him, he'd not registered my presence until that moment.

"You here, Ygnacio? This is a disaster!" His voice was flat, toneless.

"Yes, Leopoldo, a disaster of your own making. Look at what you've done! You singlehandedly undercut the morale at La Caridad and now destroyed the monastery." He shrank back. "Along the way, you destroyed two brothers. You *killed* to obtain that charter! You murdered Gelasio and Tomás!"

His shoulders jerked as if I had slapped him, and his hands again covered his face. Suddenly they dropped, balled into fists. "No, damn you, Ygnacio, I'm no murderer! I killed no one!"

I shook my own fist in his face. "Murder, compounded now by lies! You got Tomás to steal the charter, but Gelasio discovered your double-dealing. He'd have denounced you. You had to kill him, and later Tomás, who knew too much. All rooted in greed...*your* greed."

"NO! No, it wasn't like that! You're not as clever as you think, Jesuit."

"Tell that to the hangman. Don't you think you'd better confess first?"

"The Devil take you, Ygnacio! My motives were honorable. I had to do what I did to save our family's reputation and property."

"Honorable?" I moved a step closer. "A thief and a murderer, honorable?"

He recoiled, moving nearer Clara. "Let's hear about those twisted motives of yours. It may help your cause when I denounce you to Dom Gregorio."

"Denounce me for a thief if you must, Ygnacio, but I'm no murderer."

"Prove it! Your story is a string of lies. Anyone as underhanded and hypocritical as you are will have a hard time convincing anyone otherwise."

He glanced at Clara, who held out a pleading hand to me. "He's not capable of killing, don Ygnacio! Please! I'm sure he's not lying about that."

"Let *him* convince me, then. Well, Leopoldo?"

"All right! All right, you minion of Satan! If you'll listen, I *will* convince you. I don't deny my part in stealing the charter, but it was in the best of causes—my family honor, the celebrated name of Cerralbo."

"I'm listening. Go on, Leopoldo."

"Then believe what I'm about to tell you now!" His unclenched fists revealed hands shaking with emotion. He drew a ragged breath and, after organizing his thoughts, began on a calmer note. "Months ago when this quarrel began with Ciudad Rodrigo, Gelasio thought the bishop, the diocese, had a right to Robledillo. Dom Gregorio told me, around the same time, about the charter and its significance. This much was clear: whoever held the charter held power over the monastery and its possessions, as well as over the bishop and his material interests in the city.

"The family Cerralbo has diminished over the last century. I saw a way to restore it. I'd sell the charter to the bishop in exchange for a pledge in writing from His Grace."

I pounced on the word. "Pledge? What pledge, Leopoldo?" Clara echoed my words. Our combined onslaught jarred him, and he spoke quicker.

"That, beginning with me, our family be granted supreme secular authority over Robledillo and over all the lands we still possess. In addition, that I be named to a seat on the City Council of Ciudad Rodrigo with a vote in all decisions that have to do with real estate and agricultural produce. The bishop could easily arrange something like that with the Council; he has enough power and influence. No more tithes on our properties. These conditions would have allowed me to pay my debts and start marketing my herbal medicines. I want to do things that benefit people, Ygnacio, not just my family. And make money while doing it. Dom Gregorio even admitted his doubts the charter could protect the monastery for long. Better it were put to use this way."

Leopoldo's ambition and audacity amazed me. My anger gave way to cold reason.

"I can see why His Grace was dragging his feet. You'd have left the monastery, of course."

"Of course, but not the priesthood." He struck a boastful pose. "With influence like that, I would have made rapid advances in the hierarchy."

"And His Grace agreed to your terms?"

"He agreed to the major conditions. He was to give me an agreement in writing tonight."

I could not believe the wily Cuadrillero could have made such concessions without having devised a plan to counter Leopoldo's moves. Surely, there was more to the story than Clara and I were hearing. My mind turned to the charter.

"How did you get the charter in the first place?"

"The abbot showed me where he kept it. I persuaded Gelasio to steal it, telling him I was on the bishop's side."

"And Tomás?"

"Gelasio refused to search the abbot's quarters himself." Leopoldo barked a broken sort of laugh, a bitter note. "He agreed to steal, but was too honorable to break in and do it himself. He wasn't above asking his friend to do it for him, though. Tomás was part-time janitor and clever with locks."

"Why did Tomás agree?"

"You weren't there long enough to know, but it was common knowledge. Tomás loved Gelasio—too much—clung close to him when he could, and would do anything for him."

Leopoldo was breathing easier; he'd recovered his *sang-froid*, but it would do him no good. I had him. He was relaxed, unwary, caught up in his narration. He'd tell me now. "But after the charter was stolen, Gelasio had second thoughts, didn't he? What gave your game away to him? In the end, you had to kill him to get the charter. Am I right?"

His shoulders slumped. "Damn you, Ygnacio! If he'd crossed me, yes, I might have killed him, but he didn't. Didn't get the chance. You want to know what happened? This is what really happened, and since I'm the only witness, you can believe me or not; it's your choice. All right! A few monks knew about my debts and they must have talked to Gelasio. He was a smart man. He figured I wanted to use the charter for my own advantage. Anyway, we'd already agreed to meet in the bell loft that morning, at two, and he didn't change the arrangement."

"So?"

"So, I climbed the ladder at precisely two that morning and everything was silent. The bell loft was lit by a candle stuck to the bench...and nobody was there."

"A candle? How could that be, Leopoldo? Somebody had to put it there."

"I was far enough up the ladder to see splashes of blood in the middle of the room. They looked black, but I knew what they were. I froze and looked all around that chamber, but could see or hear no one."

He paused. In spite of myself, I was gripped by the eerie suspense of the moment. Clara, standing spellbound, swallowed hard. "What did you do then, Poldo?"

He gave her a dull glance. "I finished going up the ladder and went to the windows. He was down on the cobblestones below the north one, just a black form. No movement."

"So, you searched the bell loft for the charter, then went down to him," I prompted.

"Yes. I thought for sure the killer had taken it, but I needed to search Gelasio's body to be certain. First, I took a candle and lit it from the vigil light on the altar because it was so dark outside. Then I went out there. I was deathly afraid the murderer would see me and know I was...." He tapered off, as if reliving the experience.

"That much is understandable. Did you search his body? What did you find?"

"That the charter was...that he'd been thrown out the window with the charter still tucked in his belt. There was no doubt at all that he was dead. The charter was bloody—blood all over his chest and brains oozing out of his crushed skull. My handkerchief got bloody wiping the charter as best I could. I tucked the roll in my own belt, left Gelasio where he was and rushed out to the water tank. I had to get that blood off my hands. I blamed myself as if I'd killed him, because he'd never have gone up there if it weren't for me. And I was terrified the killer would get me, too."

"It was your handkerchief that tore while you were washing up at the tank."

"Yes. I was about to wet it when a corner got caught on a sharp edge between two rocks. I jerked it loose—I was in such a hurry by then—and it tore. I don't know what happened to the fragment."

"I found it later that morning, Leopoldo, still covered with Gelasio's blood. And what about Tomás?"

"I swear to God I know nothing about that. Whoever killed Gelasio killed the one who loved him, too. But I...I had no reason to kill poor Tomás."

"And after Gelasio's murder, you went right on with your plan to exchange that bloody document for favors from the bishop?"

Leopoldo's words were cold. "Our debts weren't buried with him, Ygnacio."

Clara's face showed a mixture of dismay and anger. She planted herself directly in front of Leopoldo, taking over my role as interrogator.

"I'm beginning to understand why you directed me to seduce don Ygnacio. You wanted me to compromise him so you could use him in your plan. And you drugged Dom Gregorio, as well. You might as well tell it all, Poldo."

He glanced longingly at the window where she'd thrown the charter, and sighed, shaking his head slowly.

"Yes, you're right. The charter's gone. Everything's gone." For a moment he hung his head, then continued. "Ygnacio already had amazing influence with the abbot, you see. I knew the bishop was interested in Jesuits, and therefore in him as well. If you could charm Ygnacio, get him to compromise himself as you said, I could blackmail him and he could influence both men. I was angry when I saw he resisted you. You don't often fail...Clara Eugenia."

"I'd never tried such a thing before...Leopoldo *María*." Her eyes flashed. "Only this once...and only then because I wanted to. It wasn't for you I did it."

Leopoldo stared at her in puzzlement, but said nothing.

"One thing remains," I stated, "the murderer's identity. You've explained everything else. Any ideas?"

"None. The killer's still with us, it seems." His tone was flat and disinterested, as if he no longer cared. "But come, Clara. Support me in this, our last hope. I must talk to don Cayetano. Together, perhaps we can persuade him at least to waive the tithes on our property, even without the charter. After all, without the charter, Dom Gregorio's hopes of saving the monastery have been dashed. The bishop has both of us to thank for that."

Clara hesitated. "I'll come with you, Leopoldo, but only for the sake of our reputation and our property. You've behaved despicably, and I'm ashamed to be associated with you."

He looked at her strangely for a moment, then turned toward the stairs. She gave me a slight shrug and the ghost of a smile that begged for my understanding. I did understand; she saw it in my eyes and my manner.

Then she turned and followed her brother, leaving me with a leaden feeling in my chest. I elected to stay, mulling over the dizzying events of the past hour. Leopoldo's tragic ambition had begun a chain of events resulting in two, nearly three, deaths. Thanks to the actions of just two people, sister and brother, the monastery would now wither away. My own future was as cloudy as ever.

Dom Gregorio had already written the Royal Council about my 'crime' in Cádiz. He'd requested information on the terms of my imprisonment, so I expected my limited freedom to be curtailed drastically in my near future.

As for the mysteries at the monastery, yes, nearly everything was explained *except* the murders. I struck my thigh with a fist in frustration. A fine investigator I'd turned out to be. I was no further along solving these killings than any brother in the monastery. I'd been blinded by my suspicions of Leopoldo, the obvious suspect. And now?

No answer came to me.

I took a deep breath and began to pace, avoiding the wooden frame covering a gaping hole in the floor. A pile of loose stones and a chisel told me that was the site of the repairs. The workman had left the frame unattached.

Zephyrs of cooler air were interspersed with warm against my face as the night air moved in. I paused, lost in my thoughts, and gazed down at Ciudad Rodrigo from each of the twin windows. The huge bells hung silently above, not unlike the tower at La Caridad. Only the storks were missing.

Don Cayetano was right, it was a breathtaking view. Pinpoints of light were beginning to shine from the houses, and the city panorama became more beautiful by the minute. Earlier clouds had moved away and the jumble of tiled roofs was bathed in moonlight. In the distance rose the silvered silhouette of the castle, and, to the left, the bell tower on the Church of San Isidro. Everything seemed tranquil, as if all human cares had been borne away on the wings of night.

The utter stillness of my reverie was broken by the sound of heavy and deliberate footsteps on the stairs. Could it be Bishop Cuadrillero? Perhaps he'd accepted the bargain with the Cerralbos and was coming up to show me points of interest in the moonlight.

But no, the voice with its familiar refrain was not Cayetano's.

"Damnable stairs! Bane of my existence!" A pause for heavy breathing, then, "Don Ygnacio! Are you still up here?"

"Father Plácido? What possessed you to climb all those stairs?" I went to meet him, glad of his company. "The Mass was exquisite, Plácido! Everyone was in awe. But what are you doing up here? You should be at the bishop's reception at the Episcopal Palace."

"I was there for a while, Ygnacio," he paused again, still gasping for breath, "and I'll go back in a bit. They'll never notice I was gone; there are so many people. I needed to find you, though."

The heavy arm he laid across my shoulders was damp, and he reeked of perspiration—from his efforts while conducting the Mass, I supposed, and from the climb up into the tower. I tried to move to get some space between us, but he clutched me against his side for a moment, then released me and went to the window, leaned on the railing, looking first downward and then out at the city. A distant alarm bell was clanging inside my head. Why had he needed to find *me*? What was the meaning of that rough embrace just now?

"Did my fellow choir members get off all right?" I asked.

"Yes. The coaches left right after the concert was over. The brothers seemed miffed that you had the privilege of staying. Metodio was telling everyone you were with the bishop, but Porfirio heard doña Clara invite you to the Cerralbo house for dinner."

"Then how did you know I was up here?" I leaned on the railing beside him.

"Doña Clara, in passing, told me where you were. She and her brother were just arriving at the bishop's reception."

His face was pasty pale in the moonlight as I faced him. "I still don't understand, Father Plácido. What was so important that you had to climb all those stairs to talk to me? I was about to come down."

"I had to clear the air, don Ygnacio. You see, it looks to me as though you've betrayed our Mother House to the bishop."

"*What?*" I straightened abruptly, drawing in my breath, staring in disbelief at his hulking form. "What on *earth* made you think such a thing, Plácido?"

"You remember how you came back in the bishop's coach that day, and he helped you down and embraced you like a brother? Even Dom Gregorio thought you'd betrayed us."

"Of course I remember," I snapped, "and that whole episode was painful. It was a farce, an act to make Dom Gregorio distrust me. Just what are you getting at?"

"Patience, Ygnacio! Give me a moment," he said in a quiet voice. "I'll get to it. You invited Eugenio and me into your cell and then told us how much you owed the bishop, how he'd saved your life twice, among other kindnesses. I said to you then that he had a right to ask a favor of you after all that."

"I remember. And I hope *you* remember that I agreed with you and said the bishop thought the same way you did—that I owed him a favor. He did ask me to spy on the abbot and on all of you. I refused."

"So you say." Plácido looked increasingly glum, almost mournful.

I debated how best to convince him. "Would it make a difference if I told you the charter has been destroyed? I fear that nothing any of us does will save La Caridad now." I led him to the north window and pointed down at the blackened remnant of the charter, still visible against the light gray cobblestones.

He rubbed his forehead as if his head ached, then continued in a hollow tone. "I see it. I knew already. Doña Clara told me at the reception before I left. She and Leopoldo had just come in, looking disheveled and sort of stunned. I asked her where you three had run to, and she told me the tower. Leopoldo put a hand on her arm and went on over to talk to the bishop. She motioned that she was coming, but she whispered to me, 'You know about the charter, Father Plácido? Well, I just burned it.' I couldn't quite believe that. One reason I came up here was to see if it were true."

"True enough, Father Plácido. I saw it happen, and I still couldn't believe she did it, but you say she thought you knew about the charter? *Do* you?"

He took a deep breath, straightened and faced me, pompously thrusting his chin forward.

"I-I-I know more than anyone in La Caridad, don Ygnacio. Not that it matters now." He sniffed.

Something in his words and manner was off key, as if his mind were out of balance, but I couldn't put a finger on it. At any rate, I had nothing to lose by trying to extract more information from him. Perhaps that superior knowledge he seemed so proud of could lead me to the real killer at last.

"Ah, yes, I should have guessed. Father Plácido, the spider at the center of the web. As choirmaster, you heard all the gossip, perhaps overheard private conversations. You must have known Leopoldo was conspiring with Gelasio and Tomás to steal the charter for the bishop."

He surprised me with a sudden smile. "Yes, don Ygnacio, I overheard enough to know that Gelasio was going to steal the charter with Tomás' help, and that he was going to give it to someone, but I didn't yet know who."

"Well...how did you find out?"

He returned to his dolorous mood. "By biding my time and watching. I lay in wait for Gelasio to go to his clandestine meeting on the night the charter was to change hands, and once he was in the bell loft I climbed that cursed ladder and confronted him. I demanded that he hand over the charter. My only purpose was, and is, to save Our Lady of Charity. This is a war against the forces of evil that would destroy her, you see, Ygnacio. Our Lady, our monastery, is our Mother, just as Metodio is fond of saying."

A sudden chill came over me. Plácido had been in that loft, with Gelasio! I had to tread carefully now. Unless I was badly misinterpreting, Plácido was on the verge of confessing to murdering Gelasio. His mood swings were already an indication of someone desperately troubled.

"And Gelasio refused?"

"He did, and he cursed me, don Ygnacio, he cursed me! Bishop Cuadrillero, not our beloved Dom Gregorio, was his superior, that's what he said." Plácido's eyes went out of focus, looking through me. "I fear...I fear I lost my temper and struck him across the face."

The big man sniffed again. Was he about to cry?

"His nose started bleeding a real stream. Blood spattered on the floor. I must have hit him harder than I thought. I snatched at the charter that was tucked in his belt, but he was too quick, Ygnacio, too quick. He dodged me, went to the window and climbed up on the sill. I lunged for him as he was crouching there, and he scooted backwards. I think he intended to swing down to a ledge or something, but his hand was bloody from his nose, and he slipped. He gave a short cry. I have nightmares about the noise his body made hitting the cobblestones. I can't describe it. Ghastly!"

I recalled the bloody smear on the window ledge. "If he fell that way, then no one murdered him. If it had been anywhere else but that loft...."

"That's right, so I didn't have to confess that, thank God. I started down the ladder to go see if he was dead, and to take the charter, when I heard someone coming—the person he was supposed to meet. I shrank back into the darkest corner of that antechamber, farthest from the foot of the ladder, and stayed perfectly still. The monk coming in had his cowl over his head, and I couldn't be sure, but I thought it was Leopoldo from his general shape. Hard to tell in the dark."

"He must have been preoccupied or he'd have seen you."

"Yes. I heard him exclaim, then he called out Gelasio's name even before he got to the top of the ladder. He'd seen the blood. Then he went on up and started searching the chamber above me. I slipped out and hid in an alcove just outside in the upper cloister." Plácido sighed and swallowed hard.

"Why didn't you go down at once and get the charter? If you had, you could have saved La Caridad. That's what you wanted to do."

"Everything happened so quickly. I knew Leopoldo, if it were he, would look down from the same window and possibly see me. What would I be doing out at that hour? I had no reason, you see. He came down the ladder soon enough and ran down the stairs. I followed him and watched him from the side door. He'd left it open."

The side door! The eavesdropper had been lurking there, too, listening to Metodio and me. Another small mystery solved. "That's where you heard Metodio tell me Tomás stole the charter?"

He fitted his body into the window opening beside me. I could feel his belly shake as he chuckled. "That's right, Ygnacio. How clever you are."

His sudden mirth turned immediately to grief, and he covered his face with one meaty hand. Another change of mood! Now the alarms clanged louder. I propped my elbows on the railing once again, looking out over Ciudad Rodrigo, but acutely aware of his pressure against me. The mystery was all coming together at last, but his physical familiarity frightened me.

If I moved away, I'd break the fragile spiritual contact just achieved, but moving away gracefully seemed impossible right then. Perhaps, I thought, I was doing my friend some good just by allowing him to unburden his secret. Still….

I looked down at the moonlit cobblestones below, and the image of Gelasio's crushed skull and broken body superimposed itself there, then was replaced by another image, that of a taller, emaciated figure. Its blonde-gray hair was matted with blood and brains and the blue eyes were open, contemplating the sky. Ygnacio Pfefferkorn!

I shook my head, and the illusion disappeared. I realized he was waiting for me to respond. "I never suspected you were the one listening, Plácido. How did you disappear so fast that night?"

Another chuckle. His hand came down, and he was smiling. "I dropped my cloak in the archway to delay you, and sure enough, you tripped on it and fell. That gave me a good head start. I never went into the church at all. I opened the door, then hid behind it. It threatened to close on its own, so I held it for you, don Ygnacio. You went right inside, as I knew you would. Once you were in there, I simply walked away."

"Quick thinking! I thought you'd evaporated, or that there was a secret door somewhere. But what about Tomás? Surely, his death was not an accident, too."

Did I feel him wedging me even more tightly? He paused, seeming to debate whether to take a plunge. His answer came out slowly.

"I saw you chasing him after Mass the next day, then talking to him in the plaza. He knew I was there somewhere, watching, but he didn't see me. From his gestures, I could tell he was putting you off, probably telling you he'd talk to you later." He turned his face to me, suddenly sinister. "I had to prevent that."

"Why? What would make him think you were any sort of danger to him? And why did you think he was a danger to you?" He hadn't moved, but a subtle shift of his midsection had me pinned against the window frame.

"Tomás was not a stupid man, either. He knew how fiercely pro-La Caridad I was. I'd expressed my feelings in his presence once too often. He knew I was watching him in particular...and I had plenty of information coming through the choir monks, a tidbit here, another bit there. He either feared that I'd killed his beloved Gelasio, and would kill him too, or that I'd denounce him to the one who did. He'd have told you all that, and you'd have been much closer to solving the mystery of Gelasio's death."

The frightening chill struck me again. This time I knew I'd have to move away, and quickly, but he had me wedged so tightly in place I could barely move my arms. I calmed my mind, remembering that first night at the mission in Sonora. Surely the danger of that night was far worse than this. Gently, I assumed the role of confessor, proceeding by instinct.

"So it is true, my son, that you found it necessary to silence Tomás. How did you do it?"

"I just told you, don Ygnacio, mine is a war against those evil forces that would destroy Our Lady of Charity. In a war, God forgives soldiers who kill to defend the right and the good."

"You know, Father Plácido, you'll have to confess all this formally, or your soul is bound for the fires of Hell."

His next remark was ominous, delivered with a broad smile.

"Confessing to you, Father, would be wasted effort. I'd have to confess again anyway...but I'll tell you, since you asked." He twisted then, placing a heavy arm across my shoulders. "I've been friends with Father Leopoldo for years. I've always known that someday, somehow, knowing the most talented member of the Çerralbo family would come in handy. Contacts for concerts, contributions to the monastery. You never know. And I was interested in his study of herbs, and learned—oh, months ago—how easy it is to gather belladonna and make an extract. There's plenty of it growing among the weeds in our fields and gardens, thanks to our shortage of workers."

"Yes. I thought I smelled deadly nightshade on his breath. How did you—"

"Get the poison to poor Tomás?" He chucked my shoulder. "It was a simple matter, Ygnacio. I was one of several who left the refectory during the meal and came back to finish eating later. However, I was the only one who paused and refilled his wineglass. He didn't even notice, since I was squeezing his shoulder and talking to him at the time."

Plácido's face contorted. Was he about to weep? "I checked on him several hours later. His heart seemed to have stopped beating, but he was still warm, and he seemed so peaceful. Sweetly sleeping."

"But, your grief the next morning was so convincing."

"Yes. The monks had come in to sing matins and he wasn't there. They expected me to go check on him."

He paused, looking away. When he turned back to me, his face was wet with tears. "Besides, Ygnacio, I couldn't believe he really was gone. What I'd done seemed so much like a dream by then, don't you see? When I saw him there, a *thing*, a corpse, stiff and cold and gray with his mouth gaped open, I was horrified at my own doing."

With a shudder, he regained his composure and drew himself up. "Tomás was the first casualty of the war; Gelasio was an accident. I was weeping for Tomás, for myself as well, and asking God's forgiveness. I did love Tomás, don Ygnacio, just as I love you. But I was, I am, convinced his death was a necessary part of the war. Surely, God will understand."

I drew a long breath, outwardly calm but tensed nevertheless. "Father Plácido, help me with another detail, please. During my first bout of malaria, before you so kindly made this robe I'm wearing, right after you and Eugenio and the others carried me down to the chapter room, I was lying there shivering from chills when I looked up to see a hooded monk with a dagger standing over me. Any idea who that could have been?"

"Ah, Porfirio, of course! That was a time when Metodio was spouting the most grotesque slanders against you. Porfirio took all that quite seriously. He'd have killed you, but for your obvious piety. He couldn't fit that into the picture Metodio had drawn for him, so he came to me and I calmed him. I told him you were a good man, don Ygnacio, that I loved and trusted you." He tightened his arm across my shoulders in his characteristic way, but pressed against me with such force I panicked.

I tried to duck under that arm, to put space between us, but Plácido bent his elbow in a lightning move, pulling me against his chest and grabbing my shoulder.

I gasped. I was the sparrow, held in a fist, with its head poking out between fingers.

Plácido continued in a lighter voice, smiling insanely. "But I've come to believe I was wrong and Porfirio was right that night."

"*Why*, Plácido?" I cried out. "I've not betrayed the monastery. What makes you think I have?"

He was almost caressing me with his left arm and hand, yet holding me in an iron grip, such was his strength. No nightmare had ever been worse.

"I loved you, Ygnacio. I believed in you. This double game you're playing drives me *insane!*" With the word, a jerk of his right arm around my neck nearly lifted me off my feet. My senses swirled and lights danced in my vision.

"Your game is like Leopoldo's, only worse. At least he's trying to save his estate, but you? Oh, the bishop likes and respects you, yes. That was obvious when he brought you back to La Caridad, and it's obvious now. There's too much evidence against you, Ygnacio. Just a couple of hours ago he called you out of the choir stall for a private word with him. He asked you if you had *any more information* for him. I heard him say it! That was the capstone."

"Believe me, Plácido, I—"

"And then, you ran after doña Clara to snatch the charter away from her. You and Leopoldo, together. She burned it to keep it from the two of you, I'm sure, to keep you from handing it over to Cuadrillero."

He had me in such a way, facing the railing, that I had no point of leverage, nothing to grasp. I was pinned against his belly, clawing at his huge arms. Twice my feet were lifted from the stone floor, as if he were measuring the effort it would take to throw me off the tower.

"Plácido!" I wheezed," you've got to listen to me! I'm no traitor to La Caridad!"

But he was still talking, not listening. "I am the true guardian of the monastery, Ygnacio. I must live that Our Lady Mother of Charity might live. You know too much by now, and even if you weren't the traitor you are, you'd be an intolerable danger to me." He spent a moment tightening his arm against my throat, then cried out in anguish. "Why did you join them? I *believed* in you! I *loved* you!"

His voice broke and he took three gasping breaths. His next words were flat, a monotone devoid of feeling.

"They'll find you down below here in the morning, the victim of an unfortunate accident. Or, perhaps, they'll think you despaired of your life as prisoner and ended it all. Now, I've wasted quite enough time here with you, Ygnacio. Let us finish this quickly. I must be getting back to the reception."

The arm tightened once again against my Adam's apple and I choked, knowing I'd soon lose consciousness, knowing he'd crush my windpipe or my jugular veins. My strength was feeble compared to his, but I continued clawing and kicking. He had my feet off the floor! I felt myself being bent forward, over the railing.

Suddenly I heard a woman's voice, loud and shrill. "Ygnacio! Where are you?"

Clara! It was dark beneath the bells, and the guttered torch was no more than a feeble flame, all but out. She couldn't see us.

"Clara!" My voice was hoarse and strangled. "It's Plácido, he's...."

Plácido's grip loosened momentarily. With a single, violent twist, I spun inside his grasp and bit into the soft flesh of his underarm with every ounce of strength I could muster. He roared in pain, striking ineffectually at me with his left hand to knock me loose, and staggered two paces back from the window and its railing, dragging me with him. I felt, rather than saw, the blow Clara dealt to the back of his skull. He cried out again, both hands reaching for his head, and I released him as he staggered further backwards.

His heel caught on the edge of the wooden platform covering the earthquake damage. The impact shoved the wooden frame backwards, and he fell on it with his full weight.

It buckled, and he slid, screaming, into the blackness below.

I yanked one of the fresher torches off the wall and knelt at the edge of the hole, lowering the torch to arm's length and using my other hand as a reflector. The light was minimal, but enough to see him lying some twenty feet below us, across the stone balustrade of the staircase leading up into the tower. It appeared he'd fallen on his back across the stone.

His cry was one of agony. "Ygnacio, forgive me! Father, help me! *Confiteor!* I must confess…!"

I ran to the head of the stair and charged down, the torch flickering in my hand, recklessly disregarding the darkness and danger, and reached the wretched soul in time. "*In nomine Patris, et Filii, et Spiritu Sancti, Amen.* Just recite your Act of Contrition, Plácido, I already know the rest. Time is short!"

ഇരുട

As I pronounced the final words, "*Ego te absolvo in nomine…*" his head fell backwards and the color drained from his face.

"Is he in much pain, Ygnacio?" Clara called from the opening above.

I looked down at the still form, tears of forgiveness and sorrow blurring my vision.

"No," I answered. "No."

Author Bio

Born in the high desert country of New Mexico, Florence loved exploring the wilderness on foot and horseback. Those grandiose landscapes formed her sensibility. Hidden pockets of unexpected greenery tucked away near springs in folds of barren mountainsides spoke to her of gentleness and beauty in an otherwise harsh world. She published her first poem in a children's magazine shortly after she learned to read at age four; wrote her first 'novel' at age six, entitled Ywain, King of All Cats. She illustrated the 'book' herself.

Before settling in San Antonio, Texas, she traveled extensively as an army brat during World War II. With her husband the brilliant scholar and teacher, Kurt Weinberg, she worked and traveled in Canada, Germany, France, and Spain. After earning her PhD, she taught for twenty-two years at St. John Fisher College in Rochester, NY, and for ten at Trinity University in San Antonio. She published four scholarly books, many articles and book reviews, doing research in the U.S. and abroad.

When, after retiring in 1999, she was freed from academe to devote herself to writing fiction, she produced eight novels, ranging from fantasy to historical romance and mystery. Three are in print as well as one in press: a historical romance about the French Renaissance, published in France in French translation, and two historical mysteries, starring the eighteenth-century Jesuit missionary Fr. Ignaz (Ygnacio) Pfefferkorn, two set in the Sonora Desert and one in an ancient monastery in Spain.

Her favorite animals are horses—an intense love affair over many years—and cats, her constant companions. She enjoys music, traveling, hiking, biking, gardening, riding and swimming.

Historical Appendix

These historical facts lie behind the fiction of *The Storks of La Caridad*:

Ignaz Pfefferkorn (Don Ygnacio Pferkon) was born in Mannheim, Germany, in 1725. He joined the Society of Jesus at age seventeen and sailed from Cádiz as a missionary to the native peoples of New Spain (Mexico) on Christmas day, 1755. In addition to his vocation as priest and missionary, he was a talented naturalist and fine violinist, according to the report of fellow missionary and friend, Joseph Och, S. J.

Ignaz served for eleven years in three missions in the Sonora Desert: Atí (now Atil), Guevavi, and Cucurpe. He was arrested along with his fellow Jesuit missionaries by order of King Carlos III in 1767. Expelled under the most brutal conditions, he lived through the death march across Mexico and was among twenty-seven priests who survived out of the original fifty-one arrested in the Sonora region. Sent back to Spain on a prison ship, he arrived there in 1769 and was imprisoned for eight more years.

The king justified such treatment by stating through his spokesmen that Ignaz and the other Sonoran missionaries had extraordinary knowledge of the interior of the province of Sonora, and could betray information to Spain's enemies about the mineral wealth of the area. That was the official declaration. In plainer terms, Ignaz was interrogated repeatedly about the gold of Sonora during his eight years of imprisonment. Gold and silver mines did exist in northwestern Mexico, and treasure-seekers are still digging in and around the ruins of the Jesuit missions looking for hoards of the precious metal hidden there. They have found nothing to date.

Ignaz was imprisoned in two locations. The first was the prison at the Port of Santa María near Cádiz, where he landed. After six years, he was transferred to the Monastery of Our Lady of Charity (El Monasterio de Nuestra Señora de la Caridad), near Ciudad Rodrigo, where this story unfolds. We also know that, during his incarceration at the Port of Santa María, he was held for a time together with Jacob (Jacobo) Sedelmeyer, S. J.

Fellow Sonoran missionary Bernhard (Bernardo) Middendorff, S. J., upon release from captivity, visited Ciudad Rodrigo on his way back to his homeland in Germany and saw Ignaz at La Caridad. Thereafter, Middendorff sought out Ignaz's sister, Isabella Pfefferkorn Berntges. She appealed to the Palatine Elector, Max Ferdinand, who intervened with King Carlos III. Following several months of correspondence, the king agreed to release her brother.

Ignaz returned to live with his sister and his brother-in-law in Düsseldorf, where he wrote his book, *Beschreibung der Landschaft Sonora* (Köln am Rheine, 1794-1795), in 2 volumes. He died shortly after the two volumes came out. A projected third volume containing his personal reminiscences was never published.

Most of the above information comes from the English edition of his book, *Sonora, a Description of the Province*, tr. Theodore E. Treutlein (Tucson, University of Arizona, 1989). I also gleaned information from the letters to the Abbot of La Caridad Dom Gregorio Cañada y Lobato, from the Spanish Royal Council in Madrid. These documents are in the collection of the Archivo Histórico Nacional (Madrid). I gathered background information from published collections of Jesuit documents, Jesuit and other archives, books and articles on the Jesuit missionaries of the Sonora Desert, and from assorted works covering the expulsion in 1767 and suppression in 1773 of the Society of Jesus.

Of particular interest were entries relating to Father Ignaz in the record book of the Praemonstratensian (Norbertine) Monastery, Nuestra Señora de la Caridad: *Libro de Becerro del Monasterio de Nra. Sra. De la Caridad, de Ciudad Rodrigo, Año de MDCCC*. This massive, calf-bound volume, now located in the Archives of the Episcopal Palace in Ciudad Rodrigo, was handwritten by a scribe in 1800. It presents a record of the most important events in the existence of the monastery, from its founding in 1165 to that point. These entries announce the arrival of the ex-Jesuit Ignaz Pfefferkorn *("el Ex-Jesuita don Ygnacio Pferkon")*, describe how he was treated during his two and one-half-year stay, and provide the date and circumstances of his release.

Except for his initial imprisonment at the Port of Santa María, Ignaz was sequestered in La Caridad, a Norbertine monastery. The Norbertines of Spain (Premonstratenses), officially known to English speakers as the Premonstratensians, separated themselves during the reign of King Philip II from their brothers in other lands because of the king's fear of heresies seeping in from the rest of Europe. To distinguish themselves from other Norbertines, the Spanish Premonstratenses wore black habits instead of the white worn to this day by their brothers elsewhere.

The Norbertines are a very ancient Order, founded by St. Norbert on Christmas Day, 1120, still flourishing in most of Western Europe as well as in the Western Hemisphere.

Ignaz's own order, the Society of Jesus, is relatively young. The Jesuits were founded in 1539 by a Spaniard, Ignatius of Loyola. A former military man who was later sainted, his goals included establishing missions world-wide and reforming education in Europe and elsewhere.

Pope Paul III confirmed the new Society in 1540. It increased rapidly in size and influence, establishing missions in the Far East and New World. Its schools and colleges were models of reformed educational methods. It came to wield great power and influence within the Church as well as in secular governments, politics and trade. Its success as well as its excesses led to its expulsion from Portugal in 1759.

France came next, suppressing the Society in 1764 and expelling its Jesuits in 1767. Then Carlos III of Spain followed suit, expelling the Society from Spain and all its dependences in 1767. Finally Pope Clement XIV suppressed he Society altogether in 1773.

It was reinstated in 1814.

Many of the names used in the story came from these same historical sources. During ex-Jesuit Ignaz's imprisonment at the Puerto de Santa María, Dom Gerónimo Gómez Flores was abbot of the Monasterio de San Norberto, in Madrid. The abbot at La Caridad was Dom Gregorio Cañada y Lobato, the bishop of the Diocese of Ciudad Rodrigo was don Cayetano Antonio Cuadrillero y Mota, and the noble family Cerralbo was prominent in the community there. Abbot Gregorio Cañada y Lobato received only the sketchiest instructions on the terms of Pfefferkorn's imprisonment on his arrival on July 14, 1775; detailed instructions arrived on September 6, 1776. These restricted him to the monastery, allowed him correspondence only within Spain and then only after all letters were censored by the abbot. Ignaz was forbidden contact with seculars. He was allowed association only with those Norbertines within La Caridad.

Bishop Cuadrillero, a powerful man promoted to Archbishop in 1777, also took possession of Robledillo de Gata that same year, a parish previously attached to La Caridad.

The monastery, Nuestra Señora de la Caridad, still stands. Now in private hands, it is an imposing structure whose associated buildings and immediate grounds cover 8,000 square meters. It was partially destroyed by the same massive earthquake that devastated large areas in Portugal and flattened Lisbon in 1755, but was partly rebuilt shortly afterward. The church and cloister Ignaz knew already included these reconstructions.

In other words, the monastery we now see is basically the same plant that served as his prison for two and one-half years. After Bishop Cuadrillero took possession of Robledillo for Ciudad Rodrigo, the monastery—founded in 1165 only 45 years after St. Norbert began the Norbertine Order—went into decline and closed its doors in 1814. This ended its distinguished 650-year history. Its final, fatal blow came when Napoleonic forces occupied it, stripping it of its furniture and treasures. Artifacts seen at the monastery today are antiques, but not the original furnishings.

The village of Robledillo de Gata was of great importance to La Caridad as well as to the Bishop, since its wines were both rare and valuable. Emperor Charles V declared them superior to any others in his realm, including those of more famous wine-producing regions such as the Mosel Valley and the Rhineland. Losing Robledillo was a bitter blow to the monastery, to its prestige as well as its financial stability.

The charter, which occupies such a central place in the plot of this book, is pure fiction.

The following are my translations and transcriptions of the four entries from La Caridad's records regarding Father Ignaz, preserving spelling and abbreviations as written:

"On the 24th of May of 1775, the Council sent a letter to the abbot, in which it communicates its decision that the ex-Jesuit don Ygnacio Pferkon live here sequestered, providing 100 simple pesos per annum for his needs." Becerro, p. 356.

En 24 de Mayo de 1775, expide Carta el Consejo al P.e Abad, por la q.e le comunica la resolución del mismo de q.e viva aquí recluso el Ex -Jesuita D.n Ygnacio Pferkon, mantiéndole de q.ta de las temporalidades, con 100 pesos sencillos anuales. =Caj. De Privilegios R.s Leg. 1. N.o 7.=

"On the 6th of September of 1776, the Council sent a letter to the abbot regarding the treatment of the ex-Jesuit of whom we spoke earlier. It provides that the above-mentioned have no contact or communication with seculars, but only with the community, that he write nothing without submitting the letters to the abbot, who will send them if he sees fit, except that he is not permitted to write outside this Kingdom. He is awarded up to 200 ducats above the pension he already receives, in which is included his bed, and any expenses due to illness, and clothing." Becerro, p. 357, verso.

En 6 de Sepmbre de 1776, expidio Carta el Consejo al P.e Abad sobre lo q.e ha de hacer con el Ex -Jesuita de q.n se habló anteriormte: se previene en ella, q.e el referido no tenga trato ni comunicación con seglares, y si solo con la Commd: q.e no escriva sin entregar las cartas al Abad, q.n las dará curso si le pareciere, con tal q.e no se lo permita escribir fuera del Reyno; se le señalan h.ta 200 Ducados sobre la pension q.e goza, en q.e se incluye la Cama, y qualquier gasto de enfermed.d, y Vestuario. =Caj. De Prisi ~. R.s Leg.s No 7=

"Dated the 1st of April of 1777, 2,200 reales were received to cover victuals for the year ending on the 14th of July 1776, for the ex-Jesuit don Ygnacio Pherkon, who entered this Convent by order of the King on the 14th of July of 1775." Becerro, p. 359.

Con fecha de 1 de Abril de 1777, se recivieron 2200 r~. De los alimentos de un año q.e cumplio en 14 de Julio de 76, del Ex -Jesuita D.n Ygnacio Pherkon, q.e entró en este Conv.to por orden del Rey en 14 de Julio de l775. =Lib de Arca, fol. 461ta =

"On 24 December of 1777, a letter arrived from the Council ordering that the ex-Jesuit don Ygnacio be conducted to the border with France at Irún, so he could be restored to his homeland in the state of the Palatine Elector." Becerro, p. 361.

En 24 de Diciembre de 1777 salio carta del consejo p.a
q.e al ex-Jesuita D.n Ygnacio se le conduzca á las Fronteras
de Francia por Irun, á fin de q.e se restituya á su Patria en el
Estado del Elector Palatino. =Caj. de Priv.s R.s Leg.1. No 7.=

Don't miss any of these other
exciting mainstream novels

➢ Death to the Centurion
(1-931201-26-9, $16.95 US)

➢ Mary's Child
(1-933353-11-2, $18.50 US)

➢ Unraveled
(1-931201-11-0, $15.50 US)

➢ WolfPointe
(1-931201-08-0, $15.50 US)

Twilight Times Books
Kingsport, Tennessee

Order Form

If not available from your local bookstore or favorite online bookstore, send this coupon and a check or money order for the retail price plus $3.50 s&h to Twilight Times Books, Dept. FD505 POB 3340 Kingsport TN 37664. Delivery may take up to four weeks.

Name: _____

Address: _____

_____

Email: _____

I have enclosed a check or money order in the amount of $_____

for _____ .

If you enjoyed this book, please post a review at your favorite online bookstore.

Twilight Times Books
P O Box 3340
Kingsport, TN 37664
Phone/Fax: 423-323-0183
www.twilighttimesbooks.com/